# Mud, Love, and Chemistry

Christine Layne

Edited by NICE GIRL NAUGHTY EDITS

Edited by D.P. LEHAN

Cover Designer COFFIN PRINT DESIGNS

Formatting CHRISTINE LAYNE

# From The Author

*This book is dedicated to my college girls. You know who you are, you know what we did, and you know that I will always love you.*

# CHAPTER 1

CRISP MOUNTAIN AIR FILLS my lungs as I exit the car and step into the hot July sun. Sweat immediately beads on my forehead, so I slide on my headband. Double checking that my braid is secure, I round the back of the car with a light skip in my step.

It's my favorite day of the year, Mud Down race day.

"Fuck, it's already so hot, and it's only eight-thirty," complains Lisa, my high school BFF now turned college roommate, as she meets me at the trunk.

"You can thank global warming for that."

Lisa laughs, but quickly stops when she notices I'm not laughing. "Oh, you're serious."

"Of course I am." I pull out our backpacks, making sure everything is packed securely; sunscreen, water bottles, wallets, phones. "But also, we've done this race four summers in a row. Colorado is hot in July," I say, rolling my eyes.

"*You've* done this race four years in a row. I didn't come last year."

A shaky breath bleeds through my lips before my throat closes up. I can't swallow over the lump that forms.

Lisa's eyes immediately widen when she realizes what she said, and she wraps an arm around my shoulders. "Sorry, Brynn. I didn't mean to bring him up. I was—"

"It's okay," I say, even though it's not entirely true. Refusing to let this sudden reminder of my heartache ruin my adrenaline high, I shut the trunk and link my arm with hers. "Let's wake up Jackie and Hannah. Their backseat nap has come to an end."

The frigid burst of air-conditioning blasts me in the face as we enter the huge purple and black tent. Lisa lets out a sigh of relief, while I, for one, can't wait to get out of here. I hate air-conditioning. It taints the air, giving it a stale taste. There's no comparison to the energizing feeling of fresh air flooding your lungs.

Jackie and Hannah, our friends and college housemates, are finally awake enough after check-in to take the ceremonious selfie in front of the Mud Down sign. Then, we head out to put our backpacks in a locker.

I relish the open air with a deep inhale as we step back into the warmth of the sun. Walking toward the starting area, I take a moment to survey the grounds. The same vendors from the previous years have their tents up, and eager racers already congregate near the race entrance. I admire their enthusiasm.

A pang of jealousy rips through my heart as I notice several couples dressed in matching race gear, holding hands or sharing kisses while they wait. I thought I had that. I thought I had a partner to share this race with, but he wasn't who I believed him to be.

I huff and square my shoulders. There's no sense in letting my past heartbreak get the best of me. Sure, I may have spent the last year solo and in a dating rut, but today is the best day of the year, and no memory is going to change that.

No matter how painful it is.

At the starting line, we all stretch while waiting for the emcee to begin his usual motivational speech. More people file in, and soon, we're surrounded by other racers. It's so cool that all these people are here to partake in my favorite 10-k race.

Including my friends.

"So, Jackie, Hannah, ready for your first Mud Down?" I ask as I slide into a side lunge.

"I would be if I didn't have to get up so early." Jackie glares at me mockingly. "Why'd you sign us up for such an early race time?"

I throw my hands up in defense. "Because it's going to get hotter as the day goes on. Better to get it done early." If it were up to me, we'd have arrived at eight when the event opened, and we'd already be on the course. My friends, while excited for the Mud Down, don't share my tenacity for it.

"And get used to it," Lisa chimes in. "Brynn always signs up for the earliest race she can."

I bump Lisa's shoulder with mine. "More like the earliest one you'll let me." We stick our tongues out at each other before sharing a laugh.

Hannah puts her hands on her hips. "Do you drive all the way to Grand Junction every year? Isn't there another race that's closer to school?"

"Not one with this good of a vibe," I say with extra pep.

"At least we spent the night here instead of making the five-hour drive from Greeley this morning." Lisa uses my shoulder for balance as she pulls her leg behind her into a quad stretch. "Be glad you came this year, though. Now that we're twenty-one, we get a finisher beer at the end." Lisa holds up her arm in triumph, the words "Legal Drinking Age" printed on her wristband.

After a few spirited high-fives, the four of us huddle together, arms wrapped around each other's waists, and begin bouncing on our toes as we psych ourselves up. Our uplifting affirmations get interrupted by the screech of a microphone.

"Good morning, Mud Downers!" the emcee yells from a tent next to the starting line. "Y'all ready to get dirty?"

A collective cheer goes up from the crowd, and Lisa rocks me back and forth.

"Now, before y'all get out there, let's go over the legal stuff I *have* to tell you." The emcee proceeds to explain the liabilities of the Mud Down, the safety regulations, and the partner rule. "Find the person to your right and to your left. Those are your teammates."

I look left at Lisa, then right at Jackie. We grin cartoonishly at each other.

"Remember that word, teammates. They aren't your competition, aren't your enemies. They're all running the same course, doing the same obstacles, getting dirty, just like you. So leave your egos behind."

A lightness builds in my chest. I love the Mud Down sentiment.

"Take care of each other out there. Lend a hand, work together, and be brave enough to lean on someone else if needed." The emcee leaves the tent, cordless microphone in hand, and steps into the middle of the group. "Last thing, I want you to turn to your neighbors, give them a fist bump, and say, 'you got this.'"

I turn left and fist bump Lisa, but when I turn right, Jackie isn't there. Instead, I find myself staring straight into a guy's chest. A guy's *muscular* chest.

I raise my gaze to meet the most beautiful pair of dark brown eyes I've ever seen. They're like sparkling muddy pools flashing in the morning sun. My heart skips a beat as I take in the face surrounding the eyes. This guy is gorgeous. Shaggy light-brown hair held back by a sweatband, a strong jaw covered in the right amount of stubble, and a dazzling smile that has my stomach flipping.

"You got this." His low, smooth voice is full of confidence as he bumps his fist against mine.

The second his knuckles tap my own, the spell I'm under breaks, and I blink before flexing my fingers like they're exploding. "You, too," I say, much quieter and with less confidence than he did.

His smile melts into a smirk before he turns back to his friend, and I spin to face Lisa. I suck in a breath, but luckily, she doesn't seem to notice what just happened.

To be honest, *I* don't even know what just happened. I'm usually so cool and collected, but one look at that guy and I was reduced to a swooning nitwit.

Shake it off, Brynn.

Besides, I've been off relationships and guys in general for a year, and I'm certainly not gunning for a casual hook-up. Even if I talked more to that guy, there's a minuscule chance we'll see each other again, so I move on. I focus on the race ahead of me.

That's the whole reason I'm here, anyway.

The emcee blows the whistle, officially starting the race. All the racers take off. My three friends and I begin with a liberal jogging pace, but they quickly slow down. Not on my watch. I jog a few feet ahead of them, then turn around to jog backward. When I wave them on and spout motivational phrases, I'm met with a couple of middle fingers and stuck-out tongues.

I don't give up, though.

Slowing my pace, I run circles around my friends. They complain and roll their eyes, even take a few playful swings at me, but in the end, they become fed up with my antics. Picking up their pace, we get back on track in no time.

After a half mile, we reach the first obstacle, the muddy crawl.

I take the lead. Sliding into the murky water, I dunk my head so I can crawl under the low-hanging barbed wire, then hold it up so my friends can slither through safely. That starts a chain reaction, and other racers begin copying me.

We conquer another few obstacles before coming to one that really requires teamwork. The mud mounds are exactly what they sound like; several mounds of mud over six feet tall with water-filled ditches in between. People give you a boost, then you reach down to pull them up. The slippery mud offers no footing, and it's a riot watching people slide face first into the next ditch.

The four of us jump in, and I begin giving the boosts. Lisa first, then Jackie, then Hannah, and lastly, me. This order goes on for all of the mounds, five in total. When I lift Hannah out of the final ditch, I lose my footing and go under the water. I come up immediately, ineffectively wiping my face, and reach up to grab Hannah's hand.

But Hannah's hand seems to have doubled in size.

"You got this," a deep voice says, and I forget all about the mud covering my face, whipping my head up to see my starting line hunk holding my hand. His half smile returns, and my breath shakes from my mouth, mud sputtering off my lips. "And I got you." Then he yanks me out of the ditch as if I weigh nothing.

Once I'm on solid ground again, hunky guy lets go of my hand, winks at me, and takes off running with his buddy. I'm left speechless, staring after him. I don't even know what to think. He's still as hot as he was on the starting line, even now, covered in mud.

Lisa calls my name, startling me and pulling me back to the real world. I jog to catch up with my friends. They give me concerned looks as I opt to walk to the next obstacle instead of jogging. I tell them it's because I have to pee. In truth, though, my knees are wobbling so much, I don't think I could hold a jog if my life depended on it.

Luckily, a water station is our next stop. To play out my ruse, I step into the mud-covered interior of a Porto-Potty, hoping they use environmentally friendly chemicals. I'd hate to think what would happen if one of these sprung a leak.

I run my hands over my crusty hair. What is going on with me? I don't ever get flustered over a guy.

I shake my head. It's a fluke. A hot guy happened to be in my space, and I lost focus for a bit. No big deal. I've recovered now. My legs aren't shaking anymore, my head has cleared, and I can finish this race strong. Exiting the tiny restroom, I hold my head up. I'm not going to let some handsome face deter me from my goal.

But as I move to join my friends again, the handsome, albeit muddy, face runs past me. When our eyes meet, he flashes another brilliant smile, and my heart skips a beat.

Dammit.

My three friends and I take off down the track. By the time we reach one of my favorite obstacles, the vertical wall, I've all but regained my composure. That's not to say I haven't been searching for this guy at every turn and berating myself for it. At the wall, I put my back to it and drop into a squat, becoming a step stool for my friends.

Lisa is last, and she sits atop the wall with her hand extended down. When I shake my head, she huffs. "I should've known you'd want to do this one yourself. Okay, we'll be waiting for you," she says, shrugging before climbing down the other side.

With an anxious skip in my step, I back up. I need room to get a running start so I can jump and shimmy my five-foot-five self up the eight foot vertical climb. Of course, when I get back far enough, a few other racers are now working their way over the wall, so I have to wait.

"You got this?"

I glance over to find my hunk standing next to me, his mud-covered eyebrows arched, making the mud cake into his forehead creases. A wry smirk crosses my lips, and I nod. "Oh, yeah. I got this."

As I dash toward the wall, my adrenaline pumps furiously. I scale it no problem, but instead of jumping over, I straddle the top and wave for my gorgeous race partner to follow. I watch him lick his mud-covered lips, spitting almost immediately before he takes off. He, of course, makes it up without issue, but he's also got almost a foot on me, making his climb shorter.

When he gets to the top, he copies my straddle of the wall, facing me. "I'm Sam," he says and offers me his hand.

I shake it firmly, bits of dried mud flaking between our palms. "Brynn."

He stares at me, his lips turned up in the most adorable way, melting my insides, and I can't do anything but stare back. Everything stops. I can't feel the sun baking my mud mask. I can't see the other racers topping the wall around me. I can't hear anything except the erratic beating of my heart.

"Brynn! Come on!" Lisa's sharp shout severs the moment.

I clear my throat, giving Sam a quick wink. "Gotta go!" Leaping off the wall, I jog to my friends without looking back.

"Who was that?" Lisa asks, jutting her chin over her shoulder.

I shrug, feigning nonchalance. "Some guy complimenting my climb. Guess I impressed him."

She gives me a knowing look and starts jogging.

The rest of the race goes almost as expected. While my friends dive into the ice bath, ascend the twenty-foot ladder, and scale the warped wall, I'm right there, leading them. My mind, however, is way behind. I haven't been able to get that guy, Sam, out of my head. For a moment, I consider jaunting through the electroshock obstacle. Maybe that will reset my brain, but I still have metal pins in my wrist from when I broke it several years ago, so I skip it. Since I'm not leading the way this time, my friends pass it up too.

When we cross the finish line, volunteers give each of us a gray t-shirt with the word "Finisher" across the back and a can of beer. As my muddy fingers leave their mark on the sleek fabric, my sense of accomplishment materializes in my hands. My chest fills with pride for yet another Mud Down completion.

The four of us happily cheers our drinks before heading to the food truck area. While I'm standing in line with Lisa, I find Sam sitting at a picnic table, a beer in his hand. When he sees me, he lifts his beer like he's cheersing me from afar. I nod, lifting my can as well.

"Is that the same guy from earlier?" Lisa nudges me with her elbow.

"Yeah." I can't stop the smile from conquering my face.

She shoves me in his direction. "Go talk to him."

"What? No." My adrenaline spikes at the thought.

"Just go."

Lisa pushes me hard enough that I stagger forward, and Sam notices. Now I have no choice but to talk to him. Even if reluctantly. I walk toward his table, the butterflies in my stomach fluttering a mile a minute. He watches me the entire time, his posture perking up with each step I take.

When I reach the table, I say a quiet, "Hey."

"Hey," he replies without taking his eyes off me. "Nice job finishing."

"You too."

A throat clears next to him, and Sam does a double take at his friend. "Oh, sorry. This is Walt." He motions between me and Walt. "This is Brynn."

My name sounds so natural on his tongue, so fluid.

"Sup?" Walt says, lifting his chin in my direction. "Saw you on the course today. You're fucking tough."

Sam elbows him, scoffing at his swearing.

I chuckle. "Thanks."

A silence settles between us, so Walt stands up. "I, uh, need another beer. I'll be right back." And with that, he's gone, leaving me with Sam.

Sam motions for me to sit, so I do. "Sorry about Walt. No manners, that one."

"It's okay." I shrug. "He's right, I *am* fucking tough."

Sam's brown eyes sparkle as he grins. "I like that."

Thank God I'm still covered in mud, because his flattery surely has my cheeks as red as a candied apple. "So, is this your first Mud Down?" I take a sip of my beer.

He nods. "You?"

My can stills at my lips, and I hold up five fingers.

He gapes. "Wow. So, you're like, an expert at the course then?"

I swallow my drink. "Something like that."

"You'll have to share all your secrets with me."

"No way." I shake my head. "I'm taking those to the grave."

Sam's laugh is like music to my ears.

"Besides, I wouldn't have the time to bestow *all* my knowledge onto you. My friends and I are going into town directly after this to get ice cream."

"Ice cream? No shower first?"

I laugh. "The interesting looks we get are always entertaining."

"I'll bet." Sam's gaze scans my face as if tracing the muddy outline. "I hope the ice cream is worth the attention."

"Oh, it is. There's an old timey soda shop that has the best butter pecan." My mouth waters just thinking about it.

"I'm more of a mint chocolate chip guy, myself."

The idea of tasting Sam's mintiness has me salivating, which surprises me. I haven't had that urge in a long time.

"Brynn." Lisa taps my shoulder. "We got our bags and we're going to take a picture under the finisher sign before we go. Here's your phone." She hands me my phone, winking at me before glancing at Sam. "Hey, man."

"Hey."

She turns back to me. "Hurry up, okay?"

I shoot Sam an apologetic grimace as I stand up. "Sorry. Got to go."

"Shit." Sheer panic seems to overtake Sam's face as he pats all his pockets. "I'd ask for your number, but I don't have my phone yet."

My heart skips a beat. He wants my number? "Well, here," I say, handing him my phone. "Put yours in mine."

A delighted smile slides over his face as he types and hands it back to me. I chuckle, reading what he input. "Sam Mudboy? Is that your real last name?"

He shakes his head. "It's Eastman."

"Well, nice to meet you, Sam Eastman," I say as I tap my screen. "See you around."

"Wait," he calls after me. "Do you have a last name?"

I turn my chin over my shoulder. "Guess you'll find out when you check your texts."

# CHAPTER 2

"Have you heard from him yet?" Lisa asks as we enter the ice cream parlor. The teenage girl working the counter peeks up at us.

"No. For the fiftieth time, I haven't heard from him yet," I say, rubbing my temple.

She huffs and puts her hands on her hips. "What's his problem?"

"It's been, like, thirty minutes. He probably doesn't even have his phone."

We step to the counter, and I order my usual, a double scoop of butter pecan in a waffle cone. Lisa is next, ordering her plain vanilla in a sugar cone. We giggle to ourselves as the employee keeps ducking her head to keep from staring. Jackie and Hannah come in behind us, entering the line that's built up since we walked in a minute ago.

I get my ice cream and immediately take a big lick, the sweet, buttery goodness coating my tongue. "Besides, he probably asked for my number to be nice."

"Oh, please," Lisa groans. "Guys don't ask for girls' numbers unless they want something." Her eyebrow bobbing has me groaning.

When she turns toward the cashier, I bump her out of the way. "I've got it." After I pay, we step to the side to wait for Jackie and Hannah.

When all four of us have our ice cream, we stand together and take a selfie. Jackie nudges me with her shoulder. "Did that guy text you yet?"

"No," I huff, and take out my phone to show them my screen. I'd be lying if I said I wasn't as anxious as my friends, but it's weird for me. I haven't been excited for a guy to text me since Connor and I started dating. That was three years ago. And after he broke my heart, I quit chasing love. Stopped seeking it completely.

Am I ready to start searching again?

I shake my head to clear it. "Can we go sit outside?" I'm using this question as a distraction from my love life, but it is a serious one. It is freezing in here.

"It's too hot. The ice cream will melt!" Jackie laughs.

"Then eat it faster," I say, twirling my cone around my tongue.

"Ooh, do that again!" Lisa says excitedly.

"What?"

She grabs my phone out of my hand, swiping the screen and holding it up. "Lick your ice cream."

So, I do, but in a more lackluster manner.

"No," she whines. "Not like that. Make it sexy."

"How?"

"Close your eyes, stick your tongue out all the way," she says.

"And pout a little," Hannah chimes in.

I laugh. "Those sound like contradicting actions."

"Just do it," Lisa orders.

"Fine," I say hesitantly, and do as I'm told.

"Oh, that's hot." Lisa shows me the pic, and she's right.

Even though I'm covered in mud, I look...sexy. I don't *do* sexy. Ever. Yet, there I am, with my tongue not just licking the ice cream, but caressing it. It's almost embarrassing, but at least it's only a picture on my phone.

"Now, send it to Sam."

"What?" My eyebrows shoot to the sky. "No way."

Lisa frowns. "Fine." Turning her back to me, she takes my phone with her and taps the screen.

"Lisa! No! Give me my phone!" I shout as I'm clawing to get around Lisa and trying not to drop my ice cream. Our antics elicit more gawks from the parlor patrons, but I don't care.

"Too late." She spins around with the biggest self-satisfied smile on her face.

All I can do is stare at the word "delivered" in my text messages as she hands it back to me. I wait for those three little dots to appear, but they don't. My heart speeds up, my breaths shallow, and the world around me blurs.

Lisa's arm around my shoulder pulls me back to reality. "He'll respond. Relax and enjoy your ice cream."

"I can't believe you did that," Jackie whispers to Lisa as they all walk toward a table.

Neither can I. Or maybe I can, but never thought she'd do something like that to me. She knows I like to think things through. I need to weigh all my variables, compare all my possible outcomes. I don't act on a whim.

With a sigh, I tuck my phone into my back pocket. He'll respond. Surely, he will. Either way, there's no sense in worrying about it yet. Wait for his response, or lack thereof, and I'll get my answer.

I join my friends at the table. My tension ebbs as I laugh at all the dried mud that has flaked off in a huge dusty mess all around them, but ramps right back up when my phone dings in my pocket. I don't move, just stare wide-eyed at Lisa, who's grinning like an idiot. With a deep swallow, I take my phone out and unlock the screen.

"Who is it? Is it him? What did he say about the pic? Did he love it?" Lisa's rapid-fire questions don't even register in my brain.

I'm too busy trying to quell the frenzied butterflies in my stomach. The corners of my mouth tick upward as I read Sam's message.

**SAM**: *Is your last name really Erlenmeyer?*

"Are you kidding me?" Lisa asks. "That's the first thing he says!?"

I chuckle, but it's laced with disappointment. Part of me was hoping the first thing he'd mention was my picture. I shake it off and I type my response.

**BRYNN:** *Yep, it is. Is that surprising?*

**SAM:** *Not as surprising as your picture. Is the ice cream good?*

"What's he saying that's got you smiling like that?" Jackie asks.

I shake my head. "He asked if the ice cream was good."

"Tell him it would be better if you were licking it off his chest."

I tear my gaze away from the phone to gape at Lisa before bursting into laughter. "No. I don't think I'll be saying that." I swirl my tongue around my ice cream and go back to the message.

**BRYNN:** *It's delicious. Didn't my picture do it justice?*

My stomach clenches as I await his response, those three dancing dots taunting me.

**SAM:** *It did it more than justice. I don't think I've ever been jealous of an ice cream cone before.*

Heat rushes to my face, and my smile grows so wide, more mud flakes off my cheek.

"Ooh, now what did he say?" Lisa asks.

I can't even speak the words, so I turn the phone around to show them. As my three friends read, they all have the same reaction. Intrigue at first, then wide eyes, then the giggles start. Seeing my internal feelings reflected on their faces validates me.

"He's typing!" Hannah shouts.

I whip the phone around in frantic anticipation. I haven't responded yet. What more could he have to say? The dots appear, then disappear, only to reappear again. Whatever he has to say, he's waffling about it.

"They keep disappearing." I hate the disappointment in my voice.

"Well, it's probably pretty hard to type one-handed," Lisa says before licking her ice cream.

I give her an incredulous look. "What do you mean one-hand–" Then realization hits me. "Ew, Lisa. He's not doing *that*."

She shrugs. "Wouldn't surprise me after that picture you sent."

My phone dings, pulling my attention away from my lewd friend, and I see a message that makes my stomach flip. "He wants me to call him."

"Do it!" they all shout in unison.

With a sharp nod, I step outside into the hot July afternoon. A welcome change from the frigid ice cream parlor. I know it's hot out here, but the ice cream keeps me cool, and honestly, it tastes better without the staleness of the air-conditioning tainting it.

Speaking of... I swirl my now melting ice cream around my tongue.

Tapping my phone screen, I scroll down to Sam's contact info. My finger hovers over the "call" icon as my breath begins to shake. What am I so nervous about? It's only a phone call. "Ugh, stop being dumb," I say to myself and hit the button.

My foot taps the ground wildly as I listen to the ringing. I bite down on my bottom lip, only to immediately remove it and spit dried mud onto the ground.

"Hello?" Sam's smooth voice comes through the phone.

I stand straight up, my whole body going rigid. "Sam, hey. It's me, uh, Brynn." I'm still picking pieces of mud from my tongue between my words.

"Are you okay?"

"Yeah, I am. Sorry. I got mud in my mouth right as you answered." I mentally slap myself for how stupid I sound. I've had mud in my mouth all day. Why is it an issue now? Nice one, Brynn.

"Wow. I didn't know they made mud-flavored ice cream."

I laugh. "Ew. That would be the worst. Don't worry, mine is good old butter pecan."

"Yeah, I saw your picture," he says, low and full of confidence.

I take a lick to cool myself before I can speak. "So, what's up? You still at the Mud Down?"

"No, me and Walt are back at the hotel. He's in the shower, so I thought this would be a good time to call since I'm alone."

My heart races. Why does he need to be alone to talk to me? What is he going to say? "Oh, cool." *Cool? Cool?* That's all I have to say? I'm such an idiot.

"I, uh, wanted to call and ask..." He takes a breath. A deep one from what I hear through the phone. "I know we just met, and... This is going to sound so dumb, but do you want to hang out tonight?"

My racing heart jumps into my throat, pounding in my esophagus so hard I can't speak. I try to clear my throat, but it doesn't work. I'm silent for several seconds.

Sam sighs. "Sorry. I didn't mean to be weird, but I thought maybe you'd like to—"

"Yes!" I all but shout the word, surprising even myself. Thankfully, there's no one out here except me. "I'd love to."

"Really?" The delight in his voice is palpable.

"Yeah, really."

"Awesome. Uh, I don't know what there is to do in this town, but I thought we could grab something to eat, maybe go for a walk."

I crinkle my nose. "Well, I kind of wanted to eat pizza with my friends and compare our battle wounds from the Mud Down. It's tradition."

"Oh, okay." Sam's delight is replaced with savage disappointment.

I chew on my lip, not caring one bit about the mud anymore. "How about we hang out after my friends and I get pizza? That way I'm not ditching them completely."

"Yeah, of course." I can hear the smile on his face. "Let me know when you're done and I'll come over."

"No. I'll come to you. There are three other girls in my room. We won't get a word in edgewise."

To my relief, Sam laughs. "Okay, I'll text you my hotel and room number. I'm sure we can find something to do."

I've already got a list going in my head; minigolf, a movie, the mall. My rampant ideas get cut short when my ice cream drips onto my hand. I forgot all about it.

"Sounds good," I say, trying to wear my ice cream down enough to stop it from dripping more.

As we say our goodbyes and hang up, I chomp into my cone, grinning from ear to ear. I'm sure I look like the goofiest person on the planet, but I don't care. I get to hang out with Sam.

# Chapter 3

What the fuck am I doing?

My grip on the steering wheel of Lisa's car is so tight, my knuckles aren't white, they're transparent. When I agreed to meet up with Sam, it didn't even faze me. Sure, I can go meet some guy I barely know in his hotel room in a city that's not my home. Why not?

I run my palm down my face, but tear it away as I remember I'm actually wearing makeup. Lisa insisted, so I allowed her to put the bare minimum on me. One neutral shade of eyeshadow, some light mascara, and a dab of lip gloss, but that's it.

She wanted to pick my outfit too, but luckily, I didn't bring an extensive wardrobe. I threw on a pair of comfy jogging shorts and an aqua-colored tank top. When I told her that color makes the blue of my eyes pop, it seemed to satisfy her.

As Jackie French-braided my hair, my three friends and I sat around three large pizzas as they all swooned over Sam. They giggled about his flirty text messages. They chided me for not letting him come to our room so they could meet him. They even went as far to say they couldn't wait to hear about our date. Our *date*. I told them that's not what this is.

Is it?

I date so little I have no idea. In my mind, a date is dinner and a movie, something that's planned in advance. It's certainly not a half-assed meetup at some guy's hotel room. That's more like a booty-call.

"Ugh! What the fuck am I doing?"

Slapping the steering wheel with my palm, I pull Lisa's Honda Accord with the broken side mirror into the parking lot of the Travel Lodge. At least this beat-up car will match the beat-up hotel. I could think of worse places to stay, but you get arrested for sleeping in the street.

The parking lot and sidewalks are cracked, but it seems like they've been at least spraying the weeds. Faded paint and chipped trim welcome me as I reach the entrance. Stepping inside, I hear the door chime right before I'm blasted in the face by air-conditioning. I gasp, but immediately clamp my mouth shut. The air doesn't taste like the normal staleness. Instead, this tastes...wrong.

That's the best way I can describe it.

With my lips sealed, I have to breathe through my nose and that's even worse. Now I'm getting hints of cigarettes mixed with body odor, and it makes me nauseous. Is that what I just tasted? I bite the inside of my cheek, steeling myself before I take a big breath to hold as I walk down the hall to the elevators. I have to do it again once I'm inside.

I punch the button for the third floor over and over, wanting the door to close as quickly as possible. The farther from the lobby I get, the better. I hope this breath will last me long enough to get to Sam's room. When the elevator doors finally open, I quickly direct myself toward room 305. A relieved sigh escapes me when I realize it's only a few doors down.

I knock before exhaling. As I take in little sips of air, I notice my toes tapping against the floor. A good sign that I'm actually excited for this. I haven't wanted to put myself out there in a year, and to an extent, this feels good. I don't know what's in store for me tonight, but I do know my curiosity needs to be sated.

After a few moments, I knock again.

No answer. Great. I probably have the worst timing and he's in the bathroom. What a way to begin a date.

I shake my head. This isn't a date!

Before I can argue with myself any more, the door opens, and my anxiety ebbs as Sam comes into full view.

He stands in the doorway, his hair a damp mess with curls spilling all around his head. The light-brown strands glint in the fluorescent lighting. His dark brown eyes widen before a grin spreads across his clean-shaven face.

"Hey," he says quietly.

"Hey," I respond, also quiet. So quiet in fact, I'm not even sure I heard myself. I clear my throat. "Hey." Better that time.

"I'm almost ready to go." He steps back to allow me to enter. "Do you want to come in?"

I hesitate, but the softness in his eyes reassures me, so I nod and step past him. Making sure to keep my posture confident, I say, "I found a few things we can go do, but they're all across town."

"I'm up for anything." He shuts the door before turning to face me and putting his hands in his pockets. "But I don't have a car here, and Walt won't let anyone touch his baby, so if you don't mind driving..."

Relief floods me. Not only will we be going to a public place, but I'll be the one driving. Sam hasn't given me any reason not to trust him, but I don't know him. He also doesn't know me. I wonder if he worries about me kidnapping him? "I don't mind, but that means you'd be at my mercy." I plaster on a wicked smirk.

His confident gaze stays fixed on mine. "I think I can handle that."

The gruffness of his voice makes my breath catch, so I quickly clear my throat and pull out my phone to scroll through my activity list. "Um, there's a mini-golf place, or we could walk around a park. Worse comes to worst we can always go do laps around the mall." When he doesn't laugh, I glance up to find him still staring. "Sam?"

"Oh, uh, right." He blinks several times. "Any of that sounds good, but I was actually hoping maybe you'd take me to that ice cream place you were raving about."

"Really?"

He nods. "I mean, I know you already had ice cream today, but it looked really good."

The huskiness in his voice as his gaze dips to my mouth makes me think he's not really talking about the ice cream. Heat creeps up my neck. "I'm always up for more ice cream."

Sam grabs his wallet and phone, and we're out the door. We don't talk at all during our jaunt through the hotel, both holding our breath. Once we get outside, we both let our lungs loose and turn to each other with smiles.

"You can't stand the smell, either?" I ask.

"Who could? I feel bad for the poor employees stuck in there."

With a chuckle, I lead him to Lisa's old Honda. "Sorry, it's not a Mercedes."

"You're telling me," he says as he studies the car. "Are you sure we can make it to the ice cream place?"

I tilt my head from side to side. "I can't promise anything."

When Sam's expression turns skeptical, I laugh. "Just get in." I hop into the driver's seat and start the car, making sure to roll all the windows down. "Hope you don't mind fresh air."

"Not at all," he says, buckling his seat belt. "How far is this ice cream place, anyway?"

"A couple of miles." I turn, giving him a wry look. "Why? Are you itching to get back to your hotel room or something?"

His brow furrows so fast, it's comical. "Fuck, no. Just wondering how long I have to wait to get my lips on something sweet."

The depth to his voice returns, and I have to rein myself back in to keep from swooning. I choose to nod instead of speaking as I pull out of the parking lot. If I opened my mouth, an embarrassing chortle, like Goofy's "*ha-yuck*," would probably come out. Silence is better than that.

After a few blocks, Sam breaks the lull. "Do you listen to music?"

"Yeah, why?"

"Because the radio is off. I thought maybe you enjoyed your own thoughts better."

I chuckle. "No, but Lisa and I have differing tastes, and she was the last one to decide on what we were listening to." I jut my chin at the radio. "Go ahead. Turn it on. I dare you."

"Ooh, a challenge." Sam rubs his hands together before pressing the power knob. When the lyrics to "Rock the Boat" by The Hues Corporation come pouring from the speakers, Sam looks at me inquisitively.

"I warned you."

"Fun." His tone sounds anything but amused as he presses the knob, basking us in sweet silence once again. "Your friend has...an interesting taste in music."

"She's really into oldies, but she goes through phases with the decades. Right now, it's disco."

"So, what do you listen to?"

"Honestly, a little of everything."

"Except disco."

"I don't mind it, but I can't handle it on the same level as Lisa," I say as I pull into the ice cream parlor parking lot. "One of my favorite bands is Imagine Dragons."

Sam stares at me, his eyes narrowed slightly and his lips turned up. "I love them. Walt and I saw them in concert a few days ago."

"I bet that was a great show." My heart swells at the idea we have more in common than mud.

He leans toward me. "Second best thing I've laid eyes on this week."

My mouth runs dry, heat rushes to my face, and my stomach does this weird flip thing as I sit here, stunned.

"Let's get some ice cream." Sam winks before getting out of the car.

My breath whooshes from my lips as I roll up the windows and cut the engine. If he keeps talking like this, I might need a triple scoop. I meet Sam on the sidewalk, his now easy grin relaxing me, and we step inside to a crowded shop. After ordering our cones, me with butter pecan again and him with mint chocolate chip, Sam agrees to sit outside.

A few moments of silence hang between us before he groans in delight. "I know you said it was good, but this is amazing."

"Glad you like it." Pride swells in me, but it only keeps me afloat for a moment before the heaviness of the silence hits me again. "So, Sam, where are you from?"

He eyes me suspiciously, but takes a lick. "Wyoming. Casper, specifically."

"Oh." My heart sinks, but I'm not sure why. "That's a long way to drive for a mud race."

"Well, I don't have a whole lot else going on right now." He rubs the back of his neck. "See, I joined the unemployment ranks at the beginning of summer."

"Sorry, that sucks."

He shrugs. "It's okay. It was just a job at a local hardware store. It wasn't my career, but it paid pretty well so I saved a bunch of money. So, before I dive back into the job world, I decided to take some time to hang out with Walt this summer." He sounds sad about that fact, like he's losing his friendship to a job.

"Cool." I swirl my ice cream across my tongue. "What all have you guys done?"

Sam's swallow is audible as I finish my lick. "Uh, nothing too crazy. Other than the Mud Down and the concert, we've been hanging out. Doing friend stuff."

"Do you guys have the same hobbies?"

"Mostly." He tilts his head from side to side. "We play video games, go to the bar, go to the gym, but he's into cars and I'm not."

"Three out of four isn't bad, though."

He chuckles. "No, it's not. Unless he's dragging me to a car show. He's been making me go to those things for four years, ever since we turned eighteen. I go because I love the guy, but I spend the whole time checking my watch."

"That's about the way I feel when Lisa makes me watch Christmas movies with her."

"You don't like Christmas movies?" Sam quirks an eyebrow.

"Not in August." I exaggerate my eye roll, which has Sam laughing, and the sound sends a thrill through me.

"At least we understand each other's pain."

The common sentiment has my cheeks heating, so I nod and lick my ice cream again. Sam's intent stare makes me smile. When I giggle, it seems to break his trance, and he goes back to his own ice cream. I guess I'm not the only one who needs to cool down.

Sam pops the last bit of his cone into his mouth. "That was delicious. Thank you for bringing me here."

"You're welcome." I finish my last bite with a smile, taking a long moment to chew it. I'm not sure what we're doing after this, but I do know I don't like the idea of saying goodnight. Which means I'm not ready to be done. We've connected on a few levels, and I want to see how much more we have in common. I check the time. It's only a little after seven, still plenty of daylight left. "Do you want to go for a walk? There's a park near here with a pond."

Sam's face lights up. "I'd love to."

We leave Lisa's car in the parking lot and head down the street together. Sam shoves his hands in his pockets. "So, Brynn, tell me about yourself."

I chew on the inside of my cheek. What do I talk about? I could tell him how I'm going into my last year as a chemistry major, practically first in line for my professor's internship at her environmental lab. When I get that spot, I'll be working toward preserving nature by saving it from humanity's harsh chemical usage. That's pretty exciting.

But, he didn't mention going to school at all, so maybe he doesn't? What if he can't afford it? Especially now that he's unemployed.

If that's the case, I shouldn't bring up my tutoring job. Not only am I employed, but it's flexible so I still get all the time I want with my friends. Since he thinks entering the career world will take him away from his best friend, I'm only going to make him feel bad.

Ugh, everything I have going for me sounds like I'm bragging. So, I opt for the safe route. "I like to run."

"Big surprise there." He gives me a teasing wink. "Is that all you do in your spare time?"

"No. I hang out with Lisa and my other friends, Jackie and Hannah. They're my roommates, so one of them is always around. I like to go hiking, which Lisa will do with me, but Jackie and Hannah are more into watching movies or shopping. We do go to the bar on ladies' night, though. Cheap drinks and dancing is always fun."

"Okay, that's where you lose me. *You* dance?"

I scoff. "What's so hard to believe about that?"

"Nothing. I just have a hard time picturing that tough woman on the mud course today shaking her hips…" His gaze floats toward the sky, his forehead crinkling. "Never mind. I can picture it just fine."

I giggle. "Do you dance?"

"Me? No. Not a step."

"Hm. Too bad," I say with a pout. "Few things are sexier than a guy who can move to a beat."

Sam clears his throat. "I'd be willing to learn."

A laugh escapes me, but it fades, and I stop walking. An impetuous idea has taken hold of me, and I'm fighting it. It's too outrageous.

Sam looks back, confusion spreading across his face when he notices I'm a few steps behind him. "Brynn?"

I flick my gaze away to find an empty covered patio. This crazy notion pokes at me some more, and I can't ignore it. Grabbing Sam's arm, I pull him toward it. Once we're situated in the middle of the picnic tables, I turn to Sam, excitement bubbling within me. "Lesson one."

"What?"

"You said you'd be willing to learn to dance. Here's your first lesson."

He laughs, but quickly stops when he sees I'm not laughing. "You can't be serious."

"Absolutely, I am. I can teach you how to two-step. It's real easy."

"But there's no music."

I shrug. "Sometimes it's easier to learn when you can count your own beat. Come on." I wave my hands in the air, motioning for him to remove his hands from his pockets.

Hesitantly, he does, but holds them in the air in question. "What do I do?"

"One hand here." I take his left hand in my right. "And the other, here." When I place his right hand on my waist, I have to suppress a shiver. His breath hitches, too. I lay my left hand on his muscular shoulder, fighting the urge to drag my fingers along the defined ridges. "You're in the lead position, but follow me so you can get the movement down, okay?"

He nods, his fingers digging into me.

"You walk forward with your right foot." I tug on him gently, and he follows. We go through some basics, like what is a fast step and what's considered slow. I count out loud the whole time. He only steps on my feet twice, apologizing profusely when it happens, and I can't help but smile at his vulnerability. Eventually, we pick up the pace, and I introduce the skip.

Sam's almost what I would call a natural. Sure, he makes some mistakes, but he learns from them and corrects himself each time. It's impressive. Not to mention, sexy as hell.

After a few minutes, he asks, "Can I lead now?"

"Sure." I pull out my phone. "How about some music this time?"

He nods, so I tap into my music app. The melodic guitar of "Most People Are Good" by Luke Bryan begins, and so does Sam.

It's a rocky start, but soon he's leading me around the patio like a pro. Hard to believe, only fifteen minutes ago, he was following me around like a scared puppy, worried he was going to break one of my toes. Now, he's gliding along like he's been doing this for years.

The sparkle in his eyes makes my heart rate speed up, but it's when he starts singing along to the song that it skips a beat. I feel as light as a feather. This moment is perfect. Between the setting sun, the music, and Sam's thumb caressing my hand, I lose myself.

I don't let go often, which is why when I go dancing, I dance by myself. I don't like to be led. If a guy wants to dance with me, fine, but he doesn't control me. I usually keep a tight grip on myself. Right now, though, I can't hold on. I close my eyes and let Sam lead.

As the music fades, Sam slows his pace. The song ends, and he lets go of my waist to twirl me around as our last step.

Though I miss the thrill of his touch, I step away to gape at him. "You're a fast learner, Mr. Eastman."

He hikes a shoulder to his ear. "I may or may not have danced with my mom at my aunt's wedding."

"Oh, so you lied about not dancing?" I tilt my chin up as I fold my arms.

"I didn't lie." He points upward. "I said I don't dance, which is true. I just didn't tell you that I two-stepped with my mom when I was eight years old."

My giggle is cut short when I notice our hands are still joined. I swallow, turning toward the setting sun. "Sam, it's getting dark, but I don't want this night to end yet."

"I know. Me neither." He tugs on my hand, pulling me toward him. "I don't want to sound creepy, but would you want to come back to my room and hang out some more?"

Normal, rational Brynn would say "hell no" to a request like that, but she's taking a back seat on this ride. Care-free Brynn is here, and she doesn't overthink as much. Since a million butterflies rush through me, all from the excitement of extending our date, I say, "Yes, I would."

His face spreads into a wide smile. "Let me text Walt that we'll be coming back."

# Chapter 4

When we get back to the hotel, neither of us breathe as we walk to his room. By the time we get inside, Sam's face is bright red, and I'm sure mine matches. We burst into laughter.

"Why is that elevator so slow?" I ask.

He shakes his head. "It's like they know people are trying to hold their breath."

I laugh, glancing around, and a crease forms between my eyebrows as I take in the empty room. "Where's Walt?"

"Oh, he texted me that he got his own room. Said he didn't want to spend the night in the lobby."

The crease in my forehead deepens. "Hm. Kind of presumptuous of him to think I'd be here all night."

Sam's lithe expression falls, his face paling as panic flares in his eyes. "No, Brynn, I didn't mean... I wasn't saying that... Shit."

I laugh outright. "Sam, it's fine. I'm joking." Sort of. "I get that Walt wouldn't want to be the third wheel. It's actually very nice of him to pay for another room."

"Yeah," Sam says in one long syllable as his shoulders noticeably relax. "He said I should consider it my next birthday present."

"When's your birthday?"

"March 30th."

"That's so far away!" I practically double over with laughter, but as soon as it subsides, I shiver in the chilly room.

"You okay?"

"Yeah, I hate air-conditioning."

"Oh, well, come on." Sam walks across the room and throws back some heavy curtains. "This place may not be luxurious, but it has a balcony." He opens the squeaky slider, motioning for me to follow.

I gladly step through the doorway and into the warm evening air. It may be sunset, but it's still a wonderful eighty-five degrees, and my body naturally adjusts to the temperature.

"You have a fantastic view." Sarcasm drips from my words as I take in the gas station below.

Sam laughs as he pulls a couple of chaise lounge chairs toward us. "Maybe that's the real reason Walt switched rooms."

I laugh with him and take a seat. "We can pretend it's a really boring TV show."

"I don't plan on looking at the gas station much."

I whip my head up to find Sam staring at me, his brown eyes full of an intensity that shoots right to my core. My mouth goes dry. My brain can't seem to form thoughts. Not coherent ones, anyway. "So, uh, your birthday is March 30th, huh? That's Marie Curie's birthday."

"What are you, some kind of chemistry scholar?" Sam's mouth ticks up on one side.

Something like that. "I'm impressed you know who she is, let alone that she's a chemist."

He shrugs nonchalantly. "When's your birthday?"

"May 4th."

Sitting up, he slaps his knee. "Like, as in, may the fourth be with you?"

"Ugh, yes." I'm so tired of hearing that joke, but the fact that he understands the reference makes my heart soar. "Twenty-one I just turned," I say in my best Yoda voice.

Sam throws his head back as he bursts into laughter. "That's awesome."

"Thanks." I blush, pressing my lips together. "I'm still adjusting to drinking in public. It feels weird when I order alcohol sometimes."

"Meh, that will go away. I turned twenty-two last March and I don't give it a second thought now." He gives me a sideways glance. "Do you want a drink, Brynn? I've got some cheap beers and an even cheaper bottle of tequila if you're up for shots."

I crinkle my nose.

"Or I have bottles of water, too."

"A beer is fine with me."

"Coming right up." He winks before he gets up, and my stomach does that flip thing again.

When the slider door closes, I exhale. If ice cream didn't do anything to cool me off, hopefully a beer will. My phone dings. I pull it out as Sam opens the door and I immediately cringe. "Shit."

"What's wrong?" he asks, handing me my beer.

"It's Lisa. I told her I was coming back here to hang out, and she insisted I check in with her."

"Is she one of those mother-bear type friends?"

I snicker as I shake my head. "No, usually the opposite."

"So what is she freaking out about?" he asks before taking a sip of his beer.

"She wants the hotel name and your room number. Oh, and a picture of you."

Sam frowns.

"For identification purposes. You know, in case I go missing." I lift my phone and shrug a shoulder, giving Sam a pleading look.

He rolls those dark brown eyes, but they settle on me with an intense gaze. Shifting his position in his chair, Sam angles his face and gives me the sexiest smirk I've ever seen. My mouth runs dry as I drink him in. His strong jaw line curves perfectly as his curls frame his face, and I feel like I'm gawking at a work of art.

"Um, Brynn? You going to take the picture?"

My lungs begin to work again, and I choke on my breath. "Yeah, sorry," I manage to say. With a click of the button, I take the picture and send all the info to Lisa. My phone almost immediately dings with a response. As I read Lisa's message, I feel my cheeks getting red.

**LISA**: *Ooh, girl, you better hit that tonight!*

"What did she say?"

I whip my head up, wide-eyed and head shaking. "Nothing." Tucking the phone away, I open my beer and take a big drink. Now I *know* my cheeks are red. I take another huge gulp.

"So, Brynn, where are you from? I'm guessing not Grand Junction if you're staying in a hotel."

I give him an acknowledging nod as I finish my sip. Do I tell him I live in Greeley? It's only four hours from Casper, so there's a chance we could still see each other. But that will probably segue into me going to school and all the things I didn't want to tell him about earlier. I still feel like I'd be bragging if I spill my guts about my promising future. I can deflect, though.

"I grew up in Aurora. It's a suburb of Denver." The almost-lie tastes bitter on my tongue.

"So, not close to here?"

I shake my head. "No, it's like a four-hour drive, without traffic."

"That's a long way to drive for a mud race." Sam's mocking mouth tips up.

"Yeah, but it's closer than Wyoming."

The light in Sam's eyes dims at my attempted joke. Maybe I ruined the fun by pointing out our limited time together. I also put more miles between us by lying about where I live. Good job, Brynn.

To further safeguard myself from details, I get up from my chair. "I've got to pee."

Sam motions to the slider, and I take my leave. Goosebumps immediately rise on my skin at the stark difference between the warm, welcoming evening air and the frigid air-conditioned room.

The entire time I'm inside, I'm at war with myself. I mean, technically, I didn't lie. I did grow up in Aurora, I just don't live there anymore.

But why didn't I tell him that?

I guess it doesn't really matter anyway. Sam's going back to Wyoming tomorrow, and we'll never see each other again. What does it matter where we live after that? Long-distance doesn't work. At least that's what Connor said–

I shake my head. Don't start thinking about him. He left a year ago and Sam's here, right in front of me. For now, at least.

Once I'm finished in the bathroom, I step back onto the patio, shivering as I do.

Same gives me a sideways glance.

"Air-conditioning," I say as I shrug. Then I notice our chairs have been moved. They're right next to each other, the arms touching. "What happened here?"

"Oh, the wind kicked up. A huge gust blew your chair right up against mine." Sam smiles mischievously.

I purse my lips as I glance around, playing into his ruse. "That's weird. There's not even a breeze now."

"I know. Super strange."

I round the chairs, biting my cheek to contain my excitement, but as I go to sit, Sam puts his hand on the arms of our chairs and turns his palm up. My heart flutters as I slide my hand into his, entwining our fingers. The little squeeze he gives prompts flutters in my stomach, too.

"I'm glad we got to hang out tonight."

"Me too."

His thumb caresses the back of my hand as he gazes at the darkened sky. "I really wish I didn't have to go back to Wyoming tomorrow."

Him voicing the inevitable slices through me like a sharpened blade, and I sigh. Why do the men in my life keep leaving me for other states? I don't know what to say, so I don't speak.

Sam turns his body so our eyes meet, his flicking between mine, but he keeps our hands entwined. "Brynn, if you could have one wish, just for tonight, what would it be?"

I jerk my head back. "That's a loaded question. Let me think about it."

"No, don't think."

"Ha. Overthinking is what I do. I weigh all my options against the possible outcomes, and go with whichever one would yield the best results."

"So, you treat everything like a science experiment?"

I hike a shoulder to my ear. "It's gotten me this far."

"Okay..." Sam draws out the syllables. "For this experiment to work, you have to give an organic answer. You could have anything you want, right now, but it only lasts for tonight. What do you wish for?"

I purse my lips, raising my gaze to the sky for a moment. "I don't know. How do you wish for something you know will be temporary?"

"You're a realist, aren't you?"

More like a scientist. "I guess you could say that, but I don't see the sense in having the thing you truly want for a finite amount of time. Why not wish for it to be yours forever?"

"Because that's not how life works. You have to seize the moment while you have it. Otherwise, you'll end up living in regret."

I exhale through pursed lips. "Wow, this conversation got real heavy real quick."

"Sorry. I didn't mean for it to." Sam settles back in his chair and runs his free hand through his hair. "Did I ruin our date?"

"No, not ruined." I sip my beer. "But I have to say this is one of the more unorthodox dates I've been on."

"Yeah? How so?"

"I don't know. I always thought of dates as dinner and a movie."

Sam makes a grunting noise. "It's too hard to get to know someone that way. You can't talk while you're shoving food in your mouth–" He pauses to make strong eye contact. "Ice cream doesn't count."

I laugh.

"And you definitely can't talk during a movie." He gives me a sideways glance, his brown eyes sparkling. "This is better."

"I guess I don't have much to compare it to, but this is turning out to be my favorite."

Sam's eyebrows squish together. "Not much to compare it to? You don't date?"A lump forms in my throat and I have to swallow it down before I can speak. "I've only gone on two dates in the last year. Neither of them were good. Before that, I was in a long-term relationship." I drop my gaze to watch a truck that's heavy on the exhaust drive away from the gas station. That can't be good for the ozone layer. "It didn't end well."

"I'm sorry."

"Thanks. I'm actually still kind of recovering from it."

"Well, I don't know who the guy was, but I'm going to go out on a limb here and say he's an idiot."

When I lift my head to thank him, I find the warmest, most genuine smile on his face, and my insides melt. We stare at each other for several moments, as if we're both memorizing each other's features. Every passing second, another butterfly takes flight inside me.

Sam blinks. "I, uh, I have to use the bathroom now."

When he slides his fingers from mine, I immediately miss his warmth. In fact, I miss his presence entirely. It's a weird feeling. My heart didn't come out of my relationship with Connor intact, so for me to be feeling these things about Sam, well, it doesn't make a lot of sense.

But I'm feeling them anyway.

I just met the guy today, but it's like we've known each other for a lot longer. Not like old friends, but not exactly acquaintances. Somewhere in between, and... I like it. It's so natural to talk to him, and I don't ever want to stop.

Tomorrow will come, though. And sooner than I want it to.

An idea pops into my head. It's a bold move, bolder than dancing in the park, but I can't squander this time I have with Sam. I hope I'm not being too forward, but I have to try. If I don't, I may never know if this thing between us is real.

# CHAPTER 5

THE SLIDER OPENS AND Sam steps back onto the balcony. Immediately, he pauses to study me lounging in the now single patio chair.

I shrug. "The wind again. It blew your chair all the way over there, and I didn't want to get up to get it." I point across the ten-foot space.

Sam laughs. "These gusts have been crazy, but where am I supposed to sit now?"

With a sheepish grin, I pat the seat of my chair. I watch Sam take a breath before he moves toward me. As he stares down, an intensity in his eyes, I stare back with a growing ache between my thighs.

"Can you get up?"

"What?" I ask, slightly offended that he doesn't want me in the chair.

He extends his hand to me. "If you get up, it'll be easier to situate ourselves. I'm too big, I'll crush you."

"Oh." I take his hand, allowing him to help me up so he can get comfortable.

When he does, he holds his arms open to invite me into him. I gladly accept. As soon as I'm at his side, Sam cocoons me in his strong embrace, and I snuggle up. We fit so naturally, so perfectly. I rest my head on his chest and listen to his heart beating wildly behind his ribs. Almost as wildly as my own.

"This is perfect," he whispers.

All I can do is nod. I'm so taken aback by how much I agree with him that I don't even know what to think.

"Brynn?"

"Hm?"

Sam's knuckle finds its way under my chin, and he tilts my head up. As he stares at me, I see so many things swirling in his irises, longing, desire, adoration, admiration. It's the way I've always wanted to be looked at.

"I want to kiss you so badly." Sam's voice sounds strained, like he's holding himself back. "May I?"

"Yes," I breathe.

He presses his lips to mine in the gentlest of kisses. It's soft, affectionate, not at all hungry like I expected. No, this is all tenderness and it's everything I want it to be. Brushing together, our lips caress one another.

All too soon, Sam pulls away, taking the air from my lungs with him.

"That was...amazing," he says as he presses his forehead to mine and closes his eyes.

"Sam?" I wait for his eyelids to open before I say, "Do it again."

His mouth ticks up on one side as he leans in to put our lips together once more. This time, though, he cradles the back of my head, tilting it so he can deepen the kiss. I don't mind. In fact, when his tongue slides along my mouth, I part my lips.

The longer we make out, the more I want. Not just in the kiss, but of him. I twist my fingers into his shirt and shift so our bodies make as much contact as possible. His free arm wraps around my waist, his fingers digging into me, and I moan. He devours the sound.

Our legs entwine, his thigh sliding between mine, and before I know it, I'm grinding against him like some horny teenager. The rational, overthinking part of my brain is mortified. I don't do stuff like this.

But, boy does it feel good.

So good, I'm ignoring all the alarms going off in my head and replacing them with Sam's grunts and groans. The more I move, the louder he gets, and it's so damn hot. I never knew I could make a guy feel something without being naked. It's empowering on a level I've never known. I like it.

I grind faster, harder. My hands are roaming, touching him every place they can reach. The best spots though, are where my fingertips brush his bare skin. Every single time I do, I'm set on fire. It only makes the space between my thighs wetter.

When he whispers my name against my mouth, I shatter. My body shudders as that delicious crest swallows me, but I don't stop kissing him. He doesn't seem to mind, either.

Once I'm finished, once my body has stopped convulsing, I let out a shaky breath and lock my eyes on his. The amusement dancing in his gaze immediately has my cheeks burning hot. I bury my face in my hand. "Oh my God, I'm so sorry."

"What? No, don't be sorry." Sam gently wraps his fingers around my wrist and pulls my hand away from my face. "Brynn...will you look at me?"

With a grimace, I tilt my head up to find the most adoring smile on his face. Not an ounce of judgment. Just plain, simple acceptance, and it melts away my tension.

"That was...incredible." He licks his lips, flicking his gaze to my mouth. "Do you maybe want to go inside?"

My eyebrows shoot to the sky in question.

"I'm not expecting anything, but I think we'd be better off indoors so we don't keep giving the gas station a show."

I let out a light chuckle and nod.

Sam holds on to me as he gets out of the chair, setting my shaky feet on the ground and taking my hand. He leads me through the slider and toward the bed. When he turns to sit, I don't follow. Instead, I stand there, staring at the bed like it's a ticking time-bomb.

He sighs. "Did you start thinking?"

"I told you, it's what I do." I shrug before I fold my arms across my middle in a self-hug.

"Can't you, you know, not think?"

I bark out a laugh. "You don't know me at all, Mudboy."

"I'm serious. Why can't you live in the moment?"

I lift my chin, looking to the ceiling. "Because I'm afraid of where the moment will lead me." Dropping my gaze to the bed momentarily, I give him a knowing look.

Sam raises his hands as if surrendering. "Brynn, I'm not expecting anything from you." He sighs, lowering his arms to his sides. "Do you want to hear a story?"

I nod. He pats the spot next to him, so I reluctantly sit down.

"Once upon a time, there was this guy named Samuel Eastman…"

I laugh, and he bumps me with his shoulder.

"Sam grew up in Wyoming, never really traveled much. So, when his long-term girlfriend had the chance to move to New York City, well, he was excited for her."

A familiar pit forms in my gut. Even in Sam's deliciously deep voice, that city still sounds like nails on a chalkboard. I've never visited, but Connor abandoning me to move there ruined it. I wonder if it's ruined for Sam too? "You were excited? Not sad she was leaving?"

"I mean, sure I was sad. She and I had been together for a couple of years, but I couldn't stop her from going." He folds his hands between his knees. "Besides, we decided to try long-distance."

I bristle. Connor wouldn't even humor the idea of a long-distance relationship. He outright dismissed it and me.

Sam gives me a sideways glance, but continues his story. "It worked for a few months. We talked every night before bed, did video calls, and even made plans for me to come visit."

"Did you ever make it out there?"

Sam hangs his head. "No."

"So, what happened?"

With a deep breath, he raises to sit up straight. "Over time, our calls became less frequent. She wouldn't text me back for a day or two. I honestly saw a breakup coming, but then she told me she was coming back to Wyoming for

Christmas." A sad smile tips his lips up. "She sounded really excited, and I thought everything was going to be okay."

I grimace, but don't say anything. I see where this is going; another person lost to New York City.

"When she came back, it was like nothing had changed. We fell into each other seamlessly. Spent the whole week of Christmas into New Year's together. I convinced myself that we just went through a rough patch. Long-distance is hard, so I'd just have to try harder to make it work." He sighs. "But she had other ideas."

"Oh, no," I whisper.

"Yeah." He sucks in a breath, letting it out slowly. "Apparently, she had been planning to break up with me for a while, but didn't want to do it over the phone. I appreciated that, but I didn't appreciate her sleeping with another guy in the meantime."

I feel like I just got punched in the stomach, and it's not even my story. Poor Sam.

"Needless to say, she got what she wanted. Our relationship ended."

"I'm so sorry, Sam. That's awful." I lay my hand on his, and he turns his head to face me.

"That was last January."

"What?"

"We broke up in January. And I'm not telling you this for your sympathy. I'm telling you because what you said about your heart not being intact after your last relationship? Well, I know all about that."

The sincerity in his tone grounds me. It ties me to him in a way I've not known with anyone else, not even Lisa. He knows the heartache of being betrayed by someone you love. The hurt that only your heart feels.

# CHAPTER 6

As we stare into each other's eyes, I'm lost in his sparkling brown irises. Until he leans close and whispers, "I see you, Brynn."

A delicious shiver runs up my spine, breaking the spell.

"Are you cold?"

I shake my head, my brow furrowing as I realize that's actually true. I look toward the air-conditioner. "No, I'm not. Why am I not cold?"

I turn back around to find a softness in Sam's features. "I shut off the a/c when I came in earlier. I wanted you to be comfortable if you came back in here."

How utterly adorable. Such a sweet thing for someone to do. Let alone someone I've known less than a day. Before I can think too hard about it, I throw my arms around his neck and pull him to me. Our mouths crash together in a fiery kiss.

This is different than our tender moment on the balcony. This is pure passion, lust.

It takes Sam a moment to adjust, but soon his hands spring into action. His fingers dig into my back as he hauls me flush against his firm chest. One of his hands runs up my spine to cup the back of my head, tilting it so his tongue can plunge into my mouth.

My fingers eagerly dance along his body. I trace the ridges of his muscular back and shoulders, creeping a hand up his neck to tangle in his hair. My other hand finds the hem of his shirt and dives underneath.

He sucks in a breath against my lips, but resumes our kiss without hesitation.

I'm not disappointed by what I feel under his shirt. If the muscles in his back weren't enough of an aphrodisiac, his chest and abs certainly are. Every crevice, every ridge, every nuance has my heart rate climbing and my imagination running rampant, and I can't wait another second to see for myself.

I lift his shirt, but he snags my wrist. With a delicate caress of my mouth with his lips, he pulls away, and I'm devastated. What did I do wrong? Were we not just heavily making out?

Sam brushes his knuckle down my cheek. "Let me," he says before pulling his shirt off.

I'm not only relieved, I'm entranced. He's gorgeous. Like, Adonis the Greek god gorgeous, and all I can do is stare. Hopefully, I'm not drooling.

"Brynn?"

"Hm?" I hum, but I can't tear my eyes away from his exquisitely chiseled torso. When he doesn't say anything else, I flick my gaze up to find a pleased smirk on his face, and I blush.

Without a word, he wraps his arms around me and connects our mouths once again. It doesn't take long for our passion to reignite, but now, without his shirt as a barrier, I'm dying to know what skin to skin contact feels like.

But either Sam is too distracted by our make-out session, or he's too nice to force his hand, because he's not making any move to take off my clothes. I appreciate the respect, but damn, I need contact.

I can't wait any longer, so I do what I always do— take control. I nudge him onto his back and throw my leg over his hips to straddle him and his straining pants. My braids tickle the sides of my face as we kiss. As much as I don't want to take my lips from his, I have to remove my torturous shirt immediately.

I move away from his mouth, kissing along his jaw to his ear and whisper, "My turn." As I sit up, I take in his wide-eyed, eager expression. It's adorable.

His hands fall to my hips, his thumbs brushing the skin of my stomach under my shirt.

When I lift it over my head, taking my sports bra along, I toss them to the floor without a second thought. He hardens against my apex. I fight the urge to grind against him as the need for more friction burns deeps within me. We still have way too many layers between us.

His gaze rakes over my body, like he's memorizing each and every curve. After a lingering moment on my bare breasts and a deep swallow, his eyes travel up to meet mine. "You're beautiful."

I blush, but I roll my eyes. "What a line," I say, my tone full of sarcasm.

"No, I mean it." He takes my wrists in his hands, pulling me down so our faces are inches apart. "I thought you were beautiful the moment you turned to fist bump me this morning. I thought you were beautiful when you were covered from head to toe in mud, when you conquered that vertical wall in one leap, when you showed up at my door freshly showered." He licks his lips. "You've been beautiful every minute I've known you, Brynn. It just keeps getting better."

And I keep getting wetter. Fuck if that wasn't the greatest thing he could've said. I kiss him solidly as my hands slide down his ribs to his hips where my fingers glide over to the button on his jeans. I make quick work of his fly, and he bucks his hips to remove his pants.

I giggle as we bounce up and down.

We don't break the kiss, and it seems like we're jumping right into where we left off a minute ago, but he rolls me to the side and pulls away.

"Are you sure about this?" he asks, his eyes searching mine in the sincerest of hunts.

I nod. "Yeah, I am. I mean, I've already taken off my shirt, so…"

He laughs and shakes his head gently. "You've thought it through?"

"Sam," I whisper, cupping his cheek. "I'm done thinking for tonight. If I start again now, who knows what'll happen?'

His Adam's apple bobs with a deep swallow. "Hang tight for a sec." He practically jumps from the bed, racing to his suitcase and furiously rummages through it.

I prop myself up on my elbows to watch him. My thighs clench, rubbing together to give me some reprieve from the desire pooling low in my belly. The way the muscles in his back and shoulders flex as he moves is nothing short of mesmerizing. And don't even get me started on his butt. It fills out those boxers perfectly, like it's begging to be pinched. My lower lip finds its way between my teeth, and I bite down, hard.

When he spins around, he flies back to the bed, landing in the exact spot he was moments ago, and holds up his hand. A small, square package is tucked between his fingers. "Sorry. I figured this would be a good idea."

My whole body tenses. I give a tight-lipped smile.

His excited expression falls. "Did I ruin things by being presumptuous?"

"What? No." I shake my head, dropping my chin and pinching the bridge of my nose. "It's been a long time, and seeing that made it super real for a second."

He sighs and pulls my hand from my face. "We don't have to do anything, Brynn. This is a precaution in case things get that far. I don't expect anything from you. You can tell me to stop at any time, and I'll stop. I promise."

I trail my finger along his jaw. "What if I don't want you to stop?" The words come out as a shaky whisper.

His mouth ticks up on one side. "Then I'll spend all night showing you how beautiful you are."

I'm reduced to a quivering puddle. How Sam can keep saying all the right things, I'll never know, but he delivers the lines perfectly.

As we dive into yet another extension of our make-out session, Sam runs his hand up my stomach to cup my breast. I moan at the way his fingers expertly tweak my hardened nipple, and soon I'm writhing beneath him. He massages and kneads, our grunts and moans growing louder. As his hand leaves my breast to travel down my stomach, I shudder, feeling him smiling against my mouth. When his hand reaches the waistband of my shorts, he stops.

"These need to go."

Gladly. I shuck my shorts and fling them across the room with my foot. All the while with Sam's tongue in my mouth. Once the shorts are gone, Sam's fingers glide along the hem of my underwear, and I gasp. When he runs his fingertips over my wet core, I moan.

"Brynn, I'd like to make you feel good like you did outside." He nips at my lower lip. "May I?"

I can't nod quickly enough.

Sam crashes his mouth to mine in a deep, fierce kiss as his fingers slip under the hem of my panties and inside me. One finger, then two, pulsing in and out of me while his thumb makes circles on my clit. I let out a long, low moan. I've never been touched like this before.

Pulling on my lip, Sam moves away from my mouth to pepper kisses down my jaw to my throat, and farther south to my chest. He takes one of my nipples into his mouth, and I'm set on fire. The swirling of his tongue coupled with his thumb circling my clit is brilliant.

When he moves to my other breast, I tangle my hand in his hair. I don't ever want him moving from this spot. The desire building between my thighs, though, begs to be released.

Sam wrenches himself loose of my grip to trail kisses back up my body and to my ear. "Come for me, Brynn."

I break. My dam holding back all my lustful desires cracks, and I spill over the edge. As my entire body quakes with release, Sam doesn't waver. His fingers slow, but don't stop as he allows me to ride this wave to completion.

When I'm done shuddering, he removes his fingers and plants gentle kisses along my neck. "That was fucking gorgeous," he says between pecks. "I don't think you understand how beautiful you are."

I'm so breathless, I can't even respond, so I hum contentedly.

He rolls to his side, gathering me to his chest as his hand rests on my stomach. The only sounds I hear are his heartbeat and the occasional engine revving at the gas station. When Sam's fingers begin moving, my skin prickles with goosebumps. He lightly traces lines along my body, swooping from my hips to my ribs and back again.

My relaxation quickly becomes anticipation as Sam's hand moves over my breast and his fingers pinch my nipple. With a moan, I clench my thighs.

He leans down, planting a soft kiss on my lips. "I don't want to be done, but I'll stop if you want me to. Just say the word, Brynn."

I flop my head from side to side, but only an angsty moan escapes me.

"I need words, Brynn." Sam's voice is low as his mouth moves down my throat, over my collarbone, and to my chest. "Tell me what you want." His tongue flicks my sensitive peak before he takes it in his mouth and sucks.

My back arches off the bed to get as much of me in his mouth as I can. When his hand slides between my thighs, I grab his wrist. He jerks his head up, a surprised expression on his face.

"Make love to me, Sam."

His fingers dig into my ribs. "Really?"

"Please," I beg.

With lightning speed, he flips over to grab the condom. He keeps his back to me as he yanks off his boxers and sheathes his erection. Rolling back over, he doesn't waste a second getting down to business. His hungry kiss devours my mouth, swallowing my moans and whimpers as his chest bears down on my own. He nudges his knee between my thighs, his erection resting on top of my quad, and encourages me to grind against him.

Sam's hand slides down my ribs to my hip where he tucks his thumb into the waistband of my panties and pulls them down. Once they're off, he pushes my legs apart, settling himself at my entrance. He locks his eyes on mine one last time before pressing inside of me.

I wince, a small whimper escaping me, and latch my hands onto Sam's biceps.

"Shit, Brynn. You okay? Did I hurt you?" The panic in his voice is sincere.

I shake my head. "No. You're...big."

He hums in satisfaction as he begins moving inside me. "So, I should take it slow?"

"Not too slow."

With a growl, he leans down and latches his mouth to my neck. His thrusts speed up, but every movement feels precise, which I like. The way he moves is so perfect, it has the tension building within me almost instantly, which is saying a lot.

I've never been a big fan of the missionary position. I'd much rather be on top where I can control the speed and amount of friction, but it's like he knows what I need him to do without me even saying it.

My hands scour his body, running up and down his back, across his shoulders, tickling his ribs. I can't get enough. I want to touch him everywhere. Each time my fingertips find a new ridge to trace, they burn from the contact. I finally twist my hand into his hair, pulling him closer, pressing our chests together.

The delicious pressure growing inside of me has me on the verge of another orgasm, and I can't wait. I buck my hips, moving in sync with his. The change in angle pushes me over the edge, and I tighten around Sam's cock, riding out this bliss. When the sensation ebbs, I open my eyes to find Sam grimacing, almost as if he's in pain.

He grunts, exhaling deeply. "I don't want to come yet."

I blush at his candidness, but I have to admire his resolve. Too many times was I left high and dry because Connor finished early and didn't have the "strength" to ensure I was satisfied. So, if Sam wants to keep going, I'm game.

"Can we switch places?" I ask.

His mouth ticks up on one side. "Of course." And he rolls to the side, taking me with him, but without removing himself from me.

I yelp in surprise, but I'd be lying if I said I'm not turned on by that move. Once we're settled, it's not long before he's raking over my naked body. As his gaze moves down, his hands move up to my chest. Sam's hands cup my breasts, his thumbs gently rubbing my hardened nipples. His cock jumps inside of me.

"Is this how you want it, or can I suggest something?" he asks, not looking away from his massaging hands.

"Anything."

"Can we move so I can sit against the headboard? This view is fantastic, but I'd like to be able to kiss you, too."

"I like the sound of that."

Without a word, Sam wraps one hand around my waist while the other aids him in scooting our bodies up the mattress. He slides his back up the headboard so he's sitting upright. Face to face with each other, only inches apart, our breath mingles in the space between our lips.

He tugs my lower lip down with his thumb. "Perfection," he whispers before his lips meet mine in another all-consuming kiss.

He's right. Everything about this is perfection. The way we met, our flirting, our date, and now this. The sex so far has been amazing, and now that I'm in my favorite position, it's going to get better.

I move my hips, raising up and down on my knees. Since he's already struggling to restrain himself, I don't want to overdo it right away, so I start slow. A nice, rhythmic pace has Sam panting in no time, but when I increase the speed, he's groaning into my mouth. His hands crawl up my sides to my breasts again, and it's my turn to moan.

He pulls his mouth from mine, trailing kisses to my ear. "Brynn, I lied."

My heart leaps into my throat. What the fuck does he mean he lied? Lied about what?

"I didn't want to sit up just so I could kiss *you*." He nips at my earlobe before nudging me back to take my nipple in his mouth. His tongue flicks and swirls as his fingers massage.

All I can do is let my head fall back and a groan of pleasure slips from my lips.

With a gentle kiss, he whispers, "I wanted to kiss these, too."

"You're forgiven," I say between breaths.

As Sam laves my nipples, he also moves his hips in tempo with mine. He's letting me keep control, but he's amping up the pressure that much more. It's extremely hot.

When our desires grow too intense, we speed up our movements. What was sensual lovemaking is fast becoming carnal lust. It's so intense, I lose myself in the moment. It's not like me. I'm always on top of things, always in the know, but right now, my brain is fuzzy with pleasure. I don't even know how to move myself.

Sam seems to read me. Without relinquishing my nipple from his mouth, he clamps his hand on my hip, his fingers digging into the side of my ass. His other hand wraps around my upper back, bracing me so I can stay upright. Bending his knees, his hips take over all the work.

"Let go, Brynn. Enjoy yourself," he growls against my breast.

I obey. I let him hold me, let him fulfill me. I release my grip on this moment and simply fall into another pool of desire, lust, and passion. As I call out his name over and over, I tumble into another crest, breaking with it like the tide.

My body shudders.

His grip tightens.

When my walls clench around him, he gives another few strong thrusts before he meets his own release. His cock pulsates inside of me as we both hit the peak of our climax. Soon, our movements slow. Our bodies shake together. It takes several moments for either of us to regain our composure.

With a deep inhale, he lifts his head and when his gaze meets mine, I see adoration in his languid eyes. He takes my chin between his thumb and forefinger. "You okay?"

"I'm better than okay."

"So, you enjoyed yourself, then?"

I nod. "Many times."

"Mmm," he hums as his finger traces my lower lip. "Does that mean you want to do it again?"

For the love of all that is holy, yes! "If you want to."

"Brynn," Sam says, grit lacing his tone. "I want nothing more than to watch your gorgeous body shudder with the pleasure I give to you."

I try to swallow, but my mouth has run dry, so I settle for, "Kiss me again."

And he does. All night long.

# Chapter 7

The next morning, I wake in an empty bed. It's not at all what I expect. I don't know exactly *what* I expected, but I thought I'd wake up with Sam's arms still around me, since that's how we fell asleep last night. At the very least, with him laying next to me. Instead, I'm wrapped in the thin hotel blanket, still naked, and quite confused.

At first, I think Sam is in the bathroom. I sit very still, and listen carefully, but I don't hear anything. No running water, no hum of an electric razor, not even the shuffling of a toothbrush. I'm all alone.

Panic bubbles in my gut. Which is a strange sensation considering the defeat that's weighing down my chest.

How could he leave? After everything we shared last night? After a night I can only describe as magical? Was it all a lie?

Of course it was. I'm so incredibly stupid. How could I have believed everything he said? I let some guy feed me a load of crap and I ate it up. This has got to be the dumbest thing I've ever–

The click of the hotel room door pulls my attention away from my pity party, and I gather the blankets to my chest. I expect it to be housekeeping, but instead, Sam waltzes through the doorway. He's holding a cardboard drink carrier with three to-go cups in it while a plate of breakfast foods balances on top. He tucks his keycard into his pocket and takes the plate off the stack.

I sniffle, and his head whips up. "Hey, you're awake!" The excited expression on his face falls the longer he looks at me. "Hey. Hey, what's wrong?" He walks to the bed, setting the food and drinks on the side table before taking a seat next to me.

I swipe at my dewy lashes as I shake my head. "I thought you left."

His eyebrows scrunch together in confusion until understanding dawns on him. "Oh, Brynn. How could you think I would– Well, why wouldn't you?" He squeezes his eyes shut and pinches the bridge of his nose. "I'm sorry. You were sleeping so peacefully, I didn't want to wake you, but I thought you'd like something to eat." When he finally opens his eyes, all I see is remorse.

"It's okay. I over-thought things. Again." I shrug, plastering on a big smile to show he's forgiven. "So, what's for breakfast?"

He grimaces. "Now, that is something I should apologize for." Turning to grab the plate,  he sets it on the bed between us. "The only thing that even seemed edible were the bagels, but I didn't know what kind you'd like so I took one of each."

I stare at the pile of assorted bagels, noting the cinnamon raisin one. "Anything except that one. I'm allergic to cinnamon."

"Really? I didn't even know that was possible."

"Mhm."

"All right, well then…" Sam proceeds to pull a bagel from the opposite side of the plate. "How about blueberry? It's the only one the cinnamon bagel didn't touch."

I laugh. "I don't know that I'm *that* allergic, but thanks."

Sam almost seems to get lost as he looks at me, because he quickly blinks and clears his throat. "There's coffee, but again, didn't know what you like, so I got two cups and all the cream and sugar I could carry."

I pop a piece of bagel in my mouth. "If you got two cups of coffee, why is there a third cup in the tray?"

"Oh, because as I was pouring the coffee, it struck me that you might be a tea person. So I grabbed a cup of hot water and one of each tea. You know, all four of them."

Warmth blooms in my chest at his thoughtfulness. "I do like tea sometimes, but coffee is a necessity." I eye the drink tray as he hands me a cup. "And I'd say you brought just enough cream and sugar for me."

"You're going to use all of it?" He gives me an incredulous look.

"Unless you want some."

"No, I like mine black. Puts hair on your chest." He pounds his fist against his pec.

I cover my mouth with my hand as I laugh with a mouthful of food. "What about the tea, though?"

"You can take it home. Consider it your consolation prize for having to choke down this award-winning breakfast."

We share a laugh, but as hungry as we are, we finish the whole plate of bagels. He eats three of the five, including the cinnamon raisin, and I even take a chance that the plain bagel went uncontaminated, even though it touched the cinnamon one. I live through it.

Toward the end of our meal, my phone chimes. As I lean over the side of the bed to fish it out of my shorts, I only take half the blanket with me. It slides down my torso, exposing my breasts. I hear what sounds like Sam choking, then coughing. A huge, flattered grin spreads across my face, but I groan when I read my message.

"Who is it?" Sam chokes out.

"Lisa," I reply, sitting back up. I purposefully don't cover myself. "She wants to know if I'm alive and when she's getting her car back."

Sam doesn't say anything, so I glance up from my phone to find his gaze fixed on my chest. I clear my throat, and his head whips up. I arch my eyebrows in question.

"To be fair, they were staring at me first."

A hearty laugh escapes me, making my whole body shake, and Sam's gaze drops back down.

"Uh uh, buddy. Up here," I say, putting my finger under his chin and lifting his head. I pull the blanket up again.

"Shucks." He snaps his fingers, but his forehead crinkles. "Wait, Lisa wants *her* car back? It's not yours?"

I shake my head as I type my response to Lisa. "I don't own a car. I have a license, and I know how to drive, but I haven't owned a car in a couple years."

"Why?"

I shrug. "I realized I don't really need one, and it's one more thing I can do to help the environment."

Sam hums. "So, what did you tell Lisa?"

"I said we were eating breakfast, and I'd be back in a little while." My heart sinks as I say the words. Leaving Sam is inevitable, but saying it out loud makes it real, and I'm not ready to let him go.

He must feel it too, because he doesn't say anything more as he watches his fingers pick at imaginary lint on the blanket.

We sit in heavy silence for several minutes, both filling our mouths with either food or drink as a means of avoiding speaking. Neither of us wants to address the humongous elephant in the room. You know, the one that'll eventually step between us.

When Sam swallows the last of his bagel, he picks up his coffee cup and twirls it on his thigh. "Okay, Brynn. Instead of sitting here in silent tension, we should talk about...you know."

"About how eventually we're going to have to leave this bed, and this hotel, and drive back to our respective homes without each other?"

"Yeah." His voice shakes.

I take a deep breath as I blink away the tears forming. "What do we need to say? We both knew this"–I wave my hand between us–"had an expiration. We've just hit our time limit, and now we have to face the music."

"It's such a sad song, though."

A tear breaks free and slides down my cheek. I feel silly for being this emotional over a man I just met. But when Sam wipes it away and cups my cheek, the embarrassment subsides. This feels too right to wave off. I cover his hand with mine and nuzzle into his palm.

We don't say anything more about the inevitable. What could we say? We both knew it was coming, and there was nothing we could do about it. Also, we both seem to understand there's not a future here. We haven't officially said we're not going to see each other again, but there's an unspoken conversation happening, and the theme is "this is the end."

But instead of wallowing in our sadness, we fill our last moments together with light-hearted topics such as our mediocre breakfast, the horrible smell of the hotel, and the general discomfort of the mattress. Our laughter lifts the mood. It distracts us from the knowledge of our looming deadline.

Then, the Mud Down gets brought up.

"It was a great race," Sam says cheerfully. "I can't wait to do it again next year."

A hollowness engulfs me at the idea of the Mud Down being another year away. I'm always a little sad when this weekend is over, but now I'm losing Sam, too. The idea of a long-distance relationship briefly pops into my mind. Wyoming isn't that far away from Greeley. It could work.

But after the devastating story he told last night, I know long-distance isn't something he'd go for. Besides, I've already lied about where I live, so I'd be backtracking on what I've told him. It would make me a jerk. I don't want to end our time together by apologizing for being dishonest.

"I don't want it to end," I say through more tears.

Sam gathers me to his chest, running his hand down my hair, tugging gently on one of my braids. "Me neither. I'd stay here with you forever if I could, but we can't stop time."

I glance at the clock. It's 8:47 a.m. "When is checkout?"

"Um, ten-thirty, I think. Why?"

"What would you say to us making the last hour and a half we have together really count?" I bob my eyebrows.

A mischievous grin takes over Sam's face. "You're the perfect woman, Brynn Erlenmeyer."

***

Standing in the parking lot and sulking, I sag against Sam's chest as he holds me tight. We've been loitering here a good five minutes while Walt waits in the running car behind us. I'm surprised he hasn't honked yet.

Sam finally tucks his knuckle under my chin, lifting my head up. "Hey. It'll be okay."

"How?" I choke out.

He shrugs, grimacing. "I don't know, but you'll see. Everything will work out. We'll be all right."

I snort, swiping at my nose. "You're placating me, now."

"Yeah, well, what else can I do?"

"Nothing."

"Listen, I don't want to let go of you any more than you do me. Just thinking about it has my guts twisting." He sounds angry, but it's not directed at me. "If I could take you with me, or go with you, I would in a heartbeat."

"I bet you say that to all the girls." It's a joke, but when Sam doesn't laugh, I look up to find a fire in his eyes.

"I'm not that guy, Brynn. I don't pick up random women, and I certainly don't invite women I've just met to my hotel room to have sex. This wasn't a meaningless hook-up for me. I hope it wasn't for you, either."

I swallow down my shame. "Of course not.

His expression softens, a tinge of remorse in his features. "But I also don't have a magic wand. That's not how life works."

"I know." I hate how pathetic I sound.

A warm smile crosses his lips. "And we can talk still, right? You've got my number, and I have yours. It's not like we'll never communicate again."

It's a grain of sand in an ocean, but I latch onto it with all my strength. "Yeah. You're right."

"Come here." Sam wraps me in his strong embrace and connects our mouths. It's the tenderest of kisses, much like our first on the balcony last night. Our lips caress each other's as we try to stretch this moment as long as possible.

But it's over too soon.

Sam releases me from his grip, and I'm so incredibly cold. Never mind that it's already eighty degrees outside. He slips into the passenger side of the car, his expression tight as he waves through the window. The car backs out of the parking space, moves through the lot, and pulls onto the road, driving away from me without even a second glance.

I manage to get to Lisa's car before I collapse into it and spend an exorbitant amount of time letting the tears flow freely.

# CHAPTER 8

"For fuck's sake, Brynn. Will you stop moping already?" Lisa stands in the doorway to my bedroom with her hands on her hips. "It's been a month!"

I roll from my back to my stomach, my arms hanging off the side of my bed. "I'm still sad."

Lisa huffs and sits down next to me. "Brynn, I totally understood when you cried all the way home from Grand Junction about it. I even gave you a pass when you cried off and on the week after we got home." She glides her hand down my hair, letting it rest on my back. "But you've been pining over this guy for a month. It has to stop sometime."

"You weren't there, though. You don't understand how perfect it was." I roll to my side and pick at the loose threads on my comforter. "I'm allowed to be sad for as long as I want."

"I'd almost agree with you if it weren't for one small detail."

"Which is?"

"You never even called him!" She throws her hands in the air. "You've had four weeks to reach out to the guy, but never did."

Indignation flares in me. "What exactly would I have said, huh? 'Oh, hey Sam. It's Brynn. Thanks for the great one-night-stand. Maybe we can hook up again next year after the Mud Down? Cool, have a good rest of your summer!'"

"Um, yeah. That would've been a great conversation."

I laugh, but it's stilted. "What would be the point of rehashing a night that we won't ever be able to have again?"

"You guys could have gotten to know each other more. Maybe started something serious? Casper isn't *that* far away."

"But he said he's going to be job searching. What if we got serious and made plans and then he got a job that took him clear across the country? Or even to another country? I don't think I could handle that, again."

"Not every guy is Connor."

I focus my gaze on the ceiling for a moment to keep the tears at bay. "Well, it doesn't matter. Sam didn't reach out to me either."

"Yeah, what's with that? I figured that would've been enough to make you call him. You're such a control freak, don't you need to know?"

I grit my teeth at her use of "control freak." Do I like to know what's going on? Yes. Does it mean I have to control everything around me? No. I may be a little more emphatic than most people, but that's not a bad thing. "He probably feels the same way I do about the situation. We synced that night, Lisa. We clicked. He knows as well as I do that there wasn't a real future for us. Why fight it?"

"Ugh, fine. I see there's no talking you down." She gets up and walks toward the door, but stops and spins to face me. "At least classes start tomorrow, so you'll have something to distract you."

A lightness fills me as I nod. "Yep. The only thing that sucks is I have to wait until Thursday for Professor St. James' class. But that means I don't have labs this week, so I guess it evens out."

***

With an exasperated groan, I traipse out of my first class Monday morning; English 305. I can already tell it's going to be the worst of my classes. Give me literature class and I'll read all day, every day, but an entire class dedicated to essays? No way. Unless I'm writing about pollution remediation and how the breakdown of chemicals affects nature, count me out.

As I exit the building, I'm welcomed by a warm August day. And that wonderful Greeley smell. Being an agricultural hub for the surrounding farmlands, Greeley is famous in Colorado for its Earthy aroma. After going to The University of Northern Colorado for almost four years, I've grown used to the stench of the pastures, but sometimes the slaughterhouse smell still gets to me. Being a vegetarian, I try not to think too hard about it.

Today, it's not so bad, so I relish the beautiful day as I walk home for lunch. The house I share with Lisa, Jackie, and Hannah is only a few blocks away from the UNC campus, which is enough time for me to warm up after being in that frigid English building.

Inside, I flop down at the kitchen table. Folding my arms, I cradle my head in them. "How am I going to survive a whole year of essays?" It's so depressing to think about that I've almost lost my appetite.

Almost.

I heat up some leftover pizza and try to forget that I have English again on Wednesday. Hopefully, my other classes won't be so bad. Of course, the best class is my last one of the week.

When Thursday comes, I'm beyond excited to get to my three-hour lecture class with Professor St. James. It's Organic Chemistry, supposedly the hardest of the chemistry courses, but I'm ready to be in the professor's presence again. I've had a class taught by Dr. Miranda St. James every semester since freshman year, and they're always my favorite.

The professor is brilliant. Her mind is amazing with the amount of knowledge flowing through it, and she's a great person. She also happens to own and operate an environmental research facility a few towns over. She gives the top chemistry major first chance at a spot in her paid internship every year, and not to brag, but I've basically been guaranteed that spot since sophomore year.

Working at that lab is my dream job. I've always loved nature and I can't wait to spend my life saving it.

I practically bounce through the door and across the classroom to take a seat at the front. I like to be as close as possible so I can hear and see everything going on. As students file in, I recognize quite a few. We've all had classes together for the past couple of years, so naturally, I know a lot of them.

We exchange amicable waves, but I keep to myself mostly. I've got my close-knit group of friends, and I like it that way.

When Professor St. James walks in, she heads straight to the desk, but catches me in her sight and smiles. Smiling back, I dip my head in recognition.

She checks the clock. "Since it's the first day of classes, I'm going to wait a few minutes for those who may be lost. Occupy yourselves a bit longer." With that, she begins unpacking her satchel.

I flip open my notebook and write "O-Chem" at the top with the date right next to it. As I'm writing, my mind drifts off momentarily. I think about all the great things happening for me. Senior year of college, an internship at a research facility owned by my favorite professor, great friends, and a bright future. The only thing missing is someone to share the rest of my life with.

If only that person could be–

The classroom door opens, pulling my attention away from my blank notebook page. I lift my gaze, and a million butterflies take off in my stomach as I watch the one person I least expect to walk in.

Sam Eastman.

His eyes scan the room from behind square-framed glasses. I didn't even know he wore glasses. When he finally lands on me, his face lights up, his expression surely matching my own. But then his brow furrows as he looks at the desks surrounding mine. They're all full. He gives me an apologetic shrug and tilts his head toward the back of the room.

I'm left gasping for air. My heart beats so wildly, it's drowning out all other noise. I know the professor has started the lecture, but I can't hear anything.

What is he doing here? He lives in Wyoming, so why is he in Colorado? I thought he was going to be job searching at the end of the summer. Why is he at my school? Why is he in this class?

One question puts all the others to rest...who cares?

What matters is he's here. I never thought I'd see him again, never thought we'd have a chance to be together, and now, here he is. Judging by the delight beaming from him, he's happy about it, too. I wiggle in my seat, unable to contain my excitement.

I can't wait for class to end so I can talk to him. We can tell each other all about our summers, and he can explain what in the world he's doing here.

My stomach plummets through the floor as that notion sinks in.

How will he explain it? He didn't mention anything about going to school when we met, and there's no way this is his first semester. He can't be in O-Chem as a freshman, can he? He'd have to be exceptionally brilliant.

But then how is he going to justify being here?

The bitter taste of bile creeps up my throat as I tell myself he'll have a perfectly reasonable explanation. He didn't lie. Sam wouldn't do that. Would he?

The questions won't stop coming, and I'm getting dizzy. I need to concentrate on the lecture, but I can't focus on anything. Luckily, I know Professor St. James will spend a good thirty minutes going over the class expectations and structure, but there will be actual teaching soon, and I need to listen.

Fortunately, I'm able to tamp down my worries, and manage to sit through the whole class. Unfortunately, I don't hear a lot of what is being said. I'm sure the professor would give me some notes on the lecture, but I'll have to explain why I wasn't paying attention and I'm not ready to do that.

When Professor St. James finally excuses us, everyone packs up and files out. As Sam leaves, we make eye contact, and he nods toward the door before stepping into the hallway. I shove all my belongings in my backpack and race after him.

I push through the flood of students and find Sam waiting across the hall. Even though my nerves are on edge right now, I can't help but notice how handsome he is. Better than I remember in Grand Junction.

He's got his hands in his pockets, backpack slung over his shoulder, his chin dipped. His light-brown curls hang down, framing his gorgeous face. Those brown eyes stare at me through his lashes, and a warm smile dances on his lips.

He takes a hand from his pocket to hike the backpack higher on his shoulder. "Hey, Brynn."

Even the sound of his voice is better than I remember. "Hey," I say quietly. Silence fills the hallway as the other students dissipate, leaving us to stare at each other. When Sam tilts his head, his glasses catch the light. "I didn't know you wore glasses."

"Oh, yeah." Sliding them off, he holds them out as if to admire them. "I don't wear them often, but I ran out of contacts and my order got delayed." He slips them back on. "I hate these things."

As I study how handsome he looks with the glasses, I bite my lip. "They're not so bad."

"Thanks." His cheeks tinge pink before he ducks his head. "So, uh, fancy meeting you here."

My heart leaps into my throat. I swallow it down. Right, I'm here to get answers. "What are you doing here?"

He runs a hand through his hair before rubbing the back of his neck. "Finishing my chemistry degree."

"You never said anything about going to college."

"Neither did you."

I fold my arms across my chest, annoyed at his turning the tables. "I didn't say anything because I didn't want to make you feel bad. You had lost your job, were worried you'd be losing time with your best friend. I didn't want to rub it in how good my life was."

"Oh, so you were pitying me?"

With a frown, I shake my head. This isn't the sweet, understanding Sam I met back in July. "Not pity, just...I don't know. I didn't want to gloat."

"So, you decided to lie instead?"

I scoff. "Me, lie? What about you? This isn't Wyoming, Sam."

"Technically, I didn't lie." He holds up his hand, index finger pointed to the sky. "When you asked me that, I *was* living in Wyoming. I only moved down here, like, a week ago."

"And you didn't think that was pertinent information to share? I mean, moving to Colorado couldn't have been a snap decision."

"No, it wasn't." With a sigh, he shoves his hand back into his pocket. "I transferred my credits down here at the end of last semester. That's why I quit my job. I wanted to take the summer to hang out with Walt before I moved."

My jaw hits the floor. "You lied about losing your job, too?"

"It wasn't really a lie. Mis-worded maybe, but not a lie."

An offended laugh escapes me. "You're so full of shit."

"Shh." He puts his finger to his lips as he takes a step closer to me. "What about you, huh? Greeley isn't exactly Aurora, Colorado."

I bristle, swallowing deep before speaking. "I never said I lived there, just that I grew up there. Which is true."

A dismissive look crosses his face. "Unbelievable."

"Don't spin this on me. You could've told me you were moving down here, but you chose to omit that tiny detail. Why?"

He groans as his head falls back to gaze at the ceiling. "I don't know. I had just met you, and we lived so far apart, at least I thought we did." He gives me a pointed look. "I guess I didn't think the details mattered."

I feel like I've been sucker-punched in the gut. "So, I was good enough to sleep with, but not good enough for you to share the details of your life with?"

"It's not that–"

"Then what is it?" I tighten my hold on myself, clenching my teeth. "You could have been honest, Sam."

"You could have, too." He points at me. "Instead, you made it sound like there were more miles between us." With a sigh, he removes his glasses to run his hand down his face. "And long-distance doesn't work, you know?"

"So, you lied to get what you wanted."

His hand stops on his chin as he gives me a sideways glance. "Excuse me?"

"You thought we'd never see each other again, so you decided to get some fun out of the deal."

Sam doesn't speak, he just stares at me, his mouth agape.

"All that stuff you said about not doing one-night stands was bullshit, huh? You knew if you gave us a deadline, it would raise the stakes, and saying you lived in Wyoming gave you an out." I lick my lips, bolstering myself for my next statement. "You used me."

His features soften, and for a moment, I see what I think is remorse swirling in his eyes. "Brynn, I..."

"Don't even start with your fake apologies." I hold my hands up as I back away. "Congratulations on your conquest, Sam Eastman." Spinning on my heel, I storm down the hallway, feeling sick to my stomach.

Sam calls after me, but I don't stop. I keep walking as fast as I can all the way home.

****

I spend the rest of the afternoon sobbing in my bed with my arms around a pillow. I'm so incredibly angry and hurt that the tears won't stop. It makes me even angrier to know I'm spilling them over Sam. A liar. A person who doesn't deserve my tears. Yet here I am.

I'm such a wreck that when Lisa walks in the door, she takes one look at me and rushes to my side. "Shit, Brynn, what's wrong?"

"He's here." I say through my tears.

"Who? Who's here?"

I grab a tissue and blow my nose. "Sam."

Lisa's eyebrows squish together. "What do you mean Sam's *here*? Like, in the house?"

"No." I shake my head, wiping my tears with another tissue. "In Colorado. He was in my lecture class today."

"No way."

"Uh huh. He knew all summer he was moving down here to go to school. He lied to me, Lisa." I choke out the last bit through more tears.

"That fucking skunk."

I sniffle. "And now he's here, at my school, in my class, and every time I see him, it'll remind me of what an idiot I am."

"Brynn, you are not an idiot." Lisa brings out her stern, serious tone.

"Yes, I am, considering what I did. I mean, I let some guy feed me lines, believing every one of them, and then I slept with him because I thought I felt some sort of connection. How could I be so naive?"

Lisa hums, like she's contemplating what she wants to say, before setting her hand on my knee. "Maybe your heart was exhausted."

"What do you mean?"

"This last year wasn't easy on you, Brynn. After what Connor pulled, you sort of curled in on yourself. Not that I'm blaming you. It makes total sense that you'd guard yourself pretty hardcore after that jerk, but I think it finally caught up to you."

I chew on my lower lip, but stay silent.

"I think that maybe when you met Sam, your heart took over and told your brain to take a break. You let yourself believe there was this grand connection because your heart was starved for it."

As much as I don't want it to, what Lisa says makes sense. I really did shut down after Connor abandoned me. I wouldn't let anyone in.

Until Sam came along. He was the first guy in a year to dissolve the barricade around my heart, and I let him. I'd be lying if I said it didn't feel good, though.

I tilt my head back to look at the ceiling. "It all seemed so perfect."

"I know, sweetie," Lisa says, scooting so she's sitting next to me. "But that's not necessarily a bad thing. Maybe it was what you needed to break you out of your funk. I mean, it was fun, right?"

I rub my thighs together as my cheeks heat. "It was incredible."

Lisa nudges me with her shoulder. "See? Just because Sam turned out to be a manipulative asshole, doesn't mean something good can't come from it. You had fun, got laid, and now you can move on and find someone worthy of you."

My breath comes a little easier as I mull over Lisa's words, but it gushes from my lips in a heavy sigh when I picture Sam's face. "Why did he have to be so hot, though?"

"They always are, Brynn." She pats my knee. "Hey, let's go out tonight."

"Seriously?" I ask, giving her a sideways glance.

Lisa grins at me. "Yeah, seriously. It's ladies' night at Coyote Canyon, and school's back in session so you know what that means?"

"Cheap drinks and dozens of guys willing to pay for them?"

"Bingo. You don't have classes tomorrow, right?"

I shake my head. "No, and since it's the first week of school, I also don't have any tutoring sessions yet. I have the whole day off."

"Perfect." Lisa's grin widens somehow. "Let's go out, get drunk, and maybe find you a guy to make you forget about Sam."

"He'll have to be a doozy."

"Then consider us on doozy patrol."

I laugh, feeling lighter with each chuckle. "You're a dork."

# Chapter 9

The thump of the bass in the hip-hop song fades into the twang of a steel guitar as people pair up to two-step. Coyote Canyon is by all means a country bar, but the DJ certainly knows how to mix it up.

Lisa and I scoot off the dance floor to stand under the air conditioner vent. After sweating my ass off dancing, I'll gladly accept the blasting chill. But only for a minute. I nudge Lisa to let her know I've had my fill, and we head to the bar, dismissing invites from cowboys to two-step along the way. Settling onto our stools, we order two vodka-cranberries. These will make our fifth ones of the night, but the first we've paid for ourselves.

"Here's to ladies' night!" Lisa shouts as she clinks her glass against mine.

I have to laugh. Not because of Lisa's enthusiasm, but also because I'm quite drunk. I'm feeling loose, like all the emotional weight from this afternoon has evaporated, and I can finally breathe.

I spent a lot of time thinking over what Lisa said about me and Sam. The idea that we had an insta-love connection was certainly romantic and exciting, but it was ridiculous of me to believe it. I see now that it was an insta-lust connection, and I've come to terms with that. I can forgive myself for sleeping with an extremely hot guy. It was fun, after all.

I wish I hadn't wasted so much time pining for him, though.

Picking up my glass, I swivel on my stool to give Lisa and the guy she's now chatting with some privacy. Maybe she'll get another couple of drinks out of him. Not that I need any more.

The room is already wobbling a bit as I move, but it slams to the ground when I see Sam walk through the front door. He hands the bouncer his ID, his curls flopping around his handsome face as he scans the room. He's got on an untucked, button-down shirt with the sleeves rolled up his forearms, and jeans. Even from across the bar, I can see his eyes sparkling behind his glasses.

I spin back around in my seat and latch my hand onto Lisa's arm.

She whips around, the wind from her movement brushing over me. "Brynn, what's up?"

"He's here. Sam's here," I say between breaths.

"What? Seriously?" She sits up to peer over my head toward the door. "What do you want to do? Do you want to leave?"

My eyes dart back and forth across the countertop. If I leave now, I'll avoid interacting with him, but I'll also be running away. I've let him ruin enough of my day, time to put my foot down. "No," I say, lifting my head and squaring my shoulders. "It's ladies' night, so I have *way* more of a reason to be here than he does. Plus, this was my bar first. So no, we won't be leaving."

"That's my girl!" Lisa claps her hands and waves the bartender down. "Two shots of tequila!"

I fight the urge to crinkle my nose. I'm already drunk, so doing shots isn't the best idea, but since I'm already drunk, I feel invincible.

As we down our shots, the DJ's voice comes over the loudspeaker, "All right, ladies and gentlemen, bull rides are open in ten minutes. Get your waiver signed now, and good luck!"

A huge grin spreads across my face as Lisa rolls her eyes. "You're really going to do that thing again?"

"I do it every time!"

"Okay, but I have to pee first." Lisa slides off her stool, giving me a pointed look as if to say, 'are you coming?'

I shake my head. "I want to get in line."

"Fine. I'll meet you over there."

I practically bounce all the way to the mechanical bull ring, which is a good thing because it hides the fact that I can't walk a straight line. The vodka-cranberries course through me at full force, but that tequila shot did me in. As I stand in line, I sway from side to side. I hope it seems like I'm enjoying the music.

"I knew you liked to be on top, but didn't know you liked it rough," a voice says close to my ear. Not any voice, though. This one is deep, smooth, and it sends a shiver right down my spine.

I straighten my posture and turn my chin over my shoulder. "Well, I have to make up for the last ride I got."

Sam cringes sympathetically, but keeps his stupid smug smirk. "Ooh, nice burn."

I give him a mocking sneer before turning back around, and thankfully, country music fills the space between us instead of tense silence. The line moves quickly, and I'm signing my waiver before I know it. I'm beginning to think I'll get through this line without further issue, but Sam has other ideas.

"So, do you come here often?"

I finish my signature with a flourish. Spinning around, I'm ready to tear into him about how he doesn't get to talk to me anymore and how he had his chance to get to know me, but chose to be a jerk instead, when the room spins rapidly and I lose my balance.

Sam catches me by the elbow and rights me. "Whoa, easy there. How much have you had to drink?"

"Enough." I rip my arm from his grip.

He shoves his hands in his pockets and juts his chin toward the bull. "Are you sure this is a good idea?"

"Never stopped me before."

His mouth ticks up on one side. "You sure are stubborn, you know that?"

"Hmph." I fold my arms across my chest and turn to face the bull ring.

As hard as I try, I can't stop myself from swaying back and forth. It doesn't help that I'm watching people ride a bull that's spinning, rocking, and bucking out of control. It's dizzying. I slump to my right and hit something warm and hard. When I turn my chin, I find Sam's chest against my shoulder and his stupid adorable face grinning at me.

I wrench myself upright, planting my feet firmly into the floor.

"It's okay to lean on people, you know?"

Anger seethes through me. I hate how soft his voice sounds. I hate how it makes me want to sink into his chest and let him cocoon me in his strong embrace. I hate that he smells so good right now, like lavender and sage. I refuse to let him in again.

So, as the bull ring employee waves me up for my turn, I look at Sam and say, "Too bad the last person I leaned on turned out to be another liar." Then, I'm stalking toward the bull. I don't even glance back to see if my words had any effect on him.

My hand wraps around the horn of the fake leather saddle as I put my left foot in the stirrup. Swinging my right leg over, I situate myself in my normal bull-riding position. I raise my arm in the air, and right before the bull starts moving, I find Sam. I don't mean to look at him, but my eyes betray me.

He's watching me intently as he shakes his head. It's like he's admiring me, yet admonishing me at the same time.

As the bull bucks and turns, I tighten my grip on the horn. It swivels, so I shift my weight. The operator is taking it easy on me, but I know it won't last. Once they see that I'm no amateur, they usually take out all the stops. The sound of the gears revving makes my heart race. Soon, the bull is spinning and bucking without restraint, and I'm flopping left and right. Sometimes it pays to be this drunk.

This isn't one of those times.

The operator makes a quick change in direction, and I'm toast. I go sailing off the bull, landing on the soft pads on my back a few feet away from it. Laughing at myself, I crawl across the mat because I can't stand up. Being so drunk, and now terribly dizzy, my own legs won't hold me.

At the edge of the mat, two hands grip my arms and lift me up. I'm still laughing when I stand and come face to face with Sam. Not even his concerned expression is enough to kill my giddiness.

"That was some show," he says. "But you didn't last long. Maybe next time, take it easy on the drinks."

I snort derisively. "Sometimes the drinks are what help." I point to the leaderboard, specifically the number one spot where the initials BAE are listed next to the time of twenty-seven seconds.

Sam glances at the board, then back at me with that stupid smug smirk again. I want to eat it off his face, but instead, I raise my chin in triumph.

He leans down close to my ear and whispers, "Guess I have my work cut out for me." With a wink, he backs away and strides toward the bull.

No. There's no way he's going to beat my time.

After handing the operator his glasses, Sam hops on the bull like a professional, complete with the cocky showmanship, and raises his hand in the air. The operator starts slow, like with me, but also like with me, notices Sam isn't a beginner. The bull starts moving faster, harder, wilder. It's bucking and spinning every which way, but Sam never falls off.

I fold my arms, turning away, but the urge to see the timer is strong. I glance up. The seconds tick by incredibly fast, and with every one, my heart picks up speed. It keeps climbing, and Sam keeps holding on. The crowd cheers, growing louder with each passing second.

*He's going to fall off soon*, I keep telling myself, but it doesn't happen. The longer I watch, the longer he stays on. When the timer hits twenty seconds, my eyes flick between it and Sam. Every second they're darting back and forth and I'm getting dizzy again. At the twenty-five second mark, I feel like I'm going to throw up. I can't watch anymore.

I tear away from the ring, pushing through the crowd. Air. I need air. As I break through the throng, the buzzer sounds, and I freeze. My feet root to the floor.

"We have a new record! Thirty seconds!" the DJ announces over the speaker.

I nearly collapse. I manage to reach the bar where Lisa is still chatting up the same guy from earlier. Crashing into the stool, I grab her arm. "We have to go. Now."

She spins around, wide-eyed and seemingly annoyed, but takes in my expression and nods. "Okay, okay."

I don't even wait for her to say goodbye to her new friend before I'm storming away. I have to get out of here. I *need* to get out of here. Lisa's hot on my heels as I bust through the entrance door and into the cool night air. I let it fill my lungs, hoping it will help the nausea subside.

"Hold on, I'll call the Uber," Lisa says, tapping her phone screen. "What happened in there, anyway?"

The last two minutes race through my mind. Sam on the bull. The timer. The cheering crowd silenced by the buzzer. The announcement that I'd been dethroned. It's all too much, so I scramble to the curb, and vomit into the gutter.

***

When I wake the next morning, I find Lisa sitting on the edge of my bed with a glass of water in one hand and some Advil in the other.

"Good morning, sunshine," she says cheerfully.

I wince at the brightness of my bedroom as I scoot myself to sit up. "What's so good about it?" I ask, taking the Advil and tossing them in my mouth. I wash them down with a small mouthful of water. "Thanks."

She waits until I'm finished swallowing to ask, "Do you want to maybe tell me what the fuck happened last night?"

"Why? I thought I told you on the way home?"

"No offense, but drunk, hysterical Brynn is about as easy to understand as a toddler with a mouthful of marbles."

I laugh, but it makes my head pound. "Ugh. Where do I begin?" I choose to start with Sam standing behind me in line. I tell Lisa all about our conversation, and how, even though it was snarky, the banter knocked my walls down again. The part about how his touch exhilarated me has her bouncing in her seat, but she listens all the same. When I get to the end, where Sam beat my time on the bull, Lisa practically laughs.

"*That's* why you were so upset? A stupid bull ride?"

I sit straight up, and pound my fist into the mattress. "I've had that number one spot for how long, Lisa? A year!" I yell, but it only intensifies my headache, so I slump back against the wall, rubbing my temple. "No one has beaten me in all that time."

"Dude, okay. Take it easy." Lisa puts her hands up in surrender. "But it's been a year. Someone was bound to beat you sooner or later."

"Why did it have to be *him*?"

"Why does it matter? It's a stupid bull."

"It's not just the bull." I fold my arms, hugging myself. "Do you remember the night I set that record?"

Lisa nods and puts her arm around me. "Yep, sure do. It was my birthday."

"And a week after Connor left."

Lisa crinkles her nose. "Yeah, I forgot about that part."

"Well, I haven't." I take a deep breath, my headache ebbing finally. "Connor leaving for New York broke me. I felt like such a failure, felt so out of control, and setting that record on the bull gave me something to hold on to."

Lisa squeezes my shoulder but says nothing.

"That sense of failure came back after all this shit with Sam, and I don't know, him beating my record amplified it. Like, I can't hold on to anything. Ugh, is this making any sense?"

"No." She grimaces, and I laugh. "But I know how much you like to have a handle on things, so I can see how all this Sam stuff has you turned topsy-turvy."

"I don't know what it is about him that makes me so dumb."

"Um, have you seen the guy? I'd be a bumbling idiot too if a guy like that even looked at me. Phew!" She fans herself with her hand.

A giggle escapes me. "I have seen him. *A lot* of him."

"Maybe you should hook up again."

"What!?"

"You know, a hate-fuck. Get him in your system one more time to get him out of your system for good."

"That's got to be the answer," I say sarcastically, laughing as Lisa elbows me. "There's no way that would work."

"It would at least be fun."

Shaking my head, I sigh. "No. I think the best thing for me to do is to ignore the fact he even exists."

# Chapter 10

The following Tuesday is my first lab day, and I'm both excited and petrified.

I love labs. I love being able to work on problems hands-on. It's so satisfying to see the equations from class translate into physical experiments.

But this is O-Chem lab, which means Sam will be here. And as much as I like our lab professor, Dr. Hinkle, he always gives assigned seats, and he does it alphabetically by last name. So, unless there are the right amount of people with last names that come before mine, I'll be sitting at a table with Sam. Possibly sitting next to him.

When I arrive at the lab room, students have already gathered in the hall. The door must be locked, and Dr. Hinkle must be late.

Great.

Slumping against the wall, I pull my phone from my pocket like everyone else has done. I get through three rounds of Wordle before I get stuck on a word. Three letters down, two to go. The letters I have remaining make absolutely no sense. A "U", but no "Q". No "S" or "T", but an "L"? This is impossible.

"Try 'awful,'" Sam's deep voice rumbles next to my ear.

With a flinch, I whip my head up. I don't know how I didn't notice him, nor do I understand why he's even talking to me. Our previous interactions haven't exactly been friendly. Giving him the side-eye, I scoot a few feet away.

"Sorry," he says, putting his hands in his pockets. "Didn't mean to scare you."

"Well, maybe you shouldn't sneak up on people."

His lips tick up as his gaze drifts back to my phone. "Was I right, though?"

Reluctantly, I type in his suggestion, and unfortunately, he's correct. "I would've gotten it eventually."

"That's a really strange way to say, 'thank you.'"

I sneer and turn my back to him.

"Is that what the A in your initials stands for? Awful?"

An offended gasp escapes me as I turn to stare at him with my mouth agape. "Excuse me?"

He shrugs. "It would make sense."

I don't say anything. I just stand here glaring, wishing fiery laser beams would shoot from my eyes and melt him.

With a deep swallow he takes a hand from his pocket and adjusts his glasses. "Maybe it's for AWOL since you disappeared so fast last Thursday. Didn't want to stay to congratulate me on my victory?"

I ball my fist and take a step forward, ready to give him a what-for, when Dr. Hinkle strides up.

"Sorry, sorry," he says as he fishes his keys from his pocket and unlocks the lab door.

Hiking my backpack higher on my shoulder, I file into the room with everyone else. Dr. Hinkle asks us to wait a minute before sitting so he can find his chart. I make sure to wait on the opposite side of the group from Sam.

Dr. Hinkle walks from table to table, pointing to spots and calling out names. At the second table, he says, "Dawson, Eastman, Erlenmeyer, Fredricks."

My shoulders slump with defeat as I shuffle to my chair. As much as I saw this coming, it doesn't make it any easier to swallow. The bright side is, I'm not sitting next to him, which means we won't be partners and will only have to work together when we have a table project.

It's a small victory, but I'll take it.

When Dr. Hinkle has everyone in their spots, he begins the tedious process of explaining how labs work. He goes over the agenda, the syllabus, the structure, the safety rules, and all the stuff around and in between. After that rip-roaring good time, he instructs us to use the last fifteen minutes to introduce ourselves to our group.

I take the initiative and go first. The spunky redhead across from me, Maya, goes next. She's much too bubbly for my taste, but I smile and nod at her excitement.

When Sam's turn comes, Maya gives him rapt attention. I don't even know if she registers anyone else in the room. She certainly doesn't pay much notice when our fourth tablemate, Micah, introduces himself.

I don't know why, but it bugs me. It shouldn't. I have no claim to Sam, nor do I want any. I should be happy that she's drawing his attention away from me. In fact, I should be thanking her for keeping him occupied so he can't pester me anymore. But instead, I find this weird jealousy creeping up my spine. I shake it off.

Sam flicks his gaze to me. "Cold, Brynn? Didn't think the a/c was that bad in here."

The familiarity in his tone makes my muscles tense, but the pompous smirk on his face is what boils my blood.

Dr. Hinkle saves me from making a scene by dismissing us. I all but rush out of the room, down the hall, and out the door. Frustrated tears begin to sting, but I refuse to let them out. Sam doesn't deserve any more of mine.

This whole ignoring him plan might not work after all.

Once I exit the building, my chest loosens. With the sun shining brightly and the fresh air flooding my lungs, I can work on letting go of my frustrations with Sam.

I have to stop allowing him to get under my skin. We're going to see each other every week, twice a week, for the whole year. I have to accept that he's a jerk. He's not the person I thought he was, and the sooner I come to terms with that, the better.

If Connor's abandonment taught me anything, it's that.

As my anger and frustration ebb, my annoyance with myself doesn't. Partly, because of my reactions to Sam, but also because of my next class, hiking.

I'm an idiot for waiting three years to complete my physical education requirement. At least it's hiking, one of my favorite things to do. Though, after our first class last week when all we did was go over the syllabus, I'm not exactly sure how Professor Duncan is going to fill an entire semester.

I could use a throw-away class, though.

My course load isn't hefty this semester by any means, but it would be nice to have one class I don't have to think too much about. This could be it. I already know how to prepare for a hike and what to do in case of emergencies. I even know first aid. Plus, most of our grade comes from the mid-term, final exam, and the two hikes we have to do.

Sounds like a walk in the park. Or a downhill hike.

Smiling at my cleverness, I take my seat and slouch down, allowing my tense muscles to relax. I'm already feeling better, and for the next sixty minutes, I can focus on something outside of my own personal drama.

Professor Duncan walks in, his long ponytail swinging behind his head. His untucked brown and orange flannel barely covers his Grateful Dead t-shirt as he takes a seat at the desk. As he scans the room, his head bobs. "Hey, cool," he says in his laid-back tone. "I'm glad nobody checked out of class from last week. That's a good sign."

A few students chuckle, myself included.

"I know you all had a lot of questions about the hikes, like scheduling and stuff." He pulls a paper from his satchel and holds it up "I made a list of dates for the class hike, which I'll post on the board so you can sign up for one after class." He lays the paper on the desk. "But I do want to talk more in depth about the hike you have to facilitate."

I perk up for this information, sitting straighter in my seat. My mind is already lit up with ideas for trails, most of which Lisa and I have hiked already. I'll take her with me, and this will be a breeze.

"You will not be picking your own partners."

What? Well, crap. I slouch again.

Professor Duncan takes a seat on the top of his desk. "A lot of students want to pick a friend, roommate, or relative who they know will grade them highly, no matter what happens. That's sort of like cheating, dudes. So, to circumvent that problem, I offer extra credit in my other, non-hiking classes to anyone who volunteers to be a hiking partner. That way, your grades are more organic."

Confused mumbles fill the air as Professor Duncan continues. "Your homework this week will be to figure out the days you are available and to start thinking about what trail you want to hike. If you don't have a favorite trail, might I suggest good old Google.

"Once I have your availabilities, I'll pair you up with a volunteer and give you their email address so you can get the ball rolling. So, don't wait too long. The weather can get real nasty, real quick in the fall." He gets up from the desk, grabs a dry-erase marker, and steps to the whiteboard. "Now, let's get started on our topic for today, hiking preparedness.

As the professor talks and writes, I can't help the excitement bubbling in my gut. I love hiking, and I love a challenge. Sure, I'm disappointed I can't take Lisa, Jackie, or Hannah, but this will be a good exercise to prove myself.

I just hope whoever I get paired with isn't a stick in the mud.

***

Over the next few weeks, I lean into the wind, so to speak. Instead of going on like Sam doesn't exist, which was never going to be successful, I have learned to tune him out. When he tries to talk to me, I only acknowledge him with a curt nod. If he gets too close to me, I simply walk away. It's been working wonders.

The hardest part has been lab. He sits right across from me, so no matter what I do, he's always in my line of sight. At least he hasn't been wearing his glasses lately. I hate how sexy he looks with them on.

And Maya won't stop gushing about how smart he is. Any time she's stuck, she turns to him. It's hard to ignore someone who's always being brought up in conversation, even if that person soaks it up like it's the last glass of water on

Earth. I can hardly concentrate on my work with his swelling ego crowding the room.

I don't have many options for these moments. Micah isn't a great conversationalist, not that I have a reason to engage with him. I know what I'm doing and my answers are always correct. He prefers to keep to his own work anyway, so I usually start setting up for the next problem. I don't ever look at Sam. It's difficult not to, especially when he compliments my work, but I have to stay in control.

Prepping for my hike has helped keep me occupied. I turned in my available dates right away, and Professor Duncan matched me with a volunteer the following week. I emailed the person that day. Typing "imagine a radioactive dragon" into the address field made me feel a little silly, but it was nice to know I'd have something in common with this person.

It gave me hope that this hike would be enjoyable, but I sent that email a little over a week ago. I've heard nothing since. If I don't hear anything by tomorrow, I'll email the professor. I can't be docked points if my partner bails, right?

In O-Chem lecture, Professor St. James goes over our exams from the prior week. Her tests are always through an online platform where it's available Monday, Tuesday, and Wednesday, but we only get four hours from when we log in to complete it. A lot of students love this format because it allows them to use whatever resources they want, and the time frame is usually more than enough.

I know it was enough for me. I finished in under three hours, so I had plenty of time to double check my answers. Not that I needed a lot of double checking. I always make sure to hunker down and study every day as soon as a test is announced.

Dr. St. James begins class by handing out our results. "I have to say, I am sorely disappointed in your exams," she says. "The passing percentage was the lowest I've ever seen.My stomach wrenches as she reaches my desk. She lays my result paper face-down before stepping to the next person. I lick my lips over and over, scared to even flip the page.

But I have to know.

Slowly, I peel the paper from the desk and flip it over. All the tension oozes from me as I stare at my ninety-seven percent circled several times. With a satisfied nod, I perk back up.

Professor St. James finishes handing out the results, and heads to the front of the room. "The majority of you are going to have to work very hard the rest of the semester to make up for it." And that's all she leaves us with.

When the lecture is over, and people start filing out, the professor catches me as I walk by her desk. "Brynn, may I have a word with you?"

"Yeah, absolutely." I make sure to turn my body away from the door so I don't chance seeing Sam.

"Just a second," she says, and proceeds to sit quietly until everyone has left the room. "I want to ask you for a favor."

My face lights up. A favor? From me? Professor St. James is my favorite teacher, so I'm inclined to do whatever she needs. "Sure, what is it?"

"Well, it has to do with the exam results. When I said the majority of the class would need to work hard, I really meant the *whole* class." She grimaces sympathetically. "Aside from you and your ninety-seven percent, only two other people passed, and one of those was barely even a C-."

"Oh." My eyebrows shoot up. That is a horrible passing rate. "So, what do you need me for?"

"You tutor on the side, right?"

I nod.

"I was hoping maybe I could persuade you to host a weekly peer-led study group. I couldn't compensate you monetarily, but it would be a good addition to your internship application." She gives me a knowing look, and my answer is immediate.

"Yeah, sure. I should be able to work that into my schedule."

A relieved breath blows past her lips. "That would be fantastic, thank you. You can use this room. I'll have to check its availability, but I can email you a list of days and times it's available, and you can let me know what works best for you."

"Okay, that sounds good."

"Thank you so much, Brynn. And your classmates will be thankful as well, I'm sure."

I give a tight-lipped smile, trying not to explode with excitement as I stride out the door. I'm beaming right now. The pride filling my chest has me walking on cloud 9. Not only did I pass that exam with flying colors, but Professor St. James trusts my abilities so much, she's allowing me to teach. This will certainly cement my spot on her internship team if it wasn't cemented already.

The lightness in my feet turns to lead as Sam sidles up to me.

"Hey, Brynn, got a minute?"

Was he waiting for me? What could he possibly need? With an exasperated sigh, I ask, "What do you want, Sam?"

"I thought we could discuss our hike."

My head whips up so fast, I get dizzy. "*Our* hike?"

"Yeah, I'm your volunteer." A mischievous grin spreads across his face. "Sorry, I never responded to your email. I've been busy and I wanted to make sure I'd have my contacts for it. That fucking order took forever to get here."

My head spins as I stare at him with narrowed eyes. This can't be happening. "You? Me? Hike?"

"Uh, yeah. Brynn? Are you okay?"

I stop walking as I squeeze my eyes shut and turn away. "I'm fine." The unluckiest person in the world, but fine.

"Well, should I meet you at the trailhead? Or are we going to ride together?"

The amusement in his voice makes me crinkle my nose. There's no way I'm doing a two-hour car ride with him. "Meet me there," I say curtly.

"Okay…" He draws out the syllables. "I'll see you Saturday morning at nine."

I wait until Sam is out of sight before sagging against the wall. This is so not fair. I've made great progress by ignoring him, and now, I have to spend an entire morning with the guy?

Ugh, this hike is going to suck.

# CHAPTER 11

I whip Lisa's car into the trailhead parking area and leap out. Checking my phone, I note that it's 9:06 a.m. I'm only six minutes late.

As I reach the trailhead for Dream Lake Trail, I find Sam already waiting for me. He's nonchalantly leaning against a tree with his arms crossed, his face hidden under a baseball cap. When he finally notices me, his mouth ticks up. At first, I think it's almost genuine, like he's happy to see me. But I know that can't be right.

"I was beginning to think you weren't coming," he teases.

I huff. I knew his jovial expression was too good to be true. "It's been a rough morning."

"How so?"

"My alarm didn't go off, so I didn't get the early start I wanted. Then, Lisa failed to tell me that her car was practically on E, and to top it off, I hit a bunch of construction traffic at the interstate junction. I'm sure you saw it, too."

He nods, his smile growing in self-content. "I did, but I also checked the state website for possible congestion areas last night. I knew the construction would be bad, so I left early." His chin lifts triumphantly. "Made it here with plenty of time to spare."

I fight the sneer crawling across my face and bite out, "Well, sorry to have kept you waiting, your majesty."

His shoulders bob with a chuckle like he finds my frustration amusing. "My time is important, you know. I'll have to notate this lack of punctuality in my report."

My whole face scrunches up as I scrutinize Sam, trying to read him. Is he seriously going to dock me points for being six minutes late? I wouldn't put it past him, but that's pretty damn low.

It's best if I don't think about it too hard. Easier said than done. "Let's get this over with," I say curtly and turn toward the trail, with Sam following.

"Hiking guide was less than friendly," Sam says quietly, but not so quiet that I don't hear him.

I turn my chin over my shoulder, giving him a fierce glare.

He puts his hands up. "Hey, I'm just trying to give the most honest report I can. It's not my fault you're grumpy."

"I'm not grumpy." I focus back on the trail.

"Then what would you call your cloudy demeanor?"

"Determined to get this hike finished."

"Have we even started?" he asks, as if he's not walking the dirt path with me.

I let out an exasperated breath. "Yes, Sam. Did you not see the sign at the trailhead? Do you not notice your feet moving? That means you're hiking."

"Okay, but you didn't give me any details about the hike. Didn't tell me what to expect, or how long it would be. You haven't exactly informed me on what we're doing out here."

I groan, letting my head fall back. As if struggling through my morning and dealing with Sam's teasing wasn't bad enough, now I have to listen to his valid points about how I'm sucking at this hike. I should have gone down my checklist after getting out of the car. He's right, but I refuse to let him know.

"Fine. I can see you're not going to make this easy." I turn my chin over my shoulder slightly, but not enough that I have to look at him. "There's a clearing up ahead. When we get there, I'll go over everything."

"Thank you. See? Was that so hard?"

I grit my teeth as I will my feet to keep moving. All I want to do is spin around and hightail it out of here. I want to leave Sam behind and forget this day has even begun.

But I can't. My GPA depends on it. So, I keep going.

When we reach the clearing, I slide off my backpack and kneel next to it on the ground. Sam follows suit. I don't want to look at him, but I do. And what do I see? Not the smug expression of the jerk I know him to be, but a sweet, attentive anticipation instead.

My whole body sags. "This is Dream Lake Trail. It's only about two miles, one way."

"So, you're going easy on me. Is that what you're saying?"

"I didn't know who I was going to get as a partner, so I chose a trail that's fairly easy to complete. It's supposed to take a little over an hour to hike, but I've done it in less with my friends."

"Overachiever."

I want to be offended, but his wink disarms my anger immediately, and I can't help but laugh. "Wouldn't be me if I didn't overachieve."

"Okay, what else do I need to know?"

Feeling my anger ebb, I take a moment to study his clothes. He's wearing good hiking boots and long pants. I can't tell if he's wearing a long-sleeve shirt or not, but the jacket he has on will be warm enough either way. Sunglasses hang from his jacket collar, but he already has on a hat, so those won't be needed. It's nice that he's prepared, though.

I reach up, tapping the brim of his hat. "I see you at least *read* my email."

"Oh, ha. Yeah." He takes off the hat to run a hand through his hair. "Sorry I never responded."

"It's okay. What matters is you didn't ghost me and–" A thought strikes me, and I jerk my head back. "Wait. Your email is 'imagine a radioactive dragon?'"

With a groan, he rolls his eyes, and I swear I see his cheeks pinken. "Ugh, yes. That song was really popular, and I was twelve when I created that account, so sue me."

"You've never thought about, I don't know, making a new one?"

"Oh, I have, but I'm lazy. Everything is tied to that email, so it would be an undertaking to switch everything over."

I laugh. "You're ridiculous."

"Maybe one day I'll change it." He shrugs. "Okay, so we know we're dressed properly. What's next? Do we have everything we need for a two-hour hike? What happens when we're done?"

With a nod, I stand and slip on my backpack. "I know I told you to pack a water bottle, but I've got plenty in case you run out. I also have sunscreen and bug spray reserves, two ponchos, even though it's not supposed to rain, and I packed a light snack for us to have at the end of the trail. After that, we hike back, and that's it."

"Cool. Sounds like you have everything under control," Sam says as he stands to shrug on his backpack.

My chest lightens. I'll take the compliment. It's the first genuinely nice thing he's said to me today that wasn't sarcastic or teasing. The frustration of this morning melts away, and I begin to think I'll get to enjoy this hike after all.

Sam sighs. "Glad to know this won't be eating up my whole Saturday."

My content expression falls. I should have known he'd consider this an inconvenience. With a deflated sigh, I turn toward the trail and say, "Okay, let's go."

We walk along in silence as I try to forget he's behind me. I focus on the gorgeous morning. The bright sunshine, the crisp mountain air, and the lovely aroma of the flora and fauna surrounding me. It's all so beautiful. For a moment, I actually lose track of Sam.

Until he clears his throat. "So, are you going to tell me anything about this trail?"

"What do you want to know?"

"Well, what kinds of plants are here? Anything dangerous?"

I turn my chin over my shoulder and quirk an eyebrow. "Why? Are you planning to lick a tree or something?"

"Ha, no. But, like, is there poison ivy or anything?"

"It grows here, but it's unlikely you'll run into any. Just stay on the trail and you'll be fine."

"Yeah, okay," he says, though he sounds anything but trusting.

Almost thirty minutes into our hike, we pass a couple of fishermen on their way back from the lake. They greet us with cheerful good mornings and tell us the lake is in prime beauty today. We thank them and continue on.

"So, if there's a lake with fish, does that mean there are bears, too?" He sounds downright scared.

A wicked idea pops into my mind. It might be mean if this were anyone besides Sam. "Black bears, yes. But, I'm not worried."

"Really? Why not?"

Turning to face him, I walk backwards for a few steps. "Because I'm probably a faster runner than you." With a smartass grin, I turn around and take off jogging.

"Hey, wait up!" he calls after me.

My brisk pace has him out of breath quickly, so when we round a bend and find a fallen tree trunk, I suggest a break.

"Thanks," he huffs, plopping down onto the tree.

Smiling triumphantly, I take a seat too. "So much for going easy on you, huh?"

Sam doesn't say anything as he sucks in air. Reaching for his water bottle, he groans.

Maybe I overestimated his endurance level. "Are you okay?"

"I don't feel very good. Kinda nauseous. Actually, I've been feeling a little sick for the last few minutes."

Uh oh. "Do you have a headache at all?"

"No, but I feel a little lightheaded. Why?"

"That's altitude sickness." I start digging through my backpack, pulling out an energy bar, an electrolyte drink packet, and a bottle of water. "Here," I say, handing him the energy bar. "You need to eat some carbs, and hydrate." I empty the electrolyte packet into the bottle of water and shake it.

"I don't really feel like eating." He tries to hand the snack bar back to me.

I push his hand toward him. "I know, but you need to or it's only going to get worse."

Reluctantly, he opens the package and takes a small bite.

I sigh. "We can sit here as long as you need. Take small bites, wash it down with a lot of water."

"Thanks," he says, appreciation dancing in his tone.

"You're welcome." A pang of guilt stabs me. "I'm sorry I didn't even think about you not being acclimated to the altitude. I keep forgetting you only moved here recently."

He shrugs. "It's okay. I wouldn't have thought about it either. Obviously." Chuckling, he takes another bite. "I mean, I didn't have any issues at the Mud Down."

The mention of the day we met leaves a bitter taste on my tongue. I wash it down with my own water. "Well, you were at elevation for a few days. You had probably acclimated enough at that point."

"I've been living in Colorado for over a month. Shouldn't I be acclimated by now?"

I shake my head. "Greeley is like forty-six hundred feet. So is Grand Junction. We're at almost nine thousand here. It makes a difference."

Taking another bite, he nods.

"How are you feeling?"

"Better. Sitting down has helped." He sips his water, crinkling his nose. "This is awful. What is it?"

I laugh. "Electrolyte drink mix. You know, the stuff they give kids when they get sick so they don't get dehydrated?"

"Bleh." He sticks his tongue out before smacking his lips. "Poor kids."

"Poor you, right now. You have to drink all of it."

"Seriously?"

"Mhm. Hiking guide's orders."

He feigns a gag. "This is so going in my report."

I giggle, but cut it off when I notice he's not laughing. "Wait. You're serious?"

"Of course I am. I promised I'd give an accurate account of how you handled the hike. This is part of it, and a big part, at that. It's not every day your hiking partner tries to kill you."

I scoff and stand up. If that was meant to be a joke, it sure didn't sound like one. I glance down at his energy bar. It's only halfway done, but I can't rush him. He needs to rest before we can continue. That doesn't mean I have to hang out with him, though.

"I have to pee," I lie before storming off into the thicket.

Sam has to be the most infuriating person on the planet. How I got stuck with him, I'll never know. It's like I'm being punished, but I have no idea what I'm being punished for. In fact, I feel like I've been punished enough already between dealing with Connor's abandonment and Sam's lies.

Once I'm far enough away from the trail, I put my hands on my hips and look to the sky. It's a beautiful day with a small smattering of clouds. I should be happy I'm out here. I should be ecstatic that I get to hike on a day like this. But, here I am, gritting my teeth every time Sam opens his stupid mouth.

Whenever I think he's warming up to me, and I let my guard down, he chimes in with some jerk-off thing to say. He ruins every nice moment we begin to have.

How was it so good in July, but so horribly frustrating now? Why couldn't he have stayed in Wyoming? At least then I'd have that perfect memory. It never would have been tarnished and I could have lived my life wallowing in the fact that I lost the most wonderful guy in the world.

I let out a groan, dropping my head to pinch the bridge of my nose. I'm not that lucky, I guess.

With a deep, cleansing breath, I trudge back toward the trail. I find Sam using the fallen tree trunk to stretch upon. "How are you feeling now?" I ask.

"Honestly? Still kind of shitty." His chest expands as he sucks in a big gulp of air. "I feel like I can't fill my lungs."

I chew on my lower lip. "We should call it, then. Let's turn around and get home."

"What? No, Brynn. I'm supposed to help you complete this hike." He clears his throat. "I mean, I won't get my extra credit if I don't."

Ah, there it is. *This isn't about helping me at all. It's about his grade.* "We can ask Professor Duncan if we need to make it up, but you're in no shape to keep up with the elevation changes. Let's go." With a defeated sigh, I backtrack slowly down the path toward the trailhead.

Once we're back at the parking area, I ask Sam, "Are you okay to drive?"

"I think so." He wobbles his head around. "I'm not lightheaded anymore, just nauseous and tired."

"Be sure to drink a lot of water today and rest. You should be okay in the morning."

"Thanks." He drops his gaze to the ground for a moment before looking me in the eye. There's a hint of remorse in his gaze. "For what it's worth, I'm sorry for getting altitude sickness."

I give a despondent nod. "Thanks, but it's not your fault." With another deep breath, and an even deeper exhale, I bolster myself for what I'm about to say. "It's mine."

Sam's eyes widen. "Brynn, don't think–"

"No, Sam." I put my hand up. "I should have taken into account the fact that you aren't used to these elevations. I should have been more patient and taken my time." Frustration with myself bubbles in my gut, settling in my stomach like a ball of lead. "You can add that to your report."

Before Sam can retort, I hop into Lisa's car and drive away. I don't need to hear how poorly he's going to grade me. Or worse, I don't need to hear more of his lies. He'll just say how he won't mention any of my failures, only to have my grade come back low because I wasn't prepared enough. I know I messed up.

And I don't need him digging the knife in any further.

# Chapter 12

I spend the next few days sulking about my failed hike, but as Thursday draws nearer, I perk up. It's hard not to when you know your favorite professor is going to be spotlighting you because she thinks you're brilliant. The fact that she asked me to help solidifies my standings for the internship.

I work hard to contain my excitement as Professor St. James announces the study group. "Since so many of you seemed to struggle with that last exam, I have decided to put together a peer-led study group. The group will meet in this room every Friday afternoon at five p.m., and the first one will be tomorrow."

Grumblings filter through the air. It is very last minute, but the professor and I decided the sooner we can start the better. Naturally, I'm completely prepared. I've already compiled the information from all the past lectures this semester, made the presentation materials, and read through my notes out loud several times to ensure I've got it down.

I'm going to knock this study group out of the park.

Professor St. James continues. "This will be a chance to review the information from class, maybe with a different perspective since it will be delivered by someone who isn't me."

I hear a few chuckles, and annoyance flares in me. It's not a funny topic. These people are failing and the professor is simply trying to give them another chance to succeed. How is that comical?

"Two of your fellow classmates have graciously agreed to–"

Wait. Did she say "two?" She didn't mention asking anyone else to help. And who would that be? She said only two other people aside from me passed, and one was just barely. Who is the other person?

"So…" Dr. St. James' voice reels me back in. "I would encourage you to attend these study sessions, and be sure to thank your study leaders, Brynn and Sam."

As soon as his name leaves her lips, my stomach drops so fast, I feel like I might vomit all over my desk.

Sam? As in, Sam Eastman? As in the one person on the face of this planet I've been trying to avoid for the last several weeks?

This has to be a mistake. Surely, she misspoke. I mean, if I'm getting a ninety-seven percent on my exams, then I don't need anyone to help me with the study group. I'm more than capable of delivering the information myself.

Ugh, I might actually be sick.

When class is over, I stop at the professor's desk on my way out. "Um, Dr. St. James? Can I talk to you?"

"Sure, Brynn," she says over her shoulder as she cleans the whiteboard.

"It's about the study group."

She turns around, confusion and panic on her face. "What about it? You can still do it, right?"

I nod. "Yes, but about Sam…"

"What's wrong with him?" Sam asks as he sidles up next to me. As soon as his lavender and sage scent wafts across the small space between us, a flutter runs through me.

I don't look at him, but shift my stance to take a step away. "I thought it was just me doing the group."

"That was my initial plan, yes." Professor St. James puts the dry-eraser down and joins us at her desk. "But it is a lot of work for one person. So, when Sam offered his help, I thought you could lighten the load by splitting it up."

"Oh, so like, I'll be doing one session, then Sam does the next one? We'll be switching off?" I'm disappointed by the waver in my voice, like I'm pleading instead of inquiring. Probably because I am.

Professor St. James shakes her head. "You'll be working together every week. That will ensure you're both on the same page as far as what information has been covered and can work together to field any questions the class may have."

A frown works its way onto my face.

"Again," she says, "this is a lot of work. I want to make this as easy on you as possible."

By pairing me up with the most infuriating jackass in the world? How is that making it easy? "I appreciate that, but I know the information backward and forward. I think I can handle it on my own."

Sam clears his throat, and I bristle. He's been so quiet, I forgot he was here. "It's not just about the info, Brynn."

"That's right," Professor St. James chimes in. "Sam said he's proficient with a wide range of computer programs and applications, which you've told me you struggle with."

I clench my jaw. She's right. I do a lot of things well, but technology isn't one of them. "Okay, fair, but—"

"Listen, Brynn." The professor holds up her hand. "I really do appreciate you heading up this group, but I also don't see the point in you doing it all yourself. You're brilliant, but you have an equally as brilliant classmate who can make your life easier, technologically speaking."

I glance at Sam, sneering.

"Yes, Brynn. Sam is the other person who passed the exam. With a ninety-eight percent, nonetheless."

That one percent makes me ball my fists. I bite out an acceptance of Dr. St. James' words, and all but storm out. I don't want to make a scene, but if I stand here any longer, I'll scream.

I'm not more than twenty feet down the hall when Sam runs up behind me. "Hey, Brynn, wait up."

I don't acknowledge him as I keep walking.

"Should we talk about the study group for tomorrow? We don't have much time to get our ducks in a row." He laughs, but I don't. "Brynn?"

My name rolling off his tongue echoes in the recesses of my brain, like he's a million miles away. The hallway stretches before me. If I take one step forward, it pushes me two steps back.

"Brynn?"

I stop on a dime as his voice rips through my consciousness.

Sam halts after a few more steps, turning around to face me. "Brynn? Hey, what's up?"

"What's up? What's up!?" If looks could kill, my fiery gaze would burn a hole right through him. "What's up is you always having to eclipse me."

A crease forms between his eyebrows as his eyes dart back and forth across my face. "Care to explain?"

"The bull, the O-Chem exam, the hike"–I hold out my fingers as I count–"and now, you're commandeering *my* study group."

"Let me get this straight." He pinches the bridge of his nose as he puts a hand on his hip. "You're pissed that I'm more successful than you?"

Fire rages through me. "No," I say in a quiet snarl. "I'm pissed because you keep trying to one-up me."

"Okay, how the hell does the hike count as me trying to 'one-up' you? I'm not even in a hiking class!"

Huffing, I fold my arms. "Because you used the opportunity to tear me down by picking apart every little thing I did wrong. I can't wait to see all your *wonderful* comments."

Sam opens his mouth, but I don't give him the chance to speak.

"And flaunting your one-percent lead on my exam grade? That's the bitter icing on the cake."

"I flaunted what now?"

I take a step toward him, my finger pointed and headed straight for his chest. "You, Sam Eastman, are a thorn in my side. You lie your way into my life, and then once you get here, you keep stepping on me to get ahead." His face twists from confusion into anger. "Hey, Brynn. Did you ever think that maybe this isn't all about you?"

I swallow down the sour taste at the back of my throat.

"The hike was a way for me to earn extra credit. That's it. I know I gave you a lot of flack, but fuck, all I wanted was to not work so hard in my first aid class." He puts both hands on his hips before running one through his hair. "And I'm sorry if I'm one percent smarter than you in O-Chem. That wasn't planned."

I let out a sassy snort.

"Okay, I'll give you the bull thing. I was trying to one-up you there, but as far as the study group goes? I'm not trying to 'commandeer' anything. I heard the professor tell you the study group would look good on your internship application, and I saw an opportunity."

With one arm still wrapped around my middle, I tighten my grip on myself as I shake. "You're not applying for that," I bite out.

"You bet your ass I am. Why do you think I moved down here? It wasn't for the luscious Greeley scenery, I'll tell you that."

My nostrils flare as anger seethes from my every pore. "That spot is mine."

"Don't be so sure." His arrogance is astounding. "Buckle up, sweetheart. I don't give up easily."

I clench my jaw. "Neither do I."

"Good. I like a challenge." His tone lowers, turning gritty. Stepping forward, he presses his firm chest into my trembling finger. "And I didn't have to lie to get into your life. You were all too willing to let me into that, and your panties, all on your own."

With a deep, guttural growl, I spin on my heel and sprint down the hallway. That does it, Sam Eastman. You've made yourself an enemy.

# CHAPTER 13

I'm so worked up after lecture class, I go for a run as soon as I get home. It's the best way to clear my head. I pop in my earbuds, crank up the tunes, and take off. Running is my favorite form of exercise. I can go as fast as I want, for as long as I want, and never have to worry about someone being in my way.

With the exception of traffic, that is.

A car makes a right turn without yielding even though I have the walk sign. They cut me off, nearly sideswiping me. "Asshole!" I shout, throwing my hands in the air.

With a sharp exhale, I start jogging again. If I want to get rid of all this tension, I need to keep going. Each time my feet pound against the pavement, I feel a little bit of anger release, but I can tell this will take a while.

Why does Sam have to ruin everything? And why does he have to be such a jerk about it?

I grit my teeth as his words echo in my mind, *You were all too willing...*

Maybe I was willing to let him in, but is that a bad thing? Like Lisa said, my heart was just starved for affection, and I had a weak moment, but I won't have any more.

My frustration with Sam is so high, I focus solely on it, drowning out everything else. Until my music gets interrupted by the ding of my phone. When I check it, I find a message from my Friday morning tutor client saying she needs to cancel tomorrow.

Great. That's my longest session. There goes a good chunk of money.

With a sigh, I glance at the time. Holy shit, I've been running for three hours. I didn't even notice, but now that I've stopped, the burn shoots through my muscles. Maybe it's time for a break.

As I come to a bus stop, I take a minute to stretch, and another message comes through. This time it's Lisa asking if I want to join her, Jackie, and Hannah for dinner at When in Rome, our favorite pizza place.

Pizza isn't exactly the healthiest thing to eat after such an epic run, but fuck it. I'm starving now that I think about it, and a slice of pizza—okay, maybe four slices—and a beer sounds amazing. I text her that I'm heading home, but need a shower first.

When I walk in the door, I find my roommates sprawled in the living room watching TV. I say, "Hi," but they only give me small waves, entranced in their show, so I hop right in the shower. Once I'm finished, I head back into the living room and put myself between them and the TV.

"Ready?" I ask.

They all nod and get up from the couch.

"Where the hell have you been?" Lisa asks.

"Running."

"I've been home since three-thirty and haven't seen you," says Jackie, grabbing her purse. "When did you leave?"

"Two."

"Jesus," Lisa says. "How are you still standing?"

I laugh. "I won't be much longer if I don't eat. Let's go."

The walk to When in Rome isn't long. It's only a couple of blocks from our house to the small, family-owned pizzeria, but after my three-hour tour, my legs are shot. Several times, my knees wobble, and my friends giggle about it.

"Serves you right for running that much," says Hannah as she links her arm with mine to hold me up. "Why were you gone so long?"

"I needed to let off some steam."

"Uh oh," Lisa says. "I sense a story coming on."

"First, I need a beer."

We step into the restaurant, where an employee instructs us to seat ourselves, so we choose the corner booth. A server comes over, handing us each a water, and I suck mine down immediately. Before she takes my glass to refill, she hands us menus, but we really don't need them. We know the selections by heart, and we always get the same thing; two large pizzas. One for me with cream cheese, garlic, and black olives, and one with cream cheese, Canadian bacon, and mushrooms.

After taking our beer orders, the server leaves us, and Lisa leans her elbows onto the table. "Okay, what's with the triathlon?"

"It's been a long week. Hell, it's been a long semester dealing with Sam, but today everything kind of..." I flick my fingers together as I make an exploding noise.

"What happened?" Jackie asks.

With a sigh, I tell them everything. I start with the hike, making sure to mention how Sam insisted he was going to be honest in his report. I tell them about the midterm, the study group, and the internship. I even go back a bit to explain what happened with the bull to Jackie and Hannah. All of my friends listen with their mouths agape as I finish by telling them all the rotten things he said this afternoon.

"That dickhead." Lisa smacks the table with her palm before waving our server over. "You need something stronger than a beer."

I pull her arm down. "No, not here. Let's go dancing."

"Really? I thought you had tutoring tomorrow."

"My morning client canceled so I don't have anything until noon."

Lisa's face lights up. "Sweet. Yeah, let's go dancing."

The four of us bounce in our seats as our server returns with our beers and pizza.

***

Dancing does exactly what I need it to. It distracts me. Not only from my frustrating afternoon, but also from my aching legs. I'm surprised I can even move after my monumental run, but with the pizza fueling me, I'm good to go. I'll probably regret it in the morning. Right now, though, I'm feeling loose after a few drinks and some of my favorite songs.

So loose, in fact, that when my friends want to keep dancing, I opt to sit at the table so I can catch the server to order more three-dollar shots.

I love ladies' night.

My gaze tracks the server on her way toward me when she makes an abrupt turn back to the bar. "Shit," I groan and drop my chin into my palm. I watch as she places empty glasses on the bar top before checking in with the only guy sitting at the bar, and my whole body tenses.

Sam.

Of course he's here. Why wouldn't he be? He's everywhere I don't want him.

Narrowing my eyes, I study him. He's by himself. No friends around, no girls crowding him, just alone. And he looks grumpy. His posture is slouched as he languidly nurses a beer. I wonder what's eating him? Probably that giant stick up his ass.

A sudden movement pulls my focus to the side, where I find a guy at a nearby table smiling at me. Before I can stop myself, I smile back. Idiot move, Brynn. The guy slides off his stool and heads my way, undoubtedly to ask me to dance.

Great. Now, I get to choose one of my many rejection lines. Part of me always feels bad, but it's nothing personal. I don't dance with anyone.

A traitorous flash of a memory reminds me I did dance with Sam.

My gaze flicks to him, our intimate two-step playing in my mind. A rebellious smile pulls at my lips as I think about the ambiance of the sunset, the look in his eyes, the warmth of his touch. The way my name sounded on his lips.

"Hey," a gruff voice says, ripping me out of my reverie.

Shaking my head, I blink rapidly to find the guy from the next table standing in front of me. "Hey."

"Mind if I sit down?" he asks, but doesn't wait for an answer before he slides out a stool.

"Um, sure." I turn my head between him and the dance floor, hoping one of my friends is on their way back. I'm not that lucky.

"I'm Troy."

He holds out his hand, so I shake it. "Brynn."

"Nice," he says, as a slimy smile inches across his face. "I saw you on the dance floor. Hot stuff out there."

I give him a tight smile as I glance away. When I do, I see Sam now watching us from the bar. His posture is more rigid, like he's on alert, and he's gripping his beer pretty tight, but not drinking it. Odd.

"Looks like you need a refill," Troy says, eyeing my empty glass as he waves down the server.

"Oh, that's okay. I don't need–"

"Don't mention it." He flashes me a confident smile before ordering two rum and Cokes.

Irritation bubbles inside me. I mean, I like rum and Coke, but he didn't even ask what I wanted.

"So, Brynn, do you go to UNC?"

"Yep. It's my last year as a chemistry major."

"Chemistry? Cool." His lackluster tone sounds anything but impressed. "I'm in Sports and Exercise Science with a minor in Business. I'm planning on opening my own gym one day."

My eyes scan Troy's muscular build. It's not surprising he wants to open a gym.

As I continue to smile and nod through Troy's talking, I don't really listen much. I'm too intrigued by Sam's body language. I chime in with a generic response here and there, making sure to make eye contact with Troy a few times, but I'm more focused on Sam.

His behavior is so strange. When I first noticed him at the bar, I didn't even think he knew I was here. Now, I *know* he knows I'm here, and based on his facial expression, I'd say he's not happy about it. Maybe he's just as pissed about our blowout after class as I am. Maybe seeing my face just ruined his night.

Good. He deserves it.

"Here you go. Two rum and Cokes," the server says.

As she moves to set our glasses down, Troy holds out his hands to take them from her. He slides mine to me, but doesn't let go. When I reach for it, he brushes his fingers along mine before holding his glass up. "Cheers," he says.

I clink my glass to his and take a sip.

"So, like I was saying..." Troy scoots his stool closer to me so that our knees bump, and I instinctively turn my body.

Troy's not bad looking. He's actually pretty cute, but it's the way I always react when I'm being hit on. I'm guarded, what can I say? I think the only time I haven't been in the last year was in July with Sam. Speaking of...

I glance at the bar to see Sam practically slam his bottle on the counter and signal the bartender for another. That's a peculiar way to express frustration over me being here.

My mouth pops open when a thought strikes me.

What if he's not angry that I'm here, but angry that I'm sitting with Troy? Could Sam be jealous?

No. That's preposterous. Isn't it? I guess it is possible he harbors some leftover feelings from July. We did have a fantastic night, but is that enough for him to be jealous? I have to test this.

As I turn my focus back to Troy, the dance beat fades to allow the soft melody of a slow song to rise. He holds out his hand. "Would you like to dance?"

With a quick glance at Sam, I take his hand. "Yes."

We head to the dance floor, passing a confused Lisa, Jackie, and Hannah on our way. When we get to the middle, Troy pulls me to him. He grips my right hand, and places his other hand low on my hip, but I hold back to keep some space between us. Before I know it, Troy's leading me around the dance floor.

Every time we turn, I sneakily glance at Sam, and every time I do, he's watching us. The longer we dance, the harder he stares.

It's interesting, and I want to delve deeper into possible reasoning for it, but I can't concentrate with Troy stepping on my feet every two seconds. It takes all my self-control not to take the lead. Instead, I have to keep reminding myself to let Troy guide me, but it's hard when his missteps put us off rhythm. When I try to correct our movements, he grips me tighter.

"You're supposed to follow my lead," he says, annoyance lacing his tone.

I want to retort with something snarky, letting him know I'm not follower material, but I bite my tongue. It would probably result in him ending our dance, and I wouldn't be able to complete my observations of Sam.

He's been watching us this whole time, and I'm wondering how far I can push this experiment.

Sliding my hand across Troy's shoulder, I inch closer to him. I'd prefer to keep some distance between us, but as I move, Troy seizes an opportunity. He lowers his hand so his fingers graze the top of my butt as he closes the gap completely. With a smirk, he puts his cheek to mine and continues the dance.

I have to crane my neck to see around him, but I glimpse Sam jumping from his stool, and my heart jumps too.

This is it. I've done it. I've proven that he is in fact jealous, and now he's on his way over here to cut in.

Will I let him? While I'd be grateful to be rid of Troy, I don't know that I'd accept Sam's offer. I might tell him to buzz off. That would teach him.

The slow song begins to fade out, and I'm counting the seconds until I hear Sam's voice, but it never comes. Right as the song ends, I lift my head to see Sam heading toward the exit. Before he steps through the doorway, someone enters and bumps into him, pushing him back a step.

His gaze flicks to me briefly, and I watch his features crumble as his posture noticeably deflates. Then, he leaves, and my heart sinks. That certainly wasn't the reaction I was going for.

"How about another dance?" Troy asks, pulling my focus back to him.

"What?"

"You sure don't listen well, do you?" Troy rolls his eyes. "I asked if you want to dance again."

"Oh. Um, no thanks."

He nods as if he's not terribly upset. "Well, can I get your number?"

I lick my lips, biting down on my bottom one, and shake my head. "I don't really date."

A sneer overtakes his face, but he shrugs. "Okay. You're probably not worth my time, anyway," he says, then storms off.

I don't know why, but Troy's cruel words hit me hard.

How does he know I'm not worth his time? I could be the best thing that ever happened to him, and he squandered it. Just like Connor. Just like Sam…

I frown as I slink back to my table, my gaze flicking toward the exit and, once again, a weight settles on my shoulders. My experiment didn't go as I expected. Sure, I got Sam worked up, and it seemed like any second he was going to explode in a fit of jealousy, but then, he just left.

And did I imagine the hurt on his face?

I had to have made it up. If he felt that strongly about me, surely he would have stepped in between me and Troy. But obviously, that didn't happen.

Sighing, I take a seat on my stool. Apparently, I'm not worth Sam's time, either.

# CHAPTER 14

I SPEND ALL DAY Friday at war with my emotions. One minute, I'm seething over what an ass Sam is, and the next minute, I'm being eaten away by the disappointment from my experiment last night. I'm distracted throughout my tutoring sessions. So much so, one of my students asks what's wrong, but I tell her I'm frustrated about a test.

Which is sort of true.

If basically the entire class hadn't failed, I wouldn't be in this predicament with Sam. I could go about my days, continuing to ignore him, and be a happier person. But here I am.

When four o'clock rolls around, I pack my materials and head to the O-Chem room. A relieved breath whooshes from my lips when I walk in to find it empty. I'm here first, thank goodness. I set up the almost obsolete overhead projector and organize my transparency sheets. It may be extremely old-school, but it works for me.

The door opens, and I immediately stiffen with the way the air seems to freeze. I don't need to look to know who walked in. I keep my focus on my materials, not bothering to acknowledge Sam, when I feel his presence near me. Then, the air changes. It thickens with tension, but also fills with his unfortunately delicious lavender scent.

"Hey," he says quietly.

"Mm," I respond, but don't take my eyes off my work.

I hear him sigh, but he doesn't say anything else as he walks around the desk and deposits his backpack on the floor. I keep working.

"You're not seriously going to use this thing, are you?"

I whip my head up to see disbelief on his face as he studies the projector. I immediately frown. "Yes, I am. Problem?"

He shrugs. "I guess not. Does it even work?"

"Of course it works. And it's reliable. I don't have to worry about Wi-fi cutting out, or a connection being lost, or having the right cables. You just plug it in and turn it on." With that, I go back to my organization.

"Okay, whatever you say." Sam steps back to the desk, taking a seat in the other chair and swiveling back and forth. "Brynn, can I talk to you?" he asks, a nervousness in his voice.

With a groan, I lay my marker down and turn to face him. "About what?"

"About yesterday."

For the first time since he walked in, I look at him. I mean, really look at him. I can tell by the creases in his forehead that he's concerned about something, but the pain in his eyes punches me in the gut. Maybe I didn't imagine his hurt at the bar, after all. "Okay."

"I want to apologize."

What? *Him* apologize?

"A lot of what I said to you after class was…" He runs his hand through his hair, his curls flopping back into place when he's done. "Really mean, and I'm sorry."

My lips part as if there are words on the tip of my tongue, but I can't bring myself to say them, so I settle for, "Thank you for saying that." I ignore the guilt building within me and go back to my transparencies.

"That's it? You don't have anything to add?"

"Like what?" I ask, not looking at him.

"I don't know, maybe an apology of your own?"

Now I look at him, but with a glare. "You want an apology? For what? You're the one who was being nasty yesterday."

"Hey, you dished it out, too." He points at me. "I was just reacting."

I let out a sassy snort. "Well, you reacted poorly."

"At least I have the humility to admit when I'm being an ass." Leaning back in his chair, he folds his arms.

"Care to show some of that humbleness now?"

He slowly shakes his head as his mouth ticks up in a smirk. "You are one stubborn woman, you know that?"

"Yep, and it's not surprising that you find it aggravating. Most men do."

"Did it bother the guy you danced with last night?" A bitterness laces his words, and I notice his jaw is slightly clenched.

I arch an eyebrow. "Why are you concerned with him?"

Sam's Adam's apple bobs with a deep swallow before his features relax, a sly grin taking over his face. "Just worried he didn't know what he was getting into. I mean, you do have a history of sharing intimate moments with men, only to turn on them later."

"Hmph." I narrow my eyes. "Well, you can rest assured knowing I didn't give him the chance. I've got enough emotional sewage to wade through after you."

Sam jerks his head back, his eyes wide. Then, I watch as his whole face softens, like his heart just split right down the middle. "Brynn, I—"

Before he can finish, the classroom door opens, and students file in. I can breathe once more. That conversation was getting too heavy, and I'm glad it flew through the doorway before it became cemented to the floor. I go back to finishing my lesson plan as we wait for everyone to take their seats.

Sam leans over into my space, and I hate, that even after our bickering, I still like his nearness. "Do you need me to do anything?"

I stand instantly, shaking my head. "I've got this."

"Of course you do." His lips press into a flat line and he nods.

Giving him a sharp glare, I step to the projector and begin the study session. It's a sixty-minute time slot, which goes by super fast, and before I know it, people are leaving. As I pack up all my transparencies and markers, I smile proudly. That felt like a really good session. It was productive and informative, and I know grades on the next exam will improve. I'm still beaming when the last student leaves.

"Brynn, can I say, you're brilliant," Sam says, still perched in his chair.

I ignore the warmth his praise makes me feel, the bright smile I almost shine his way, shrugging instead. "Yes, you certainly can."

"You're also very modest." He chuckles, getting up to walk to the desk. "But can I also say, and I mean this in the nicest way possible, that lecture was fucking boring."

My mouth drops open as I frown. "Excuse me?"

"All that info was spot on. You know your stuff and it shows in how you deliver it." He shoves his hands into his pockets. "Which you did exactly the same way as Professor St. James."

I blink in disbelief, unable to form words.

"She's brilliant, too. Don't get me wrong, but she's also fucking boring."

I scoff. "You're incorrigible."

"Why do you think the whole class failed that exam? They were all probably lulled to sleep by her mechanical, robot voice. You can't tell me you don't hear it."

My forehead scrunches as I think. I've never thought she sounded like a robot, but I guess she does tend to drone on when she gets stuck on a tangent. "Maybe she is a little robotic sometimes."

"A little? The woman makes Siri sound like Oprah."

I snort a laugh. "Well, when you put it like that..."

Sam smiles, his gaze lingering on me. "Can I make a suggestion?"

"Only one."

"What if next week, we do something different? Like a game?"

"A game?"

"Yeah, we can split the room into teams and play Jeopardy, or something."

I crinkle my nose. The idea sounds good, but executing it sounds like I'm going to struggle on a computer. "Do you know how to do that?"

"Yeah." He nods, the smile growing in smugness. "It won't take too long. We could knock it out in a couple hours."

I jerk my head back. We? "You mean, like, us meet up to work on it?"

"Well, yeah. We could meet at the library or the coffee place down the street."

My heart leaps into my throat. That isn't anything I want to do. "Um, can I email you the info and you put it together?"

His excitement falters. "Oh, um, yeah. That works too."

I choose to ignore the strange disappointment on his face as he picks up his backpack, hikes it onto his shoulder, and heads for the door. He doesn't even say goodbye as he leaves.

***

The following Friday, when I get to study group, I don't have anything to do. Sam made the presentation, so he's got everything on his computer, and I have nothing. I mean, I supplied all the questions and answers, but I have no physical contribution.

I plop down into the desk chair and swivel around. I hope this session goes well. Sam's idea wasn't terrible, even if what he said about my presentation was. I still can't believe he called me boring right after he apologized for the crap he said the day before. I'd be lying if I said I wasn't still miffed about it.

What am I going to do about him? Things between us are so weird.

It's his fault. One second, he's doing something sweet like telling me I'm brilliant only to negate it the next second by saying something stupid. It's confusing to no end. I don't know what happened to the guy I met in July.

Oh wait, that's right. He doesn't exist.

At least not the sensitive, emotional side of him. Physically, he's the same person, and I can't deny my attraction to him. I mean, the guy is hot. Downright gorgeous, actually. But a handsome face isn't enough when you're a jerk on the inside. Some of the things he's said have been incredibly harsh, so I can't blame myself for reacting the way I have. And after all the lies and manipulation, he deserves every bit of pain I inflict.

Though, he did initiate the apology. That was nice of him.

Not nice enough for me to completely forgive him, but maybe enough for me to keep things civil. At least while we're working on the study group stuff. I mean, we're going to have to work together no matter what, so why make it more difficult than it has to be?

I'm feeling better about the situation when Sam walks in the room. He shoots me a smile, and something in my brain ticks. Something from a few months ago when I first met him and thought he was someone special. It warms me. I don't want to like the feeling, but I can't help it. Even if it's rooted in vanity, it's still comforting.

And I'd rather have that than all this antagonizing tension.

He sets his backpack in the chair. "Hey."

"Hey. All set?"

He nods. "Yeah, I want to go through it real quick to make sure it's all still there." Pulling out his laptop and several cables, He sets them all on the desk. "You want to help?"

"Me?" I'm sure the incredulous look on my face is ridiculous. "I don't know how."

"I can teach you." He gives me a teasing smirk. "If you're not too stubborn to learn."

That was almost nice. "That's okay. You should probably do it. I'll just be in the way."

"Suit yourself." Sam gets down to business. He plugs in the different cables, connecting the computer to the projector, and soon the presentation is on the screen. He clicks through all the slides to ensure the questions and answers are all there in the right places.

"You did that very quickly," I say, begrudgingly impressed.

"It's pretty easy once you know how to use the program. I can't believe you've gone so long without learning."

"It's not like I've *never* used it." I fold my arms. "I've always made the most basic of presentations and used it as more of a guide."

"I can't imagine you doing anything basic." His tone is low, gravelly, as his eyes flick between mine. "Not after what I've seen."

My mouth has run dry, but it doesn't matter. I don't know what I would say to that even if I could speak. The air is so thick between us, suddenly, I can't breathe. I sit here with my mouth agape as I try to not choke.

When the door opens, the spell is broken, and we return to co-hosts of a study group, which goes extremely well. Much to my chagrin, the Jeopardy game is a hit. Everyone is engaged and actively answering the questions. Sam even brought candy as a reward for the winning team to make it fun. As much as I don't want to, I have to hand it to Sam. He did well. Several people even compliment us on their way out, including Maya.

She stops at the desk, leaning her hip against it. "Good job tonight, Sam."

"Thanks, but Brynn helped too."

Is he giving me credit for something?

"Oh, yeah. Of course." She flips her hair over her shoulder. "Thanks, Brynn."

"Don't mention it." Seriously, don't.

The look Maya gives me could almost be described as grateful, if it wasn't for the sneer on her lips. She turns her burning gaze back onto Sam. "This was way better than last week."

No, really, Maya. Don't mention it.

Sam gives me the side-eye. "Yeah, well, it was the first week. We worked with what we had."

Maya blinks, her head jerking back. "No, Sam. I didn't mean last week was bad or anything, I just–"

"Maya, it's okay." Sam laughs. "I'm not offended, but we do have to clean up and get going, so..."

"Oh, okay. Yeah, of course." Maya adjusts her satchel strap as she backs away toward the door. "I'll, uh, see you later, Sam. Bye, Brynn." My name doesn't leave her lips quite as melodically as his does.

When she's out the door, I let out a heavy breath. "I thought she'd never leave."

"Not your cup of tea, huh?"

I shake my head. "Too bubbly. She seems to like you, though." I hate the jealousy underlying my words, and I hope Sam doesn't notice it. I have no reason to be jealous. Sam isn't mine, and I don't want him to be.

Sam grunts, but says nothing as he ties up his cables and puts them in his backpack.

I swivel back and forth in my chair. "So, tonight went really well. I hate to say it, but you were right."

"Hold on," Sam says as he whips out his phone and holds it up, facing me. "Say that again."

"Why?"

"I want it on video so I have proof."

I scoff, smacking him playfully with the back of my hand. "I'm serious. Everyone seemed way more engaged. There was a lot of laughing even though the competition got a little intense. You did good, Sam Eastman."

"Thanks." A prideful smile graces his face before turning into something more sheepish. "I've got other ideas. You know, so we don't have to play Jeopardy every time?"

"Okay, like what?"

"Different things." Rubbing the back of his neck, he glances at the floor. "I could show you, if you want."

"Sure." It comes out as more of a question because I'm not positive where this is heading.

"Maybe you could come to my place one day and we–"

My eyelids peel back. "Your place? What happened to meeting at the library or the coffee shop?"

"We can still do those places, I guess. But it's easier for me not to have to lug my computer around."

I chew on my lower lip. Me? Alone with him? Even he has to know this isn't a good idea. We can't spend five minutes together without fighting. Okay, tonight was an exception, but we were distracted with the presentation. Who knows what'll happen if we're alone together.

Maybe we need to do it once to prove it won't work. "What the hell. Sure, why not?"

His entire face lights up briefly before he reins it back in, clearing his throat. "Cool. Um, I'm free on Saturdays."

"As in tomorrow?"

"Yeah."

"You don't work or anything?"

"No. My parents said as long as I keep my grades up, they'd help with my finances." He tilts his head from side to side. "My student loans also help, though."

Quickly, I do a mental check of my schedule. My Saturdays are always free unless a tutoring session gets rescheduled like last week, but I didn't have any cancellations today. I sort of wish I had, though. "I guess I could do that," I say, albeit reluctantly. "What time?"

He pulls out his phone, tapping the screen. "Maybe, like, one o'clock? Right after lunch?"

I nod. Daytime is a good idea. It'll still be warm as long as the sun is out, and I can be out of there before nightfall. I definitely don't want to be walking home in the dark, and more than that, I don't want to be anywhere near Sam at sunset. A romantic backdrop to our study group prep is the last thing we need.

My phone dings, so I grab it from my bag and see a message from "Sam Mudboy" pop up. It's the first time I've seen his contact in my phone since we texted in July. A warm nostalgia washes over me, but I quickly shake it off.

"That's my address and apartment number."

I click the message and copy the address to Google Maps. "That's on the other side of campus from me. Should only take me about fifteen minutes to walk."

"Walk? Don't do that. Let me pay for an Uber or something."

I shake my head. Partly, to dismiss his offer, but also because of the weird protectiveness in his tone. "I like walking, Sam. Outside, remember?"

"Okay, but just so you know, I don't even have my a/c on anymore."

A sprinkle of appreciation settles in my chest.

"Well, let's get out of here." He shrugs on his backpack and holds his hand out, inviting me to exit first.

As we walk down the hall together, we pick apart our study group session. We discuss the things that went well, and the ones that didn't quite work. All in all, we call it a success.

To be honest, just walking down the hall and holding a civil conversation seems like a success, too. We make it all the way through the building and outside without arguing. Maybe we can get through prepping the presentation with no issues.

I still don't know if we'll ever be more than classmates, but maybe we could be friendly classmates. Even that feels like a stretch, but if I want to survive this year and graduate with an internship, I've got to try.

# CHAPTER 15



"Are you sure this is a good idea?" Lisa asks as we eat breakfast at our kitchen table.

I scoop up a spoonful of cereal. "No."

"Then why are you going? Did something happen between you two that you're not telling me about?"

"Ew. No way." I shove the spoon into my mouth.

"So, you guys are friends, then?"

"Not exactly," I mumble.

Lisa throws her hands in the air. "For crying out loud, Brynn. What are you doing with Sam?"

I swallow my food and sigh. "We're not friends. After all the lies and shit he's pulled, I don't know if we ever will be." Staring at my bowl, I stir my cereal. "But I want to do this study group thing right. I don't want to disappoint Dr. St. James and have my internship on the line."

"The same internship Sam's vying for?" Lisa folds her arms, leaning back in her chair.

"Yes, but I'm her favorite student." I stab my spoon into my bowl. "If I fuck up this study group thing, though, I might be taken down a peg. I don't want to give Sam an advantage."

"But doesn't helping him succeed with the study group improve his chances too?"

"Of course it does, but it's way better if I help. I'll continue to be Professor St. James' favorite student, I'll get the internship spot, and then I can rub it in Sam's stupid, handsome face."

Lisa wiggles in her chair, biting down on her lip like she's holding something back.

"What?"

"You still think he's handsome?"

"Ugh." I drop my face into my hands. "Why do I talk to you?"

"Because no one else will put up with your shit."

I glare at her through my fingers. "Ditto."

"Brat." Lisa sticks her tongue out. "When are you going over there? Want a ride?"

"No. Thanks, though. I'm supposed to be there at one, and I'm looking forward to the walk. It'll give me a chance to clear my head about the whole thing."

***

The walk does the opposite. Instead of clearing my head, I simply clog it with more outrageous thoughts of Sam. Talk about overthinking.

My breath is so short and fast, I can't enjoy the fresh air. It almost burns instead of cleansing like it should. I'm chugging my water to quench my dry throat, but I know it's going to make me have to pee.

How could I think this is a good idea? If being alone with your enemy isn't bad enough, being alone with your enemy, whom you not only think is handsome, but also slept with, has to be terrible. But it's not like I'm going to act on anything. There's nothing wrong with finding someone attractive.

At the stoplight, I close my eyes and try to regulate my breath. I've got to get my heart to stop pounding. It's thumping so powerfully, I can hear it. By the time the chirping of the crosswalk signal sounds, I'm a bit more relaxed. I can at least hear myself think now.

This is going to be fine. We're going to work on the presentation, that's it. We don't even have to talk about anything other than chemistry. I'll get in, get the work done, and get out. Easy peasy.

The closer I get to his complex, the more my anxiety ebbs. That may be due to the fact that I can't concentrate on anything except my full bladder. Every step gets harder to take. I want to run the rest of the way, but I can't chance peeing my pants. I'll have to distract myself.

What was I thinking a minute ago? Oh, right. Sam and I are classmates. We are adults. We are capable of lasting two hours to finish a presentation without killing each other. We're two colleagues working together on a project that will solidify which one of us gets a coveted position integral to our respective futures—

Breathe, Brynn. Breathe.

So much for decreasing my anxiety. I suck in copious amounts of air as I lean onto the railing of his apartment building. The stairs in front of me seem like Mount Everest; an arduous trek into unknown territory that I'm grossly unprepared to enter. And at the top, who knows what I'll find.

Taking the stairs slowly, I creep to Sam's door and force myself to knock immediately. No sense in delaying the inevitable.

Sam whips open the door with a half-eaten sandwich in his hand. "Hey," he says through the mouthful of food. "Sorry. Come in." He swallows and steps back to allow me to pass.

As I cross the threshold, I enter a total bachelor pad. There's nothing on the walls aside from the 80-inch television, and the only pieces of furniture are a couch flanked by two mismatched side tables, and a coffee table in front. I crane my neck toward the small kitchen and find a breakfast table, but with two mismatched chairs.

"Nice place," I lie, feigning cheerfulness.

Sam laughs. "Don't mock me." He shuts the door and rounds the couch, holding out his hand to invite me to sit. "I'd give you the tour, but you've seen eighty percent of it, and the last twenty is just as bad."

"Well, I do have to pee."

"Oh, um, that door." He points across the living room. "I cleaned it," he says as I scurry away.

He cleaned for me? The thought doesn't linger long before it's shoved away by the pure joy that comes from emptying one's bladder. I can't believe I made it all the way here.

As I sit through the longest pee ever, my gaze wanders around the small bathroom. It's not much bigger than the one I share with my roommates, but it's way more organized. On the counter rests one toothbrush, one tube of toothpaste, a can of shaving cream, and a razor. That's it. Our counter at home has four times as many items, and that's not including the toothbrushes.

And everything is clean. Like, actually clean. We try to keep ours tidy at home, but with four girls sharing one bathroom, it's destroyed in a matter of minutes. One of the disadvantages of having only one bathroom with a shower.

When I'm finished, I step back into the living room, and Sam greets me with an eager expression. "Better?"

"Much," I say, joining him on the couch. "And you did a good job cleaning, by the way."

"It really wasn't that hard. Doesn't get too bad since I live alone."

"Must be nice not to have roommates, though."

"I guess." He shrugs. "Gets kind of lonely sometimes."

A pang shoots through my heart at how sad he sounds. "Well, you should come clean my bathroom sometime. When you share one with three other girls, things can get messy."

He chuckles. "But you've always got someone to talk to."

"True. I guess it was a weird adjustment for me. I'm an only child, so I never had to share."

"Oh, so that's what's wrong with you."

"Excuse me?" I shake my head. I'm not sure what he's getting at.

"Only child syndrome." Sam smirks. "See, I know how to share. I grew up with an older brother and a younger sister."

A sly grin spreads across my face. "Is that why you are the way you are? Middle-child issues?"

He snorts, but doesn't do anything except keep that stupid adorable smirk going.

"So..." I say, turning my focus toward the computer on the coffee table. "What kind of ideas do you have for the next study session?"

Something resembling disappointment flashes across his face before he flips open his laptop and presses the power button. "I was thinking we could do another game. That seemed to work really well."

"Yeah, there was a lot of competitiveness going on last night." Snippets of my classmates hollering at each other and high-fiving their teammates flash in my memory, making me smile. "What kind of game?"

"Similar to Jeopardy," he says, opening the application. "But this would be a puzzle." He clicks through a couple of screens and a picture pops up. It's a jaguar lounging in a tree. "See, we cover this image with a blank page cut into puzzle piece shapes. Each one has a question on it, and if they get it right, the piece slides off." He taps the keyboard, and a puzzle icon glides across the screen to reveal part of the image underneath. "They keep going until they get a question wrong, and the team that gets the last piece wins."

"Huh, that's cool." I'm genuinely impressed. This is way more intricate than anything I've ever done. "How do we keep one team from dominating, though?"

"I figured we could do five puzzles. They don't take that long to get through, and that way, everyone would get a chance to play."

"That's a really good idea." I'm genuine in my statement. It is a good idea, and the fact that Sam can make such a seamless presentation for it piques my interest. If he can do it, why can't I?

"I know."

His arrogance makes me hesitate to ask my next question. "Would you... Would you show me how to put the presentation together?"

Sam's lips spread into a beaming smile. "You want to learn something? From *me*?"

"You know what? Forget it." I huff, grabbing my notebook.

Sam grabs my wrist, the tingle from his touch stopping me in my tracks. "I'll teach you, if you really want to learn." His heated stare burns into me.

"I do," I whisper, swallowing roughly.

We spend the next few hours putting the puzzles together. Selecting the images to use is easy. The process of creating the puzzle isn't. The questions and answers aren't the problem; I know all that information backward and forward. The tech side of everything is what gets me.

I can read a textbook, take notes, fill out quizzes, or perform lab experiments without batting an eyelash, but put me in front of a computer and I freeze. It's like my brain can't wrap itself around what's going on. If I can't see the way it works, I can't understand it.

Maybe that's why I like chemistry so much. I can physically see the work happening in front of me instead of a computer doing all of it and showing me the results. It's why I like the Mud Down. Seeing my obstacles and being able to map out my action plan makes things so much easier.

That doesn't explain why I don't know what to do about Sam, though. He's right in front of me. I should be able to study him and make an informed decision on how to proceed, but I can't. Ever. It's like he inhibits my brain from functioning.

"Brynn?"

I whip my head up from the computer. "Hm?"

"You do the next one."

My lower lip works its way between my teeth. I just watched him create a puzzle. He even talked through all the steps as he did it, but am I ready? "Can you do one more? I get too flustered when it comes to computers."

A warmth appears in his eyes as he nods. "I'll walk you through it, but you do all the clicking."

"Okay, fine." I frown, but let it fall quickly to show I'm joking.

"First thing's first, pick which image you want for the puzzle."

I pull up the internet browser with the online site we've been using for images. Thinking for a moment, a wicked idea pops into my mind and I type "imagine a radioactive dragon" into the search bar.

Sam groans. "Seriously? You're never letting me live that down, are you?"

"Nope," I say, emphasizing the p sound.

He narrows his eyes, but smirks. "Well, then I get some say in what image you pick. Move over." Scooting closer, his hip bumps mine, and he playfully knocks my hand out of the way.

I hope he doesn't hear my breath catch. Just the gentle brush of his knuckles on my own sends a thrill through me. And don't even get me started on the burst of lavender and sage that blasts me in the face as he moves.

It's all so heady, but too much, so I inch away.

When he approves an image of a green-glowing dragon with laser eyes, he leans back. "Okay, you take it from here," he says, clapping me on the shoulder. His hand lingers a moment too long, and when he pulls it away, I miss the warmth.

Get it together, Brynn. Finish the damn slide and you can leave.

As if he senses my tension, Sam moves farther from me as he guides me through the rest of the process. Pointing to which icons to click or which commands on the keyboard to use, he's surprisingly patient and understanding when I ask questions. And I ask a lot of them.

After he helps me add a few puzzle pieces, he sits back and lets me take the reins. I'm able to do one on my own, but I screw up the next one. I don't even know how. I swear technology hates me.

I glance at Sam, an incredulous look on my face. "Well?"

"Well, what?"

"Aren't you going to say some smartass remark about me screwing that up?"

A sympathetic crinkle forms in his brow. "Brynn," he says, leaning forward. "A lot of sarcastic, albeit witty, things may come out of my mouth, but I'm not going to berate someone who's trying to learn. Even if that person is the most stubborn woman on the planet." He nudges my hand out of the way to take over the keyboard, but when our fingers graze, it steals my breath again.

I need to get a grip on myself. Sam isn't anything more than my enemy.

But even that doesn't feel right, at the moment.

Sure, he knocked me out of my first place standing on the bull, infiltrated my study group, and is my competition for an internship that's basically been mine for three years, but does that make him enemy material?

Maybe rival is a better word for what he is to me.

After what seems like a painstakingly long time, my puzzle is finished. Sam clicks through all the slides, showing me what buttons to press to reveal the questions and answers. Everything seems to be in place.

I stare at the screen in awe. "I can't believe it works."

"You see? You're not completely hopeless."

With a roll of my eyes, I give him a sideways look as I muster up the will to say, "Thank you for showing all that to me."

"No problem." He hikes a shoulder to his ear, a blush rising in his cheeks. "Well, we survived this together. Do you maybe want to do this every week?"

My spine stiffens. "You mean, me come here every week?"

Nodding, he rubs the back of his neck. "Yeah. It's nice to work with someone in person rather than communicating through email. And you can get some more practice with the apps."

With pursed lips, I take in his offer. It's not the worst idea, but it's not the best.

"And, I don't know, maybe you and I could work toward becoming friends?" The hope in his voice shines through as his deep brown eyes beg me to say yes.

I can't, though. I want to, but I just can't. Not after our muddy history and all the lies. "The best I can give you is frenemies."

His mouth ticks up on one side, and he holds out his hand. "I'll take what I can get."

# CHAPTER 16

THE NEXT FEW WEEKS fly by. Between classes, homework, tutoring sessions, and the study group, my time is completely eaten up. I barely hang out with my friends, and Lisa has been voicing her opinion on that fact almost daily.

"I'm sorry," I say as I ready my backpack for lab day. "This semester's kicking my ass."

"Yeah, yeah." Lisa waves me off. "I know you're busy. I just want a girls' night once in a while. Is that too much to ask?"

Guilt weighs me down. "No, it's not, but I don't know when that'll be. After classes and study group this week, I'll be hunkered down all weekend since midterms are next week."

"You're racking up quite a tab, you know?"

"I know, I know. Tell you what. You pick any day after next Friday, and I'll scrap whatever plans I have to do a girls' night."

Lisa sits straight up on the couch. "Really?"

"Really. I owe you some friend time." The truth is, I could use some, too.

"The following Saturday night, then."

I jerk my head back. "That was fast."

"It's Halloween weekend." A sly grin spreads across her face as she nods. "You're coming out with us and I'm picking our costumes." When I start to protest, Lisa jumps from the couch to clamp her hand over my mouth. "Uh uh.

You haven't gone out for Halloween in years. I'm pulling my card. No excuses, Brynn."

My whole body slumps with defeat. "Fine," I say, the words muffled under Lisa's hand. "Don't make us into a bunch of sluts, please."

***

Lab is fairly uneventful. With midterms coming up, Dr. Hinkle only gives us individual assignments for the day, and when we're finished, we're supposed to study. I appreciate the extra time to brush up on my O-Chem. Besides, it helps keep Sam out of my hair.

Hiking class doesn't do much to combat my boring Tuesday. When I walk in, I see Professor Duncan at his desk reading, and the words "Study Day" written on the white board. As if I didn't just do a mini-cram session in O-Chem lab, now I'm going to be studying for my hiking midterm, too? And what exactly do I need to study? This is *hiking,* for crying out loud.

With a groan, I slouch in my chair.

Professor Duncan closes his book before grabbing some papers. "As you can see, I'm giving you a study day to prepare for midterms next week. You can either do this alone, or in a group. It's up to you."

I fight the urge to groan. I'll be studying alone, thank you.

He rounds the desk, flopping the papers in his hand. "But before we get into that, I've got some of your individual hike reports to pass out."

This information perks me up. I've been nervously awaiting my report for weeks. I can't say I've been looking forward to it, since I know Sam most likely gave me a C or lower, but I have to know. I need to prepare myself for how much of a hit my GPA is going to take. How hard am I going to have to work to bring it back up? Will acing the midterm be enough, or will I have to plow through a bunch of extra credit? I will *not* let hiking class be the end of my straight-A's.

My stomach knots itself as Professor Duncan moves toward me. He says nothing as he sets a packet, face down, on my desk.

I deflate. This can't be good.

I inhale deeply to bolster myself before flipping the packet over. As soon as I do, I'm smacked in the face by the letter A written on the top line next to my name.

An A? Sam gave me an A?

I have to know exactly what he said, so I scour the rubric for his comments. Each one I read has me melting with appreciation.

*Hiking guide was late, but made light of her situation and proceeded with professionalism.*

That's a nice way to say I was grumpy, but I'll take it. I move on to the next ones.

*Hiking guide was knowledgeable of the trail, plant and animal life, and made me feel like I was in expert hands.*

*Hiking guide listened to my concerns, letting me take breaks as needed.*

So far, Sam seems to have put me in a kinder light than I would have put myself. There's one big issue he hasn't mentioned. The fact that I rushed him and made him sick. I swallow down my nerves and continue reading.

*When I developed altitude sickness, hiking guide was well prepared with ways to combat my symptoms. She made sure I ate and stayed hydrated, gave me plenty of time to rest, and even cut the hike short in order for me to get home to recuperate.*

*She took full responsibility for the occurrence, but it is my own fault for not listening to my body. Hiking guide put concern for my health and safety above her grade and shouldn't be docked points for not being able to complete the hike.*

I almost want to cry. All of these notes put a positive spin on all the ways I failed. Not one mentions anything about me being short with him, or rushing him, or being difficult to work with. Sam has only good things to say.

The smile that breaks across my face is irrefutable. I can't help it. This is better than I expected from him, and I certainly need to say thank you.

I pull out my phone, ready to send a text, but I stop. This is something that needs to be done in person. I'll thank him on Thursday.

***

Unfortunately, Sam is late to O-Chem on Thursday, so I don't get a chance to thank him beforehand. Then, he leaves with Maya, and there's no way I'm getting close enough to speak to him with her around. I'm forced to wait one more day.

The following night, when I arrive at study group, Sam's already waiting for me. "Hey. You're here early," I say, confusion lacing my words since he always comes in after me.

"Just wanted to see your face."

I crinkle my nose at the affectionate tone of his words, even if they do warm my chest. "Excuse me?"

"Oh, uh..." He clears his throat. "I mean, the face you're making. I wanted to see your confused face."

"Okay," I say, increasing the pitch of the second syllable. "Have you set up yet?"

He shakes his head. "I'm making you do it."

"What?"

"The last three group nights you've watched me plug everything in, watched me connect to the wi-fi and all that." His stupidly adorable grin takes over his face. "It's time for you to put your knowledge to the test."

I groan. "Fine." Standing here, I wait for him to move. "Where is everything?"

With a flick of his wrist, he points at his backpack, but says nothing as he leans back in the chair, folding his arms.

An exasperated sigh escapes me. These are the only times I doubt myself. Well, this and on any date after Connor left, but that doesn't have any bearing on right now.

I pull Sam's laptop and all the cables from his backpack, laying everything out on the desk. I organize them by order of operation and set to work. Right off the bat, I struggle to get the first cable into the computer port. After a few seconds, when it becomes obvious I don't know what I'm doing, Sam gets up.

"I don't know what I'm doing wrong. I've tried every port on this stupid thing, and it doesn't fit." The unflattering whine in my voice grates at my nerves, but I can't help it. I'm frustrated and it's been less than a minute.

"That's because you've got it backward," Sam says quietly as he slides the cable from my fingers. He flips it around. "Try this end."

Embarrassment floods me. Why didn't I think of that? Stupid Brynn.

As I sheepishly take the cable from him and plug it in, I struggle to find the right words to thank him for my hiking report. A simple "thank you" doesn't seem like enough. "So, uh, I got my hiking report back the other day." I glance over to see him sitting stock still, like a deer in headlights. "And I need to say thanks."

He swallows and clears his throat. "You're welcome."

I refocus on my task, running the cable down to the projector hub. "Can I ask why, though?"

"Why what?"

"Why did you give me such a stellar report? I was late, I rushed you, which gave you altitude sickness, and I wasn't exactly pleasant." After plugging in the last cord, I finally look at him. "Why did you praise me?"

His expression is that of disbelief. "Really, Brynn? What would have been the point of me rating you low? I'm not competing with you for a hiking internship."

"Oh, yeah." I don't know why, but his words stab me. "Well, thanks either way."

I finish setting up the computer, open the application, and to my utter surprise, everything links up. The presentation pops up on the screen, and I forget about my disappointment.

"Hey! It worked! I did it!" The look on my face is probably that of a kid who won a goldfish at the fair, but it doesn't matter. I'm proud of myself.

"I knew you weren't helpless," Sam says, holding his hand up for a high-five.

I slap his palm, but Sam wraps his fingers around my hand. I think it's meant to be a way to show me how proud he is, but the instant his warm hand winds tight around my own, the air in the room changes. Fire builds between our palms. It radiates down my arm and into my chest, making my heart pound.

An image of him yanking me to him and pressing his lips to mine flashes before my eyes, but I shake it away. I wriggle my hand from his, wiping it on my jeans. "Thanks for your help." My voice quakes.

Sam's mouth presses into a tight line as he nods.

Thankfully, before things can get any more awkward, the door opens and our fellow classmates file in. The mood returns to normal. Sam and I move forward with our presentation, neither of us acknowledging our weird moment.

Since it's the last study group before midterms, we've opted to extend it to two hours instead of one. While it is a successful session, and everyone is very appreciative of our help, I'm exhausted by the end.

Sam has me undo everything, too. He says I not only need to know how to set up, but how to tear down as well. It's much easier than before. The biggest thing I have to remember is to save the work before shutting down the application. From there, it's just turning off the computer and projector before removing the cables. Easy peasy.

"Good work, tonight," Sam says.

"You, too." I don't look at him. I can't. The burn of his touch is still seared into my palm.

"I'm proud of you, you know."

This makes me whip my head up. Him? Proud of me? Maybe he misspoke. Maybe he's proud of himself for being able to teach a technological disaster such as myself how to use a computer.

But as I stare at him, he leans in ever-so slightly. With bated breath, I stand here, completely frozen as I anticipate the feeling of his lips on mine. I know I'm supposed to hate the guy, but I remember his kiss. It's amazing.

Is it so wrong that I want to experience it again?

It must be because before we get too close, the classroom door bangs against the wall as the cleaning lady drags her cart inside. I jump away from Sam and watch him reach over to grab his laptop.

Is that all he was doing? I stood here, my heart about ready to burst, and all he wanted was his computer? I'm the biggest idiot in the world.

"Ready to go?" he asks.

With a nod, I blink away the stinging tears of embarrassment and rein myself in for the walk down the hall. Usually, we spend this time picking apart our presentation. We talk about what we could do better, or what worked. This time, I don't feel like talking. My throat is so thick, I don't know if I even could.

"That went pretty well," Sam says proudly.

"Mhm."

"I think everyone enjoyed the format."

"Yeah," I whisper.

"Maybe we can do this one again, but tweak it so it's not exactly the same."

I only nod.

"Feel free to jump in with ideas at any time." His annoyance shines through in his tone.

Irritation bubbles in me as I glance at him, but pull my attention back to the floor. "Sorry. I'm tired."

"I know that was a long session, but you could at least feign interest." He huffs.

Right before we reach the exit doors, I stop walking and turn my frown on him. "Interest? I'm sorry, who's the one supplying *all* the questions and answers? Oh, right, that would be me."

Sam folds his arms. "And who has been putting all those questions and answers into engaging presentations? Not to mention, teaching a certain stubborn someone how to create said presentations?" His eyebrows arch in challenge.

"What do you want? A thank you?"

"No, you've already said that, but it would be nice if you'd contribute to the conversation. Some sort of feedback would be helpful."

An offended laugh escapes me. "Okay, how's this for feedback?" I lick my lips. "Your presentations are great, but they wouldn't be shit without my knowledge on the subject."

Sam's mouth falls agape. "Oh, yeah? Well, if it weren't for me, the entire class would still be failing due to your titillating lecture delivery."

"Screw you," I bite out, and spin to shove the exit door open. It isn't until I get across the parking lot that I let my frustration out. "What a fucking prick!" I practically growl to myself.

How could he possibly think he's doing so much more work than me? I'm the one scouring the textbook for adequate information. I'm the one forming that info into questions and answers to align with the units we're covering. All he has to do is input it into the computer. He's acting like he's the golden child. Well, he's sorely mistaken if he thinks I'm going to let him have this one.

# Chapter 17

My feet pound against the pavement. With every stride, I feel endorphins shoving out my shitty mood. Ever since my blowout with Sam last night, I've been itching to get outside. I need to get this frustration out. I would have gone for a run afterward, but it was dark, and I didn't want to chance being run over by a car.

Now, it's mid-morning. The sun is out, the breeze is not, and the brisk forty-five-degree temperature is keeping me perfectly comfortable. I've been running for thirty minutes already, and I have no intention of stopping any time soon.

Not when Sam's egotistical expression from last night keeps popping into my mind, fueling the anger coursing through me.

Who does he think he is? I'm the one toiling over these presentations. Sure, he's the one putting them together, but after watching him do them, it makes his contribution seem like a cake-walk. I, on the other hand, have to study the textbook for information that would make good questions. I'm not pulling stuff out of my ass. I have to think it all through.

He has no idea how exhausting that is.

A stoplight turns red, so I opt for a break. I fold my arms behind my head and pace as cars turn the corner in front of me.

And he knows technology isn't my thing. Yes, I've made presentations before, but I told him I only did basic ones. These fancy games aren't easy for me. So, not only am I providing the material, but I'm also learning too. It's mentally taxing, and I don't need him teasing me on top of it.

When I get the green light, I'm all worked up again. I need to leave this foul mood behind. Taking off at full speed, I blaze down the street, turning into a neighborhood to get away from the busy traffic of 8th Ave.

I'm so glad we're not meeting today. With midterms next week, we don't have a study group, so we don't have a presentation to make. It's a good thing, too. I don't think I could stand being in the same room with him.

Judging from the irritation in his tone last night, I'm sure Sam feels the same way.

Maybe we jumped the gun on even being frenemies. I mean, things have been going well for a few weeks. Our arguments are down a ton compared to where we were at the beginning of the semester, but obviously that doesn't matter. All it takes is one dumb comment from him, and we're right back where we started.

Is that my fault, though? Am I the one who's over-reacting?

I shake my head, balling my fists. No. I'm not blowing things out of proportion. He says some really stupid shit sometimes. And maybe I'm a little emotional about it, but he's the one who started all this with his lies. So, no, I'm not taking blame for this.

Why is the guilt eating away at me, then?

"Ugh." I tighten my fist, pressing my nails into my palm.

I will my feet to go faster, but they're already fighting me. My legs scream for rest. I ignore them. The more I push, the more the fire in my muscles burns away my frustration, and I want it turned to ash.

If I stop, though, it'll come back. So, I keep going, because I may not be able to run away from Sam, but I can run until I'm too exhausted to think about him anymore.

***

On Tuesday, as I anxiously await Dr. Hinkle's arrival, I chew off all of my fingernails. Even though I haven't seen Sam since we bit each other's heads off Friday night, I'm still not ready to face him. Nor do I want to. Running helped, but when I was finished, I was right back where I started– embarrassed over the mistaken kiss and seething anger from our argument.

Maybe, since it's midterm week and this is an optional lab day, he won't show. I'm here because extra lab time pads my accolades on the internship application, and I'll do anything to get ahead of him on that front. That intern spot is mine, has been for years. I won't give it up easily.

As lab time inches closer, a few other students walk up, but Sam isn't one of them. A weight lifts from my shoulders. Maybe my luck is changing.

Think again, Brynn.

Sam strides around the corner, but he's not alone. Walking in step with him is Maya, and she's doing her best rendition of a coquette. She flips her hair, laughs at Sam's every word, and goes as far to touch his forearm at least a dozen times. It's sickening. Especially because he soaks it all up. His ego must be the size of a watermelon right now.

When they reach the door, Sam stops. "Hey, Brynn."

"Hey," I say through a clenched jaw. I don't want to, but when I look up, I meet his amenable gaze and inwardly shrink.

"So, Sam. What were you saying about The Broncos? I think football is so cool." Maya all but pulls on his arm, tearing his gaze from mine.

Even if she does like football, her obvious attempt to steal Sam's attention makes me want to gag. As does his quick reaction. He doesn't even hesitate to resume their conversation.

Whatever. I'm just glad to have the focus taken off me. Sam strode up here all nonchalant, like nothing happened last week, and it's so fucking irritating. I hate how unaffected he is by all this, and yet, here I am, stewing over something as dumb as a petty argument. I don't let things go very easily, but maybe this is one time I should. Sam's not worth me fretting about.

Maya can have him.

When Dr. Hinkle finally arrives, only half of the lab class is present, so he gives us all individual assignments, and I couldn't be happier. This is my time to shine. I don't have to worry about sharing the work with my lab partner, or waiting for another group member to finish their calculations. I can simply do my work without any annoying interruptions.

"Aw, boo." Maya pouts. "My lab partner is so helpful. Will you still check my answers, Sam?" she asks, batting her lashes.

"Of course."

I glance at Sam to see a self-satisfied smile on his face, and I want to puke. I don't know what's worse; Maya's constant, obvious flirting, or the fact that he doesn't seem to get his fill of it. If this continues too long, I might actually be sick.

"Besides Maya, you're easy to work with. Some people can be as *stubborn* as a mule." Arrogance drips from Sam's words, but I don't give him the satisfaction of reacting.

Instead, I dive into the assignment. It's fairly straightforward. We are to write out our steps and show our measurements and calculations before performing the actual experiment. No problem.

As I'm listing out the amount of chemicals to be used, Maya's giggling infiltrates my ears. I look up through my lashes and find Sam leaning toward her, his mouth next to her face as he whispers something.

"Oh, Sam. Stop," Maya playfully whines before giving him a light smack with the back of her hand.

I narrow my eyes. This amount of philandering is a bit much, even for them. I wonder if there's more here than meets the eye?

Telling myself that I don't care, I decide to show Sam that I'm perfectly capable of ignoring him, and turn to Micah. "Hey, do you want to work on the next part together?"

My lab partner does a double take at me. "You *want* to work with me? On an individual assignment?"

"Sure, why not?" I ask, but it's clear I'm out of my element. If I could work alone on every experiment, I would, and everyone knows it. Micah's reaction is completely understandable.

His gaze flicks from me to his paper. "Um, okay. This is what I have so far."

As he slides his work toward me, I note the jumbled mess of calculations. There doesn't seem to be any rhyme or reason to his organization. With a sigh, I try not to sound condescending as I suggest ways to keep the information neat. I'm honestly trying to help, but Micah seems to be a bit sensitive whenever he receives criticism.

He pulls his paper back. "On second thought, I'll just finish it up myself. Thanks, though."

I deflate, my shoulders sagging, so I put my focus back on my work. Maybe *try* to focus is the better way to put it. Between Maya's giggles and Sam's whispers, I can't concentrate long enough to get anything done. Reaching into my backpack, I pull out my earbuds and pop them in. As I click the play icon on my phone, I'm basked in sweet melodies instead of shameless flirtation, and I'm back on track.

I finish the measurements portion and move onto the calculations when Dr. Hinkle taps me on the shoulder. Taking out an ear-bud, I look at him.

"Sorry, Brynn. No headphones. I need all your attention on your work," he says.

With a despondent nod, I put them away. Great. I'm right back where I started.

"Now you can contribute to the group, Brynn," Sam says.

I whip my head up to glare at him. "And what exactly do I need to contribute?"

He nonchalantly shrugs a shoulder. "You're, like, the second smartest person at the table. Your input might be useful."

If I was a lithium metal, Sam's words would be water. They ignite a fire in me, exploding from deep within my gut to radiate throughout my body. I want to leap across this table and tear that smug smirk off his face.

But that's what he wants. He wants me to react so he knows he got to me. Well, too bad.

With a deep breath, I turn a friendly, albeit fake, smile on him. I pitch forward to look at his paper. "Well, it's a good thing you asked." I point to his first calculation. "You've switched your chemical amounts here. If you mix these like this, it'll ruin your result."

Sam narrows his eyes before he scans his work. His skepticism turns to disdain as he realizes I'm right. Grimacing, he sighs. "Thanks."

"Don't mention it," I say in my most bubbly voice.

Our heated glares threaten to set off the fire alarm until Maya butts in. "Don't let it get to you, Sam. It was a silly mistake. Now that you've got it sorted out, Brynn can go back to her own work." The bite undercutting her words pulls me out of my angry staring contest.

She and Sam return to their own little world, and I'm left to myself. I should be glad. Obviously, Sam is still miffed from our fight last week. Probably even more so now that I've one-upped him in front of Maya, but he seems to recover quickly, falling back into their whisper-giggle routine.

I guess this is my sign that I imagined the attempted kiss. Relief should be flooding me.

So, why do I feel the weight of disappointment settling in my chest?

# Chapter 18

"I can't believe I let you talk me into this," I say, hiding my face in my hands.

"Shut up," Lisa says as she applies her bright-red lipstick. "You're hot. And we can't have a complete Village People line up without the cop."

I pull my hands away from my face to observe myself in the mirror. I'll hand it to Lisa; she did a fantastic job on my makeup. The smoky eye she gave me really makes my blue eyes pop, and thankfully she went easy on the blush. Even the lipstick shade is a more muted red. My hair is cute too. The loose curls spill out from under the police hat like a waterfall as they cascade onto my shoulders.

But this costume, if you could even call it that, isn't anything more than full-coverage lingerie. The hem of my dress doesn't even cover my whole ass. The fishnet tights only add to the effect, as does the zipper in front that stops halfway up my torso. If I bend over even slightly, people will see everything I usually keep under lock and key.

"I'll probably be arrested for indecent exposure," I joke, but Lisa glares.

"No one is going to complain." She puts the finishing touches on her makeup, fluffs her hair, and pulls me in for a side hug. "We're going to be the hottest girls there. Come on, let's get Jackie and Hannah."

The Halloween party Lisa is dragging us to is only a few houses down the street. Makes for an easy walk home, though it's cold enough, I'd be fine paying for an Uber, too. The four of us stroll down the street, trying not to break our ankles in the hooker heels we're wearing, and giggling the entire way.

When we reach the house, I'm not at all surprised to hear the music blaring through the speakers, or to see people crowded into every square inch. A lot of people means more eyes to witness me in this ridiculous costume. I tug on the hem of my "dress" as we ascend the front steps.

Lisa pats my shoulder. "Get a grip, Brynn."

"Tell that to my outfit," I say, wriggling the costume down as much as possible. "Whose party is this, again?"

"A guy from my Econ class."

"A guy? Or a guy you know?"

Lisa rolls her eyes. "Yes, I know him. His name's Brent." A smile pulls at her lips. "We sit next to each other and talk every day. He's cool, don't worry."

I'm not worried about Brent. I'm worried about the hundred pairs of eyes that will be ogling all the square inches of my exposed skin.

As we enter the house, we step right into the living room, the beat of heavy bass thumping against the soles of my feet. This is apparently the dance hall. Through the throng of costumes, I see two huge speakers flanking a bay window.

I stiffen as I scan the room, not recognizing anyone here. It's not surprising if this is an Econ student's place. Besides my roommates, I don't know a lot of people who aren't chemistry majors.

"Let's get a drink," Jackie practically shouts in my ear, and I eagerly nod.

Halfway down the hall, a door opens to reveal a clam-baked office. Smoke pours through the doorway, making me cough. I'll stay out of there. Passing the mudroom, we get a glimpse of a beer pong tournament happening in the garage. That could be fun later, though.

When we finally reach the kitchen, we find the holy grail of self-serve drinks. Half of the counter is stacked with every kind of hard alcohol one could ever want, and the other half has all the mixers. There are also three coolers on the floor. One is labeled "beer," one is labeled "water," and the last is labeled "other."

My eyebrows scrunch as I wonder what that means. Before I can investigate, Lisa claps a guy in a vampire costume on the back. When he spins around, his face lights up as he wraps his arms around her waist and picks her up. He staggers back a bit, but doesn't fall down.

"You made it!" he shouts, setting her back on the floor.

Lisa adjusts her construction worker shorts. "Of course I did! Thanks for the invite." She turns to motion to the three of us. "These are my friends."

The guy shakes all of our hands. "Hi, I'm Brent."

We exchange pleasantries, and Brent offers to mix us all drinks, which we happily accept. Soon, Lisa falls deep into conversation with him while Jackie, Hannah, and I watch from the sidelines. He seems like a nice guy, and certainly has an eye for her. She's never mentioned him before, but she's got a little more pep in her attitude while talking to him.

An acute sense of dismay settles in my chest as I watch them. It would be nice to have a guy of my own to share that sort of thing with. The closest I've got is arguing and bickering with Sam.

Sam...

God, I wish he wasn't such an ass. Three and half months ago, I would have begged to have him by my side, but now he's just a thorn in it. He pokes at me, sharp and irritating.

I sip my surprisingly delicious drink.

Unfortunately, Sam being the most aggravating person on the planet doesn't negate the fact that he's the hottest guy I've ever met. Those springy curls that frame his face so perfectly. His strong jaw line. Ugh–and his beautiful brown eyes. I hate that I love the way they look when he wears his glasses.

A longing builds within me, threatening to become a heated desire, so I gulp down the rest of my drink to douse the flames. I motion to Jackie and Hannah that I'm going to refill, and head to the bar. I stop dead in my tracks before I get there.

A cowboy with dark curls peeking from under his hat steps into the kitchen. My breath hitches as I anticipate seeing Sam dressed in chaps, but when he lifts his head, disappointment hits me hard.

It's not him.

I shake my head. Good. I don't want to see him.

After pouring myself a more-rum-than-Coke, I rejoin my friends. I find Lisa still in the throes of conversation with Brent while Jackie and Hannah stand to the side, looking bored beyond belief.

"Want to go play pong?" I ask as I make a swoosh gesture with my arm.

Their heads turn between me and Lisa before nodding. "Please," they whine in unison.

With light giggles, Jackie, Hannah, and I scoot off to the garage. As we walk through the mudroom, a couple of inmates are on their way inside. I turn sideways, pressing my back to the wall to allow space for them to pass.

"I wave my rights, officer," one of them says, his voice low and confident. Almost familiar.

I whip my head up, squinting in the dim light. "What?"

"Please, take me away," he begs, and holds his hands out like he wants to be cuffed.

"Dude, don't be creepy," his friend says. "Sorry, ladies." He shoves the other inmate forward, and they leave the mudroom, laughing. As they step into the well-lit hallway, I get a better look at the guy.

He's not Sam.

Why does that matter? Was I expecting it to be?

I frown. Both at the disappointment beginning to overwhelm me, and the fact that I shouldn't be disappointed in the first place. The last thing I need is Sam showing up to ruin my night.

Jackie nudges me. "See? Lisa was right. You look hot."

"Yeah, guess so."

Inside the garage, Jackie and Hannah take the first game while I stand to the side. I don't mind being a spectator. It's better than watching Lisa flirt with Brent.

But when Hannah's body language turns sexy, I know she's set her sights on her opponent. The guy is cute, tall with blond hair, muscular, and he's been paying more attention to Hannah than anyone. That's a sure way to win her heart. I must be right, because once their game is over, the two of them disappear to get better acquainted.

I track them all the way to the door, my face scrunched with concern.

"She'll be fine," Jackie says, grabbing my arm. "Come on, I want to play again."

With a sigh, I accept that Hannah is an adult who can make her own decisions and saddle up to play beer pong. I'll text her in a bit anyway. I tip up my cup, finishing my drink, and look across the table at our lone opponent.

He searches the room with his hands in the air. "Who's up? I need a partner!"

"I'm in!" a voice shouts from the crowd.

A figure emerges, and I'm immediately distracted by his costume. This guy is wearing a suit. No, not a suit. A tuxedo. Complete with a bowtie and everything. As I scan his length, I note how well he fills out the tux. My interest piques until I turn my gaze to the face attached to the body, and my mood goes south.

Sam is here. And he's wearing his glasses. Dammit.

I'd swallow down the sour taste at the back of my throat, but my mouth has run dry. And my cup is empty.

He fist bumps the other guy before turning to me and Jackie. When he sees us, or me, particularly, his mouth curls into that smug smirk of his. As he rakes over my costume, however, his smirk falls, and he takes his bottom lip between his teeth.

I fight the urge to squirm under his fiery gaze, but when his Adam's apple bobs, I think this game might be fun, after all.

Since the guys won the last game, they get the first shot. The other guy steps up to shoot. He rarely missed any during the last round. He's so accurate, I've started calling him Ace in my head, so it's no surprise when his first toss plops right into the front cup.

Sam steps to the middle, moving his arm back and forth like he's practicing. He shoots and sinks it in the same cup. Their hollers of victory ring out as they high-five each other before Sam looks at me. "Drink up, ladies."

Gladly. Jackie picks up a corner cup as I grab the one with the ping-pong balls inside, raising it into the air. "Take a good look, boys. You won't see us drinking much after this." I remove the balls, and toss back the warm, cheap beer.

"And we get our balls back," Sam says, holding out his hand.

I snort, my sinuses burning with the carbonation of the beer, and watch Sam's cheeks redden.

He clears this throat as he pulls at his collar. "We get another turn."

"I'm aware of the rules," I say, bouncing the ping pong balls across the table before setting my cup to the side. "But try to hold on to your balls next time."

Sam narrows his eyes, but I see amusement dancing on his lips.

Over the next few turns, Jackie and I make most of the shots, but the boys aren't far behind. We now have six cups on the table. Sam and Ace have four. We're in the lead, but I'd like a solid gain. When Ace steps up, he sinks his shot, no problem.

Shit. If Sam makes it, we'll be tied. And if he makes it into the same cup, they have a chance to move ahead. We need a distraction.

I fluff my hair, pulling some strands over my shoulder, and tip my chin toward my cleavage. "Oh, no!" I cry. "Jackie, my hair is stuck in my zipper!"

Jackie does a double take at me, but catches on quickly. "Oh, shit. Let me see." She turns me so I'm facing the boys, and pretends to struggle with the false tangle.

I glance up to find Sam frozen in place, his lips parted and his eyes fixed on my chest. Good.

"Come on, man. Take your shot," Ace groans.

Jackie tugs a little more on my zipper. "I can't get it to budge. Move a little for me."

I do more than just move. I start bouncing on my toes, twisting my torso from side to side. When I look up again, Sam's mouth has fallen even further, and a maniacal idea crosses my mind.

"Go on, Sam. Shoot already," I whine, clasping my hands in front of me to push my boobs together.

He shakes his head, like he's just woken up, licks his lips, and shoots. The ping-pong ball bounces off the rim of the cup and falls to the floor.

With a triumphant cheer, Jackie and I hug.

"No fair. That was blatant interference," Ace says.

Clearly, he was not fazed by my half-naked body, but Sam was, and that's all that matters. I zip my costume back up. "I don't see your partner complaining. Right?"

I shoot Sam a pointed look, but as spirited cheers go up around the room, embarrassment floods me. Apparently, *no one* is complaining. Whatever. We won. With a shrug, I pick up my ping-pong ball. "Game on."

Jackie and I mop the floor with the boys after that. We clear their cups while they only manage to get one of ours off the table. Watching Sam and Ace cringe their way through the rest of the warm beer is the most satisfying thing ever.

Ace gulps down his last bit and slams the cup on the table. "Round two?"

"I'm up for a rematch," Jackie says.

I shake my head. "I've had enough cheap beer. I need something with flavor." I pat Jackie on the shoulder and turn toward the door.

"Better leave while you're on top," Sam says. "Since it's your favorite position."

With an offended gasp, I spin around, ready to glare my pretty little head off. When I meet Sam's gaze, though, he winks. Snippets of our night in Grand Junction flash behind my eyelids with every rapid blink, and I feel heat rising in my cheeks. I swallow down my anger and step into the house.

I need something to drink, and fast.

# CHAPTER 19

AFTER REFILLING MY COCKTAIL, I wander around, searching for signs of my two missing friends, Hannah and Lisa. Between the thumping music and the flowing drinks, I've practically forgotten Sam's quip about me being on top. He is right, after all.

With my confidence back, I opt to ride this high of beating Sam at beer pong for as long as possible. I even dance my way across the living room. I don't think anything will bring me down. When I get through the crowd, I find Lisa on the couch with Brent's tongue down her throat.

Ew.

At least I found her. Dancing my way back through the room, I pull my phone out and text Hannah. I haven't seen her at all since I came back in. Knowing that she left the garage with some guy I've never seen before has my hackles up.

When my phone dings a minute later, I relax as I see a string of emojis. It's our secret message way of communicating. As long as she sends specific emojis in a specific order, I know she's okay.

With my friends all accounted for, I finish off my drink and head back to the kitchen. I'm on a roll tonight, so why not celebrate? As I'm nursing my fourth...or maybe fifth, rum and Coke. I lean my head back against the wall and shut my eyes.

"Oh, I didn't realize there was a cheaters-only section of the kitchen."

My eyes pop open, finding Sam perched in front of me with his head cocked to the side. "Excuse me?"

"Oh, nothing. Just referencing your little show out there." He juts his chin toward the garage.

I snort before sipping my drink. "You're just mad I beat you at something." Leaning my head back, I shut my eyes again.

"You had help."

When I snap my head up to glare at him, the whole room spins, and I'm glad the wall is sturdy. "So did you, but even Ace couldn't save your lack of skill."

"Who?"

"Your partner out there. He hardly missed."

"So, you gave him a nickname?" Sam quirks an eyebrow. "How drunk are you?"

I scoff and take another sip. "Not drunk enough to put up with you."

"But drunk enough to strip in front of a bunch of people?"

I'm taken aback by his tone. He sounds almost, I don't know, jealous. "Hey, it's not my fault you're so easily distracted."

"I think the whole room was distracted by you."

The burn of desire in his gaze makes my stomach flutter. "Yeah, but you're the one who missed his shot." In more ways than one. I tip up my cup, ignoring the slight wince in Sam's expression. As I finish my drink, I push off the wall. "I need another one," I say, but the room spins again, and I stumble forward.

"Whoa, there." Sam catches me by the elbows. "Are you sure you need more?"

"I'm fine. It's these damn heels," I lie.

His gaze slides down my length to my shoes and back up. "Those are tall. Can you stand?"

I shrug out of his grasp. "Yeah, thanks," I say, smoothing out my costume. As I raise my head, I drag my gaze up his gorgeous tuxedo-covered frame. "What are you supposed to be?"

"007."

"Who?"

He leans down and puts his lips to my ear. "Bond. James Bond."

I shudder as his hot breath spills down my neck, but reel myself in as he stands back up. Staring at his handsome face, I can't help the wave of longing that washes over me. I reach up to tap the edge of his glasses. "Does James Bond need these?"

He ducks his head. "Not normally, no. But I didn't want to risk passing out here and sleeping in my contacts."

"Smart thinking."

A blush rises in Sam's cheeks at my compliment, but he covers it by downing the rest of his drink. "Who's your favorite Bond?"

"No idea." I shrug. "I've never seen a James Bond movie."

"What? That should be illegal." Something like offense slides across his face before melting as he rakes over my body. "As should your costume. A cop, right?"

"Not just any cop. I'm Ray Simpson." That's right, I Googled him.

"Who?"

The outrageously confused expression on his face makes me laugh. "The cop from the Village People. Lisa's into disco music, remember?"

"Oh." He licks his lips. "Well, I think you fill the outfit better," he says, his voice gruff.

My stomach flips and desire pools low within me.

"So, where are your other villagers?"

"Well, you saw the sailor in the garage. Was she still shipwrecked on Beer Pong Island when you came inside?"

Sam chuckles and nods.

"The other two... I'm not sure where the cowboy, I mean, cowgirl went. She must have rode off into the sunset"–I sigh–"but the construction worker is in the living room, busy getting her foundation laid."

Sam snort laughs, nearly choking on his drink.

Pride over my cleverness puts a lightness in my chest. "Are you here alone?"

"Nah, I came with a couple of buddies. They're still in the garage. I saw you when I came in for a refill. Speaking of, do you really want another one?" Sam takes my cup when I nod, brushing past me to mix us both another beverage, and I drink him in.

There's something completely sexy about a guy in a tux, and Sam is no exception. In fact, he might be my new favorite version. I know what his body looks like under the tux, so it's no surprise he fills it out perfectly. I wish his jacket wasn't so long. I'd love to get a glimpse of his ass in those slacks.

BRYNN! Get a hold of yourself.

"So, Brynn," Sam says, drawing out my name as he hands me my cup. "About last Friday..."

My heart leaps into my throat. There are so many things he could bring up about last Friday. What will it be? The success of the study session? My imagined kiss? I *really* hope he's not going to rehash our argument.

"Mid-terms went well, so I guess our extended study group was a success." He tips his cup to his lips.

I blow out a forceful breath. "Yeah, I mean, the professor said the majority of the class passed with a C or higher, but that doesn't mean they all passed."

"Still better than the first exam."

I beam inwardly. *I* did that. *I* helped the class earn better grades, but when a nagging little voice in the back of my head reminds me that Sam also helped, I grimace.

"You okay?" he asks.

I turn my grimace into a tight smile. I can't take all the credit, but that doesn't mean I have to give him any praise. "Yeah, just thinking about how we still have work to do."

"So you think the professor wants us to keep the study group going?"

"Probably. She'd say something like 'never stop working as long as there are improvements to be made.'"

"You sound exactly like her." Sam rolls his eyes.

I scoff. "Well, I've only had her every semester since I was a freshman."

"My condolences." Sam lifts his cup, tilting it toward me before taking a sip. "So, I guess this means we're stuck with each other for a while longer, huh?"

"Unfortunately, yes." My lips curl into a sly grin as an idea comes to mind. "Unless you want to hand everything over to me."

He shakes his head, curls flopping about. "Ha! Nice try. I'm not about to give up something that's going to land me that internship."

"That internship is mine," I bite out, putting my hands on my hips. "I've been first in line for almost three years; there's no way you're getting it."

Sam's face twists into mock sympathy. "Aw, Brynn. You're so cute when someone knocks you down a peg."

"Excuse me?"

"The look on your face right now is exactly the same as that night at the bar when I got on the bull. And it's also how you looked when you found out about my ninety-eight percent. It's adorable."

My red Solo cup crinkles as I tighten my grip on it. Nostrils flaring, I glare at Sam and his stupid self-satisfied expression.

Seemingly unaffected by my anger, he opens his mouth to speak, but his attention flicks to the side and the teasing glint in his eyes turns to panic in one second flat. He grabs my wrist, pulling me around the corner and through a doorway. Before he shuts the door, I grab a glimpse of boxes and cans of food.

"Um, Sam, why are we in the pantry?"

With a groan, he lets his forehead fall to the door. "Because Maya just walked in."

"Maya? From lab?"

"Yeah." He flicks the light switch, bathing us in low, incandescent light. "If she would've seen me, she never would've left me alone."

I fold my arms. "Would've saved me some trouble."

He turns, a glare on his face, but says nothing.

"What? I say that because you and I were about to rip into each other again. Technically, Maya stopped what would have turned into a brawl."

His mouth ticks up on one side. "I think I could take you."

"But you're afraid of Maya?" I say in a teasing tone.

"No. I'm not afraid," he bites out. "Just exhausted. She never stops talking."

I throw my hand over my mouth to muffle the laughter that bursts from me.

"Why is that funny?"

I hold up my finger, signaling I need a second to catch my breath. "I thought I was the only one who felt that way."

"Well, you're not." He folds his arms and leans against the shelves.

"So, what's your plan? You going to hide out in here all night?"

"No, *we're* only hiding until the coast is clear."

"Ha, no way I'm staying in here with you any longer than I have to." I take a step toward the door, but Sam doesn't move. "Excuse me. I'd like to leave now."

Sam shakes his head. "You're not leaving until I say so. You'll blow my cover."

"Um, try again. I'll leave when I'm good and ready, which is now." I lift my cup to twirl it in the air. "I'm going to need a refill soon."

"There's juice in here." His head turns in all directions as is he's surveying the selves.

"Nope. No way. I'm going to need something stronger if I'm stuck in here with you."

A flash of hurt graces his face before being replaced with mischief. "I can think of worse company." His gaze scans my length again, this time lingering on my half-covered chest.

I self-consciously wrap my arms around my middle, but that only emphasizes my cleavage. I drop my arms. "And Maya is that worse company? I really thought you enjoyed her attention."

"Hey, there's nothing wrong with being flattered by a pretty girl flirting with you." He runs a hand through his curls. "But being able to hold an intelligent conversation makes all the difference."

The smolder in his eyes makes my mouth run dry, so I take another drink. I keep drinking until my cup is empty, then turn it upside down. "Time for a refill. Move please."

"Nope."

"Sam. Get out of the way."

"Uh uh."

I narrow my eyes at him. When I catch his gaze flick down to my chest again, an idea pops into my head. "But Sam…" I purr, pouting my lips and batting my fake lashes. "Please?"

"What are you doing?"

"Nothing." I exaggerate the syllables, letting my tongue slide between my teeth.

He swallows deeply. "Stop it, Brynn."

I clasp my hands in front of me and use my biceps to push up my breasts. "Why? You liked it earlier."

He downs the last of his drink, crushes the cup, and tosses it to the side. With one big step, he closes the gap between us. One of his hands loops around my waist, yanking me to him and making my stomach flip, while the other cups the back of my head.

I drop my cup and splay my hands across his chest, a thrill shooting through me, both from shock and desire.

"I still like it," he growls before crashing his mouth to mine.

At first, I want to protest, but I quickly fall into a swoon. His kiss is as I remember, tender with notes of passion laced through it. With a moan, I thread one of my hands into his hair, and the other grips onto his muscular shoulder.

As he slowly unzips my costume, the anticipation of his touch builds within me. When he slides his hand along the bare skin of my stomach and up my ribs, I'm on fire, but he's not done.

He brushes his fingers over my lacy bra, and hums. "So sexy." His warm palm runs over my hardened nipples, the sensation almost too much to bear.

My knees buckle, but he catches me. He braces me against the shelf, running his hand over my ass and under my thigh to hike up my leg. I hook it around his waist so that our hips meet. His hard length presses against my apex, and I gasp. I've forgotten how good that feels.

How good *he* feels.

He very gently grinds against me, sliding his hard cock up and down. I'm moaning my head off, but luckily, the party is loud enough I'm sure no one can hear us. When he presses harder, my head flops back. Sam takes full advantage.

Peppering kisses along my cheek and jaw, he nuzzles into the crook of my neck. His hot breath cascades down my skin as his hand slides down my body. It settles between my thighs, his fingers caressing my soaking wet lacy panties.

He pushes the fabric aside and slips two fingers inside me. With a shudder, he whispers, "So wet. All for me?"

My response is to moan and twist my fingers tighter into his hair, pulling him closer.

He continues to suck, kiss, and nip at my neck and shoulder. His fingers work their magic as his thumb massages my swollen clit. The pressure building inside of me has me digging my nails into his shoulder, but it doesn't seem to faze him. He keeps his tempo, rubbing me the right way. I'm so close to my climax, but I don't want it to end yet.

Sam ends it for me when he bites out, "Come for me."

I meet that glorious crest head on. My body shudders with release as I cry out his name, but he doesn't stop. His tempo slows, but he keeps moving his fingers until I'm completely finished. Slowly, my grip on him eases. He releases me from his embrace, allowing me to stand on my own.

As I steady myself on my own two feet, I look up at him through my lashes. The adoring, longing expression on his face rips the air from my lungs once again. I want nothing more than to pull him in for another searing kiss so I can ride him cowgirl style until the cows come home.

But before I can act, the pantry door opens, and light spills in. Some drunk guy dressed like a pirate steps through the doorway, but stops immediately when he sees us. Realization spreads across his face in the form of a shit-eating grin.

"Sorry," he says, snickering. "Thought this was the bathroom."

"Well, it's not. Get the fuck out!" Sam shouts, but it's too late.

Getting caught made everything suddenly very real for me. I run, as best I can in these heels, straight out the door, not bothering to zip my costume. Sam calls out after me, at least I think he does. The music is too loud, but the pounding of my panicking heart is louder. It's drowning out everything around me.

I bolt through the house and out the front door, not giving two shits about the freezing air as I tear down the street. Within minutes, I'm back home. I fling the door open, crashing it into the wall, and slam it shut. In my room, I flop onto my bed, covering my face with my pillow and screaming into it.

What the fuck was I thinking? Bottom line is, I wasn't. Yet again, Sam Eastman busted through my walls and kept me from weighing the consequences of my actions. It's like he impairs my ability to think things through.

I'm sure the alcohol didn't help, but even when I'm drunk, Lisa says I'm still an annoying over-analyzer. So, what's my problem?

"Ugh," I groan into my pillow. How am I going to face Sam in class after this?

I need Lisa, but I don't want to ruin her fun. I pull out my phone to text her that I'm home and that everything is okay, that I'm just tired. My drama can wait until tomorrow. Maybe a good night's sleep will help me sort things out.

# CHAPTER 20



THE NEXT MORNING, I'M awake by six. It's certainly not intentional since I didn't get home until after one, but I had such a fitful sleep, I can't stay in bed any longer. So, I get up, make a pot of coffee, and read.

One of my guilty pleasures is reading romance novels. There's something about a hot, perfect leading man who gives the female character all her wishes and desires that calls to me. I guess in a way, I'm waiting for my perfect leading man. I've yet to find him.

I read for over two hours before Lisa and Jackie come downstairs. They look like hell, and I have to stifle my giggles. "Good morning, sunshines."

Lisa flips me off as she yawns, her lipstick smeared down her chin. From the way her eye makeup is smudged, she's probably been rubbing her eyes. I confirm this when she gets close enough for me to see she's only got one fake lash still on. Her ponytail is barely holding it together as she lumbers down the steps.

"Is Hannah still asleep?" I ask.

Jackie shakes her head and shrugs. Her makeup isn't in as bad of shambles as Lisa's, but I'd say she's winning the walk of shame since she slept in her costume. I shoot them both a questioning look laced with concern.

"She left with that beer pong guy," Lisa says.

I chew on the inside of my cheek. "I knew she left the garage with him, but I didn't know she *left* with him."

When my concern doesn't waver, Jackie sighs. "It was someone she knows from class. She texted me last night when she got to his house, and she already texted me this morning that she's alive." She pulls out her phone to show me the messages, complete with the slew of emojis. "Happy?"

I nod in approval as she absentmindedly tries to slide her phone into the nonexistent pocket on her costume. It hits the floor with a sharp *thwack*. She bends down to pick it up, and a ping pong ball falls out of her cleavage. The three of us watch in silent awe as it bounces across the room.

"How did you sleep with that in there all night!?" Lisa asks through laughter.

"No idea." Jackie shrugs before sniffing at the air. "Do I smell coffee?"

I nod. "I made another pot, like, fifteen minutes ago. Help yourselves."

They happily scurry into the kitchen. While they're pouring their cups of self-medication, I finish the chapter I'm on, and put my book away. They both come back to the living room and snuggle on the couch with me.

"What happened to you last night?" Lisa asks.

"I texted you. I got tired," I say, lifting my mug to my lips.

She shakes her head. "No, I mean at the party. One minute, you were there, and the next, you were gone."

"First of all, you were so enthralled in conversation with Brent, you probably didn't even notice me, Jackie, and Hannah go to the garage." I shoot Lisa a pointed look, but she smiles. "Then, when I came inside, you and Brent were...getting familiar." I bob my eyebrows to encourage her to elaborate. I'm not quite ready to dive into the story about me and Sam, so I'll divert to her.

Lisa lets out a contented sigh. "Ladies, I think I'm in love."

"What?" Jackie and I shout in unison, both sitting upright at full attention.

"Mhm. Brent is perfect."

"But you're not even dating him." Jackie crinkles her nose. "Wait, is there something you haven't told us?"

Lisa shakes her head. "I haven't been secretly dating him, no. We've been hanging out before and after class, seeing each other in passing. But when we're together, we click." Lisa stares off into the room, a contentedness in her features. "He asked me out last night."

Jackie and I burst into giddy giggles, with Jackie bouncing in her seat as I try not to spill my coffee. "I'm happy for you, Lisa," I say, and I am, but I'm also a bit skeptical. Lisa has flitted from guy to guy for years, never really being into one more than the other. I hope this isn't another fleeting relationship. "But no wonder you didn't notice where I was."

"Yeah, about that..." She turns to face me, and Jackie leans over her shoulder to listen in. "Your turn to talk about your night."

"Well..." My lower lip works its way between my teeth. "While you were busy sucking face with Brent, Sam found me."

Lisa's eyes widen. "Sam was there!?"

"He played beer pong with us," Jackie teases, grinning at me.

"Did you whoop his ass?"

"Of course, we did." I high-five Jackie. "But then I went to the kitchen for another drink, and he came inside. We ended up talking."

Lisa makes a noise like she's impressed. "From what you've told me about him, I'm surprised you didn't choke him out."

"I have *some* self-control."

"You guys have been hanging out, though?" Jackie asks. "Are you still enemies?"

"We agreed to frenemy terms."

They both chuckle before Lisa nudges me to continue.

"So, he came to say hi, and we discussed the study group and celebrated our success with a few drinks." I spill the whole story from the initial civil conversation, to him making us hide from Maya, all the way to me needing a refill. "When he wouldn't leave the pantry, I started teasing him."

"Teasing him?" Lisa arches an eyebrow. "Explain."

I groan. "Okay, in my defense, I was on my, like, fifth or sixth drink."

Jackie wiggles in her seat. "Ooh, this ought to be good."

"I was making pouty faces and squishing my boobs together to get a rise out of him."

"I bet he rose." Lisa nudges Jackie with her elbow, and they giggle.

With a roll of my eyes, I continue. "We started making out, and I…sort of…let him finger me." The last part comes out quietly as I hide behind my coffee mug.

"Ahhhh!" They both squeal, and I wince at the pitch.

"How was it?" Lisa asks, her face lighting up.

"Fantastic." I release a contented sigh before I yank myself back to the present. "But what am I going to do, now?"

"I think the more important question is, what do you *want* to do?" Lisa asks.

I stare at her blankly, but say nothing.

Lisa groans. "Do you like him?"

"Not in the way you're thinking."

Jackie's mouth drops open. "But you said you let him—"

I hold up my hand. "I know what I said, but that doesn't mean I have feelings for him. I just like the way he touches me."

"So, do you want him to keep touching you?" Lisa asks, wiggling her butt in her seat.

This isn't an easy decision. Chewing on my lower lip, I squeeze my eyes shut and breathe out the word, "No."

"No?" they both ask in unison.

I open my eyes to find the most ridiculously incredulous looks on their faces. "I don't want a relationship with Sam, and I don't want to lead him on."

"Then what are you going to do?" Lisa asks.

"I'm going to tell him we can't be alone together anymore. We'll have to do our study group prep at the library or something." It sounds so easy, so simple. I hope I can say the words when the time comes.

***

All day Tuesday, I psych myself up for an unpleasant chat with Sam, only to be thwarted by Maya. She gets to lab early, ambushing Sam the second he rounds the corner, and then waits for him to leave with her when class is over.

Part of me is relieved.

The other part writhes in anguish about delaying this conversation. I'd like to get it over with so I don't have it weighing on my mind any longer than I have to. It leaves too much time for me to think.

On Thursday after lecture, I try my best to follow Sam out the door. Yet again, my path is intercepted by Maya. I'd swear she's his shadow if her hair wasn't so bright.

I'm about to skulk away in defeat, when I hear Sam say something about a meeting with another professor, then he parts ways with Maya to walk in the opposite direction. I wait a few seconds so it doesn't seem like I'm following him before I do just that. I may walk a little faster than necessary. I don't want to lose him, but when I round the corner, I almost crash into him.

"Whoa, Brynn. What's the rush?"

"Sorry," I say, collecting myself. "I... Wait, why are you hanging out over here?"

He runs a hand through his curls. "I'm waiting for the coast to be clear before I can leave."

"Are you hiding from Maya? Again?" I try not to laugh.

"She doesn't have class after O-Chem, so she walks me to my next one *every* day. And she doesn't stop talking for a second of it."

The defeat in his voice almost makes me feel bad for the laugh bursting from my lips, and I practically double over.

Sam snorts. "Glad you think it's funny."

"I'm sorry," I say between breaths.

He tilts his head to the side. "Actually, what are you doing over here? You never leave this way either."

My jovial expression ices over, and I clear my throat. "I need to talk to you."

"Okay, about what?"

"Um, well..." I drop my gaze to my feet, watching as I dig my toe into the low-pile carpet. "We need to..." I lift my head, the words on the tip of my tongue, but when I meet his deep brown eyes, I lose what little confidence I had. "We never prepped for tomorrow night."

"Oh," he says, the light in his eyes dimming.

"I have all the questions and stuff ready. I could email it to you. If you don't mind putting the presentation together, that is."

He shakes his head, his lips pressed into a flat line.

"Okay, thanks." I take small steps backward. At the corner, I peek around the edge. "I think the coast is clear."

Relief takes over Sam's face. "Cool, thanks. I think I'll hang here for another minute or two, though. Just to be safe."

I nod and turn the corner, letting my embarrassment fuel me as I practically run away.

# Chapter 21

The next day, I make sure to arrive at study group at 4:55 p.m. so I don't have to be alone with Sam too long. As I walk through the door, I let out a dramatic sigh, insinuating I didn't intend to be late. I flop my bag onto the floor, plopping into my chair.

"You okay?" Sam asks, his eyebrows raised with curiosity.

I nod. "Just a long day of tutoring." It isn't a complete lie. I did have a long day of tutoring, but it wasn't nearly as stressful as I'm letting on. "Sorry I'm late."

"No problem. Everything's ready to go." He motions to the computer and up to the projector screen.

As I give him an approving smile, a lull finds its way between us. Hanging in the silence is the conversation I know I must have, but don't want to have.

Luckily, I'm saved when our classmates arrive and the room explodes with conversation. Sam and I begin the session where we play a fun game similar to Family Feud. Sam presents the questions and the teams can either answer or pass to the other team. It ends up being a riot with how competitive this class is.

When our time is up, everyone leaves. Well, almost everyone. Maya lags behind the group, coming to linger at the desk where Sam and I are packing up.

"Are you doing anything after this, Sam?" she asks, a glimmer of hope shining in her tone.

A pained look comes over his face, and I can tell he's struggling to find the right words to say. I'm overcome with pity for the poor guy, so I chime in, "Actually, we do need to talk about next week's study group."

Sam shoots me a thankful look, but clears his throat. "Oh, yeah, you're right, Brynn. Sorry, Maya, not tonight."

"Oh, of course. No problem." She smiles sweetly at him, batting her eyelashes before turning a not-so-sweet smile in my direction. "See you guys later," she says, and exits the room.

Sam noticeably relaxes. "Thanks. I owe you one."

"Don't mention it." I shrug. "But we do really need to talk about next week."

"Okay, but we can do that tomorrow."

"Yeah, well…" I chew on the inside of my cheek. "I kind of wanted to talk about that, too."

Sam stares at me, a slight panic in his eyes.

Reluctantly, I say, "I don't know if it's a good idea for us to be alone together anymore."

"Why?" Sam zips his backpack and sets it on the ground. "Is this about what happened on Halloween?"

"Of course it is." I fold my arms, hoping I can hold down the heat rising within me. "We're supposed to be colleagues, classmates. We can't casually hook-up and retain our professionalism."

"Why not?"

I jerk my head back like it's the most absurd question he could ask. "What do you mean, why not? Lots of reasons."

"Name your best one."

"Well, there's the fact that we hate each other's guts."

"Right, that." His gaze bounces around before meeting mine again. "Lots of people who hate each other have sex. Next point."

I scoff at how casually he brushed that off. "Sam, are you actually suggesting we become fuck-buddies?"

"That term implies the two parties are friendly." He tilts his head from side to side, a grin spreading across his face. "I was thinking more along the lines of fucking-frenemies."

A laugh bursts from my lips. "You're joking."

"Not in the slightest." His seriousness makes my heart race. "Let's check the facts, shall we." He bends his leg to sit halfway on the desk. "You and I are both single, both busy fourth year college students who, let's face it, don't have the time or energy to date. We already see each other on a regular basis, already know each other fairly well. We don't necessarily get along, but that's a non-issue in the bedroom."

I tear my gaze away from his as I bite down on my lower lip. He's not wrong in any of what he's saying, but do I agree with him?

"Plus, it's obvious we enjoy each other's bodies. At least, I assume you enjoyed having my fingers inside you last weekend." The gravel in his tone makes me shudder, and he grins.

I lick my lips. "But that would be it, right? All physical, no feelings?"

His Adam's apple bobs with a deep swallow as he nods. "Of course. We'd be two consenting adults who happen to enjoy having sex. That's it."

"But what do we say if people ask about our relationship?"

"Who says anyone has to know? You already come to my place once a week. We can hide behind the study group prep guise."

"Really?"

"Sure, why not?" He shrugs. "We can bang out our frustrations before we bust out the presentation." The self-satisfied smirk on his face is both adorable and infuriating.

But I laugh all the same. "No way. It's absurd."

"You think so?" he asks, lowering his voice to a soft growl. He slides off the desk to brace his hands on the arms of my chair and caging me in. His face hovers inches from mine. If I tilt up a bit, our mouths will meet, and how I long to feel his lips on mine again. Slowly, he moves his head so his mouth grazes my ear, and his hand slides up my thigh. "Tell me to stop."

A shaky breath escapes me, but I say nothing.

His hand inches higher, his fingertips brushing the crease where my thigh meets my hip. "If it's so absurd, tell me no, Brynn."

My eyes flutter closed, but I stay silent.

He slips his hand between my thighs, barely touching my apex. "Are you already wet for me?" he whispers, and I break.

My eyes pop open, and I swat his arm away. I sit straight up, my chest heaving as I struggle to fill my lungs. As I collect myself, I watch Sam lean his hip against the desk, his arms folded confidently across his chest.

"Why don't you sleep on it?"

"What?"

"Go home and think it over. Just don't think too hard about it." With a wink, he leans down to grab his backpack. "If you decide you want to give it a try, show up at my place at one o'clock tomorrow like normal. If not," he says, hiking his pack onto his shoulder, "then I'll meet you at the coffee shop down the street at one-thirty."

I'm pretty sure there's going to be a permanent crease between my eyebrows from the amount of thinking I'll be doing, but I nod in agreement.

"Cool. See you tomorrow." He leaves the room, and I'm left a breathless, confused wreck.

***

The entire night all I dream about is Sam's nearness. Not dreams of us having sex, no. Just dreams about the way his body heat feels, the way he smells, the way I burn with desire when he's close to me. All the things to build up my anticipation without granting me any sort of release. It doesn't make this decision any easier.

At breakfast Saturday morning, I mostly push my cereal around instead of eating it. Lisa notices.

"Hey, what's wrong with you?" she asks.

"Hm? Oh, nothing." I sigh. "Okay, well, something. Can you swear to keep a secret? Swear to not tell anyone, including Jackie and Hannah?"

Lisa's face lights up as she crosses her heart and makes a zipping motion across her lips.

I chuckle and shake my head. "Something happened at study group last night."

"Ooh, drama." She wiggles her butt in her chair. "Did you and Sam make out after group, or something?"

"No, there wasn't any making out, but he did offer me an interesting proposition."

"He propositioned you? Like a hooker?"

"Ew, no!" I let out a mock-offended laugh and swat her leg. "He asked if I wanted to casually have sex whenever we hung out."

"So, fuck-buddies?"

"He called it fucking-frenemies, since we don't actually like each other."

Lisa giggles. "Are you going to do it?"

"I don't know. I mean, he made a *very* convincing argument last night." I clench my thighs as I think about how close he came to convincing me. "But now that I've had time to think about it..."

"Stop thinking, Brynn."

With a snort, I say, "Easier said than done."

"You think too much. This time, leave your brain out of it, and go have some *fun*."

I sigh. "God, do I want to have some fun with him." I bite my lip at the thought of knowing how good that kind of fun really is.

"Clearly." She grabs my hand. "I know Connor broke you, but I think you should let Sam fix you."

I crinkle my nose.

"Sam may not be 'the one,' but if he's what you need to get yourself back, then go do him until you feel like you again."

Lisa's words may be a little edgy, but they make a lot of sense. "You're right. So what if he's not my forever, or even my next year? He can be my right now, and that's good enough."

"Atta girl." Lisa pats my leg. "Now, can I help you pick out what to wear?"

# Chapter 22

It's an unseasonably warm November day for my walk to Sam's apartment. My Colorado Avalanche hockey hoodie is almost too heavy, but I don't dare take it off. The outfit Lisa had me wear can barely even be considered one.

As I stroll along, I decide not to look a gift-horse in the mouth and enjoy my time outside. The sun is shining, but the light breeze blows softly across my skin and keeps me cool enough. A faint aroma of burning leaves wafts into my nostrils. I soak up the beautiful autumn day, letting it quell my anxiety.

I've been trying not to think too hard about the situation I'm about to walk into, but that's as easy as prying a bear trap open. I mean, I've made up my mind, as stupid as it may be. Lisa was right, though. After what I went through with Connor, I deserve some fun, and what Sam is offering sure does sound fun. There's nothing wrong with what we're about to do. Like he said, we're both consenting adults who are aware of our actions.

Doesn't make my nerves any less strained.

The thoughts burst to life before I can stop them. How is this going to work? Are we going to have sex first? Or should we work on the presentation beforehand? That is the main reason I'm going to his apartment in the first place. If we do the presentation first, though, I'll have all that time to think things over and change my mind. But if we have sex first, will that make the presentation stuff awkward? Will we work on it while we're naked?

Shaking the thoughts from my mind, I let out a groan.

Why didn't we talk about how this would work beforehand? I mean, I should have asked questions so I would have all the information upfront. That would have made this decision easier to make. At least, I think it would have.

"Get a grip, Brynn," I mumble to myself before I push the crosswalk button. My toes tap the pavement as I watch for the light to turn. The little stick figure lights up, guiding me across the intersection.

Maybe that's what I should do. I should let Sam guide me. This was his idea, after all, and he should be the one to tell me what to do, but what if he doesn't know either?

A frustrated sigh escapes me as I climb his apartment stairs. Fuck it. I'm taking the reins on this. We're going to have sex first to get it out of our systems, and then we'll work on the presentation. That way I can't talk myself out of it.

With a reaffirming nod, I knock on his door.

When he opens it, he has a cavalier air about him. "Glad to see you didn't think about it too hard."

"I'm not inside yet," I say in challenge.

He takes a step back and bows, motioning for me to enter. Before he gets the door shut, I'm already stripping off my sweatshirt and tank top. My hands are tangled in my shirts above my head when Sam turns around.

"Oh," he says, almost choking on the syllable.

"What?" My eyes follow his as they flick up to my hands, then down to my lacy camisole tank top.

He juts his chin at my torso. "That's nice."

I drop my arms, covering myself with my inside out garments. "Well, I wasn't sure how this was going to work. I mean, I figured we should, uh, you know, first so I don't have time to overthink things, but if you–"

Sam takes one big step, closing the gap between us, and plants his fingers on my lips. "Shh," he whispers. "Brynn, I'll absolutely get naked with you right away. Just...stop talking."

I smile behind his hand, and he lowers it. "Then kiss me already."

His mouth is on mine within the next breath as he grabs the back of my head and tears my sweatshirt from my arms. Spinning our bodies, he pushes me against the back of the couch. His hands are all over me, hungry for the touch as they devour my body from my hips to my waist to my ribs and around to my back, driving moans from my chest that are just as starved.

I run my fingertips along the hem of his shirt, tugging on it. He grunts and lifts his arms, allowing me to slide it off. My knuckles brush against his warm skin, and I'm set ablaze. I grab his shoulders, pulling him to me so our chests collide, and roll my hips against his.

He reaches down, sliding his hands under my thighs, and lifts me to sit on the back of the couch. Stepping forward, he settles himself between my legs.

I hook my ankles behind him. I want him as close as possible, and I don't want him leaving.

His hands slide up and down my back as he peppers kisses along my jaw and down my throat, nuzzling into the crook of my neck. When I twist a hand into his hair, he groans. He grips me tight as if bracing me, and runs a hand up my ribs to cup my breast. Palming my hardened nipple through the lace, he nips at my collarbone.

"Sam," I breathe.

"What do you want, Brynn?"

"You," I whisper.

He moans against my skin, the vibrations giving me goosebumps. "Tell me what to do."

Yes, sir. "Fuck me, Sam."

A deep growl emanates from him as he lifts me from the couch and carries me to the only room in the apartment I haven't seen; his bedroom. He sets me on the bed and crawls over me, my body immediately warming beneath him. His mouth latches onto my throat as he unbuttons my jeans which I promptly shimmy out of. When his fingers brush over the matching lace panties, he pauses his sucking on my neck and pulls back to scan my form as if admiring a work of art.

I squirm in the awkward moment, but when he turns and locks his eyes onto mine, I melt. The sincerity in them eases all my tension, but the fire in them builds desire within me. I grip his shoulder and pull him onto me. I want to be crushed by his weight. I need it.

He works his knee between my legs, pulling one of mine up and around his waist. His hips lower to meet mine, and his delicious hardness presses against my apex.

With a moan, I arch my back, my head flopping to the side.

Sam kisses down my body and stops at the neckline of my camisole, running his tongue along my skin above the fabric. "As much as I like this aesthetic…" He takes the lace between his teeth, snapping the elastic. "I like it better when you're naked."

I tilt my chin down and lift my arms to help him remove it.

With a chuckle, he rears back, pulling me to sit up. Once I'm upright, he slips the camisole from my body, and a shaky breath escapes him. Connecting our mouths again, he eases me onto my back. His warm palm finds my breast, and the skin-to-skin contact leaves a path of fire in its wake.

Each time I moan into his mouth, he swallows it down. As he leaves my mouth to kiss his way to my breasts, his hand moves south to settle between my thighs. His fingers slide along the lace of my panties, pressing gently, and it makes me squirm.

I'm burning for release, and we haven't even started yet. I buck my hips, but Sam "tsks" against my breast.

"Not yet," he whispers, and slides his hand under the waistband of my underwear. When his fingers graze my seam, he hums in delight. "So wet for me already. I like that."

All I can do is breathe his name as I continue to buck my hips. He finally grants me some release and slips a finger inside me. When he slides another finger in, he begins swirling my clit with his thumb, all the while sucking my nipples. I lose a hand in his curls, pulling his head closer to my breast.

"Sam," I plead.

He kisses my nipple before working his way up my chest and neck, all the way to my ear. "Beg all you want, sweetheart. I'm not fucking you until you come."

I groan in ecstasy. I mean, how can I be mad at that?

"Just enjoy yourself, Brynn." He kisses his way back to my breasts, taking a nipple between his teeth. "I certainly am."

When he speeds up the pace of his fingers, I can't help myself any longer. I give in. I let go of the hold I have on my body and drown in the waves of a delicious orgasm. It's amazing. My body quakes with pleasure as the tension breaks, and I melt into the sensation.

Sam rides the wave right along with me. He slows his motions, but doesn't stop until I do, and when I do, I'm like a limp noodle. Removing his fingers from me, he takes off my panties. I hear the jingle of his belt buckle and the ripping of a condom wrapper, but my eyes won't open. I have to imagine what's happening.

Before I know it, Sam's hovering over me once again, lightly peppering kisses along my collarbone. "You okay?" he breathes against my skin.

"Mhm," I hum, ready for more.

"Good. Any requests for how this goes?"

That gets my attention. I pop my eyes open, confusion spread across my face.

"Both of us are supposed to have fun," he says. "I'm going to, no matter what, so I want to know what's best for you."

"I like to be on top."

"Of course you do."

I scoff. "Hey, you asked."

With a quick nip at my collarbone, he rolls our bodies to the side. I yelp, gripping his shoulders as I'm thrown over to straddle him. When we're settled, I stare at Sam in amazement, the stupid self-satisfied grin on his face making me want to laugh, but only for a moment.

Quite suddenly, the mood changes. His eyes darken and his grip on my thighs tightens. My mouth and throat run dry. He cups the back of my head and pulls me down to connect our mouths once again. As we kiss, I adjust my hips so the tip of his cock hits my entrance, and I hover long enough to elicit a needy groan from him. Sliding down his hard length, I take him fully inside me.

It's as breathtaking as before. He fills me completely, fitting perfectly and making me shudder.

"Still okay?" he asks.

I nod and sit up. I watch the expression on his face turn from concern to heated desire as his gaze rakes over me. When I move my hips, his eyes close and his hands run up my sides to cup my breasts, his thumbs circling my nipples. My head falls back, his name spilling from my lips. Leaning back slightly, I rest my hands on his thighs and dig my fingers into his skin.

That's when he starts moving with me. He thrusts slowly at first, still letting me lead the pace, but when I start losing myself in the moment, he takes over. One hand stays on my breast while the other snakes around my waist to hold me up. His hips thrust faster.

Our breathy moans fill the room, soon becoming grunts and groans full of lust. We both want to hit that crest, both want to feel that burst of release that comes when we do. But we don't at the same time. At least, I don't.

I want to savor this feeling of our connection. His nearness. The friction. I don't ever want it to end, but I know he won't last forever.

It's obvious he's close when the hand around my waist slides to my stomach and dips lower. His thumb settles on my clit, gently circling the sensitive bundle of nerves.

I gasp, clenching my hands around his thighs. "Sam," I moan into the air.

"Fuck, Brynn. Say it again," he orders between grunts.

So, I do. Over and over, I let his name roll off my tongue, each time getting louder.

He shows his appreciation by pressing harder on my clit. "Come for me."

I tumble over that edge so fast, my head spins. I'm practically screaming his name as I tighten around his erection, my entire body shuddering as my release hits me head on.

Sam latches his hands onto my hips, thrusting into me with intense, passionate movements before succumbing to his own orgasm. His cock pulses inside me as he slows.

I collapse over onto him to rest my head on his shoulder. Our chests press into each other's with the huge gulps of air we're sucking in.

Sam tilts his head and kisses the top of mine. "You good?"

I note the sweet, affectionate action, but choose to ignore it. I'm so blissed-out right now, I can barely think. All I can do is hum a one-note syllable that sounds more like a caveman grunt than an affirmation to his question.

My head shakes with his laughter, the deep tone vibrating through his chest. "I'll take that as a compliment."

We fall into comfortable silence as we lie together. One of his hands brushes up my back while the other stays tucked under his head. With my ear against his chest, I listen to his heartbeat steady itself.

This moment is reminiscent of our time in the hotel. The way he's holding me. The warmth of his body next to mine. His soft breath moving my hair and tickling my neck. It's all so serene. I hate that I enjoy it so much.

Suddenly, I feel him tense beneath me. "Can you move?"

"Probably," I mumble against his chest.

"Well, can you? Because I need to get up."

The harshness in his tone surprises me. It's vastly different from the Sam I was just fucking, and as much as I don't want to admit that it hurts me to hear, it does. I roll to the side, releasing him from me, and curl into a ball, immediately missing his warmth.

Without another word, he gets up from the bed and heads for the bathroom.

I don't have time to pick apart his abrupt change in demeanor, so I jump out of the bed to get dressed. After all, our agreement has been fulfilled. Now that the sex is over, we can get to the presentation which is really why I'm here. I have to keep reminding myself of that.

Sam and I are not friends. We are not a couple. There are no feelings between us other than the desire between our legs which we've satiated.

# Chapter 23

Once I'm dressed, I hurry to the living room to set up the study group materials. I'm in the process of starting up the laptop when Sam comes into the room. He waltzes in wearing his jeans and no shirt. I have to swallow down my racing heart as I think about having his muscular torso pressed against me only minutes ago.

When he doesn't say anything, I flick my gaze up to find a sultry smirk on his face. "What?" I ask.

"I like that top." His voice is full of grit, and it makes me squirm.

I glance down at my camisole, my nipples barely visible through the lace. "Sorry," I say, and grab my tank top from the floor, pulling it on. "There. Better?"

"I wasn't complaining in the first place." He rounds the couch and picks his shirt up off the floor. "But that's not much of a shirt either. Do you want another one? I have more."

It's a sweet gesture, and I want to accept, but all of his shirts probably smell like him and the last thing I need is his scent saturated into my skin more than it already is. "No, but thanks. I'm fine like this."

"You sure are." Joining me on the couch, he pats my thigh.

I whip my head up, my eyebrows furrowed.

"That was really fun in there," he says, nodding toward his bedroom.

I snort and push his hand from my leg. "Yeah, well, now we have work to do."

He chuckles, rising from the couch. "Coffee?"

Damn, that does sound good. "Yeah, thanks."

I hear him in the kitchen, packages rustling and mugs clinking against the counter. Soon, the delicious aroma of hazelnut fills the air. My mouth waters as he returns with two mugs in his hands.

"So, what is your idea for this week?" I ask.

Sam dives into his plan for the presentation. It's like Wheel of Fortune this time, and he's already found the perfect spinner icon. We whip it out in no time, each of us downing three cups of coffee in the process. I'm certainly awake and focused by the time we're finished.

"That didn't take long at all," I say, tilting my cup up to drain the last few drops.

"Glad the coffee was good."

"Coffee is always good." I set my mug down. "But now I'm going to be up until midnight."

Sam's lips curl into a mischievous grin, and he scoots closer to me. "I have an idea of how we can burn off some energy."

I do a double take at his bobbing eyebrows, laughing. "You're not serious, are you?"

"Hey, no one ever said there was a limit."

My mouth opens, but I can't form any words. I'm a little flabbergasted at his proposition. I mean, we just had sex, and don't get me wrong, it was fantastic, but are we really going to do it again? "I don't know, Sam..."

"We don't have to make it a big thing." He leans in, putting his lips on my shoulder. "Let me fuck you on the couch."

"What?" I pull away, my eyes widening.

He gives me a look like he's offended or something. "I'll still make sure you come." The offense melts away to a saucy expression. "That's my favorite part."

Well, when he puts it like that, how can I not be flattered? But it's still an outrageous idea, right? "You really want to have sex again?"

"Brynn, asking a guy if he wants to have sex again is like asking Isaac Newton if he believes in gravity. The answer is always 'yes.'"

I laugh, shaking my head in disbelief. "Okay, then."

"Really?" The excitement on his face is adorable.

I nod. "I mean, why not?"

With a content moan, he wraps a hand around my neck and pulls my face toward his, stopping when our mouths are millimeters apart. "Leave the lace on this time."

***

I spend the next two weeks in a haze of sexually fulfilled bliss. Sam started a trend of us having sex both before and after the presentation prep, and I have to say, it was a brilliant idea. In more ways than one. Not only are we both enjoying ourselves, but our daily interactions have become less tense.

For one thing, he's actually speaking to me during lab, instead of just making snarky comments. For the last few months, he's rarely consulted me on anything, unless it's been a table project where we're forced to work together. Mostly, he has stuck to talking to Maya.

I've never minded because I always found him infuriating, and her to be supremely annoying. I thought they'd be perfect together. Even if I did feel a strange prick of jealousy over it.

But now, Sam's talking to me for nearly the whole two hours of lab time. He's still technically not my lab partner, but he walks into lab with me, leaves lab with me, and checks his answers against mine as much as possible. It's getting me the icy glare from Maya, but I don't mind.

In fact, I'm finding myself enjoying his attention. Which is absurd, because I still hate his guts, but I think I hate him a little less. It's both relieving and irritating at the same time.

I don't want to like him. We're rivals. We're both vying for a coveted position at the end of the year, and I *will* be the one who gets it. No amount of his attention or mind-blowing sex is going to change that.

The Friday before Thanksgiving, Sam and I are wrapping up our study session and heading out the door. "See you tomorrow?" he asks.

I shake my head, an incredulous look on my face.. "Um, next week is Thanksgiving."

"Yeah. So?"

"There's no school Friday, which means no study group."

Understanding dawns upon his features quickly followed by disappointment. "No labs either." He shoves his hands into his pockets. "So, I guess we won't see each other for, like, almost two weeks."

"I guess so."

An uncomfortable silence settles between us, like disappointment clogging the air. Sam licks his lips. "Do you still maybe want to come over tomorrow?"

I jerk my head back. "So, now I'm what? A booty-call?"

"No." He chuckles.

"Well, the reason we started this arrangement was the study group, and since there's no study group..." I quirk my eyebrow in a pointed expression. "I'd be coming over to have sex. In essence, a booty-call."

He takes his hands out of his pockets and crosses his arms. "We could order pizza and watch a movie."

I frown, skeptically narrowing my eyes.

"I'll lay it out for you, okay? I don't want to wait two weeks to have sex again. Do you?"

My lower lip works its way between my teeth as I shake my head.

"Okay, then. You can come over at our usual time, we'll do our usual thing, and then we can watch a movie instead of working on a presentation." A sly grin spreads across his face. "Or we can spend the entire time fucking, which I'm also okay with."

I scoff at his candidness. "A movie sounds good."

"Shucks." He snaps his fingers before winking. "See you tomorrow, Brynn."

My name slides from his lips a little more tenderly than normal, but I don't linger on it for long. "Yeah...tomorrow."

****

Biting wind nips at my cheeks. I pull my scarf farther up my face to cover my nose. The walk to Sam's apartment is only fifteen minutes, but today is brutal. Thirty degrees, gusty winds, and a cloudy sky aren't exactly ideal weather conditions. I know Mother Nature is screaming at me to turn around right now, but I don't listen.

I cup my hands around my mouth, blowing hot air into my palms. What am I doing? I mean, I know what I'm doing, but is it a good idea? This arrangement of mine and Sam's is about making it easier for us to work together. There aren't supposed to be feelings involved, and up until now, we've kept it strictly professional.

This feels like a date. Sandwiching dinner and a movie in between bouts in the bedroom feels like something a couple would do. Fuck-buddies, or fuck-enemies, whatever we are, should not simply hang out. The terms were clear. This blurs the lines, and I don't like it.

But I do like the sex.

Too many variables rush through my mind, and it's far too cold to focus on any of them for very long. I speed up my pace. If I freeze to death before I get there, the awkwardness won't matter.

When I reach his building, I take the stairs two at a time, and knock on his door without a second thought. In fact, the only thought I have is to get inside and out of the freezing cold.

Sam opens the door, a pleased expression on his face, but it turns to shock when I push past him and into the living room. "Uh, yeah, come on in," he says with a chuckle.

"Sorry," I say through my chattering teeth. "I had to get out of the wind."

"Did you walk here?" His tone is pure concern.

I give him a questioning look. "Yeah. I don't own a car, remember?"

"You could've called an Uber."

"For a mile drive? That would be a waste of money."

"I would've paid," he says out of the corner of his mouth before clearing his throat. "Do you want something to warm you up? Tea, coffee?"

"Coffee sounds great, thank you."

"Okay, hang tight. Um, you can take off your coat. I have blankets in that basket next to the couch," Sam says, pointing as he walks to the kitchen. "You want some Irish cream in your coffee?"

That would be a nice way to take the edge off. "Sure, that sounds good." I reluctantly shuck my coat, laying it on an armchair that wasn't here last week. "Nice chair."

Sam looks up from the coffee pot. "Oh, yeah. I did a video call with my parents earlier this month and my mom was appalled by how barren my place was." He laughs. "She sent me some money to go furniture shopping."

"So you bought a chair and a blanket basket?" There's a mocking tone in my voice as I grab the first blanket and wrap it around myself. It's the thickest, softest, most comforting blanket I've ever felt in my life. "Actually, I approve of your purchases."

"Just what I wanted, your approval," he says sarcastically. He comes out of the kitchen with two mugs in his hands and a bottle tucked under his arm, setting everything down on the coffee table. "I wasn't sure how much Irish cream you'd want."

"Thanks," I say as I take the bottle from him. Pouring a generous amount, I fill my cup to the brim. It's so full, I have to lean over and slurp some off the top before I attempt to lift the mug. When I sit back up, I find Sam watching me intently, a fire in his eyes. I clear my throat. "I'm sure this will warm me right up."

"No problem." He shifts to lean his back against the arm of the couch, and blows across the top of his mug.

I take a sip, licking the delicious taste from my lips. "Mmm. This is really good."

"Thanks. I don't splurge often, but coffee is non-negotiable."

"Glad you have your priorities straight."

He chuckles and leans over to set his mug down. "Speaking of priorities, how soon before you take your clothes off?"

I nearly spit out my drink. "Excuse me? You literally just poured me a cup of coffee."

He hikes a shoulder to his ear. "I'm eager, so sue me."

"Plus, I haven't warmed up yet."

Scooting a bit closer, he trails his fingers up my thigh. "I could help with that." He continues moving closer, practically crawling over me.

My heart races. Is he really going to start while I have a mug in my hand? Second degree burns are not the way I want to kick off this rendezvous. I shift back as much as I can without spilling.

His mouth curls into a devilish smirk as he lifts his arm to reach around me. Within seconds, a fireplace roars to life. I do a double take between it and him.

He sits back, waving a tiny remote in his hand. "Something else I bought with my mom's money. Electric fireplace."

"You're ridiculous, you know that?"

"I do."

A smile breaks across my face, and for once, it's not sarcastic or mocking. It's genuine. This entire interaction with Sam has been enjoyable. We don't usually spend time together before we get naked, so I don't ever see this side of him until afterward. And then, I chalk his amicable mood to endorphins. I can't say I hate seeing it right now.

But that isn't necessarily a good thing.

I lean forward to set my mug down, locking eyes with him. "I'm warm now."

"Yeah?"

"Mhm," I hum as I crawl across the couch to him. His hands grab my hips, and I watch his eyes darken. Hovering my face an inch from his, I whisper, "But I want you to burn me."

# Chapter 24

"You want popcorn for the movie?" Sam's deep voice rumbles through his chest, echoing in my ear resting against him.

I tilt my chin up, pouting. "I was promised pizza."

With a laugh, he pats my hip where his fingers have been drawing circles. "That you were. Okay, I'll order it." He rolls to the side, grabbing his phone from his pants on the floor. "What do you want on it?"

"Depends on where you're ordering from."

Sam rolls his eyes. "Where do you want to order from?"

"When in Rome."

"Do they deliver?"

"No, but Door Dash does."

Sam laughs. "Okay. What do you want on your pizza?"

"Cream cheese, garlic, and black olives." I don't even hesitate to answer.

"That's it?" He jerks his head back. "No pepperoni or sausage?"

I shake my head. "I'm a vegetarian."

"Really? I had no idea."

"Well, we don't talk much, Sam." I sound more disappointed than I intend to.

"Right," he says, remorse lacing his tone. "Well, let me order this and we can pick a movie."

We both get up from his bed and get dressed. As much fun as naked movie time sounds, it's not a good idea. The pizza and movie are nothing more than a replacement for the presentation we usually work on. Cuddling isn't an option.

Being Saturday, the pizza takes forty-five minutes to arrive, which ends up being a good thing because Sam and I cannot agree on a movie to save our lives.

"How do you not like Batman?" Sam asks, seemingly offended. "He's the greatest superhero."

"But he's not a *super*hero. He's a rich kid with cool toys."

"All right, Miss Know-It-All. Who do you think is the greatest superhero?" Leaning against the arm of the couch, he folds his arms.

I purse my lips, glancing at the ceiling as I contemplate. "Captain America."

"Oh, fuck." Sam exaggerates a groan. "You're a Marvel fan?"

"Of course. They're the best movies!"

He sits up, holding out his hand to use his fingers to count on. "Batman, Superman, Wonder Woman, Aquaman... Not to mention The Joker, Bane, Lex Luther... Come on, Brynn."

I shake my head. "No way. Marvel has The Avengers, X-Men, The Fantastic Four. I mean, Spider-Man alone trumps all of DC."

"What!?" Sam practically tumbles from the couch he jumps so fast.

I laugh, thinking he's adorable when he's passionate about things, but I shake it off. I put on a serious face and act like I'm getting up. "Well, I guess I'll see myself out, then."

Sam grabs my wrist, keeping me in place. "I can accept your flaws."

My mouth runs dry with the intensity in his eyes. What was a light-hearted discussion has become a heavy moment, and it makes my heart race.

He clears his throat and lets go of me. "I mean, at least long enough for sex."

Right. Great sex is all we are to each other. The headiness in the air dissipates. My heart rate slowly returns to normal, and I exhale slowly.

A knock at the door startles us, and we laugh off the awkwardness. Sam pays for the pizza, setting it on the coffee table, but doesn't sit. "You want a beer?"

I nod. "Sure, that would be great."

Sam hurries off to the kitchen, returning with two bottles, which he opens. Handing one to me, he clinks his bottle against mine. "Cheers."

"Cheers," I say, and take sip.

"How about Planes, Trains, and Automobiles? That's a good Thanksgiving movie."

I blink at him in awe. It is a good movie for Thanksgiving, but it's also super old. I'm surprised he even knows about it. "I love that one."

The corners of his mouth lift into a pleased grin. "Cool."

We spend a good fifteen minutes eating the pizza before settling into our spots on the couch. We're on opposite ends, not touching each other at all. I'm good for a while, but halfway through the movie I'm getting uncomfortable in my curled up position. I stretch my legs out a bit thinking it'll give me some reprieve, but all it does is make me want more room.

This goes on for several minutes before Sam groans, sits up, and pulls my legs over onto his. He flops back against his arm of the couch. "Better?" He floats his hand over our crisscrossed legs.

"Thanks."

With a crisp nod, he turns his attention back to the movie.

As our beers dwindle, I notice his hands begin to fidget. At first, he plays with the label on his bottle, then he plays with a frayed edge of his t-shirt. Eventually, his fingers migrate to my ankle and up my calf. The brushing of his fingertips gives me goosebumps, and I shiver.

"You cold?" he asks.

I nod, unwilling to explain the truth.

Grabbing the blanket I was wrapped in earlier from the back of the couch, he spreads it over us. He makes sure to cover my legs completely, including my toes. When he's satisfied, he slides his hand under the blanket, continuing his grazing of my skin. It's oddly affectionate, but I don't want it to stop.

It's probably the beer. Maybe he gets fidgety when he drinks. Lots of people have weird ticks when it comes to alcohol whether it's getting the munchies or getting talkative. This must be his.

That's what I tell myself for the rest of the movie, anyway.

When the credits roll, Sam stretches his arms over his head. "Man, that movie's great."

"Yeah," I say, pulling my legs off his. "Good choice."

"I'm actually surprised we agreed on it."

I shrug. "Just a fluke. I doubt we'll have anything else in common."

"Maybe."

An awkward hush falls over the room, the only sound is the music of the credits. I fling the blanket off my legs and stand. "Well, I guess I should get going."

"You're leaving?" He sits up, gripping the back of the couch tight.

"The movie's over. That ends our night, right?"

"What about second sex?"

A laugh bursts from me. "Second sex? What are we, hobbits?"

"I'm glad you caught that."

"That's an easy one." I sit back down, barely on the edge of the cushion. "I wasn't sure if we'd do that since this isn't a normal night."

"Brynn," Sam says, scooting closer to me so I can feel his body heat. "I'm not going to see you– I mean, we're not going to have sex for two weeks. I want as much as I can get to hold me over."

I can't help it, I blush. His words aren't exactly romantic, but I can get behind the sentiment. "Well, then what are you waiting for? Kiss me."

Sam doesn't kiss me right away, though. He snakes his arms around my waist, pulling me to him in a tender embrace, and I throw my arms around his neck. He spends the next few moments staring at me. His eyes roam my face as if committing details to memory before he lays his mouth on mine.

Not the fiery, hungry ravaging I expect. No, this is soft, full of affection, and it's dizzying. He's *kissing* me. Legitimately, delicately, attentively kissing me. I give in to the headiness and allow his strong arms to cradle me as his lips caress my own.

He eases me onto my back, crawling over me and hovering, careful not to crush me. His hand runs down my side, dipping under the hem of my shirt. When he cups my breast to palm my hardened nipple, I suck in a breath. He's being weirdly gentle. I can't complain because there's something incredible sexy about a man who can be tender when he wants to be, but I don't know that I want Sam to be that guy.

I don't have much time to think about it because he sits up, pulling me with him to remove my shirt. He takes the initiative and tugs my bra off too. Laying me back down, he reaches behind his head to yank off his own shirt which he tosses across the room. Instead of crawling over me again, he undoes the button on my jeans and removes them.

As I lie here in my underwear, I squirm under his intense gaze. Again, he scans my length like he's memorizing every curve of my body. When he looks me in the eye, I watch his irises darken, a desire burning in them, but he doesn't make a move. He just stares.

Trailing his palms up my legs, he leans down, coming back to hover once more. He brings his face close to mine. His eyes flick back and forth briefly before he connects our mouths. The same tender kiss as earlier, but this time, I melt when his lips touch mine.

Even the way his hands move is different. He's not groping or pawing, he's massaging. He's caressing. It's like I'm a porcelain doll and he doesn't want to scratch my delicate finish. I'm eating it up.

When his hand slides between my thighs and his fingers brush over my very wet panties, I moan.

He swallows the sound and presses harder against my apex. Peppering kisses across my cheek, he puts his lips to my ear. "I want to make this last. So you have something to think about for the next two weeks."

All I can do is nod, as I'm lost in a haze of desire.

"I'm going to take the lead, okay?" He waits for confirmation before he continues. "If you want me to stop at any time, just say the word, Brynn." He goes back to kissing lightly down my throat to my chest, stopping to suck on my nipples before moving down my stomach. When he gets to the waistband of my panties, he pauses to slide them off.

After dropping my underwear to the floor, he runs his hand up one leg while kissing his way up the other. His lips brush the skin of my inner thigh as he lifts my leg over his shoulder.

With bated breath, I watch him spread me open and rest his fingers on my clit. My head falls back. The sensation is always great, but with the way he's been touching me tonight, it's heavenly. His name rolls off my tongue in soft whispers.

"I love the way you say my name." He slides his fingers inside me, pulsing them slowly but deliberately. "I want to hear you scream it, though." With that, he glides his tongue over my clit, laving it gently.

I practically come on contact.

Neither of us has gone down on the other, but I'm damn glad he's doing it now. I don't know how the guy does it, but every time he touches me, whether in a new way or not, it's sensational. His tongue moves in circles, varying the pressure every few seconds. His fingers move in and out of me so fluidly. I'm bucking against his mouth within minutes.

When he hums, it vibrates through me, and I come undone. My whole body shudders with release. Sam grabs onto my hip with his free hand and holds me in place. He slows his movements, his tongue making languid circles as his fingers slowly slip out me. Once I'm done convulsing, he gently kisses my center before backing away.

"Beautiful and delicious," he whispers against my skin.

That can't be what I heard, right? "Hm?"

"Nothing." He crawls over me, peppering kisses all the way to my collarbone. "I want to do that all the time."

"Deal."

He chuckles, and his breath on my skin elicits goosebumps. "But I can't help but notice you weren't screaming my name."

"Too busy coming."

A choking sound emanates from his throat, and I giggle. His lips brush down my chest to my nipple, which he flicks with his tongue. "Can I try again?"

"If at first you don't succeed..."

He takes my nipple fully into his mouth and slides his palm down my inner thigh. I twist a hand into his hair, pulling him closer. His fingers glide up my slit, grazing my still sensitive clit, and I gasp.

"Too much?" he asks with my nipple between his teeth.

I shake my head. "Just still thrumming."

"Good. I can take my time, then." He pulls away, sitting up to shuck his pants and boxers. He pulls a condom from his pocket, tears it open and rolls it down his hard cock. Turning back to me, he grabs my hips and nudges me over onto my stomach. He helps position me so I'm bracing myself on the arm of the couch, and he sidles up from behind. The tip of his cock teases entrance.

I press my ass backward, inviting his tip inside, but he grabs my hips and holds me still. "Not yet," he whispers.

I feel the absence of his dick, but his fingers replace it. They slip inside me and begin pumping hard and fast. Pressure builds quickly, making his name spill from my lips.

"Louder," he orders, and pumps into me faster.

I moan out his name in one long syllable.

"Almost there." His voice is a deep growl now.

"Sam... Please..." I beg, needing to feel him. All of him.

"Please what?"

"Fuck me, Sam." Before I finish the words, his cock thrusts inside me. His grip tightens as he furiously pounds against my hips

The tenderness is long gone. This is primal. This is animalistic. This is fucking. And I like it. I like it so much, I let myself go and shout his name. The more I scream, the faster he thrusts. The sound of skin slapping skin mingles with my shouts and his grunts. It's a damn fuck-fest in here.

Sam leans over, pressing his chest to my back, and one of his hands snakes between my thighs. His fingers find my swollen clit once more. "Come on my dick, Brynn."

I love the way he orders me to orgasm. So much so, I obey every single time he does it. My body shudders, but this time, Sam doesn't stop.

He slows down enough to flip me onto my back again. He adjusts his position without removing his cock from me until I'm settled. "Comfortable?" he asks.

I nod.

"Good." He lifts my leg to hook his elbow under my knee, and leans down so his lips brush mine. "Now, let's finish with something we'll both remember." Closing his mouth over mine, he begins thrusting.

I'm expecting the hard and fast type of fucking we just did, but once again, I'm surprised. Sam thrusts into me, but it's slow and deliberate. His whole body ebbs and flows in one fluid motion. And he kisses me the whole time. Even when he speeds up, his lips never leave mine.

My hands roam everywhere. I can't get enough of the way he feels under my fingertips. So soft, yet so hard at the same time, I crave the sensation of skin to skin with him.

With one strong kiss, Sam lifts up, but continues to thrust. I search his eyes, wanting some hint as to what he's thinking, but all I can do is get lost in the deep brown irises. The deepest of muddy pools that sparkle in the setting sunlight.

"I want to watch you while you come," he whispers.

One huge breath shakes from my lips, and I close my eyes. I let the sounds of his grunts and groans fill my ears. His lavender and sage scent infiltrates my nostrils, tantalizing my brain. His warmth radiates off him, burning my skin. I want it all. I want him. Every bit of him I can get.

His thrusts speed up, so I roll my hips. I feel his hair tickle my chest as he dips his head. "Sam," I moan softly. Digging my nails into his back, I buck my hips against his and repeat his name in increasingly louder increments.

He lets out a strained growl, and slides his hand between us, his thumb finding my sensitive nub. "Come for me, baby."

His use of an endearing nickname doesn't have time to faze me because, like always, he tells me to come, and I do. But this time, it's different. The sensuality of the moment, the tenderness of his touch, the soft tone in his voice, it's enough to not only make me orgasm, but to put stars in my vision.

Maybe it's because it's my third one of the night, but it feels better than any one I've had before. It's not only an orgasm, it's an orgasmic experience. I'm wracked with waves of pleasure as I clench around Sam's erection. I want this moment to last forever.

But it doesn't.

Sam holds out as long as he can before he pulses inside me, shuddering with his own release. He collapses onto me, both of us struggling to breathe. When he finally regains enough strength to move, he rolls to the side, cupping my cheek and turning my head.

Adoration pours from his eyes, but I chalk it up to his high endorphins from the intense sex we just had.

Sam's thumb strokes my cheek. "I wish I could keep this moment forever."

"What?" I jerk my head back, all three centimeters it'll move.

"I, uh... I mean this." He gestures down my naked form. "You're fucking beautiful when you come."

"Oh." I roll my eyes behind closed eyelids. I don't know what I thought he meant, or what I *wanted* him to mean, but that wasn't it. Remember, Brynn, this is an agreement, not a relationship.

# Chapter 25

"Brynn, can you pass the potatoes, please?" my uncle, Albert, asks. He dips his head in thanks as I pass the bowl. "So, how's school?"

Here we go. The conversation always starts this way at family functions. School gets brought up first, then my social life, and eventually somebody asks if I'm dating anyone. Ever since Connor and I broke up, my family has been very interested in my love life. Maybe I'll get lucky this time. "School is fine."

"What classes are you taking?" Albert spoons a heaping mound of mashed potatoes onto his plate.

"Well, I only have one left for my major, but it's Organic Chemistry and it's a doozy." I sip my wine.

"I'm sure you're not struggling, though."

I shake my head. "I'm managing with my ninety-five percent average."

"That's my girl," Dad says, holding up his wineglass in cheers to me.

Lifting my glass to him, I take a sip, licking the drops from my lips. "But I have a few classes I've been putting off that I have to take now."

"Like what?" Aunt Barbara asks.

"Ones I should have taken freshman year; English lit, creative writing, and hiking."

"What do you do in hiking?" Mom asks.

As soon as her question leaves her mouth, I cringe at the memory of my hike with Sam. Why did I mention hiking? I take a small bite of my food, chewing for a beat before I answer. "Mostly sit in class and learn how to hike. The safety precautions, how to pack, the dos and don'ts, stuff like that."

"Do you do any actual hiking?" Uncle Albert asks.

With an inward groan, I say, "Yes. We had a class hike early on in the semester, and I had to facilitate one myself."

"Did Lisa go with you?" Mom asks, and I know it's because she doesn't like me hiking alone.

But it still makes me grimace. "No. I couldn't take friends. My professor said they would be biased in their grading." I reach for my wine, but choose to change the subject right away instead. "Besides, Lisa probably would've been busy with her boyfriend."

"Oh, how lovely," Mom says, her eyes dancing with excitement. "When did that happen?"

"When did what happen?" my grandma chimes in, her meek voice barely audible.

My mom leans over to loudly say, "Brynn's friend has a boyfriend."

"Brynnie has a boyfriend?" My grandma's face lights up, but I inwardly recoil.

That wasn't the turn I was hoping for. I meant for the conversation to steer into Lisa's love life, but that plan backfired.

Mom must notice the pain on my face, because she clears her throat and turns to my younger cousin. "Mary Beth, have you decided which colleges you want to apply to?"

I shoot my mom a tight smile and mouth a "thank you" in her direction. Magically, the rest of Thanksgiving dinner moves forward without the conversation spinning back on me. Poor Mary Beth gets the brunt of the interrogation, though.

I remember being in her shoes almost four years ago. Hell, even two years ago, my relatives would focus on my studies instead of my relationships. I suppose that was because I was serious with Connor so there wasn't anything to talk about. That changed quickly after he left.

At first, it was condolences and making small talk about how life will get better, but it quickly became offers to set me up on dates. Aunt Barbara knew a woman from church with a son my age. Or there was Dad's new coworker who had just finished college. I knew deep down they were just trying to help, but it only twisted the knife further.

My relatives shoving dating prospects in my face simply reminded me that I was dumped. If I hadn't been, I wouldn't have needed to meet anyone new.

When dinner is finished, I all but jump at the chance to help Mom clear the table. I gather plates and take them into the kitchen. Setting them down with a heavy breath, I turn on the faucet to fill the sink and pump some dish soap into it.

"You okay, honey?" Mom asks as she steps through the doorway with the turkey platter in her hands.

"Yeah, I'm fine." But the despondent tone in my voice says otherwise.

"You know Mimi didn't mean anything by what she said, right?"

"I know."

Mom sets the platter down and wraps an arm around my shoulders. "She's stuck in a time when you were young and played a lot of 'house.' You used to go on and on about getting married and having a baby. In fact, I seem to recall you were going to have fifty babies." We share a laugh, and she squeezes me against her side. "She remembers that version of you, that's all."

I nod. Shrugging off her arm, I begin sliding plates into the sink water to soak.

Mom sighs. "Do you still want those things, Brynn?"

"I think so." My shoulders slump as if a weight has been dropped onto them. "But why is it such a big deal that I haven't settled down? Not everyone meets their soulmate at seventeen like you."

"Your father and I were lucky, but for the record, we're quite proud of your academics." She tucks her finger under my chin and turns my head. "You've accomplished a great many things, boyfriend or not."

Pride swells in me, but it quickly wilts, and I turn the faucet off. I let my fingers fall to the mountain of soap suds built up, brushing the peaks. "It's not like I don't want to find someone."

"I know, honey. I think everyone worries about you after what happened with Connor."

My insides twist at the mention of his name.

"Have you dated anyone since he left?"

"No," I say out of the side of my mouth. It's not a lie. Sam and I aren't dating, we're fucking, but I don't need to explain that to my mother. "I've tried, Mom. I went on a couple dates, but they sucked." And one very good one that led me to sleeping with my enemy. Though, that's not what he was at the time.

"Every failed date is a step closer to the right one."

Tears prick my eyes. I thought Connor was the "right one." Then I thought Sam was. "What if... What if there's no one for me?"

"Oh, Brynn." Mom wraps me in a tight bear hug. She runs her hand down my hair, and I nuzzle into her shoulder. "I'm a firm believer in there's someone for everyone. You just have to keep your eyes open."

"They're open, Mom. I'm not seeing anything." I sniffle and lift my head.

She puts her hands on my cheeks. "Sometimes you find diamonds in the muddiest of puddles."

My eyes flick between hers as I try to make sense of her words.

"Now, come on. Let's finish cleaning up." She pats my cheek. "Aunt Barbara brought her famous pies."

I make it through dessert and card games without another issue, but that night, in my old bedroom, I lie in my twin size bed and stare at the ceiling. The light from lamppost outside streaks across the popcorn texture.

As I gaze upward, I mull over my mother's words from earlier. Is there really someone out there for everyone? If so, where do I find the one for me?

I don't often let myself feel these emotions. In fact, ever since Connor left, I've actively avoided thinking about the future of my love life. I've switched gears to focus solely on my academic future. It's more concrete. I can see exactly what's in front of me, and I know exactly what I need to do to get what I want. There's been no gray area.

Except now, Sam has blurred things.

For three years, I've had my sights set on the internship with Dr. St. James. There's been no question in my mind that I'll get it. That's what I've been working toward and the path to get there has been clear as day. I've had no competition, no distractions, until now.

And what's worse is it's not even about the internship anymore. I'm beginning to like Sam. I don't want to, but I can't help it. Our intimate goodbye sex last weekend didn't help anything, either.

I still can't get over the look in his eyes, or the gentle way he touched me, or the tenderness of his voice. It doesn't even feel right to say we had sex. That's not what we did. We made love, and I'll be damned if it wasn't the best we've had.

What am I going to do? I certainly don't want to stop having sex with him. That's not even an option for me. And I can't tell him I'm growing feelings for him. That would ruin everything. He'd probably call off the whole arrangement, and then where would I be? Alone and sexually unfulfilled, that's where.

No. The best action to take is no action at all. I'll go on like nothing weird happened. I'll keep my feelings to myself, and who knows, maybe it was a fluke. A one-time thing that sparked some long-buried desire to be in love again. I know Sam's not the one for me, but I'll have to make sure my heart stays on board.

***

When I round the corner on my way to lab the following Tuesday, I'm surprised to find Sam already waiting at the door. My heart skips a beat as I drink him in.

Luckily, he's distracted by his phone, so he doesn't see me right away. With his back leaned against the wall and his chin dipped, his curls fall around his face to frame it perfectly. Even though he's wearing a coat, his broad shoulders still fill it out. I have to swallow as my eyes fall to his hips and my mind replays the delicious ways they move.

When I get closer, he lifts his head, and his whole face lights up at the sight of me. He tucks his phone into his pocket. "Hey, Brynn." My name slides off his tongue like satin. "How was your Thanksgiving?"

Dammit. I missed him over the break. "Good. No drama. How was yours?"

"Really good. Got to see all my siblings, and Walt. Actually spent a lot of time with him."

"That's nice." I give him a tight-lipped smile. It's all I can do not to throw myself into his arms.

He shoves his hands in his pockets and sighs. "It's nice to see–"

"Sam!" Maya's voice cuts through the air, making both Sam and I wince. She sidles right up to him, not paying me any attention. "How was Thanksgiving?"

He does a double take in her direction. "Um, hi, Maya. Thanksgiving was good. *Brynn* and I were just talking about ours."

Maya's gaze flicks between us, confusion on her face. "Oh, sorry."

"It's okay, Maya. Mine wasn't that exciting, anyway." As I back away to give them some privacy, Sam shoots me a look I can only describe as longing. He's not pleading with me for help. He seems almost disappointed that I'm leaving. The expression quickly fades, though, and he turns to engage in conversation with Maya.

His entire demeanor changes as soon as he does. The laid-back Sam I spoke to is gone, replaced with an animated, jovial version. I don't know whether to be disheartened or not.

I don't get much time to think because Dr. Hinkle comes around the corner and opens the lab door. We all shuffle in, taking our seats while the professor hands out the work for the day. When Sam sits down across from me, we catch each other's gazes and he winks. My stomach flips, but I set my focus on my tasks.

Part way into our setup, Sam leans over the table to spy at my measurements. I playfully slap my hand over my paper and shake my head. A sly smirk spreads over his face, so I arch my eyebrow in challenge.

"Sam, hey. Sam, I have all the numbers right here," Maya says in her bubbly voice.

Sam reluctantly slides back into his chair, but keeps his smoldering eyes on mine until the last second. He turns to Maya, seemingly forgetting about me.

I huff, turning to my lab partner, Micah, and continuing our setup. Once we're ready, Micah goes to fetch the supplies, and I'm left alone with Sam and Maya. Really, I could say I'm left alone, because Maya keeps such a tight leash on Sam, he can't even glance in my direction. But I stare at him all the same.

I don't know if I've never noticed before, but he has the cutest curl to his lip when he laughs. And the way his hair bounces back after he runs his hand through it? Ugh, so adorable. When his tongue darts out to lick his lips though, that's when I feel a familiar ache between my thighs. I bite down on my cheek and avert my eyes. I'm not doing myself any favors.

Sam and Maya finish their setup, so Sam goes to collect their supplies. I'm not even going to deny that I stare at his ass the whole time he's up. It isn't until Maya clears her throat that I look away.

"Do you need something, Maya?"

She purses her lips as she folds her arms. "Don't think I don't see what you're doing."

"Uh, I'm sitting here."

"Nuh-uh." She shakes her head. "I see you staring at Sam."

My stomach drops. I feel the need to defend myself. "I was just staring off into space, Maya. I didn't even realize he was–"

"Oh, shut up." She rolls her eyes, letting out an exasperated sigh.

I await an explanation, but Micah returns with our samples, and I'm forced to switch gears. Not soon after, when Sam comes back to the table, I do my best to ignore him. I can feel Maya's death glare and I don't need to add fuel to the fire.

The rest of lab time creeps by. Me trying not to look at, or engage with Sam in any way, is exhausting. Micah and I are one of the first groups to finish, so I bury my nose in my O-Chem textbook. I'm deep into a section on polar covalent bonding when a hand grips the top of my book and pulls it down. I lift my gaze to find Sam smiling at me.

I scan the room to see everyone packing up. "Is lab over?"

"Yeah, brainiac." Sam chuckles, but glances over his shoulder at Maya returning their equipment. "Can you help me out? I need to get Maya off my back."

I nod as she comes back to the table. "Okay, Sam. All cleaned up. Ready to go?"

"Uh... well..." He rubs the back of his neck. "You see..."

"Sam, we really need to work on the presentation for study group this Friday since we didn't this weekend," I chime in.

The immediate fiery glare I get from Maya is negated by the appreciation pouring from Sam. A comfortable warmth radiates through me, melting my insides. The only way it could get better is if I were also being warmed by his strong embrace.

He blinks and turns to Maya. "She's right. We really need to get that done."

Maya's mouth opens for a rebut, but she snaps it shut and smiles. "Sure. See you later." Before she leaves, she shoots me with one last sneer that could freeze over Hell.

I whistle a descending tune. "Wow."

"Yeah, I know." Sam stands, hiking his backpack onto his shoulder. "Thanks. I owe you one."

When he turns to leave, I leap from my seat, skipping to catch up as we enter the hall. "Can I cash that in tonight?" The words spill from my lips before I can stop them.

He stops mid-step, looking at me with furrowed brows. "Tonight?"

Ugh. He's probably going to tease me for being antsy. I shouldn't have said anything. "You know what? Never mind," I say, picking up my pace.

"Brynn, wait." Sam grabs my arm, stopping me in my tracks. "What did you mean, cash it in tonight?"

The curiosity in his tone contrasts with the concern on his face, and a pit of guilt settles in my gut. I shouldn't have said anything, but I can't back track now.

"Listen, Sam, I'll be honest with you. It's been a long week and a half, and I could use a little…" I swallow my nerves. "Release."

His mouth ticks up on one side. "Wouldn't that be a violation of our agreement?"

I shake my head. "We can still work on the presentation. That does need to be done, but first I want to do you."

"I like the sound of that." A full-face grin spreads across his features as he rubs his chin. "Okay, my place, five o'clock." He leans down, putting his lips to my ear. "And wear that lacy number again."

# Chapter 26



Sam whips open his apartment door, grabs my wrist, and yanks me across the threshold. "Get your ass in here," he says with a grin. My stomach flutters at his clear excitement. Once I'm inside, he shuts the door and pins me against it, his strong arms framing me in. "That's better."

"You're telling me. It's freezing out there."

He pinches the bridge of his nose. "Did you walk here, again?"

"No. Lisa dropped me off on her way to her evening class, but it was still a cold walk up the stairs."

Sam chuckles, lowering his chin and shaking his head. When he raises it up to meet my gaze, his eyes flick between mine and I watch his irises darken. "Allow me to warm you up." Taking my lips with his in a deep kiss, he hurriedly unzips my coat.

I shimmy out of it and let it fall to the floor. Throwing my hands around his neck, I pull him closer until our bodies meet and his chest presses against my lacy top. I didn't even bother wearing a shirt over it.

He breaks the kiss to scan my torso. "Such a good listener, you are." Claiming my mouth once again, he wraps his arms around my waist, squeezing me tight.

When my feet come off the floor, I hook my ankles behind him, but my mouth never leaves his. Carrying me to his bedroom, Sam kisses me solidly. He devours me like I'm a burst of fresh air and he's been holding his breath.

Inside his room, he kicks the door shut before tossing me onto his bed. When he reaches back to tear off his shirt, the sight of his bare torso rips the air from my lungs. His naked body is such a turn-on. Even more so now that I haven't seen him in over a week.

As much as I enjoy the view, I grow impatient waiting for him to make a move. "Um, Sam?"

"Huh?" He shakes his head, blinking his eyes as if he was entranced. "Sorry, just taking in the sights." His gaze slides down and up my length.

I brush my fingers along the low-cut neckline of my top. "See anything you like?"

"Sure do," he says and takes two giant strides across the room. He flops onto the bed, bouncing me around.

"Whoa, there, big fella." Giggling, I splay my hand on his chest to steady myself. As soon as my fingertips touch his skin, they burn with the desire for more. With tentative movements, I creep my fingers up his pec to lightly graze his collarbone.

He grabs my hand, squeezing it. "If you want to touch me, Brynn"–he presses my fingers down harder–"just do it."

The grit in his tone makes me shudder, and I crash my mouth to his. He runs his hands all over my body, touching me in places he hasn't touched in a while, but takes his time. It's almost like he's savoring every nuance. I'd be lying if I said it wasn't super hot.

I tell my impatience to shut the hell up.

As he slides a hand down my thigh, I let out a whimper, but he swallows the sound. I roll my hips to guide his fingers between my legs. He pulls it away. I break the kiss, turning a confused glare on him.

He chuckles and taps the button on my jeans. "These are in the way."

"Oh, yeah." I duck my head, blushing at my eagerness.

Sam makes quick work of not only my pants, but his as well before he rolls on top of me. God, how I've missed his weight. Missed the warmth of his body. Missed *him*.

He latches his mouth to my throat, his hands roaming over every inch of my body. When I moan his name, I feel him harden on my thigh. I shift so the growing bulge in his boxers is between my legs, sitting at my entrance. He scoots himself to kiss his way down my torso.

Again, super hot, but my impatience will only listen for so long, and the desire pooling inside me begs for release.

Sliding my hand down his ribs, I make a turn at his hip to palm his erection through his boxers.

He turns his hips away.

I don't want to ruin this sexy, albeit excruciatingly long moment, but I have to make my frustration known. I settle for a strained groan.

Sam chuckles against my skin. "Am I taking too long?"

"Just a bit," I bite out.

"Sorry." He peppers kisses up my ribs and across my collarbone. "But I've missed you," he whispers softly.

So softly, I'm unsure I heard him correctly. "What?"

"I, uh…" He clears his throat. "I've missed the feel of you is what I meant."

"Oh." I sink into the mattress, chewing on my lip. Something inside me says that's not what he meant, but the ache between my thighs doesn't want to waste time worrying about it. "Well, I *need* to feel all of you. Like, now."

The corners of his mouth tick up. "Yes, ma'am." He reaches into the drawer of his side table, grabbing a condom and tearing the package open with his teeth. Holding it out to me, he says, "Want to do the honors?"

I bite down on my lower lip and nod. As I hold the wrapper, Sam starts to take off his boxers, and an idea pops into my head. He missed the feel of me? Well, I can give him all the feels. I put my hand on his forearm, stopping him.

He turns to me, a question in his gaze, so I give him a coy smile. "May I?"

"Be my guest." He lifts his hands.

"Will you stand up?"

Sam gives me a curious look, but rises from the bed. He lets me position him so he's standing between my legs, his hips at my eye level.

"Um, Brynn?"

"Shh," I say. "Trust me." Sliding my fingers into the waistband of his boxers, I yank them down. Sam tenses as his erection springs forth to stare me in the face. His breath shakes from his lips, and I watch his fists ball at his sides. I glide my fingers along his hard length as I look up at him through my lashes.

He stares down at me, his brown eyes full of intensity.

When I grip him, he gasps, but when I kiss his tip, he shudders. His body practically quivers as I take him into my mouth, caressing him with my tongue. I run my hands around the backs of his thighs and pull him closer, which makes my name roll off his lips in a strained moan.

I pick up my speed.

"Fuck," he bites out.

Hallowing out my cheeks, I increase the pressure.

Sam's hips move in tempo with me, thrusting gently, as he twists a hand into my hair. When saltiness hits the back of my tongue, Sam tightens his fist and pulls my head back. His face is contorted in what looks like reluctant self-restraint.

After a moment, he composes himself and opens his eyes. With one hand still tangled in my hair, he runs his other thumb over my bottom lip. "Careful. That pretty little mouth will get you into trouble."

"Better be safe, then," I say, and remove the condom from the wrapper. I roll it down his shaft before shaking my head loose of his grip and easing onto my back. I crook my finger, wiggling it in the air to beckon Sam to me.

I expect him to lunge, but he doesn't. Instead, he drops to his knees and takes my ankles in his hands. As he kisses his way up my leg, his palms slide over my shins and up my thighs. The closer he gets to my center, the heavier my breaths come.

He pushes my legs apart, runs his tongue along me, stopping to swirl my clit.

My head falls back as I melt into a puddle of glorious anticipation, but then, Sam pulls back and continues to kiss his way up my stomach. I lift my head to glare at him.

He doesn't so much as glance in my direction.

I narrow my eyes and see his mouth curl. He knows I'm staring at him and he knows why.

When his gaze flicks to mine, he winks before sliding his hand between my legs and slipping two fingers into me. His thumb circles my clit, and I'm reduced back to puddle status. Sam kisses up to my breasts, taking a nipple into his mouth. As his tongue swirls, so does his thumb and soon, his name spills from my lips in whispers.

"Mmm," he hums against my breast. "I missed that sound. Say it louder." He presses harder on my clit.

I obey and let his name roll off of my tongue in sensuous moans. My hips move, bucking against his hand. While his touch feels amazing, I need more. More friction, more pressure, more him.

"Louder," Sam orders.

"Then fuck me already." My impatience has won. I want him inside me. Now.

He rears back, amused surprise on his face that fades to sultry mischief. Kissing his way to my ear, he whispers, "Not until you come, sweetheart."

His hot breath on my neck has me coming undone in moments. Closing my eyes, I grip Sam's shoulder. I let go of my resolve and allow the waves of pleasure to crash over me. He peppers kisses along my jaw and down my throat as I ride out my orgasm.

"I fucking love the way you look when you come," Sam growls against my skin before flipping me onto my stomach. He grips my hips, pulling them toward him. "But I promised you something." He eases his hard cock inside me.

I let out a satisfied moan as I dissolve into the mattress. The way he fills me is nothing short of perfection. Always has been. I can't deny it, nor do I want to.

Sam works slowly, sliding in and out of me with rhythmic thrusts. His hands stay planted on my hips where his fingers dig into me to hold me in place. When he picks up speed, I twist my fists into the blanket.

He runs his hand up my spine. "So sexy." Leaning over, he puts his mouth to my ear. "And all mine."

The words break my bliss. *His*?

Sam quickly pulls me back into the moment by thrusting hard and fast into me. He's grunting and groaning, his hips working overtime. When I shout his name, a strained "Fuck," escapes him, but he keeps his pace.

This is raw and real and I'm loving every second of it. We've had hard, fast sex before, but this is almost carnal. I knew I was starved for him, but it seems like the instant he got another taste of me, his own hunger consumed him.

He slides a hand around my waist, between my thighs, and pressure builds low within me. The precipice of another orgasm teases my senses. I want it so badly, but I don't want this to end. Sam's insatiable desire is so addictive. I need it. I crave it.

With his fingers circling my clit, he whispers, "Come for me, Brynn."

The grit in his voice breaks me. Practically screaming his name, I shatter into a million pieces, each one shuddering as they fall.

Sam continues to swirl my clit as he gives a few quick pumps before I feel him tense. His cock pulses inside me and his whole body releases. As his chest heaves against my back, his hot breath blows across my neck. "You good?"

I roll my head as I hum contentedly, then turn over to face him, but keep my eyes closed.

He drags stray pieces of my hair from my face before cupping my cheek. "I could do this forever," he whispers.

"What?" My eyes pop open.

Sam doesn't stutter, doesn't falter as he says, "Hold you in my arms after making you come so hard you see stars."

I let out a breathy chuckle, but it's stilted. I'd read further into the tenderness of that statement if he hadn't attached it to our naughty activities.

He gathers me to his chest. "Give me a few minutes, and I'll do it again."

It's not our usual protocol, but I also don't want to argue. The idea of having any part of him inside me already has me clenching my thighs again. So what if he tacked on a tender thought? Endorphins are running high. It makes sense he'd be a little more affectionate right now.

I will myself not to overthink it as I snuggle into Sam's warm, firm chest to wait for round two.

# Chapter 27

"Have you eaten yet?" Sam asks as he twirls a lock of my hair around his finger.

I give him an incredulous look. "Like, as in dinner?"

"Exactly like dinner."

"No."

"Good, me neither. You like Chinese?"

I nod. "Oh, yeah. Vegetable lo mein is my favorite. Bonus if they have tofu."

He rolls to his side to grab his phone from the side table. Scrolling quickly, he taps call and puts the phone to his ear.

"You have them in your contacts?" I ask in disbelief.

He shrugs, but instead of answering me he says, "Hi, can I place an order for delivery?"

A few minutes later, our food is ordered. When we get dressed, Sam offers me one of his shirts, and this time I accept. It's huge on me, hitting mid-thigh, so I don't put on my pants. As I strut into the living room, Sam watches me intently. I make sure to exaggerate the swing in my hips.

I take a seat on the couch and giggle at Sam still staring. "Careful. You're starting to drool."

In a panic, he wipes at his mouth, but when his hand comes back dry, he mockingly glares. "Just thinking about dessert." With a wink, he turns on the fireplace, but I'm already on fire.

He grabs what has become my favorite fuzzy blanket and tosses it to me. I don't hesitate to wrap it around myself. If anything, just to cover my bare skin so I'm not distracting him anymore.

Once I'm covered, Sam pouts before placing his fingers on his laptop sitting on the coffee table. He doesn't open it. "I had an idea for this week. What if we played charades?"

"How would that work?"

"Well, we'd split the room into teams, but you and I would be the only ones acting stuff out."

I frown. "That doesn't sound like any fun for me."

"I just thought it would be something different." His cheerful expression falls, and guilt slaps me.

A grimace takes over my face before I say, "I guess we could try it, but what would the presentation be?"

"There wouldn't be one, necessarily. You and I would load the clues into a random number generator and spin to see what we get." He taps the laptop gingerly. "It wouldn't take very long to do…"

"Which would give us more time to do what?" I ask in jest. I know exactly what he wants more time to do, and to be honest, so do I.

Sam locks eyes with me, an intensity burning in them that makes my body temperature rise even more. "Satiate our appetites."

I don't need this damn blanket. I swallow, ready to accept his offer, but a knock at the door startles me. Sam stands, his gaze lingering on mine as he steps past the couch to answer the door. As he returns to the couch, he sets a paper bag on the coffee table, and the delectable aroma of Chinese food fills the air.

My mouth waters until he pulls several Styrofoam containers from the bag. Then, I frown.

"What's wrong?" he asks.

"I just can't wait for the Styrofoam ban to take effect."

"Ah," he says, setting a container in front of me. "Well, it won't be much longer, right? As of the first of the new year?"

I grunt and nod, but don't say anything as I open my container.

"Why does it bug you?"

"Because Styrofoam is so damaging to the environment," I mumble with a mouthful of lo mein. Swallowing, I continue my rant. "They think it takes five-hundred years to decompose, and even then, they don't know how quickly after that it would be gone. So it's just sitting in the landfills, being broken into tiny pieces for animals to mistake for food."

Sam grins at me, but his eyebrows are sky high. "I didn't realize you were so passionate about that stuff."

I shrug, scooping another forkful of noodles into my mouth. "Nature's been in my blood ever since I was little. My mom said even as a baby, I was happier outside. As I grew up, I learned all about the atrocities of humans and their effect on nature." I hold my fingers out as I list them. "The depletion of the Ozone layer, deforestation, global warming, The Great Pacific Garbage Patch–"

"The what?"

"Garbage patch. It's a huge collection of trash floating around the ocean, roughly twice the size of Texas."

Sam's eyes widen. "Whoa."

"So, from a young age, I knew I wanted to do something with my life that would help the environment."

"That sounds like the Brynn I know." Sam shoots me a quick smile before taking a bite of his orange chicken. "Already had her life planned out by age eight. Am I right?"

"Not exactly." With a sigh, I settle against the couch, setting my food in my lap. "I knew I wanted to help the environment, but I didn't know how. There were a lot of options, I just couldn't decide. Then, my friends started applying to colleges, my parents pestered me about scholarships and loan applications, and even my teachers were questioning what path I was taking." I pause, stirring my noodles. "It was a lot of pressure."

"Sounds like it."

I look up to find sympathy on Sam's face and have to take a steadying breath. "One day, I decided to go for a hike to do some serious thinking. So, I headed to Red Rocks. I guess there was a concert happening that night, because it was already crowded, so I had to park down the hill. I passed this old, beat-up truck, and honestly wouldn't have thought anything about it, but a rabbit scurried out from under it. Its little feet left black tracks in the dirt."

"Black?" Sam scrunches his face.

I nod. "Yeah, I thought it was weird, too. When I looked underneath, there was a good-sized black puddle on the ground. The truck was leaking oil."

"Oh, shit."

"So, I called the Denver Parks and Rec to report it. Turns out, based on the speed of the leak, the truck had been sitting there for like three or four days."

"You stayed until the service people showed up?"

"You bet your ass I did," I say authoritatively as I swirl my fork in my noodles. "I watched them assess the situation and was enthralled with the remediation process. I knew right then and there, that's what I wanted to do. So, I went home and began researching career options, which is how I found out about Professor St. James' lab.

After reading how her lab is one of the top in the country for environmental research, and how their work has advanced tons of green initiatives across the country, I knew I had to be a part of it." I chuckle to myself. "I even told my dad to sell my car shortly after the Red Rocks thing. I didn't want to contribute to pollution anymore."

"That's admirable, Brynn." Sam's tone is soft and endearing. "I understand why that internship means so much to you now."

"It's the reason I applied to go to UNC. Working at the lab is my dream job, and getting my education from the woman running it seemed like the obvious thing to do."

Sam lets out a breathy, one-note chuckle. "And here all I saw was a prestigious job opportunity that could further my chemistry career later on." Exhaling sharply, he stands from the couch and heads to the kitchen. He returns with two plates and hands one to me.

"What's this for?"

"To transfer your food to. That way, you don't have to look at these Styrofoam containers anymore."

I melt with appreciation. "Thanks."

Sam nods, but says nothing as he clears the trash from the coffee table. When he sits back down, his expression is sullen. "I wish there was something else I could do other than throw all that stuff away."

"It's okay." I pat his knee. "Hopefully, with the ban, the amount of Styrofoam and plastics will diminish quite a bit. Things will improve."

"I'm sure you'll see to that." The adoration pouring from Sam's eyes steals my breath.

We spend the next few minutes finishing our meals. By the end of it, I'm stuffed. I lean back to stretch out. "Oh, man. That was great. Thank you for ordering."

"Don't mention it."

"How much do I owe you?"

Sam shakes his head, holding up his palm as he chews his last bite.

"No, seriously. Let me pay for mine."

Still chewing, Sam puts his knuckles to his mouth as he mumbles, "No. This was my treat. Besides, you didn't offer to pay for the pizza last time."

I shrug. "That's because it was your grounds for me coming over. Tonight, we had the presentation to work on."

He swallows his food between chuckles. "Maybe you should have gone to law school."

"Who says I'm not?"

His eyes narrow as he collects our dishes. "I wouldn't be surprised with how smart you are," he says before walking to the kitchen.

A lightness blossoms in my chest and radiates through me. I shouldn't be flattered by his compliments, but who doesn't like a hot guy stating facts about them? I hear the clink of dishes against the sink, and watch Sam saunter back into the living room to his spot on the couch.

"Thanks," I say.

"Like I said, don't mention it."

"No, not just for the food. I mean, thanks for being nice to me."

"Brynn," Sam says, leaning back against the arm of the couch. "Contrary to popular opinion, I'm actually a nice guy."

I giggle, ducking my head. "Is my opinion really so popular?"

"Fuck, I hope not."

A laugh bursts from me, but as it ebbs, a lull takes over the room and all I can hear is the crackling of the fire. Clearing my throat, I reach for my phone on the coffee table. "I should see if Lisa can come get me."

Sam puts his hand on mine, stopping me. "You could stay."

"What?" My mouth opens and closes as if I can't form words. "You mean, stay the night?"

He nods.

"Sam... That's not what this"–I gesture between us–"is about."

He runs a hand through his curls. "I know, but it's dark and cold, and you're already here." His eyes flick between mine. "And I'm not ready for you to leave."

My breath catches.

"I mean, we haven't even had our post-study prep sex yet. Who knows how long that'll last. Besides, do you think Lisa wants to drive all the way over here again?"

Arching an eyebrow, I ask, "Couldn't you take me home?"

"I suppose." Defeat hangs in his words. "Do you want me to take you home?"

My heart races. He put the ball in my court, gave me the challenge. It's my decision whether or not to stay, and although every rational fiber of my being is screaming for me to leave, my rising desire for Sam wins. "No. I want to stay."

His mouth ticks up on one side. "Good, because I wasn't about to be driving you home at midnight."

"Jerk," I mockingly scoff as I smack his thigh. I glance at the clock. "Sam, it's only seven-thirty. How long are you planning on lasting?"

He sits up, scooting closer to me. "Brynn, I went over a week without fucking you. Now that I've gotten a taste for it again, I want to do it all night long."

I want those words to be true, and true only for me, but we're not exclusive. We're not a couple, and yet there's a loyalty in his words I haven't noticed before. I have to test him. "You could have called Maya if you were so hard up."

He lets out a disgusted grunt. "I told you in July, I'm not that kind of guy."

"Yeah, you did," I say quietly, anticipation of his next words bubbling in my gut.

"Well, it's true. I don't sleep around just to get laid." He sounds offended. "You and I may not be in a relationship, but there's no one else, Brynn. It's you and me. For as long as we have this arrangement, at least." That last bit comes out a little on the defeated side, but he recoups quickly. "Now, am I going to have to take off your clothes for you?"

***

I wake the next morning with the sun. Light pours through the thin curtains, streaking the air like sharp blades as dust lightly floats in and out of the streams. Closing my eyes again, I stretch, but something gets in my way.

Something warm. Something firm.

I realize I'm encased in Sam's arms with my back against his chest. His steady breath tickles the back of my neck. He's still asleep.

Panic creeps up my spine. "Shit, shit, shit," I whisper.

We're not supposed to cuddle. Cuddling leads to feelings, and feelings lead to relationships, and relationships lead to...well, nothing that I'm interested in doing with Sam. I knew spending the night was a bad idea, but I was so swept up in the incredible sex that I didn't even consider the consequences. And now those consequences have me wrapped in their embrace.

I've got to leave.

Slowly, ever-so slowly, I lift Sam's arm and shimmy away from him. He grunts and smacks his lips, but doesn't move otherwise. With a relieved sigh, I gather my clothes and quickly dress before leaving the apartment, but then guilt pokes at me.

We shared quite the intimate night. I mean, I opened up to him in ways I haven't since July. And I don't just mean spreading my legs. I told him why the internship is so important to me, and he seemed to really understand. It was a nice moment of connection.

But that doesn't mean we should have cuddled all night.

Still, I should've at least woke him up to say goodbye. If anything so he could lock the door behind me, but that would've opened up a whole slew of other issues. He probably would've wanted to have sex again.

Okay, so maybe that wouldn't have been so bad, but what if he invited me to stay for breakfast? Would we have had sex again after that? Then he probably would've offered lunch and more sex. I would've ended up spending the whole day with him, too!

Well, I suppose at some point, I'd have to leave for class. I wonder if he has classes on Wednesdays. We've never talked about our classes other than in regards to scheduling for the study group stuff. I don't even know what he's taking besides O-Chem.

I guess there's a lot I don't know about Sam.

No. That's not completely true. I know he's taking a first aid class with Professor Duncan. That's how he became my hiking partner. And I know he likes Imagine Dragons, but happens to be an unfortunate fan of DC Comics. Just one of his many flaws.

I giggle to myself. I suppose he's not entirely flawed. I mean, he is incredible in bed. His sense of humor isn't all that bad, either. At least when he's not teasing me.

As I walk, a crease forms between my eyebrows. I know more about Sam than I realized, and for some weird reason, I like that.

# CHAPTER 28

Friday afternoon, I chew on what's left of my fingernails while on my way to study group. After sneaking out of Sam's apartment early Wednesday morning, I felt like such a sleazeball. He texted me to make sure I got home okay, but that was it. I don't know if he was mad about it, or just indifferent, but I avoided him all the same. I even managed to get into O-Chem lecture early and be the first to leave yesterday.

I wasn't ready to talk about what happened. Honestly, I'm still not.

Spending the night is not part of our agreement. We're supposed to be having sex to make working together more tolerable, and it's been successful. We don't argue anymore. We don't disagree nearly as much, and when we do, it's a light-hearted discussion. We're on much better terms than we used to be.

But that doesn't negate the fact that we cuddled. All. Night. Long.

We usually cuddle for a few minutes post-sex, but that's mainly to make easing back into reality less stressful. We don't do it because we like each other.

I shake away the jumbled mess of thoughts and emotions as I walk through the O-Chem doorway. I find Sam already here, waiting for me. "Oh, hey," I say as I shut the door behind me.

"Hey," he replies without looking up from the computer.

The guilt punches me again. "Is everything ready?"

"Mhm." He nods, but doesn't look at me.

With an exasperated sigh, I slide my backpack off my shoulder, and plop into a chair. I swivel the seat back and forth with my hands folded on my stomach. My gaze keeps unintentionally flicking to Sam, but he's laser-focused on the computer. I can't blame him for being mad.

"All set." He slaps the desk and turns to me. "Sorry, I wanted to make sure it was actually going to work before everyone got here." His brow furrows. "You okay?"

I give a tight smile and nod.

Still eyeing me suspiciously, he leans back in his chair, mimicking my posture. "I think this will be fun tonight."

"I'm sure it will be."

"I can't wait to see what happens on the next test. The mid-term grades improved so well, I wonder if they'll improve more or stay the same." There's a sparkle in his eye, like he's excited to discover new data. Like a true scientist.

"Maybe if everyone gets A's, we won't have to do these groups anymore." As soon as the words leave my mouth, I regret them. Even more so when I see the hurt on Sam's face. "I didn't mean that. What I meant was—"

Sam holds up his hand. "Nah, I get it. This eats up a lot of time." The hand that's in the air floats back to run through his hair.

I wince at the defeat in his tone, but I nod. "Maybe we shouldn't have any more impromptu meetings, then."

He opens his mouth, but a knock at the door stops him. Getting up, he stalks past me to unlock it, but stops and bends down. "For the record, I don't mind you eating up my time." With a wink, he steps away to open the door.

I stare after him, my mouth hanging open at the audacity of his confession. I decide it's best not to think too hard about it, especially right now when we're supposed to be teaching, so I turn my attention to the class.

Charades is a huge hit. Between my awful rendition of compound molecules and Sam's hilarious, yet strangely accurate, display of synthesis, we have the entire class rolling on the floor. Several students even ask us to do charades for another study group session.

As bad as my acting is, I enjoy myself quite a bit. It helps that Sam's laugh is infectious. From the first muffled guffaw, I find it incredibly difficult to keep my composure. Half the time, I end up breaking character to laugh along with him.

But that's not all I learn about him tonight.

I also notice he's different when he's laughing. Like, actually laughing. The kind where you can't catch your breath and tears well in your eyes. When he laughs like that, his smile is brighter. I don't know exactly how to describe it, but I know I haven't seen him smile like that before, and it's cute.

*He's* cute. The whole session he's been playful, fun, and a giant goofball that maybe I knew was in there, but haven't paid attention to. I know Sam is funny. He's clever, anyway, but I'm not familiar with that side of him. Now, I want to be.

By the time the last of our classmates are out the door, Sam and I are all packed up. He hikes his backpack onto his shoulder, giving me a grin. "We were a hit tonight."

"Yeah, we certainly were something." I shake my head. "At least you were, I don't know what I was doing."

He chuckles. "You did pretty good."

"I made people laugh, but I don't think that's the point of these sessions, is it?" I crinkle my nose, making an exaggerated confused face.

Sam laughs harder, and I revel in the sound. "No, but I'm sure it'll help some of them retain the information. They'll come to a question on the next test about the molecular makeup of adrenaline, and all they'll have to do is picture you doing jumping jacks and running around in circles."

"Ugh." I drop my face into my palm. "I hope no one got that on video."

"Hey, maybe you'll go viral."

I remove my hand, looking up at Sam. "Ha, just what I need."

He smiles sympathetically and sighs. "Brynn, I want you to know I meant what I said earlier about you taking up my time."

My breath catches. "Oh?"

"I don't mind. In fact, I think I enjoy it. Because of the sex, that is."

A laugh bursts from me, but I quickly reel it in with a sharp inhale. "I'm sorry for taking off without saying goodbye Wednesday morning."

"No worries. You staying the night isn't our normal protocol."

"Yeah, but I should know how to act like a decent human being. I could have at least woken you up so you could have locked the door behind me."

Sam licks his lips, his gaze flicking away before meeting mine again. "So, why did you leave then?"

"I don't know." I let out a heavy sigh. "Waking up still in bed with you freaked me out. I didn't think things through the night before, and I wasn't prepared for the outcome."

"And what was the outcome?" Sam asks, his voice quaking with curiosity.

My pulse flutters as I stare at him. I want to tell him the outcome was me enjoying waking next to him. That I slept better than I have in a long time because of his arms wrapped around me, and I want to do it again. I want to explain these feelings bubbling within me.

But I can't.

It violates our agreement, so I settle for, "That I panicked because I had to rush to get home in time to get ready for my classes."

Sam's shoulders sag as he slowly nods. "I can see how that would be stressful." With a deep breath, he says, "No more meetups during the week, then. We'll stick to Saturdays only."

As much as I know I should feel relieved, I'm almost disappointed. But I know it's for the best. "Thanks, Sam."

"So..." he says, rocking back and forth on his heels. "I'll see you tomorrow?"

"One o'clock."

"Awesome." He juts his chin to the door. "Come on. Let's get out of here."

***

It's a beautiful day for a walk. Sure, it's only thirty-five degrees, but the sun is shining and there's no wind. Plus, there was a light snowfall last night, and the ground glitters in the sunlight. It's fitting scenery for my uplifted mood.

After my talk with Sam yesterday, I feel so much better. Knowing that Wednesday wasn't as bad as I thought takes a weight off my shoulders I didn't realize I was carrying. His understanding about only meeting on Saturdays helped too. I'm lucky to have such a great frenemy.

I practically skip around the corner to Sam's apartment. As I reach the stairs, his door opens, and I whip my head up with a smile on my face to greet him. Was he watching for me? He must be as excited as I am.

The smile drops from my face when a woman's laughter stabs my eardrums. In a panic, I duck into alcove for the lower-level apartments, pressing my back to the wall. Footsteps sound on the stairs, so I peek.

I see Sam's Converse sneakers walk down first, in step with a pair of fuzzy Uggs. His jeans and sweatshirt then come into view, contrasting the form-fitting leggings under a plush sweater next to him. When they reach the bottom step, I see his arm around her shoulders as her long blondish hair cascades down like a waterfall.

My chest constricts around my palpitating heart. It's beating so loudly, I can't hear what they're saying, but I can hear her giggling at his every word.

Is this really happening? Is Sam with another girl? After everything he said about not sleeping around, he goes and bangs some bimbo

He lied. Again.

Nudging her toward the parking lot, they turn their backs to me, so I make my escape. I tear away from the alcove. My jelly-like legs don't let me get far, though, and I end up collapsing behind a nearby tree. I bang my head against it.

How could I be so stupid? I fell for all his charm again.

My lungs struggle to work. I can't seem to suck in enough oxygen. I need to get out of here.

When I peek around the tree, I see them chatting next to a car. Sam's back is to me, but the blondish girl is facing me, and she has the happiest expression on her face. She looks like she's just had the best time of her life.

If she was with Sam, I understand why.

My stomach drops when she throws her arms around his neck and pulls him in for a strong hug, planting a gigantic kiss on his cheek. I lurch, but hold down the nervous vomit threatening to rise. Clamping my hand over my mouth, I lean against the tree once again.

With my eyes squeezed shut, I fight the urge to cry. I refuse to shed any tears over this. Over him.

A car door shuts and an engine roars to life. My eyes pop open. I lean over to watch Sam wave his hand in the air before shoving it into his pocket as the car drives away. The huge smile on his face when he turns around makes my jaw quiver. The fucking snake is happy about this.

What do I do now? I can't go up there after witnessing that. There's no way I'd be able to look him in the eye, let alone have sex with him. Ugh, I might actually puke.

That gives me an idea. I pull out my phone.

**BRYNN:** *Hey, I can't come over today. I think I have food poisoning or something.*

**SAM:** *Oh, shit. That sucks. Do you need anything?*

Dammit, why does he have to be sweet right now?

**BRYNN:** *No, thanks. Lisa is here to take care of me.*

**BRYNN:** *But I'll send over my notes for the study group in a little while.*

**SAM:** *Yeah, sure, whenever. No rush. Get some rest, and if you need anything, let me know.*

**BRYNN:** *Okay, thanks.*

I let my head fall back against the tree as my arm falls to my side. I'm in the clear for now, at least. I need to get home and figure out what the fuck I'm going to do about this. With a deep, bolstering breath, I climb to my feet and begin the long trek back home.

After I burst through our front door, I slam it behind me and flee to my room. I flop onto my bed and scream into my pillow, but I don't cry. I can't. My blood boils so furiously that my tears evaporate before they even reach my eyes.

Beating my fists into my mattress, I scream some more. The anger swirling inside me has taken control of my body and mind, and I can't stop myself. I can't even think straight. I'm sure I look like a toddler throwing a temper tantrum, but no one is here to see.

How could he? How could he betray me like that? After all the things he's said to me, not to mention all the things we've shared and done. He used me.

Again.

He told me all the things I wanted to hear and, like an idiot, I ate them up. I let my guard down. I trusted him when I knew I shouldn't. He showed me who he was when he showed up in O-Chem, exposed all his lies, then became my enemy. I knew better, and yet, here I am. All because I gave him the benefit of the doubt.

Like Connor.

I roll over, flopping my arm over my face, and the tears finally come. Am I destined to be that girl? The one who's only good temporarily? The one who's great for warming a bed, but not for loving?

Fuck, I hope not.

But when will I get my chance? I've already proven I'm no good at character judgment. The one guy I thought was my forever left me for bigger and better things, and the guy I thought was my insta-love story turned out to be a lying prick. Twice.

The sobs lurch out of me so violently, I curl into the fetal position.

I don't know how long I lie in bed crying, but it's long enough for the sun to go down. When my stomach rumbles, I realize I haven't eaten anything since lunch, so I head downstairs. I search the fridge, coming up empty. My stomach may be hungry, but I have no appetite.

I settle for a bowl of cereal, which I eat on the couch while watching trashy reality TV. I need something mindless. Curling up under a blanket, I nurse my cereal and let the drama on the TV negate my own.

It isn't long after I finish my cereal that the front door opens and Lisa strolls in with Brent hot on her heels. I try my best to wipe my face and plaster on a happy expression. "Hey, guys."

Lisa does a double take. "Oh, Brynn. I thought you'd be at Sam's." She frowns as she watches my jaw quiver. "Oh, shit. What's wrong?"

I raise my gaze to the ceiling, blinking away the stinging tears, but I can't speak.

Lisa runs to my side. "Brynn, what happened?"

"He did it again." I drop my chin, locking my watery eyes on hers. "He lied."

She grimaces and turns to Brent. "Can you give us a minute?"

"Oh, uh, yeah. I'll wait in your room," he says, then  heads upstairs.

When we hear the door to her room shut, Lisa turns back to me. "Okay, spill it."

Through more tears, I let all the details come pouring out. Lisa knows about my agreement with Sam, but she doesn't know how well things have been going. So I tell her. I tell her everything from the mind-blowing sex, to how much I've come to like Sam, to our intimate Wednesday night. Each sentence is painful to say, but I feel better after every confession.

Until I get to the end. "Which brings us to today." I take a deep breath and swallow. "When I got to his place, I saw him walk a girl out."

Lisa gasps. "No."

I nod. "She even kissed him goodbye, and when he turned around, he seemed so happy about it."

"That sack of shit."

I don't defend him. He doesn't deserve it. "So, I texted him I was sick, and came home to cry all afternoon."

"What? Why didn't you confront the prick?"

"I don't know." I drop my gaze to my lap, wringing my hands. "I think that if I confront him, then all this becomes real. I'll hear the lies come out of his mouth and it'll solidify the fact that I'm alone."

Lisa takes my hands in hers. "Then let's not be alone."

"What?" I sniffle and lift my head.

"Let's go out."

"Tonight?"

"Yeah. I mean, I know it's not our usual Thursday ladies' night, but we can still get you hammered enough to let another guy take your mind off Sam."

I chuckle, wiping away a tear. "But you have plans with Brent. I can hang out with Jackie and Hannah."

"They went to Denver for that concert, remember?" She shrugs a shoulder. "And Brent can come with us. That way, he can scare off creepers."

"Are you sure? I doubt that's what he wants to do with his Saturday night."

"You obviously need to do something or someone"–she pauses to wink at me–"to get over Sam. You're my best friend. You will *always* come first."

I gawk at her. "You're pretty confident."

"I get it from you," she says with a smile, and pats my leg. "Now, go take a shower and get ready. Brent and I can have our night together before we go out." She bobs her eyebrows.

I crinkle my nose. "I didn't need to know that."

# Chapter 29

Lisa was only half right. Even though it's not ladies' night, I've had plenty of drinks, but I'm not having any luck finding someone to take my mind off Sam. To be honest, I'm not trying. How can I? Everything with Sam is so fresh, and while the six cranberry vodkas coursing through my veins are helping, they're not magic potions.

Every time a guy smiles at me, I turn away. I've refused the few that have asked for a dance, and I even turned down a guy who wanted to buy me a drink. When I think about trying to flirt or dancing with someone, it feels too much like cheating on Sam, which I know is ridiculous since he's the one who did it first.

I take a long draw, finishing off my seventh drink. I can't think things like that. We aren't a couple. Never were, and never will be, so why am I so hurt?

As I flag down the bartender to order another cocktail, my eyes fall to Lisa and Brent sitting on the bar stools to my side. They're so involved in each other, they've barely spoken to me. I can't really blame them. Lisa doesn't usually stay with a guy for long, but she seems to really like Brent. I'm happy for her.

I am, but I can't watch them for long. Their gooey facial expressions are sickening, but it's more so the fact that I want what they have. I want someone to look at me the way Brent looks at Lisa, like I'm the only one in the world who matters. It's the way Sam looks at me.

Fuck, I need some air.

Tossing back my newest drink, I tap Lisa's shoulder and point to the patio. Her eyes flick from me to the bathroom, as if asking whether she should come, but I shake my head and hold up a finger. I'll only be a minute. I need to clear my head, and what better way to do that than by stepping into the frigid December air. Luckily, my eighth cranberry vodka is keeping me warm, if not a bit unstable on my feet.

A blast of winter smacks me in the face as I open the patio door. Unlike air-conditioning, though, the air is fresh and crisp. It seems to open my airways instantly when I breathe.

Taking up residence under an outdoor heater, I stare at the twinkling stars peppering the night sky. I used to wish on the stars as a little girl. I wished for all kinds of crazy things, as all kids do, but the one wish I made over and over again was to fall in love.

I never wanted a fairy tale, didn't need a handsome prince to come save me. I knew I was perfectly capable of saving myself. My life was going to be an adventure, and I wanted someone to share that with. I wished and wished for a partner, an ally, a soulmate.

Still do, but I haven't found one yet.

With a heavy sigh, I spin to head back inside, but the patio swirls around me. I have to brace myself on a nearby stool. Hopefully, the world will stop spinning soon so I can get inside before the alcohol wears off and I'm able to feel the cold

"Brynn?"

I freeze, and not from the chill in the air. That voice isn't one I've heard in a while, and it's one I never thought I'd ever hear again. One I never *wanted* to hear again.

Turning to the side, I find the absolute last person I'd like to see tonight. "Connor? What are you doing here?"

All the possibilities rush through my mind. Did he move back? Is he here to apologize for all the heartache he put me through? Is he here to ask for forgiveness? Even if he is, would I? If he walks over here and wraps his arms around me, will I let him?

I choke down a sudden rush of bile at that thought. Even as drunk as I am, I know where my convictions lie.

He shuffles toward me, hands in his pockets, shoulders hunched. "It's Brian's birthday, so I flew out to celebrate."

"Oh."

"Hey, man. We're going back in," Connor's friends say as they head toward the door.

He acknowledges them with a nod. "Cool. I'll be there in a minute." Turning back to me, his dark blue eyes soften under the patio lights. "Didn't think I'd see you here tonight. It's not your usual Thursday ladies' night."

"Well, things change."

Connor's head bobs with a despondent nod. "It's good to see you, Brynn."

"Connor, don't," I bite out before I can think about it.

His head jerks back, his shoulders suddenly tense. "Don't what?"

"Don't give me the 'it's good to see you' pleasantries like we're old friends who are going to get coffee later to catch up on life."

"Well, aren't we old friends?"

The noise that escapes me is a mixture of offense and disbelief, followed by a laugh. "No, we are not. You're the guy who had my heart for two years before you ripped it out of my chest and stomped it into the pavement. So, don't stand there and say it's nice to see me."

"Fuck, Brynn." Connor takes a hand from his pocket and runs it over his short, dark-brown hair. "You're a piece of work, you know that?"

I lift my chin, hesitantly letting go of the stool to stand up straight, and fold my arms. "Obviously, I was too much work for you."

"Don't start with that shit," he groans. "You knew I was leaving. Hell, you even started researching jobs and grad schools in New York the day after I told you about my acceptance letter."

"I wanted to know what my options were."

"Two years in advance?" He throws his arms out to the side before slapping his outer thighs. "Come on, even you know that's a little insane."

I take a steadying breath, keeping my tone calm as I say, "What's insane is you dumping me without warning."

"Oh, please." He rolls his eyes. "It's not like me moving to New York came as a big surprise."

"No, but you breaking up with me after two years because 'long-distance doesn't work' was." I make air quotes with my fingers as I use a stupid-sounding voice to mock him.

Connor narrows his eyes. "See, it's shit like that snotty attitude of yours that told me we'd never work."

I fight the quiver in my jaw as my thin hold on my resolve bends. "So, if you didn't think we were going to last, why date me at all?"

He shrugs. "When we first started dating, it was fun. You were hot, smart, funny." Connor takes a deep breath. "Things were going well, until I noticed how much of a control freak you were."

His phrasing makes me clench my fists. "I am not–" I take a step forward, but the world spins again, and I stumble. Unfortunately, right into Connor.

"Whoa, careful." He catches me by the forearm and guides me to sit on a stool. "Too many cranberry vodkas, huh?"

The fact that he even remembers what I like to drink infuriates me. He's the one who abandoned me, he doesn't get to be familiar with me anymore. I rip my arm from his grip. "I'm fine, thank you."

Connor lets out a one-note chuckle as he licks his lips. "This is what I'm talking about. You always have to be the strong one. You can't ever let go. It's like you don't need anyone. You certainly didn't need me." The last part comes out harsh and cold.

"Then why make it two years? Why not break things off sooner?" I ask through gritted teeth.

"Because I really liked you."

He *liked* me? "So, you were lying every time you said 'I love you' to me?"

Hanging his head a moment, Connor meets my gaze again with a shrug. "Isn't that what you say when someone says it to you?"

I didn't think it was possible, but my heart breaks even more. Pieces of it chip off and the shards prick my veins. He didn't mean any of it. Our entire relationship was a ruse. I wasted two years of my life on a guy who never intended to be my forever. My mouth opens and closes, but I can't speak.

"Look, Brynn. I never meant to hurt you like that," he says before letting out an exasperated sigh and lifting his gaze to the sky. "When I realized you weren't ever going to change, though, I had to do something."

"That's not fair." My voice shakes, showing my cracking confidence.

"No, what isn't fair is how much I walked in your shadow. You always had to take the lead, and I always came in second." He runs his tongue along his teeth like he's debating what he's going to say. "And it all sort of came together when we did that stupid Mud Down race."

His words stab me right through the heart. "*That* was the tipping point?"

"You had me all hyped up about it, and I thought 'hey, maybe this will be my chance to shine.' I could finally show you that you didn't always need to be number one. Then, when the day came, you proved how self-sufficient you were by scaling all the obstacles without me. You let me eat your dust."

"We did all of them together," I huff.

"Did we? Or did we do them adjacently?" Connor takes a step toward me. "Face it, Brynn. You are too independent to be with anyone seriously. I mean, what kind of guy would put up with that for the rest of his life?"

"Hey, there you are."

I whip my head over to see Sam stepping through the patio door with a smile on his lips and two beers in his hands. The smile falls as he studies my face, and his gaze flicks to Connor. "I, uh, got you that beer you wanted. Sorry it took so long." He walks to me, handing me a beer before turning to extend his hand to Connor. "Hey, man. I'm Sam."

Connor clears his throat as he shakes Sam's hand. "Hey. I'm Connor."

"Nice to meet you." Sam turns his gaze on me, concern lacing his features. "Everything okay?"

I nod. "Connor was...just leaving."

With a quick sneer, Connor says, "Good luck, Brynn."

I hear the music from inside suddenly swell before it fades to muffled thumps once again. When Connor is gone, my entire body goes slack, and I have to use Sam as a crutch.

"Shit, Brynn. Are you all right?" Sam holds me up, helping me to the railing.

My chest heaves as I focus on the ground in front of me, though I can't see much through my watery eyes.

"Who was that guy?" Sam asks.

I shake my head. I can't speak, let alone explain the cataclysmic blow I just took. "I... I need to get out of here."

"Yeah, sure." Sam takes the beer from my hand and sets it with his on a high-top table. He wraps an arm around my waist and directs me toward the door. "Let's go."

"But your beers."

"Leave them." Sam holds on to me as we navigate our way through the crowded bar. Once we get our coats and get outside, he leads me to his car, and I hear the locks click. He opens the passenger side door, but I hesitate, giving him a questioning look. He sighs. "I haven't had anything to drink yet. Those beers I brought out to the patio were the first ones I ordered tonight. And they're still full."

I narrow my eyes, but give a playful smirk as I climb in the sedan. As the door shuts, I take a quick second to observe my surroundings. It's clean. Cleaner than I'd expect for a college guy, anyway.

The way it smells, though, is the worst.

It smells like Sam. Lavender and sage saturate every inch of the interior. I couldn't avoid thinking about him even if I tried. I breathe deep and close my eyes, allowing his scent to envelop me, but they pop back open as the driver's side door shuts.

"Where to?" Sam asks, leaning onto the steering wheel. "Home?"

Staring straight through the windshield, I debate my answer. I need something to distract me from Connor. From the tantalizing aroma of Sam's cologne wafting into my nostrils with every inhale, but if I go home, I'll lay in bed and sulk.

I shake my head, both in answer to his question and to clear it.

"I can take you to my place."

I whip my head up to look at him, half expecting to see his eyebrows bobbing. All I see, though, is a sympathetic crinkle in his forehead and concern lacing his eyes. It takes every ounce of self-restraint not to throw myself at him. I know he would do a damn good job of distracting me from Connor, and as drunk as I am, I'd let him. But I'm still pissed about this afternoon. The only reason I'm with him now is because when I needed a way to escape the bar, he was it.

My rumbling stomach gives me an idea. "I'm hungry. Can we go to the Double Clutch Grille, please?"

"Where's that?"

"I'll navigate. You drive."

# CHAPTER 30

As Sam drives away from Coyote Canyon, he doesn't try to engage in conversation with me. He doesn't prod me about my mood or ask about what happened with Connor. Aside from my directions every few minutes, it's completely silent in the car. The radio isn't even on.

I don't mind. In fact, I'm grateful. My brain is such a jumbled mess of thoughts, I don't even know if I could hold a coherent conversation. I'm still struggling to process what I saw at Sam's apartment, and after Connor's attack, I can't think straight. I'm angry, hurt, and embarrassed by both men. Yet, here I am, relying on one of them to get me away from the other.

What a cluster-fuck.

When we pull into the parking lot of our destination, Sam's forehead crinkles. "A twenty-four-hour truck stop?"

"Mhm. They serve breakfast all day," is all I say as I exit the car.

Sam jumps from the driver's seat and rushes around to meet me, but I push past him. I'm still unstable on my feet, but he's not the person I want to lean on. He follows me inside and to a booth in the back corner. As I slide into one side of the booth, he hesitates like he wants to sit next to me, but instead takes the other side.

A server comes over, sets two glasses of water down, and hands us menus. "You kids know what you want?"

"I do," I say, looking at Sam expectantly.

"Uh…" He scans the menu. "I'll have whatever she's having."

The server turns her frustrated, exhausted gaze to me. "What'll it be, sweetie?"

"A pot of coffee and two French toast platters," I say, turning my gaze away from Sam to hand her the menus.

She leaves with the menus, but returns fairly quickly with our coffee, two mugs, and a little tray with a whole slew of sweeteners. "Cream?" she asks, and when I nod, she brings us a metal carafe of half and half.

Then, Sam and I are alone.

Focusing on slowly tearing open the packages of sugar, I pour them into my coffee. I stir each one before opening the next, staying completely silent. After I've emptied my usual four sugars, I pour the cream until my black coffee turns a nice shade of taupe.

"So, this place has good breakfast?" Sam asks, an eagerness to his tone like he's trying to break the ice.

All I do is nod. My whole body teems with confusion. I'm still angry with Sam, so I don't want to talk to him, but I'm stuck with him right now. That doesn't mean I have to look at him. Instead, I watch my hand as I absentmindedly stir my coffee.

Sam clears his throat. "I still don't know how you can take your coffee like that."

I lift my gaze to glare at him, but when I find a look of adoration on his face, my shoulders slump. I guess the shock of seeing Connor took all the fight out of me. "It's better than yours."

Sam's mouth curls into a smirk. "So, are you going to tell me what happened back there?"

I pick up my mug and blow across the rim. He's obviously not going to just let me sit here in silence. Connor isn't my preferred topic of conversation, and Sam's the last person on the planet I want to talk to about my ex-boyfriend. But I'm also not ready to bring up what I saw at Sam's apartment.

With a sigh, I set my mug down, keeping my hands wrapped around it. "Connor is my ex."

"Oh," Sam says, sounding like he put the pieces together. "You want to talk about it?"

No, but yes. Just stating who Connor is opens the floodgates, and the alcohol in my system makes me want to spill my guts about this fresh wound he carved into me. I take another sip of my perfectly mixed coffee and lick my lips. "Connor and I met my freshman year. He was a junior, but we hit it off instantly, and within weeks, we were dating." I drop my hands to my lap to wring them. "When he was in his last semester, he started applying for grad school and got accepted to NYU."

"Wow, that's pretty awesome, right?"

I nod. "Yeah, it was one of his top choices. We were both very excited, but after graduation, he changed."

"How so?"

Chewing on the inside of my cheek, I ponder whether to tell him. It's none of his business. And after today, I don't know if I want to tell Sam anything personal ever again.

But he does look genuinely curious, and he's never been outwardly mean when I've opened up to him. It also helps that Sam sort of came to my rescue at the bar. I don't think that means I've forgiven him, though. I'm still mad. Just maybe not seething anymore.

"He was super distant, didn't return my texts or calls, sometimes until the next day. I chalked it up to him being busy preparing to move, so I didn't say anything." My throat constricts so I take another sip to let the hot liquid soothe it. "We ran the Mud Down that summer. I thought it was a great day, a good memory to end our summer with. But then, the next week, Connor broke up with me."

Sam doesn't say anything, but I watch his face twist with sympathy.

It's a disarming look, to say the least. So I keep going. "I was devastated. I thought he was my forever, and when he left, well, I sort of shut down." I pick up my spoon to fidget with it. "That's why I went on all of two dates last year. It's also why, when you and I met, I was single."

"Did he give you any reason for the breakup?"

"Mhm." I blink several times. "He said it was because long-distance never works, and two years was far too long to keep anything serious going."

Sam sucks in a sharp breath. "Ouch."

"Yeah." I drop my gaze to my lap.

"So, what was happening at the bar, then? Was he trying to win you back or something?" The hint of jealousy in his voice gets garbled in his sip of coffee.

"No." I let out a derisive snort. "I sort of bit his head off when he tried to give me the 'it's nice to see you' line, and then he told me the truth behind our breakup."

"Truth?" Sam's eyebrows shoot up. "Long-distance wasn't the reason?"

"Nope," I say, emphasizing the p. "He broke up with me because I'm too stubborn and too controlling."

A forceful breath blows from Sam's lips, puffing his cheeks out a bit. "What an entitled dick."

I smile, but it fades. "He has a point."

"No, Brynn, he doesn't," Sam says with such an authoritative tone, it makes my eyes widen. "You are a born leader. I've seen that in so many instances, from the Mud Down to our study group. You don't make people follow you, you lead the way."

The smile works its way back to my lips. Okay, so maybe flattery works. The understanding and support Sam's given me through this entire conversation isn't bad either. With each word I speak, I feel lighter.

"And yeah, you may be the most stubborn woman I've ever met, but you're a challenge, and that's cool as fuck."

I blush and tuck my chin. "Thanks."

When I lift my head, I meet Sam's gaze and my mouth runs dry. He's doing that thing where he looks at me with such intensity, it makes me feel like the only person in the room. I hate that I like it. Especially right now.

"Here ya go," our server says, sliding our plates in front of us. "Careful, the plates are hot."

"Thanks," we say in unison, catching eyes and smiling at each other.

"Here." I pick the bacon off my plate and lay it on Sam's. "You can have this."

"Awesome." His face lights up.

We dig in, and soon, Sam's moaning in delight, but it makes me clench my thighs. Those are the sounds he makes when we're in bed. When he's feasting on me.

Heat creeps up my neck, but quickly ices over as I remember the girl I saw him with. I wonder if he made those sounds with her? It's a disparaging thought, so I shovel food into my mouth to distract myself. After a few minutes, I catch Sam watching me.

He arches an eyebrow. "Glad to see you recovered from that food poisoning." He doesn't even try to hide his sarcasm.

With a grimace, I swallow my mouthful and wipe my mouth with my napkin. I haven't been fair to Sam. He's been more kind to me tonight than he ever has been, and I'm holding a grudge over something I have no right to. "About that..."

"It's okay, Brynn. You don't have to explain, but also, you can tell me if you don't want to come over."

"It's not that."

His forehead crinkles. "What is it, then?"

"Ugh," I groan, raising my gaze to the ceiling. "I saw you today. Walking that girl out of your apartment."

I watch as understanding dawns on him, followed by more confusion, and finally a grimace. "Brynn, you've got the wrong idea."

"No, don't feel like you have to explain. You and I aren't together, so you have every right to be with whoever you want, whenever you want. I just wish you would have been honest with me."

Sam sighs, sounding amused. "No, Brynn. You seriously have the wrong idea." He shakes his head, pinching the bridge of his nose. "That girl was my sister."

"Your sister?"

"Yeah, she was on her way to Denver to meet some friends for a concert and stopped by to visit for lunch. I really didn't want her to be around when you came over, so I made sure she left by one."

I feel so strange. A weight lifts off my shoulders, freeing me from this emotional turmoil I've been in, but then a pit of guilt forms in my stomach. "Sam, I'm so sorry."

He waves me off. "No big deal, but were you really *that* jealous?"

"No." I bristle. "Maybe."

Instead of chiding me with laughter like I expect, a satisfied grin spreads across his face. "I told you, Brynn. I'm not seeing anyone else."

"*We're* not seeing each other, though. That's the thing." I sip more coffee. "When we made this agreement, there weren't supposed to be feelings involved."

"You have feelings for me?" He sounds hopeful.

"No, but I'm getting attached." I fold my arms, suddenly feeling empty at my next thought. "I don't think we should do this anymore."

The light in his eyes dims as his expression falls. "Oh, okay."

"Sorry."

"No, don't be. You're right." He takes a deep breath, running his hands down his thighs. "This arrangement was for nothing more than to make working together more tolerable. If you're uncomfortable with it, then we should stop."

I chew on my lower lip. "No hard feelings?"

"None."

"Okay, thank you."

Sam nods and takes another few bites of his meal. "But, we still have a presentation to put together for next Friday."

"You didn't do it today?"

"No," he says, tilting his head to the side. "Someone never sent me her notes for it."

I slap my forehead. "Shit, I'm sorry."

"It's okay. We can meet tomorrow at that coffee place down the street. If you still want to, that is." The despondency in his voice hurts my heart.

"Yeah, I think that will be fine."

"Sounds good." He finishes his last bites, and leans back against the booth. "That was delicious, by the way."

I hold my chin up triumphantly. "Told you."

# CHAPTER 31

The next day, I arrive at Cuppa Joe's to find Sam waiting for me. He's standing outside with his coat zipped all the way up, his hood on, and his hands in his pockets. His posture is so rigid, he'd be like a statue if it weren't for his shaking.

"Are you cold?" I tease as I walk up to him. "What are you doing waiting out here? It's, like, twenty degrees."

"Well..." he says through chattering teeth. "I was going to wait inside, but before I opened the door I peeked through the glass and saw Maya behind the counter."

I gasp. "No way. She works here?"

"Evidently."

"We can go to the library if you want."

He shakes his head. "Too quiet and not enough coffee. Besides, you're here now, so I'll have a buffer."

"I'll do what I can," I say, saluting him like a soldier. "Come on, let's get inside before you ice over."

He laughs, then opens the door and steps inside. I trail in behind, and witness Maya's elated expression turn sour as her eyes flick from Sam to me. A mild sense of pity takes root in my chest, but I get over it quickly.

Sam and I head to the counter where Maya greets us. I should say she greets Sam, because all I get from her is a curt, "Brynn." We order our drinks, and Sam tries to pay, but I don't let him. Since it's my choice not to meet at his place anymore, I feel like it should be my treat.

"So, what are *you* two doing here?" Maya asks as she takes my credit card.

"Just working on the study group presentation," I say.

"Oh. You don't usually come in here to do that, do you?"

"No, but we needed a change of scenery." Picking up the house roast she slides across the counter, I hold it up. "And a hot drink to warm up." I pass the cup to Sam.

"Thanks," he says. "I'll go grab a table."

Maya hands me my card back as she longingly looks at Sam, but she doesn't say anything. My name is called at the other end of the counter, so I head there to pick up my order, then to the table Sam claimed. I sit down and use a frustrated breath to blow on my hot drink.

"Everything okay?" Sam asks.

"Mhm. I'm glad Maya's not my lab partner."

He chuckles. "Maybe we should switch partners."

"Oh yeah, I'm sure Micah would *love* that." I roll my eyes.

"Are you kidding me?" Sam turns between me and his computer, his eyebrows scrunched. "He'd be ecstatic. Have you seen the way he looks at her?"

I stare at him in confusion. "No. I had no idea."

"That actually doesn't surprise me. You're always so engrossed in your work, you don't notice a lot."

I fold my arms. "I do too. I might not look, but I notice things."

"You've never noticed me staring at you," he says quietly out of the side of his mouth.

My forehead crinkles as my lips part slightly. He stares at me? Since when? "That's because I didn't want to see your annoying face."

To my relief, Sam laughs. "Yeah, okay. Whatever you say." He opens his laptop, sipping his coffee as the computer warms up.

The silence hanging heavily between us gives me time to think. I don't know that I ever properly thanked Sam for last night. He not only saved me from Connor, but he also hung out with me and let me vent my frustrations. He was also more understanding about my confusion with his sister than I expected him to be.

That all deserves to be mentioned.

"Sam?" I wait for him to acknowledge his name. "I need to thank you for last night."

His brow crinkles sympathetically, but he doesn't speak.

I drop my gaze to my coffee cup. "Even after I lied about being sick, you still helped me through what happened with…" I swallow. "With my ex. I want you to know that I really appreciate what you did." When I glance up, I'm greeted by a warm smile on Sam's face.

"Brynn…" My name spills from his lips with such longing, I'm surprised I don't melt into a gooey puddle. With a small wince, Sam pats my thigh before turning back to the computer. "You're welcome."

When he removes his hand, the spot on my thigh aches for his warmth, so I rub my palms down my legs.

"How are you doing, anyway?" he asks, not looking at me.

I lean forward, clasping my hands around my knees. "Fine."

He tilts his head. "Fine?"

"Better."

"Good." He continues clicking the mousepad. "I'm glad I was able to help."

"Me too." I chew on my lip as my next question niggles at me. "How did you know I was on the patio?"

Licking his lips, Sam rubs the back of his neck. "I saw you sitting at the bar with your friend, and was on my way to inquire about your food poisoning…" He gives me a pointed look, a smirk appearing. "But you stumbled your way outside before I could get to you."

"So, you opted to get a couple beers before coming to find me?"

"Ha, no. I was about to follow you, but your friend saw me first."

The misery in his tone tells me Lisa was anything but nice, and a small pang of guilt hits me, but I'd be lying if I didn't find it funny.

Sam must notice me struggling to contain my amusement because he nods at me. "Yeah, that was interesting. You've got a good friend there, you know that?"

"I do."

"Well, she jumped off her stool and charged right at me, finger pointed and everything. She didn't give me any details as to why you lied about being sick, but she used some colorful language to make it abundantly clear that you were upset with me." He makes a pained face as if the memory is replaying in his mind.

I can't help it, I giggle. "Sorry."

"No, don't be. She was just protecting you."

"So, how did you convince her to let you talk to me?"

Sam swallows deeply and rubs his chin as he seems to be contemplating. "I, uh, told her that I wanted to hear things from your mouth, and apologize for whatever it was that I did. That seemed to satisfy her."

I nod even as I wonder why Lisa didn't mention any of this.

"So, I bought a couple of beers as an olive branch before coming out to the patio. You know the rest." He clears his throat. "I'm just sorry I didn't get there sooner."

He sounds incredibly defeated by regret, I feel the need to comfort him, so I place my hand on his shoulder. His muscles instantly tense under my touch, but then relax. "It's okay. I think I needed to hear all that shit from Connor."

Sam gives me a sideways glance. "Really? Why?"

"For the last year, I've been thinking he left me because I was too weak to hold on to him. But really, he left me because he couldn't handle my strength." I squeeze Sam's shoulder. "You helped me to see that. So, thank you."

As we stare at each other, the silence falls between us again. This time, though, it's not heavy. It's warm, like we've opened the curtains to a bright, sunny day. I get lost in Sam's eyes. The adoration pouring from them makes my heart race.

When he reaches up to lay his hand on mine, his touch sears my skin. So much so, it breaks the spell, and I flinch away. What the hell was that? I clear my throat. "Um, we should get started on the presentation."

With a deflated nod, Sam scoots his chair closer to me, turning the computer so I can see the screen, and my whole body tenses. We're so close, I can feel his heat. A rush of adrenaline courses through me as I recall how warm he is when he's pressed against me. If I adjust my position, I could feel that again.

"What do you think about this?" Sam's voice wrenches me back to reality, and I shake my head to clear it.

Take it easy, Brynn.

As he walks me through his latest idea, which is a play on Twenty Questions, I slowly relax. The presentation is a nice distraction from my growing desires. We need to get back to this. Back to focusing on the study group and not getting naked.

His idea is a simple design, but it'll be effective. I tilt my head, and when he notices me staring, he gives me an incredulous look. "What?"

"Have I ever said thank you for all the work you put into these presentations?"

His lips curl playfully. "No."

"Well, I'm saying it now. Thank you, Sam."

"Wow, two 'thank you's' in one day. I should go buy a lottery ticket," he says with a wink.

I smack his arm playfully. "Hey, I mean it. You've made the study group really successful."

His cheeks tinge pink. "Well, I couldn't have done it without your expert knowledge."

"Whatever. You're just as smart as I am. You're the only other person to challenge my test scores."

"Does all of this make us even, then?" He locks his eyes on mine, not taunting me, but almost like he's pleading. "Can we stop being enemies?"

The air is stolen from my lungs, but I whisper, "Sam, we haven't been enemies for a while."

"Good." He noticeably relaxes before turning back to the computer to shut it down. "Come on, let's get out of here. I can feel Maya's glare burning a hole right through me."

My laugh cuts any lingering tension, and we pack up to leave. Sam heads for the door, but I walk toward the counter to throw my cup away. As I do, Maya waves me down. Hesitantly, I walk to the other end of the counter to meet her.

"Hey, Maya. What's up?"

"You win."

"Excuse me?" I quirk an eyebrow.

She huffs and folds her arms. "You win, okay? Sam is all yours."

"What?" I close my eyes and pinch the bridge of my nose. "Maya, you've got things all wrong. There's nothing between me and Sam."

"Oh, shut up, Brynn."

My eyes pop wide open to see her rolling hers.

"You can stand there and tell me all about how you don't think there's anything between you two, but I just spent a good two hours watching you." She licks her lips, tucking her bottom lip between her teeth. "I saw the way he looks at you. He doesn't look at *anyone* like that."

My lips part. "Maya, we're classmates. That's it."

"Yeah, whatever. Keep telling yourself that, Brynn." She waves me off before returning to work.

I'm left in awe. I don't know what's more surprising, the fact that Maya talked to me, or that she thinks Sam is interested in me. At one point, there might have been something growing between us. Hell, I even felt a strange sensation today while we worked, but it's all residual feelings from our recently ended arrangement. I'm sure of it.

I shake my head to clear it, and step outside to meet up with Sam who is waiting patiently for me. We walk side by side to the end of the street where we exchange pleasant see-you-laters, then we both head to our respective homes. It's not a romantic goodbye filled with angst and longing. Just two people parting ways.

Whatever Maya *thought* she saw was left over from the last time we slept together. You know, less than a week ago...

# Chapter 32

With only two weeks left before winter break, I'm furiously working to get everything done. Technically, the semester goes until mid-January, but I like to have all my loose ends tied up. If I don't, I'll ruin my break by dwelling. The majority of my classes are straightforward. A test to study for in O-Chem, a review of my favorite hiking trails for hiking class, but my latest essay for English is going to kill me.

If I could have chosen my subject, things would be fine, but it was chosen for me. My English professor thought she'd go easy on us by assigning "fun" topics. For me, it's anything but fun. Maybe others would enjoy writing about how the hippie movement shaped history, but I've been struggling to develop a cohesive argument in order to relay the information properly, and it shows. My paragraphs are all over the place. They're disjointed, choppy, and lack any sort of general flair.

I'm frustrated with myself, but Brynn Erlenmeyer doesn't quit.

Hunkered down in my room, which happens to be on the main level of our house, I commit myself to this paper. I have three hours until I meet Sam. Plenty of time. All my resources are readied, websites opened, books stacked. I just need to concentrate on rewording these sentences so they make sense.

Twenty minutes into working, Lisa opens my door without knocking. "What'cha doing?" she asks, popping her gum.

Drumming my fingers on my desk, I don't look up. "Writing a paper."

"Ooh, you sound super excited about that." She snickers. "Do you want to grab lunch later before you meet up with Sam?"

I shake my head, still keeping my focus on my work. "I need to finish this. I'll just have a sandwich or something."

"Okay, fine." She sighs, but doesn't leave my doorway. "What's the paper about?"

"Hippies."

"What?" She practically laughs the question out.

"My professor assigned us topics, and mine is about how hippies shaped history. I hate it."

"Why? It sounds fun. I love the music from that time. If you want, I can–"

"Lisa," I say curtly as I finally turn to look at her. "I don't need help right now. I just need you to leave so I can finish."

Her face crinkles with annoyance. "Yes, ma'am," she says, saluting me with her middle finger before walking away.

I groan and get up to close my door. I know I pissed her off, but I'll apologize later. I have work to do. As I settle back at my desk, I don't read more than two sentences before "Where Have All the Flowers Gone?" by The Kingston Trio comes blaring from our living room stereo.

I clench my jaw to power through the noise, but after the song ends, it starts again. It repeats three times before I realize Lisa is playing hippie and having her own form of protest.

"Ugh." I drop my face into my palm and take a deep breath. "It's okay. I can work through this."

Thirty minutes later, I've heard the song at least ten times, but it's faded into background music at this point. In fact, I've come to consider it almost white noise. I'm feeling better about my ability to finish this paper when thumping sounds from the room above me, and I slump in my chair.

Lisa has taken over the living room, so Hannah must be doing her workout. In her bedroom directly above mine. It's a normal occurrence when you have three roommates with varying schedules, but why does it have to be right now?

With a frustrated groan, I shut down my computer and pack my materials. I can't concentrate under these conditions. It's bad enough I hate my essay topic, but now with the same song on endless repeat and my bookshelf rattling every five seconds, I'm at my wit's end.

I leave my room, striding through the living room toward the front door. Lisa lounges on the couch scrolling her phone, and I send a glare her way. She twiddles her fingers in the air as I storm out the front door, slamming it behind me.

Once I'm outside, I breathe in the brisk December air. After a few days of twenty degrees or below, this forty degrees feels like a heat wave. I briefly shut my eyes, taking a moment to bask in the sun before setting off for the library.

The precarious ice patches make my walk longer than normal, but by the time I reach my destination, my angry frustration has ebbed. I don't have anyone to blame except myself. If I hadn't been rude to Lisa, she wouldn't have commandeered the living room and Hannah wouldn't have been doing jump squats eight feet above me. Maybe if I had apologized right away, I'd still be in the comforts of my own room, and not in the library.

At least it's quiet in here. This could be a good thing. Sometimes a change of scenery is all it takes.

It worked with me and Sam.

After we started meeting at his place, things improved between us. Okay, so that may have been due to us sleeping together, but it was an improvement nonetheless. Even now, without having sex, we're still in a good spot. Meeting at the coffee shop has been great. Granted, today will only be our second time, but Sam and I don't argue anymore, we don't pick at each other. In fact, we seem to have completely let go of our hatred and are getting along better each time.

The thought buoys my mood as I take a seat at a computer station. Digging through my backpack for my student ID, I come up empty. That's odd. It's always in the inside pocket. I don't put it anywhere else...

Shit.

I took it out when we went to Jackie's art show last weekend. She won a competition that landed her a temporary spot in a gallery, and students got in for free on opening night. I remember tucking my ID into my pants pocket.

The pants that are currently sitting in my hamper.

With a heavy sigh, I trudge to the front desk to get a temporary login. It should be a simple task. All I need is for a librarian to print me off a code so I can log into our school server. Except, there aren't any librarians anywhere.

I wait for what feels like forever before I track one down and it takes all of twenty seconds to get a pass code. When I finally sit down at a computer, I notice it's been thirty minutes since I left my house. I've wasted half an hour just trying to get started again.

I still have plenty of time to dedicate to this paper. It'll be okay.

Popping in my ear-buds, I set to work. The steady stream of hard rock songs drowns out the noise around me, and surprisingly, I fall into a steady flow. I manage to not only read through, but rewrite the majority of two pages. In only forty-five minutes nonetheless. A smile pulls at my lips as I let the weight of the past two hours slide from my shoulders.

That is, until my music suddenly stops. "What the...?" I pull my phone from my pocket to see a black screen. "Awesome," I groan. Guess I forgot to charge it last night.

I tell myself it isn't the end of the world and dive back into my paper, but concentrating proves harder than I thought. I lose focus more times than I can count. The idea that I'm unreachable niggles at me.

What if there's an emergency? This could be the one time my parents need to contact me, and they can't. Sure, they could call Lisa, but I left without speaking to her, so she doesn't know where I am.

I lean my elbow onto the desk, dropping my face into my palm. I'm usually so much better prepared than this. How I even forgot to plug in my phone last night is beyond me.

It's just an off day.

With a deep breath, I begin the same paragraph I've reread at least six times. I'd like to finish it before I have to leave...

Crap. What time is it?

I glance at the clock on the computer. "Twelve-forty!? Shit." I hurriedly log off and throw my materials into my backpack. The coffee shop is a short walk from my house, but the library is on the other side of campus, so now I have twice as far to go.

Racing out of the library, I speed walk down the street. If I keep this pace, I'll make it to Cuppa Joe's just in time. It's a good thing I run for fun.

As I come to an intersection, the light threatens to turn, so I speed up. I'm not paying attention when I step off the curb onto a patch of ice I expect to be sturdy, but my foot goes right through. I shake the water from my snow boot, patting myself on the back for deciding against sneakers.

That sense of pride slowly fades as my sock becomes wet. Great. I have a hole in my boot somewhere. A moist sock has to be the most uncomfortable feeling in the world, and I don't have time to run home.

Frustrated tears sting my eyes. This day has not gone at all how I had hoped. All I wanted was to finish a paper that I don't want to look at anymore, but I couldn't even get that done. And now, I'm late to study group prep.

When I get to Cuppa Joe's, I find Sam waiting outside again. A smile ticks up on his lips, and all my tension releases. Dammit. Why do I find him so comforting? I didn't used to. In fact, it was the opposite. Whenever I saw him, it irritated me and I couldn't wait to get away from him, but things have changed. It's one thing not to hate him, but counting the minutes until I see him again? I shouldn't be doing that. We're nothing except classmates, now.

As I get closer, the cheerful expression on his face fades, instead turning to concern. "Hey, is something wrong?"

"I'm having a really shitty day." I sniffle, swiping at my dewy lashes before eyeing him suspiciously. "Why are you outside? Hiding from Maya again?"

He snorts out a laugh. "Is it that obvious?"

"No, you're just predictable."

"Ouch." He lays his hand on his heart, but winks before he opens the door. "After you."

Sam steps to the counter while I head straight to the bathroom. I not only need to pee, but I spend a minute using the hand dryer on my sock. Standing on one foot shouldn't be this difficult. I'm hopping from side to side, leaning all over as I try not to touch the bathroom floor with my bare toes.

When my sock is dry, I bend to slip it on, but lose my balance. I end up over-correcting as I hop backward, and bang my elbow on the sink counter.

"Fuck!" I shout. Could this day get any worse?

Once my boot is back on, I go order my drink. After this shitty day, I deserve something fun, so I order one of their holiday specials. One I've never had before. When my name is called, I grab my cup, but instantly pull my hand away. It's piping hot, even through the paper cup.

Groaning inwardly, I slip a cardboard sleeve around my drink and join Sam at a table. I plop into my seat, letting out a heavy sigh.

"Do you want to talk about it?" Sam asks in his most gentle voice, and it disarms me.

So, I let it out. I start at the top, telling him about how I pissed off Lisa all the way to the hole in my boot. "And, to top it off, this coffee is way too hot to drink, so now I have to wait."

The sympathetic look on Sam's face doesn't waver throughout my entire vent session. "Well, how about you sit there and listen while I talk about the presentation? You don't have to do anything for a while. Maybe that way, nothing else will go wrong."

I chuckle, nodding. "What's your idea for next week?"

True to his word, Sam does all the talking for the next several minutes. Diving into the presentation information, he goes over all the details, but never opens his computer. He gives me all his attention even though all I'm doing is listening.

And boy, I could listen to him talk all day. His deep voice is so smooth, it wraps me in velvety softness. A few times, my mind wanders, and I conjure the sound of his voice when he's talking dirty in my ear. Even with these extra layers on, I get goosebumps.

When he's finished, he picks up his coffee. "So, what do you think?"

"I think it all sounds good." I tentatively wrap my hand around my cup, elated when I find it cooled enough to touch. "Finally," I say in a breath.

Sam laughs. "You sure are excited about that coffee."

"Well, I wanted to try something new."

"Really? What did you get?"

"Gingerbread latte," I say, lifting my cup to my lips.

Sam snatches the cup from my hand, yanking it away like I was about to drink acid.

"Hey!" I shout. "What the hell?"

"You're not drinking this."

Is he joking? If so, it's not funny. "Want to bet? Give it back." I reach across him, but he scoots his chair back, shaking his head. "Sam," I say, folding my arms. "Give me my drink back."

"Brynn, you *can't* drink it."

"Why the hell not?"

"Because they top it with cinnamon. See?" He pulls the lid off to reveal a fluffy mound of foam sprinkled with brown powder.

My eyes widen. "Oh, shit." I slump back into my chair. "I didn't even think to ask."

"Yeah, obviously. You really want to top off your bad day with a trip to the hospital?"

I squeeze my eyes tight, flashes of my almost future playing behind my eyelids. My body temperature rising. My throat constricting. My tongue swelling. It hasn't happened since I was young. I've been so vigilant, so meticulous about ingredients. Until today.

"You need to be more careful."

I bristle at what sounds like Sam chiding a wayward toddler, but when I open my eyes, the fear on his face confuses me. As I stare at him, I let his words replay. The tone of his voice echoes in my mind, sounding more and more like concern each time.

He wasn't berating me. He was scared, and he protected me the only way he could.

My anger slowly ebbs as his regard for my safety warms me. "Thank you," I say, ducking my chin.

"No worries. It's what friends are for."

I whip my head up. *Friends?* Only a few months ago, that word would have made me scoff. Now, it hits me like a rock to the gut, but it's my own doing. I called off our arrangement. I friend-zoned myself.

With an accepting nod, I sigh. "Sorry I got mad."

Sam's expression softens, his mouth curling into a sweet smile. "Hey, it wouldn't be you if you didn't fight me about it."

# CHAPTER 33

I DON'T MISS SAM. I don't miss Sam. *I don't miss Sam.*

If I say it enough, eventually it'll become true, right?

I've been repeating it all week, it has yet to sink in. It's making me question my choice to end our arrangement. I thought that was the best thing to do. I was struggling with my feelings, so the natural solution was to cut myself off from the temptation.

And it was working. Everything was going swimmingly.

Until he ruined it by labeling us as friends.

Now, all I can think about is how *friends* don't do the things we were doing. Classmates casually hooking up? No problem. Fuck-buddies calling each other out of the blue? Sure thing. Hell, even as enemies I was fine with some hate sex, but this new label changes our circumstances.

I may have shut the door on us, but he locked it.

Sitting here, watching him dole out questions for our latest study group isn't helping, either. All the little things I ignored about him before are catching my attention. For instance, when he's nervous, he clears his throat. It's something small you wouldn't notice otherwise, but I've become attuned to it.

I've also learned the difference in the way he smiles. When his lips are closed, he's doing it to be polite. It's how he smiles at Maya. I get full-faced grins where his mouth stretches from ear to ear and his eyes light up. Even the smirks he gives me show a little teeth.

As Sam wraps up the presentation, he turns that devastatingly great smile on me. "Well, that was fun," he says as he shuts down his computer. "I don't know if we can top it next week."

A pit of disappointment settles in my gut. "We don't have to."

Sam turns to me, eyebrows furrowed. "What do you mean?"

"We don't have a study group next week, remember? It's the week before Christmas break, and we have a test."

His expression falls. "You're right."

"Ooh, say that again," I tease.

He scoffs, rolling his eyes before going back to packing up.

I swallow deeply. "And no lab, either."

His shoulders noticeably sag. "So, I guess I'll see you in O-Chem next week."

"Yeah, I suppose so." I hate the despondency in my voice, but I can't help it. I wish we had a study session next week. I wish I had an excuse to hang out with Sam one more time before break.

But I'm not that lucky.

Sam turns to face me as he hikes his backpack onto his shoulder. He doesn't say anything, but his mouth ticks up on one side. When he juts his chin toward the door, we both shuffle out. Walking down the hall in silence, we fall into step together. He could easily out-stride me, but he keeps my pace until we reach the door, which he opens for me.

We step outside and into a light snowfall. Big, fluffy, white flakes float around us, shimmering in the lights of the building. I close my eyes and dip my head back. Snowflakes gently land on my face, sticking to my lashes and making me smile. When I open my eyes, I find Sam watching me with an adoring look on his face.

I quickly brush off the flakes. "Sorry. I just love a good snowfall."

"You don't have to be sorry," he says in a low voice as he steps to me, lifting his hand to brush snow from my cheek. "It's nice to see you happy."

His hand lingers at my jaw, and my skin burns under his fingertips. The intensity in his gaze has my heart racing as I flick my eyes to his mouth. If I tip up onto my toes, our lips will touch. It wouldn't hurt anything, right? Just a simple goodbye kiss.

As my chin tilts up, Sam drops his hand and steps back. "Have a good weekend, Brynn. I'll see you next week."

Defeat fills me to the brim, but leaves me empty as I watch him walk away. I don't know what exactly I was expecting. I called off our arrangement, and he cemented it with his label. So why did I think it would be appropriate to kiss him?

Feeling like an idiot, yet again, I trudge home through the snow to spend my weekend hunkered down in my room, studying.

Alone.

*** 

"Good God, Brynn. Did you go running *again*?" Lisa asks as I walk through the front door.

"Yes," I huff between breaths. I shuck my gloves and slide out of my shoes before pulling off my ear warmer. "It's not so bad out now. This morning was worse."

"I can't believe you got up and went for not one, but two runs today. And you went on one yesterday!"

I nod. "And one on Sunday, and one on Saturday. What's your point?"

"My point is you're crazy." With a dismissive wave, she goes back to flipping through Netflix. "What's got you so wound up lately?"

I sigh and take a seat on the couch next to her. "I haven't had sex in three weeks."

"What?" Lisa's jaw drops and her eyes widen. "What happened to your arrangement with Sam?"

"I called it off."

"Dude..." she groans. "Why didn't you tell me?"

I shrug. "It didn't seem like a big deal at the time."

"Wait, you've still been meeting him on the weekends. What are you guys doing if you're not fucking?"

"Literally nothing except working on the study group stuff." I hate how frustrated I sound. "But it's been so good, Lisa. We're getting along really well, but I miss the sex."

Lisa snorts. "I bet you do."

"Ugh." I drop my face into my palm. "What do I do?"

"Tell him you want to start fucking again," she says it so nonchalantly as she picks up the remote.

"I can't say that." I chew on my lower lip. "Besides, he friend-zoned me."

Lisa's entire face scrunches. "How in the hell did you guys go from one-night stand material, to mortal enemies, to fuck-buddies, to just friends?" She lets out a heavy breath. "This is getting too complicated."

"That's just it, though. It's not complicated anymore. We're friends." I slouch into the couch, letting the cushions swallow me. "Boring, platonic friends."

"Brynn, there is no way you two are platonic. You've been sleeping together for months. That stuff leaves behind residual attachment you can't get rid of. You of all people should understand that. It's science."

I chuckle, but it fades. "Yeah, but the whole point of us sleeping together was to make us hate each other a little less, and it worked. I don't hate him anymore."

A knowing grin spread across Lisa's face, and her eyes light up. "So, you like him?"

I take a moment to examine the question. I do like Sam, but is that romantically or physically? I've left our past behind, and managed to become friends with him, but I think that's where it stops. "Not *that* way. I just like him when he's naked."

"Same difference."

"No, it's not," I say, shaking my head and putting a finger up to make a point. "Liking someone means you have feelings for them, which I don't. The feelings I have for Sam aren't from my heart, they're only from between my thighs."

A laugh bursts from Lisa and she practically chokes on it. "Okay, that's fair. I've seen the guy and I can't blame you for that."

My smile fades. "But I hate the idea of using him for sex."

"Trust me, guys don't care as long as they're getting laid."

"Some guys might not care, but Sam doesn't seem like that kind of guy. I don't know. I've gotten to know him better, and I feel like me only wanting to be physical would hurt him."

"What about doing it one more time to get it out of your system?"

My eyes narrow. "You've had that idea before and it still sounds terrible."

"No, think about it." Lisa shifts her position to face me. "It's the Tuesday before break, and we're not going home until Sunday. You and him can pick a day to meet up, fuck each other's brains out, and then you'll have almost a month to get over him before classes start up."

I hope the pure skepticism on my face comes through clearly. "Lisa, that is the worst idea you've ever had. I can't sleep with Sam again if I want to get over him." I nod curtly to myself. "I'll have to be strong."

"Better buy some new running shoes, then."

***

"Overall, I was very, very pleased with the outcome of this test," Professor St. James says as she wraps up her recap of our exam. "So, for the next few weeks, don't even think about Organic Chemistry. See you all next year."

There's a collective cheerful ovation from the class as everyone gets up to leave. I pack up quickly so I can make it out before Sam. I've decided it would be best if I don't see him in case I lose my resolve and take Lisa's advice.

Before I make it to the door, Professor St. James stops me. "Brynn, can you stay for a few minutes? I'd like to talk to you and Sam before you leave."

I inwardly groan. "Sure. No problem."

As I stand at her desk, the professor turns away to wipe the white board, and Sam sidles up next to me. "How'd you do on the test?" he asks.

"Ninety-eight percent," I say proudly. "You?"

He smirks, but it turns into a grimace. "Eighty-seven."

"Wow, that's low for you. What happened?"

"I was just…" He clears his throat. "Preoccupied."

I suck in a breath as I nod. I wonder what he was preoccupied with? And why is he nervous to tell me? Maybe he was with another girl. Has he moved on since our arrangement has been over for a few weeks? I know he said he's not the type to sleep around, but it has been a while. I guess I can't blame him.

But why does that sting?

"Okay, thanks for sticking around," Professor St. James says as she turns to face us. "I wanted to tell you both how much I appreciate the work you have put into this study group. The test scores have improved drastically. I couldn't be happier."

A beaming smile overtakes my face, dulling the pain of Sam replacing me.

"I know I said I couldn't compensate you for your time, but I wanted to do something to show my gratitude, so here." She hands Sam a small envelope. "It's not much."

He opens it and slides out a gift certificate to a local Italian restaurant. "Wow, a hundred bucks? Thank you."

"Well, I thought you two deserved something, and while I can't technically pay you, I could at least buy you both nice meal." She shakes our hands. "Enjoy your holidays. I'll see you next year."

Sam and I both profusely thank the professor before we leave the room. As we walk the hall, Sam studies the gift certificate. "I can't believe she did this."

"I know. It's really nice of her. And I love that restaurant."

Sam's gaze flicks between me and the certificate. "Well, then, here." He holds it out to me. "You take it. You can go have a girls' night."

"What? No, Professor St. James gave it to *us*. You deserve to use it as much as I do."

A flash of appreciation blazes in his irises. "Would you want to use it tonight?"

"Tonight?"

"Yeah, I mean, unless you have plans."

"No, no plans." I shake my head, more so to clear my confusion than anything. "I just wasn't expecting to use it so soon."

He hikes a shoulder to his ear. "Well, I'm leaving early Saturday to go home, so it's either tonight, or January."

Him putting it that way makes a sense of urgency rise within me. "Tonight is fine. Can we meet at, like, six?"

"Sure. I've got one more class today, and it goes until four-thirty, so six is perfect. See you later," Sam says before turning to walk in the opposite direction.

All I can do is stare after him. What am I doing? I spent the whole last week avoiding the guy so I could get him out of my system, and here I am agreeing to dinner with him. I must be crazy.

# CHAPTER 34

LISA PULLS HER BEAT-UP Honda up to the curb in front of the Italian restaurant and sighs. "Well, here you go. Are you sure about this?"

"No." I shake my head slowly, staring at the lit up sign front.

"It is sort of the opposite of your plan to avoid him until after the holiday break."

I roll my eyes at her judgmental tone. "I know that."

"It's not too late," she says melodically, like she's trying to persuade me. "I can still drive away if you want."

"I don't think I want you to."

She sighs again. "Then what do you want?"

"Lasagna," I say flatly.

Lisa laughs. "I guess you're in the right place."

I turn to her, my face stoic as I try to hide the fear and doubt. "Am I crazy if I go in there?"

"No, Brynn. You're not crazy. Confused, maybe, but not crazy."

"That's the understatement of the year." I blow a piece of stray hair from my face.

Lisa puts the car in park. "Can I ask you something? And I want an honest answer. None of your variable weighing nonsense, got it?"

I nod.

"Do you have feelings for Sam? Like, honest to goodness feelings in here." She taps my heart.

I let my head fall back to gaze at the roof of the car. That's such a loaded question. I mean, with the way things started between us, I'd have to say yes. But when you factor in all the lies, it gets muddy. Then, after sleeping with him for months and coming to genuinely like him as a person, I suppose I'd go with–

"Brynn!" Lisa's voice reverberates off the car windows, and I snap my head over. "I said no overthinking."

"It's not an easy answer."

"Well, I don't want to sway your answer in any way, but I want you to know that I've always liked Sam."

I scrunch my eyebrows. "Really? Always? What about all the times you called him a prick?"

"I was validating my friend who was hurting." She raises her nose in the air before giving me the side-eye and laughing. "But seriously, I do like him."

A warmth builds within me, but dissipates as I remember what Sam said about her confronting him at Coyote Canyon. "Hey, why didn't you ever tell me about you seeing him at the bar that night I ran into Connor? Sam said you really chewed him out."

"Oh, that." Lisa makes a face, a guilt-stricken expression like she's been caught. "Well, you didn't ever ask, and you seemed so much better after that, I didn't see the point."

"What did he say to you?"

Lisa grimaces, her eyes pleading with me to let it go.

"I want to know," I say sternly.

"Okay, fine." She sighs. "I laid into him pretty hard, telling him about how hurt you were and what an asshole he was. I didn't tell him why. I said you were upset and he needed to leave you alone."

"So, how did he convince you otherwise?"

"Oh, Brynn. He had the best answer." A wry smile crosses her lips. "He said he needed to know how he fucked up, and would spend as long as it took to fix it because he couldn't stay away from you even if his life depended on it."

My eyelids peel back, my heart stuttering "What?" That can't be right. Or at the very least, it can't mean what Lisa thinks it means. I'm sure it's nothing more than a physical pull.

"Mhm." Lisa nods. "Now, I'm not a hundred-percent sure, but I'd say that boy has it bad for you."

I scoff, waving her off. "That's where you're mistaken. He friend-zoned me, remember?"

"I bet you're wrong," she says melodically.

I shift in my seat, folding my arms.

"And all this back-and-forth with him, the hating and not hating, the fuck-buddy thing, it makes me think you've got it just as bad."

My toes tap the floorboard as I avoid eye contact with Lisa.

"I've never seen you happier than when you've been with Sam. I mean, sure, you two went through a rough patch for a bit, but I've seen so much more of the real Brynn since Sam's come around. Especially after you started sleeping together."

I let out an airy chuckle and turn my appreciative gaze on her. "I have felt more like me lately."

"See? I bet Sam has had a lot to do with that." She pats my leg. "And I know you think he's just a good lay, but I think you'd be doing yourself a disservice by shutting the door on him completely."

I sigh. "He locked it, though. How am I supposed to open it now?"

"If you go into this dinner with a fresh outlook, he might turn the key. Things between you and Sam have gone from great, to bad, to terrible, and back again. You're in a good spot with him, don't let that go to waste."

Sucking in a huge breath, I nod.

"Now, get in there and have fun, but call me if you need rescuing."

"Thanks, I will." I hug her before exiting the car to take the hardest steps of my life.

As I near the entrance, the door opens, and Sam waltzes outside to hold it for me. I take a second to drink him in. His maroon button-down shirt and black slacks make him such a different version of himself. He's sleek, sophisticated, and not like the usual laid-back, casual Sam I know. It's enticing, to say the least.

"After you," he says, bowing slightly.

I roll my eyes, but smile. "Thank you, sir."

Once I cross the threshold, I'm reminded of why I love this little restaurant. The entryway is lit with white Christmas lights dangling from the ceiling, and their reflections in the shiny floor tile makes it seem like I'm walking on stars. There's always soft music playing. Mostly instrumental Italian music, but a few crooners like Dean Martin work their way in too. The delectable aromas filling the air complete the entire effect. It's like being transported across the sea within a few seconds.

"You look nice," Sam whispers next to my ear as he slides off my coat.

I shudder at his warm breath on my neck. As I turn to thank him for the compliment, I find him raking over my length only to pause on the scooped neckline of my dress. My heart races.

I tug at the slinky, emerald-colored fabric. "Thanks." Running my hand over my capped sleeve, I inwardly shrink. "We didn't talk about dinner attire, so I'm glad you and I are on the same page." I float my hand up and down, motioning to him. "You clean up nicely."

He leans in to whisper, "I'd say you have me beat." When he pulls away, he finally looks me in the eyes, and I can see his smoldering.

I swallow. "I'll take that victory," I say as confidently as I can before turning to the host. "Hi, table for two?"

The host grabs a couple of menus and leads us toward the back of the small restaurant. As we walk, I try to figure out what I want from this night. Do I want to prove Lisa right or wrong? If she's wrong, and all Sam wants is to be friends, then I'm good. He's already given us that label, so I'll just have to learn to move on.

But if she's right, then what?

"Here you are," the host says as he seats us. He then explains the specials and ensures us our server will be right over. When he leaves, it's just me, Sam, and the awkward silence as he stares at me.

I pick at my nails under the table so I don't squirm under his gaze. "So, how was your other class today?"

"Fine. Sort of a throw-away class, though. I really could have skipped it."

"Why didn't you?"

He shrugs. "I needed something to keep me occupied until I got here."

I narrow my eyes. Was he anticipating this dinner? I'll never admit that I was, but if he was too, then maybe we do have a chance together. I don't know how to be certain, though.

"Hello, you two," our server says as she sets two water glasses down. "Have you perused the menus? Or do you need a minute?"

I give Sam a pointed look. "I know what I want."

"Of course you do." He licks his lips and picks up his menu. "Go ahead, I'll find something quick."

"Sam, I can wait—"

"No, you go ahead," he orders. "I'll find something."

Well, that wasn't gentle. Feeling defeated, I turn to the server. "I'll have the lasagna, please."

"Sure thing. Do you want that with marinara or Bolognese?"

"Marinara, please."

She writes it down, then looks at Sam. "And for you, sir?"

"The pesto chicken, please." He hands her the menu. "And can we order a bottle of wine?"

My eyebrows shoot up. "A whole bottle?"

"Why not? Professor St. James set us up."

"Our wine list is right there." The server points to a leather-bound menu on the table. "I'll go put your orders in while you decide."

Sam's eyes flick to the wine list, so I grab it. "What kind do you like?" I ask.

"Doesn't matter to me. Whatever you want."

I give him an apathetic stare before returning to peruse the menu. At the bottom of the list, I find an interesting caption. "It says here Thursday is two for one. If we buy any bottle at regular price, we get a bottle of the house wine for free." I lift my excited gaze to Sam's.

"What's the house wine?"

"Chianti."

"So let's get a white wine to have with dinner. That way, we're getting a little of both."

I nod. "Good idea."

After ordering our wine, the server delivers it rather quickly, and Sam and I raise our glasses in a toast.

"Here's to our success as study group tutors," Sam says. "Without us, many of our classmates would've changed majors already."

I chuckle. "Cheers, then." Clinking our glasses together, I take my first sip of a crisp and refreshing Chardonnay. "Mmm. This is good."

"It is," Sam says before tipping his glass up to finish off his pour.

"Whoa, slow down. We've got a whole dinner to get through."

"Yeah, and another entire bottle of wine." An excited grin takes over his face. "Don't worry, I took an Uber here."

I shake my head. "Okay, whatever you say." There's no way I'm drinking two bottles of wine in one dinner.

"So, Brynn," Sam says as he pours himself another glass. "How have you been?"

The nonchalance of his question catches me off guard. "Um, fine." The lie tastes bad on my tongue, but I don't want to get into all the angst I went through in the past week. "You?"

"All right, I suppose." He lifts his glass to the smirk on his lips. "Hard to tell when I don't see my nemesis all week."

A blush rises in my cheeks, so I pick up my glass. "Why would that make a difference?"

"Well, without you to argue with, I can't tell whether or not I've lost my snark."

I laugh, nearly spitting out my wine. "I'm sure your snark is intact."

"How can you tell?"

"Hmmm. We need something to argue about." I purse my lips and fold my arms. This is the perfect test. I'll show Lisa that Sam and I would never work as a couple, because we can't ever agree on anything. I just have to pick the right topics. "We've already established that you're wrong about DC being better than Marvel, so…"

Sam hangs his head as his shoulders bob with laughter.

"Ah, I've got it. How do you feel about pineapple on pizza?"

His face scrunches with playful curiosity as he shakes his head. "I'm going to go with no way. Fruit doesn't have any place on my pizza. What do you say?"

Well, that backfired. "The same," I say quietly.

"Give me another."

I take a long draw of my wine as I think. "Do you read?"

"Are you asking if I like to read?"

I nod.

"Yeah, actually, I do."

"Okay, physical book or e-book?"

A sly grin spreads across his face. "That's actually a harder question. E-books are nice in terms of convenience, but nothing can ever replace the way a physical book feels in your hands, you know? The sound of the pages when you turn them, the smell…"

My mouth falls open as I listen to him. His words combined with the whimsy in his eyes make this moment surreal. He's describing exactly how I feel about reading. I need more wine.

"It's kind of magical," he says with a shrug.

The goosebumps rising on my skin dissipate when the server brings our food.

"Here you go. Bon appetit," she says.

I tilt my glass up and finish the last of my wine, a warmth spreading through me. When I lower my head, I find Sam staring. "What?" I ask.

Shaking his head, he says nothing as he refills my glass. He then empties the bottle into his own glass. "Should we go ahead and drink the free one, too?"

"Sure, *wine* not?" I instantly cringe as the words leave my mouth. "Sorry, that was terrible."

He chuckles. "I wouldn't say terrible, but it wasn't *grape*."

His pun eases the pain of my own. "Thanks."

"Let's eat," Sam says, holding up his fork.

We dig in and, as usual, the food is delicious. Both of us are lost in flavor heaven, not saying a word as we take bite after bite of Italian bliss. I know Sam feels the way I do, because I hear his soft groans of delight.

After a few minutes, he wipes his mouth with his napkin, and picks up his glass. "This is fucking great."

I shake my head. "Eloquent way to put it."

"Well, what would you say, then?"

"Probably something like 'this is delicious.'" I give him a pointed look. "Something with less 'fucks' in it."

Sam laughs. "So, you don't give a fuck?"

"Only when it counts," I say, and lift my wineglass to my lips.

He stares at me for a moment before clearing his throat. "Okay, give me another debate topic."

"What?"

"We never found anything to argue about, remember? I'm still wondering about my snark."

"All right, let me think." While I do, I sip my wine. I need something that will undoubtedly end in an argument. Something with a wide variety of answers so we couldn't possibly agree. As I reach my decision, I finish off my glass and set it on the table. "Okay, favorite Disney movie."

"Ooh, that's a good one." Sam crinkles his forehead as he pops open our bottle of Chianti and fills my glass. "Are we talking original animation, or Pixar?"

"Either or."

He thinks for a good while, finishing his Chardonnay with a deep sigh. "You're going to laugh."

"I promise I won't," I say, making an "X" over my heart.

"*The Princess and the Frog.*"

My breath catches in my throat. Did I hear him right? All my readied arguments fall to the floor in pieces, as I stare at my recent enemy who just claimed *my* favorite Disney movie as his own.

"Before you say anything, let me make my points." He runs a hand through his hair. "I watched it a lot with my little sister. She loved it from the first time she saw it, so it was always on whenever she was home. I've seen it so many times, I know all the songs by heart."

I bite down on my lower lip, unsure of whether I want him to continue or not. So, I grab my wineglass and let the bold Chianti do its magic on my nerves.

"The more I watched it, though, the more I came to really love the story." Sam watches his fork as he twirls it in his side of spaghetti. "I mean, Tiana and Naveen didn't start off on good terms. They were two opposites who came from different worlds so at the end, you knew they really were in love because they had seen each other's truest sides. They had to work for it, you know?"

When he lifts his gaze from his food, his vulnerability astounds me. There were no lies in what he said. It was the honest truth, and a beautiful way to view my favorite movie.

He groans, leaning back in his chair and picking up his wine. "Go ahead, tear me to shreds with your argument."

I feign a frustrated sigh. "I'd love to, but I can't."

"What? Why?"

"Because you've given me another reason to love my favorite Disney movie."

A smile slowly spreads across his lips, like my words sink in, and his face lights up. "Yeah?"

God, I love that look of his. "I don't know that I ever dissected it like you, but there's something about that movie I've always loved."

Without taking his eyes off me, Sam tilts his glass to mine, making the tiniest clinking sound. "Well, then cheers."

"To what, this time?"

"To me not needing my snark, anymore."

Heat rushes to my cheeks, and this time, I know it's not from the wine.

We finish our dinner, and the second bottle of wine with Sam asking for the check shortly thereafter. Our gift card more than covers our bill, so we both chip in a good amount for a tip. On our way to the door, Sam hands me the gift card.

"What's this for?" I ask.

He shrugs. "There's, like, twelve bucks left on it. That's enough to pay for you and Lisa to come have a girls' dessert night, or something. Just don't order the coffee cake."

"Why not?"

"Because it was labeled as *cinnamon* coffee cake."

A lightness rises in my chest that he made sure to check the ingredients. "Thanks. That's *sweet* of you." I give him a sideways glance.

He shakes his head. "Do you always speak in puns when you're drunk?"

"Who said I'm drunk?" I ask, but as I turn to face him, I trip over my heels.

Sam catches me by the elbow, righting me and throwing his other hand around my waist to steady me. "Whoa, easy killer."

When I get my bearings, I look into those deep brown eyes that have captivated me from day one. The twinkling lights reflect in his irises, making them sparkle. Behind the sparkle though, is an intensity. It's one I've seen before, and one I quite enjoy. It's passionate, and hot, and makes me squeeze my thighs together.

To Hell with just being friends.

I lick my lips. "Take me home, Sam."

He lets out a shaky breath. "Sure thing. I can have the Uber drop you off first, and—"

"No, Sam," I say confidently, running my hand over his shoulder. "Take me to *your* home."

# CHAPTER 35

SAM OPENS THE CAR door for me, and I slide across the backseat to make room for him. As soon as he's at my side, I lay my hand on his thigh and squeeze. I watch his Adam's apple bob.

"Buckle up," the driver says, but it falls on deaf ears.

The second I turn my chin toward Sam, his mouth collides with mine in a kiss that leaves me breathless. It takes every ounce of self-restraint I have not to tear off his clothes, or to let him tear off mine. I want so badly to throw my leg over his lap. I want to ride him all the way home.

We make out for the duration of the Uber ride. When the car lurches to a stop, our driver looks less than enthused as he glares at us from the rearview mirror. We collect ourselves, thank him, and exit the car. He takes off as soon as the door closes.

"I don't think he was very happy with us," I say, biting my lip.

"He was probably jealous." Sam taps away at his phone, but tilts his head to give me a wink. "Besides, he's getting a good tip."

"That's nice of you."

Sam tucks his phone into his pocket, takes my hand, and yanks me to him. "Well, I've got to make up for what I'm about to do with you." He claims my mouth once again before tugging me up the stairs to his apartment.

As we ascend, the world spins. I have no idea how I make it up the steps without tripping, but as I wait for Sam to unlock the door, I have to brace myself on the wall. When Sam opens the door, I'm thankful he offers me his hand. Pulling me inside, he kicks the door shut.

Before I can think, his hands are on me, tearing off my coat. He nudges me backward until my ass hits the back of the couch, and he pins me against it with his hips, his growing erection pressing into my thigh. Our lips reconnect and the passion reignites. I throw my hands around his neck, keeping him close and losing a hand in his hair.

As the spinning stops briefly, I begin unbuttoning his shirt. The first button is so infinitesimally small that it slips from my fingers several times.

With a groan, Sam grabs my hand. "Here, let me," he says against my mouth, and finishes the rest of the buttons.

I slide the shirt over his taut shoulders and down his arms, my fingertips brushing his skin and burning for more.

He peppers kisses along my jaw and down my throat to nuzzle into the crook of my neck. His hands slip the straps of my dress down, so he can kiss across my collarbone.

As my head lolls back, the spinning returns, and I have to snap my head up.

Sam pulls back. "You okay?"

"Mhm." I nod, but halt when I feel like I'm going to fall over.

"Maybe we should stop."

I pout. "What? No. I don't want to stop."

I reach for him, but he grabs my wrist. His eyes narrow as they flick between mine.

"Sam," I breathe, dropping my gaze to his mouth. "Kiss me, please."

He huffs, still scrutinizing me, but doesn't make a move.

I bite down on my lower lip and thrust my chest out. "I need you."

With a shudder, he steps forward to pin me again. He cups the back of my head and wraps the other around my waist as if to steady me. His kiss is more tender now. The passion from a minute ago isn't there. It's still a great kiss, but it's different, like he's handling me with kid gloves.

Well, I'm not going for that kind of night. I want this to obliterate our friend-zone.

I push him backward until his back hits the door. The force of the collision makes him grunt, but his kiss doesn't waver. When I hike my leg up around his hip, he grips my ass firmly to keep me pressed against him, and the passion returns.

I'm moaning, groaning, and grinding my way toward an orgasm when suddenly, my body goes slack. I can't even hold my head up.

"Whoa, Brynn," Sam says, his voice full of concern as he holds me up.

I mumble something, but even I don't know what I'm trying to say. I simply fall into Sam's embrace, trusting him. The last thing I remember before the world goes black, is Sam telling me he'll take care of me.

And I believe him.


***


"Sam?" I say, though my voice is weak. My mouth and throat are so dry, I can't even swallow. As I sit up, I rub my eyes, trying to get them to focus in the muted sunlight streaming through the curtains. Scooting up to rest my back against the wall, I drop my gaze to the side table to see a glass of water and two aspirin tablets. I toss them back, exerting all my self-restraint to not chug the water. With a long exhale, I knock my head against the wall. I'm in Sam's bed.

Alone.

What happened last night? I remember most of it, though the end is a bit hazy. I know I told him to bring me home, and while I don't remember exactly what happened once we got here, I know it was getting hot and heavy. Did it get hotter and heavier? How far did we go?

I throw back the blanket, relieved but confused when I see I'm not wearing my dress. Instead, I'm clad in a pair of what seem to be Sam's sweatpants and a t-shirt. I don't remember putting these on. Did Sam undress and re-dress me?

Pulling the neckline of the t-shirt out, I dip my chin down to also see I'm still wearing my bra. Confusion washes over me. So, I didn't get naked, but I didn't put these clothes on either. What the hell went on here last night?

As if he hears my question, Sam strolls through the bedroom door with a mug in one hand and a plate in the other. His face lights up when he sees me. "Hey, you're awake."

"Yeah. I woke up a few minutes ago."

"That's good. I was afraid you'd sleep all day." He walks to the bed and takes a seat, setting the mug on the table and handing me the plate. "Here, I made you some toast. I figured you'd need something in your stomach before you take the..." His eyes drop to the side table. "Aspirin."

"Too late," I say, snatching the toast and taking several bites. "Thank you."

"You're welcome. There's coffee, too."

I groan as my stomach turns. "I don't know if I'm ready for that yet. Maybe the rest of the water first." I set down the half-eaten toast. "Sam, what happened last night?"

His mouth ticks up on one side. "You don't remember?"

"The details are kind of fuzzy after we got here."

"Ah, then allow me to fill in the missing pieces." He clears his throat. "You insisted that I bring you here, and who am I to turn down a beautiful woman's request?"

"Did we actually make out the whole ride home?"

He nods. "And the Uber driver wasn't too pleased."

"Ugh." I drop my face in my hands. "Then what happened?"

"Well..." He rubs the back of his neck. "We sort of threw ourselves at each other, but you got real woozy, so I put you in bed."

I lift my head, arching an eyebrow. "Is that how I got these?" I pinch the t-shirt fabric between my fingers. "Did you dress me?"

"Mhm. And let me tell you, getting you out of that dress and into those clothes was no easy feat."

"So, we didn't have sex?"

He shakes his head. "By the time I got you into those sweats, I was so tired, all I wanted to do was sleep. I mean, I laid here for a while to make sure you weren't going to stop breathing, or puke, or anything, but eventually, I fell asleep."

Appreciation blooms in my chest, radiating warmth through me.

"I didn't let go of you until I woke up this morning, and the only reason I got up was because I had to piss."

The warmth intensifies, no longer comforting but stifling instead. "Wait, we cuddled all night?"

"Well, yeah, basically."

"Dammit, Sam." I flop my head back to hit the wall, groaning in agony from the collision.

"What?"

"We should have had sex," I say authoritatively as I rub the back of my head.

His brow furrows to the point of his eyebrows touching. "Are you mad that I didn't fuck you while you were unconscious?"

"No, of course not. But I..." Squeezing my eyes shut, I cringe at what I'm about to say. "I wanted to get out of the friend-zone."

"The what?"

With a heavy sigh, I open my eyes to see even more confusion on his face. "After my cinnamon incident, you labeled us as friends, and it made me question my recent decisions."

"You mean calling off our arrangement?" He waits for me to nod before his lips quirk up. "Brynn, if you wanted to have sex, all you had to do was ask. I don't care what we label each other, I will always be up for naked time with you."

I perk up, my shoulders relaxing and my chest loosening. "Really?"

"Really. Just because we're not enemies anymore doesn't mean we can't still hook up. It's just sex."

The lightness in my chest disappears, a weight settling in. Clearing the hurdle of being friends with benefits was one thing. Now, we have the issue of keeping feelings out of the picture. "We're not supposed to cuddle," I say quietly.

"Brynn, I didn't really have a choice. You weren't exactly awake."

"Yeah, but you didn't have to hold me all night, or dress me, or make me fucking toast."

"What's wrong with toast?"

"All of that isn't what this"–I wave my hand between us–"is about."

Sam straightens up, folding his arms. "What do you think *this* is, then?"

I look at him like he asked the dumbest question in the world. "It's an arrangement. An agreement." I huff and get up from the bed, wobbling on my feet as I pace the length of it. "We agreed this would be purely physical, no feelings, and here you are acting like you really care about me."

A flash of hurt whips through his eyes, but he blinks and it's gone. "So, what was I supposed to do?"

"Leave me in my dress. Let me sleep on the couch. Offer me aspirin, and coffee, and food *after* I wake up, not preemptively."

"Oh, right." He rolls his eyes. "Because that wouldn't make me a dick at all."

I stop pacing, looking down at him sternly. "This isn't about being a dick or not. This is about setting boundaries. You're treating this like a relationship when it isn't."

"Isn't it, though?"

My eyes widen as my breath catches.

Sam licks his hips, flicking his gaze to the side. "I mean, we're doing all the things people do in a relationship. Why not own it?"

"Because that's not what it is." My jaw quivers as I speak.

He stands, stepping forward to close the gap between us. His eyes flash as he stares down at me. "Then what do you call it?"

With a deep swallow, I say, "Two people scratching an itch."

His mouth curls into a smirk as he runs his knuckle down my cheek. "An itch I've had since July," he says softly.

Did he say what I think he said? I back away. I'm almost too afraid to ask, but I squeak out, "What did you say?"

Sam grabs my biceps, holding me in place. "I said I've had this itch since July, Brynn. Ever since our night in Grand Junction, I've done nothing but think about you. You've been all I've wanted for six months."

I can't say anything. All I can do is breathe, and it's shaky at best.

He lets go of me, turning to the window, and sighs. "When I walked into O-Chem that first day and saw you, I thought my wildest dreams had come true. Then, after our initial conversation, I knew I was fucked." He runs a hand through his hair. "I never thought you'd end up hating me, though."

I squeeze my eyes shut as I wince. "Sam, I…"

"Don't, Brynn. You don't have to apologize. I was the one who wasn't honest in the first place, so I only have myself to blame." He turns around and shoves his hands in his pockets. "But I wanted to make it up to you. I thought maybe if we spent more time together, if you saw the real me again, that maybe we could have what we had after the Mud Down. Which is why I volunteered to help with the study group."

My eyes pop open, along with my mouth. "I thought you wanted to get ahead for the internship."

"At first, I did. It's the whole reason I transferred down here, after all." He hikes his shoulders to his ears. "But I'm not applying for it."

"Why not? You're brilliant. You would be a shoe-in."

"Yeah, maybe, but you deserve it. After what you told me about your dream of saving the environment, I couldn't fathom trying to take it from you, even if I thought I had a chance."

Disbelief spills from my lips in a forced chuckle. "I can't believe you would do that for me." My eyes search the room as my forehead crinkles. "Wait. Were you going to use that as leverage to get me to date you?"

"No." Panic streaks across his face. "I would never do that. I just wanted you to have what was rightfully yours."

So, then what was his angle? "And what about the fuck-buddy thing? Was that in your master plan to get me to like you again?"

"No. Never in a million years could I have planned that." He laughs, raising his gaze to the ceiling. "But I knew there was something here. I could feel it whenever we worked on the presentations, but I had no idea how to bring it up. I kept waiting for an organic opportunity, and finally got one on Halloween." He tilts his head from side to side. "Though that wasn't exactly what I had thought was going to happen."

"I don't think either of us thought *that* would happen." My cheeks heat as I remember the night.

"Afterward, I was even more hung up on you, and I didn't want to lose the momentum I'd stirred, but the fuck-buddy idea was a spur of the moment thing, I swear. You tried to back out of our Saturday meetings, and I panicked. I never thought you'd go for it, but I'm glad you did."

"Me too."

Sam steps to me and takes my hands in his. "Brynn, I never meant for this to escalate the way it did. All I wanted was to be near you, to spend time with you."

My eyes well with tears as I stare up at him. All the things I thought I knew about this man were wrong, and all the things I convinced myself weren't real, were. "I'm such an idiot," I choke out, dipping my head.

"No, you're not." He tucks a knuckle under my chin and lifts my head so our gazes meet. "You're incredible, intelligent, headstrong, passionate, beautiful, to name a few."

I swallow deeply, a small smile curling on my lips as a tear breaks free and rolls down my cheek. "A few what?"

Sam wipes it away. "A few reasons why I love you."

I jerk my head back. "You what?"

"I love you, Brynn Erlenmeyer. I fell in love with you in July, and haven't stopped for one minute since."

My heart pounds hard and fast as my eyes flick between his. He's in love with me? He's been in love with me for six months? How the hell did I not know? I truly am an idiot.

But I won't be anymore.

Words tickle the tip of my tongue. The same ones that describe the feelings I formed in July. God, how I fought these words with all my might for months. I didn't want to believe them. Couldn't fathom how I could be feeling them after such a short time with Sam.

Now, they're stronger than ever before, and I can't hold them in any longer. "I love you, too."

"I know."

I scoff. "Jerk," I say, playfully smacking his arm.

He wraps his arms around me, pulling me to him and laying his lips on mine in a tender kiss. This time, we claim each other. It's not one-sided, it's mutual.

Sam loves me.

Though, he may be challenging, argumentative, and irritating to no end, I love this man with all my heart. With our muddy history behind us, the trail ahead is much drier as we step forward together.

# Epilogue

"You got this," Sam whispers in my ear.

"I know." Taking off at a full sprint, I leap mid-step to scramble up the vertical wall. My muddy shoes slip against the surface, but I grab the top and hoist myself up. Once I'm settled, I wave for Sam to follow.

With a huge grin, he runs toward the wall. He barely even has to jump as tall as he is, and within seconds, he joins me at the top. We sit, straddling the wall, facing each other.

"Nice to see you again," Sam says with a wink before studying our perch. "Isn't this where it all started?"

"Yep. You were sitting there, and I was here when you held out your hand and said, 'I'm Sam.'" I use my deepest voice to impersonate him, but it's still several pitches too high.

"I don't really sound like that, do I?"

"Thankfully, no. If you did, none of this would have happened."

A mischievous grin takes over his face. "Think of all the trouble I could've saved myself."

"Shut up," I say, playfully smacking his chest.

He grabs my hand, holding it to his heart. "Best trouble I ever could've asked for."

I roll my eyes but let them settle on his. "I'm glad you're here."

"Me too." As he pats my leg, crusty mud flakes off my pants. "I'd kiss you, but you have a little something right here." He reaches up to smear mud down my cheek.

Yelping, I jerk away as he laughs.

"Come on, you two!" Lisa yells. "No one wants to watch your PDA!"

Thankfully, I'm covered in mud because I know my cheeks are red.

Sam and I jump down from the wall, and join our friends in our jog to the next obstacle. This is the biggest group I've ever done the Mud Down with. Lisa, of course, is here, but she brought Brent along, and he seems to be enjoying himself so far. Jackie and Hannah surprised me by wanting to come again. Even Walt drove down from Wyoming to join in.

The seven of us complete obstacle after obstacle until we finish the race. To my utter disbelief, Lisa actually joins all the guys as they rush through the electroshock wires at the end. Hannah, Jackie, and I meet them all on the other side. I can't wait to see the pictures of their faces later.

As we collect our newest t-shirts, I can't help but notice how different this feels. It's the same shirt we get every year, the same fabric, the same fit, and yet, the sensation of having it in my hands is better than ever before. I don't know how to describe it.

Until I look at Sam.

He's the difference. He's the reason this accomplishment feels so much more incredible than any other year. We've completed our first Mud Down together as a couple. He was right next to me the whole time either cheering me on or offering to help if I needed it. Though, I didn't need it much. He was my partner through the whole thing. He never tried to one-up me, didn't sulk when I completed an obstacle without him. In fact, he high-fived me every time I did.

Because he's proud of who I am.

As we head off to get our finisher beers, Sam leans over and gives me a peck on the cheek. "I'm going to grab our bag so we can take a picture. Be right back."

I sigh contentedly as I watch him jog away.

"He's still swoon-worthy?" Lisa whispers to me.

I nod. "Absolutely."

"Well, like I said, I've always liked him." She wraps an arm around my shoulders. "I'm happy for you, Brynn."

"Thanks," I say, resting my head on her shoulder. "It's been a crazy seven months. I mean, we went from not being able to stand sharing the same space, to being in love, to living together."

"Don't forget working together, too."

"Yeah, I still can't believe Professor St. James opened up another intern spot just for him."

We step forward to order our beers before stepping aside to wait on the rest of our group.

"How do you know Sam wasn't her first pick, and the second spot wasn't for you?" Lisa arches an eyebrow.

I give her a pointed look. "Yeah, right."

With a laugh, Lisa cracks open beer and tilts it toward mine. "Cheers."

"We should wait for Sam."

A sly grin spreads across her face. "He's already here," she says, jutting her chin behind me.

Confused, I turn around to find Sam kneeling in the dirt. His adoring smile blinds me. That's when I notice something small in his hand. I gasp, my hand flying to my mouth, my eyes immediately tearing up.

"Brynn," Sam says. "You know I love you, right?"

I nod, unable to speak.

"And from what I've gathered in my own research, you love me, too."

A laugh bursts from my lips, but tears accompany it. I wipe them away, smearing the mud further across my face.

Sam keeps smiling. "This may seem sort of sudden, considering our rocky start, but I've never been surer of anything in my life. I know without a doubt, I want to spend the rest of my days making you happy, and building our future together."

I'm making all kinds of faces to stop the happy tears from streaming down my face, but it's all in vain. They slip out, one by one.

"So, Brynn Erlenmeyer…" He swallows, taking a moment to compose himself. "Will you please make me the luckiest man on the planet by being my wife?"

"Yes," I choke out.

With the biggest self-satisfied grin on his face, Sam stands and slides a rose-gold silicone ring onto my finger. "Don't worry, you'll get a real one later. I didn't want to risk losing it in the mud."

"It's perfect," I say, and throw my arms around his neck, pulling his lips to mine.

Cheers and applause go up all around us as we seal our commitment with a tender, albeit muddy, kiss.

Sam pulls back and presses his forehead to mine. "Oh, and I'm absolutely taking your name."

I chuckle. "We can hand out flasks as our party favors."

"I love you so much, Brynn Erlenmeyer."

"I love you, too, Sam Mudboy."

The End

# Preview of TBD



## Chapter 1 – Holden

I wince as the chime of the door splits my head in two. Pressing my fingers to my throbbing temple, I step through the doorway of Caffiends, my favorite local coffee house. I welcome the cool air-conditioned air blowing across my body. Walking four blocks doesn't seem like much, but when you do it in the heat of August in Denver, Colorado, it's excruciating. Especially at eleven in the morning amidst the throes of an immense hangover. As I search the cafe for Leon, the room bustles with Saturday morning business, but I manage to find him sitting at a table in the far corner.

He waves me over when he sees me. "Hey, man. Glad to see you're alive," he says as I sit down.

"Barely," I croak.

"Well, here." With a smirk, Leon slides a mug toward me. "Start with some coffee. Nice and black, just the way your boring ass likes it."

"Thanks." I lift the mug to my lips, taking a second to inhale the delicious aroma. It awakens my senses, if only for a moment. I take a sip. "And just what do you mean boring? Did I, or did I not do shots with you last night?"

"Sorry, maybe vanilla would be a better description."

I roll my eyes, taking another sip of my coffee.

"I mean, just look at what you're wearing." He floats a hand up and down, gesturing to my outfit. "A Spongebob t-shirt? Your twenty-six for fuck's sake."

Smoothing down my shirt, I scoff. "It's ironic."

"Moronic is more like it."

"Fuck off." I lean back in my chair, folding my leg to rest my ankle on my knee. I jut my chin in his direction. "What exactly would you call your look, then?"

With a smug smirk, Leon runs his fingers down the lapel of his navy blazer, pushing it back to slide his hands into the pockets of his perfectly creased slacks. "Sophisticated."

"Sounds like complicated if you ask me."

"Good thing no one asked you, then."

I snort a laugh. "You're just jealous it takes me five minutes to get ready, instead of an hour like you."

He arches an eyebrow. "Jealous? Of a librarian?"

"Hey, man. Say what you will, but my life is pretty sweet." My playful mood dims as my shoulders sag. "Well, at least it was."

A sympathetic expression slides over his face, but he doesn't say anything.

"Aren't you supposed to tell me everything will be all right, or some other comforting bullshit? Isn't that what best friends are for?"

Leon's face twists into wry amusement. "That's not my style." He claps me on the back. "Helping drown your sorrows when you're hurting by shoving shots down your throat, that's more my method."

"Ugh." I grimace as Leon's slap rattles my brain around in my skull. "Do you have to help so loudly?"

He laughs again, this time squeezing my shoulder. "Maybe the pain in your head will make you forget about that pain in the ass."

I give him a dry look. "You mean Rosalind?" Even though her name is like a thorn in my heart, I still feel the need to defend her. Slightly. "You really shouldn't talk about her like that."

"Why not? You'd rather me praise the bitch who broke off your three-year relationship after moving thousands of miles away?"

I sigh dejectedly. "No, no need for praise, but you don't have to be so crass."

"Crass?" Leon throws his head back, almost cackling. "Oh, man. I can see breaking you from her curse is going to take some work. Last night was just a stepping stone."

I groan and drop my head into my hand. "Well, then it must have been slippery."

"Speaking of slippery, what happened with you and that chick?"

Taking a sip of my coffee, I lick my lips. "I don't know what you mean."

"Don't give me that bullshit," Leon says, leaning forward in his chair. "You know damn well what I mean."

Boy, do I ever. My mouth curls into a smile as snippets of my night flash before my eyes. The bar. The shots. The beautiful dark-haired, tattooed vixen that I chatted up. Our whirlwind Uber ride back to my apartment. The amazing, mind-blowing, passionate sex. I feel the front of my pants tighten as I picture her riding me.

I blink myself back to the present and clear my throat. "I don't kiss and tell."

"Oh, come on." He scoffs, flopping against his chair-back and folding his arms. "Fuck."

"Do you really want me to tell you the ins and outs of me having sex?"

Leon feigns a gag. "No, but you can tell me about her without describing you. I mean, you've got to give me something, Holden. Especially since that woman you took home was the stark opposite of Rosalind."

My mouth ticks up on one side, but falls quickly as my ex-girlfriend pops into my mind. I close my eyes and picture her green irises looking back at me. The way her cream-colored blouses would contrast her tanned skin, and the sound her heels made on the tile. Her perfectly high-lighted hair always pulled back in a bun or twist. She was so well put together, it was amazing.

Until she stomped on my heart.

I open my eyes, but stare into my coffee instead of looking at Leon. "That was the whole point of the night, right? To find someone who *wasn't* Rosa?"

"Mhm. And it was your idea, not mine, so talk."

I take a long sip of my coffee as I glance around our table to make sure no one is within earshot. I lean over and say quietly, "It was the best sex I've ever had."

"Ha! Yeah, son!" Leon punches me in the arm not so playfully. "How were her tits?"

I feel a burning sensation in my face. "Dude!"

Leon rolls his eyes. "Man, what happened to you? We used to be able to shoot the shit, not giving a fuck what anyone around us thought. Then, Rosalind came into the picture, and you changed."

"Well, excuse me if I don't want anyone in here thinking I'm some kind of sexist pervert."

"You mean like me?" He arches an eyebrow.

"Exactly like you."

Chuckling, Leon turns his head from side to side. The cafe has cleared out quite a bit, leaving the tables surrounding us empty. "No one's around, Holden. You can speak freely."

With a groan, I take one more look to ensure he's right, and reluctantly swallow my morals. "We had sex four times."

"My man!" Leon holds his hand up for a high-five, but when I shake my head, he lowers his arm. "I didn't even know you had that in you."

"Ha, me neither. Rosa and I never had sex more than once a week."

Leon shifts in his chair, his eyes lit up in eager excitement. "So, how did it feel to get laid four-hundred percent more than normal?"

I twirl my mug on the table, watching the dark coffee swirl around. "Really good."

"Sounds better than good, I'd say."

My mouth ticks up. "Okay, it was pretty fucking incredible." For more reasons than just the sex, but I know Leon well enough to know he won't humor my romanticism.

"So, when are you going to hook up with her again?"

The slight smile on my face disappears. "Never."

"What do you mean never? If the sex was that great, I'd be making plans to booty-call her in advance."

"Can't booty-call someone you don't have a phone number for."

"You didn't get her number?" He folds his arms. "Did you even get her name?"

I nod. "Mara."

Leon arches his eyebrows as if asking for me to elaborate.

"She didn't say much else." I hike my shoulders up. "She was twenty-four and had recently moved here."

"Didn't say much, or your drunk ass didn't listen?"

I furrow my brow as I think. "She and I made small talk at the bar. Nothing too interesting, though." The crease in my forehead deepens and I rub my hand along the stubble on my jaw. "We didn't discuss work, or personal life at all."

"She wasn't a talker?"

"Kind of hard to talk when your tongue is rammed down someone's throat."

"Nice." A knowing grin spreads across Leon's face, but falls. "You two didn't talk this morning?"

"She wasn't around to talk to."

His eyes widen. "She skipped out on you?"

"Mhm." I nod lethargically. "I woke up this morning to an empty bed. No note. No phone number. Nothing."

"Yikes."

"I know. I mean, how do you ditch someone so easily after such incredible sex?"

"Incredible for you," Leon says out of the corner of his mouth.

"What was that?"

He takes a deep breath like he's bolstering himself. "You said it was the best sex *you* ever had. Maybe it wasn't for her."

My mouth drops open, but I can't speak. I let my gaze fall to the table as I grip my coffee mug tighter. Could it have been so one-sided? I don't see how. We went through multiple positions, several of which had her screaming my name in ecstasy. I know because I made sure to ask if she came. Did she lie? Was it all faked?

I shake my head, smacking Leon's shoulder with the back of my hand. "You're a dick."

"Hey, I'm just trying to keep your ego from over-inflating." He holds his hands up in defense. "But maybe I'm wrong."

Nodding my head, I chew on my lower lip. "She could have just been embarrassed. I mean, a one-night stand isn't exactly something you boast about."

"Unless you're me." Leon grins, hiking a shoulder to his ear.

I chuckle, but a lump forms in my gut. "But why didn't she leave her phone number?"

Leon sighs. "Look, Holden. Last night you went into that bar to do two things: get drunk, and get laid. You succeeded. Be happy." He leans forward, squeezing my shoulder. "Besides, were you really into that girl, or was she just the complete antithesis of Rosalind?"

"Good word." I smirk, but it's stilted. "I guess you're right. All I wanted was to strike Rosa from my memory for the night, and Mara did just that." I picture Mara's dark clothing. Her nose piercing. The eyeliner surrounding her sparkling brown eyes. The seductive crease of her cleavage peeking out from her low-cut top. I shake my head to clear it. "Yeah, that's all she was. I mean, she and I would never fit in each other's lives, I'm sure."

"There's the rational thinking Holden Hayes I know." Leon tips his mug back, emptying it. "Now, let's talk about where we're going out tonight."

Chapter 2 – Mara

"Mara? Is that you, sweetie?"

"Yes, Tía Ana," I answer as I gingerly shut the front door.

Ana comes around the corner from the kitchen, wiping her hands on her floral-print apron. Her wrinkles deepen on her foreheard as she scrutinizes me. "I hope it was a fun night."

"Yeah…" I kick off my shoes and tuck them under the bench next to the door. "How is she today?"

Ana sighs. "She had a rough morning. Asked for your father a lot. She's napping, now."

A pang of guilt rips through my chest. The nurses don't come on Sundays, so it's up to us to care for Mamá, but Ana shouldn't be the one tending to her, I should. But what was I doing instead? Sneaking out of my one-night-stand's house and performing an extended walk of shame at nine in the morning.

"Sorry, Tía Ana."

She shakes her head, holding up her hand. "No, Mija. Don't be."

A small smile quirks onto my lips. I may not be her daughter, but she's always treated me like one.

"You're a young woman, and you should be out having fun. I'm perfectly capable of taking care of my sister." She narrows her eyes, a smirk crossing her face. "But these late nights better stop when you start school."

I drag my finger across my heart in an "X" motion. "Promise."

The smirk grows into a smile as she waves me toward her. "Come on, there's leftover apple empanadas if you're hungry." She pats my back as I pass her and enter the kitchen. "When do classes begin?"

"The week after next, but I only have classes on Mondays, Wednesdays, and Fridays."

"What will you do with all your free time?" Ana shoots me a knowing look and hands me a plate.

As I pile up empanadas, my mouth waters "Probably work." I don't even wait to sit down before biting into the flaky pastry crust. Ana's cooking is quite literally the best. Breakfast is by far my favorite, but since moving in with her four years ago, I've always had a satisfied belly.

Her brow crinkles. "Working? I thought you quit that job."

"I did," I mumble through a mouthful of cinnamon apple filling before swallowing. Delicious. "But I'm still going to need some money. If anything, to help you with bills and groceries."

Ana frowns and puts her hands on her hips. "Now you listen here, bribona. I told you once we got the government assistance money for your mamá, you were to go back to school. That's what I want you focusing on. I don't care about the bills. Your Tío Luis and I have made our payments for years before you came along, and we can do it again."

I press my lips into a flat line as I nod. Ana always tries to be stern with me, but I know she's a big softie on the inside. "Thank you, Tía." I take another bite, chewing it slowly before asking, "What if I just did something super part-time? That way I could have spending money for myself."

She quirks an eyebrow at me.

"You think Tío Luis would pay for me to go out with my friends?"

Ana laughs, shaking her head. "No, he probably wouldn't." She sighs. "Okay, get a job if you really want to." She walks to me and takes my hands in hers. "But if it gets to be too much, you can quit. I want you to succeed in school. Nothing is more important."

I close my eyes as she presses a kiss to my forehead.

"Phew, you smell like a trough," she says, pinching her nose. "Go shower."

Pulling my black cabbie hat tighter to hide my surely tangled mess of hair, I scoot past Ana toward my room, my cheeks burning.

Inside my room, I take two steps toward my bathroom before flopping onto my bed. Now that my stomach is full, exhaustion hits me. It was a late night, an early morning, and I already took a long walk. I'm beat.

I throw my arm over my eyes, and flashes of the night play behind my eyelids. The bar. The drinks. Holden's tongue down my throat.

I shudder, popping my eyes open.

Okay, so it was a fun night. *Really* fun. I hadn't gone out with the intention of hooking up with anyone, but Holden just sort of happened. I don't even remember how we started talking.

Furrowing my brow, I play back the night step-by-step.

It was my turn to buy the round. As I waited at the bar, some guy in a cheap looking suit tried to hit on me. It didn't work, though. I remember spouting off something snarky, and him telling me it was my loss.

Yeah, right.

After the suit left, Holden leaned over to apologize. Apparently, the suit was his friend. That struck me as odd. Not only because I hadn't noticed anyone sitting there, but also because he didn't look anything like his friend. Loafers peeked out of the bottom of his khakis, and he had a gray cardigan on over his shirt.

What did the shirt say? I giggle as I recall it. *I hate two things; t-shirts and irony.*

I don't remember much between that moment and what felt like a few minutes later when we were making out in a booth. I know we talked. I can't remember what about, but I know it was easy. Holden had this air about him that relaxed me, made me comfortable.

I have no idea why, though. Maybe it had to do with how many drinks I'd had. Or maybe it was his warm smile.

A tingle flutters through me as I picture it.

I shake my head. Whatever it was, it worked. We made out for I-don't-know-how-long before he invited me back to his place. Or maybe I asked him to take me home? Fuck, I don't know. All I know is once we got there, it was on.

My eyelids flutter shut as I let the events of the night transpire in my memory.

Holden spun me around to pin me against the door as he kissed every inch of bare skin he could find. His hot breath cascaded down my throat every time he whispered my name. He took off my clothes one piece at time at a pace so painstakingly slow, I thought I would explode.

It was so methodical, like every movement had a purpose. A risqué purpose.

When he had me down to my underwear, he picked me up and carried me to his bedroom. I remember thinking how hot that was. I squirmed, rubbing my thighs together as I anticipated glimpsing the muscles that lifted me effortlessly.

I didn't get what I expected, though.

No washboard abs or rippling biceps. No corded forearms. No pecs I could bounce quarters off of.

I'd be lying if I said I wasn't a little disappointed, but it's not like Holden was flabby. He was lean, but still muscular in all the right places. His stomach was flat, just undefined, and I know his arms were strong because he picked me up like I weighed nothing. The body under the cardigan wasn't bad, but I had hoped to see those V-shaped muscles that lead to his...

I bite my lip.

Talk about not getting what I expected. All those romance novels I read as a teenager led me to believe the best sex came from a ripped dude, so when I saw Holden naked, my hopes dipped. Boy, was I ever wrong.

What Holden may have lacked in the muscle department, he made up for with his cock. And man, did he know how to use it. Just thinking about it now has my heart racing and a familiar ache building between my legs.

Sliding my hand down my stomach, I dip into my pants. I wiggle my fingers into my underwear and slip them along my seam, wetting them so I can glide them over my clit. I picture Holden above me. His intense brown eyes locked onto mine as he thrust into me again and again. The pressure builds surprisingly quick. I must be more turned on than I thought.

With my other hand, I tweak one of my hardened nipples and think about how good Holden's tongue felt as he swirled it on my breast. That magic tongue of his.

I think about all the things we did last night. And we did *all* the things. I don't know if there was a place his tongue or fingers didn't touch, and I'm perfectly okay with that. He tended to my needs, ensuring I came every time. He was sensual and passionate, but also masculine. Holden did everything right, and even now, in my fantasy, he's doing it all right again.

My crest hits all too soon when the deep rumble of his voice echoes in my consciousness, *Mara.*

A whimper escapes me as I shudder with release. When my ragged breathing settles, returning to normal, and my heart slows, I open my eyes. "That's going to be a handy new trick."

The idea puts a smile on my face, but it quickly fades as a sourness creeps up the back of my throat, and I remember why I went out in the first place last night.

Alicia and Everly wanted me to formulate a plan on how to win my ex-boyfriend back. They made some convincing arguments as to why Az and I should be together. I'd be lying if I said I didn't sort of agree. I'm just not sure it's what I want.

With a groan, I grimace. Is going home with a random guy and fucking him five times what I want, though? It's certainly not the way to another man's heart. Az definitely won't take me back if he finds out I'm with someone else.

Have I fucked everything up?I take a deep, steadying breath. It was one time. Holden and I aren't dating. Hell, we can't even booty-call each other because we never exchanged numbers. It's not like this will ever happen again. Everything will be okay.

Unless I keep masturbating while picturing Holden between my legs.

"Ugh," I sigh, slapping my palm over my face. "I need to shower."

In the bathroom, I'm not surprised to see my makeup smeared across my face. Black eyeliner runs down my cheek and my mascara has created dark rings around my eyes, making it look like I haven't slept in weeks. My lipstick is long gone, but that probably happened before I even left the bar.

No wonder Aunt Ana frowned at me.

Laughing at myself, I finger-comb my long, black hair, the fading blue streak catching my eye as I do. Time for a touch up. Maybe a different color? Purple would be fun.

# Also by Christine

Because of Blake : https://a.co/d/5mFhtEN
Love Hops : https://a.co/d/295bogt

# Acknowledgements

Third time's a charm! Publishing this book was infinitely easier than my other two, but that's not to say it didn't come with its trials and tribulations. I cannot, nor will I ever be able to do this on my own. I am so grateful for all the support I receive, and I would personally like to thank the following:

**To my loving, supportive husband:**

Thank you for continuing to read my books, even though it has become abundantly clear you are not a romance reader. I appreciate the support you have given me, and I thank the future you for the support I know will come.

**To my children:**

Thank you for being some of the best kids I have ever known (and I'm not just saying that because I'm your mom). I love you both so very much. Thank you for cheering on your mom when she was feeling down.

**To my awesome critique partners, Shayna Astor and Tara Brodbeck:**

I feel like I'm on repeat when I say that you two are the best writing partners I could ever ask for. I have grown so much over the years of working with you, and I cannot wait to see what we accomplish in the future. Thank you for always being up to reading for me. Thank you for your invaluable advice. And thank you for being amazing friends.

**To my wonderful writing group:**

Thank you for keeping me accountable every week!

**To my fantastic editors, Mackenzie and D.P.:**

Thank you for your continued hard work and dedication to make my books better each time. I appreciate your advice and guidance.

Thank you **Coffin Print Designs** for my gorgeous cover!

**To my ARC team:**

Thank you for your support before the book was even released! I appreciate you taking the time to read and review it so the world can get a glimpse. You give authors our start, and we wouldn't get very far without you!

**And, most importantly, to my readers:**

It doesn't matter if this is your first time reading one of my books, or your third time. What matters is that you gave me a chance. I cannot stress enough that authors would not be authors without readers. Art cannot exist without someone to view it, and I thank you for viewing mine.

# About the Author

Christine Layne is a romance author who loves to tell stories about people falling in love against the odds. Though writing is her passion, Christine also enjoys painting, spending time with her children, or watching movies with her husband, as long as she has a cup of tea in her hand.

Check out my Linktree! Links to my books, newsletter, and social medias for the latest updates, teasers for upcoming novels, giveaways, and more!

Linktree: linktr.ee/christine.layne.author